an 3
weate
Flannery or
S. M.
Ress
Jessie
fr. 0. 9

Bl.

Irene Carr was born and brought up on the river in Monkwearmouth, Sunderland, in the 1930s. Her father and brother worked in shipyards in the North East and her mother was a Sunderland barmaid.

KATY'S MEN

An independent, bonnie lass, Katy flees the drunken wrath of her father and gets a job with the Ashleigh family in an import and export warehouse in Newcastle-upon-Tyne. But when young Charles pays her attention, Katy is forced to work for Spargos, a dishonest haulage company in Sunderland. Rescued by a glamorous but evil conman, Katy once more finds herself on the streets — this time with child. She finds work and refuge with ex-soldier Matt Ballard who runs a rival haulage company across the river from the Spargos. But trouble lies ahead . . .

IRENE CARR

◆

KATY'S MEN

Complete and Unabridged

CHARNWOOD
Leicester

First published in Great Britain in 2000 by
Hodder and Stoughton
London

First Charnwood Edition
published 2001
by arrangement with
Hodder and Stoughton
a division of Hodder Headline

The moral right of the author has been asserted

British Library CIP Data

Carr, Irene
    Katy's men.—Large print ed.—
    Charnwood library series
    1. England, Northern—Social conditions—Fiction
    2. Love stories
    3. Large type books
    I. Title
    823.9'14 [F]

    ISBN 0–7089–9284–6

Published by
F. A. Thorpe (Publishing)
Anstey, Leicestershire

Set by Words & Graphics Ltd.
Anstey, Leicestershire
Printed and bound in Great Britain by
T. J. International Ltd., Padstow, Cornwall

This book is printed on acid-free paper

1

WALLSEND-ON-TYNE. DECEMBER 1890.

'Not another lass?' Barney Merrick was the first man in Katy's life. He glowered down at his newborn daughter, her pink face contorted and squalling under a little cap of black hair. His own voice came out strangled, in mingled disbelief and rage, from his face suffused with blood. He was a man on whom glowering fitted naturally. Barney had crinkly hair lying close to his bullet head. He was not tall nor broad but his chin always stuck out pugnaciously. His fists were clenched now as if ready to strike.

'Hell's flames! There's no bloody justice! That's three lasses now!' His red-veined, pale blue eyes shot furious glances around the room. There was little to see. It was on the ground floor of a two down, two up house in a long terrace of fifty or more, one end of it almost in the dirty waters of the Tyne. Another family lived in the two rooms above. There was a bed, a chest of drawers and a chair, and underfoot was cracked, old and cold linoleum. A fire burned in the grate, a rare luxury, only lit because of the confinement of the woman in the bed. Ethel Merrick lay exhausted, the first delight at the birth now gone. In truth there had already been four girls, not two, but one had died at birth and another after only a few weeks of life. Ethel's heart had been broken more than once. She was a thin, dark-eyed, gentle woman. She smiled pleadingly at her husband as his enraged gaze rested on her and it won her some small clemency.

He turned that glower accusingly on Betty, the mid-wife, who cradled the child in her arms. 'Another lass!' But this time the rage was tinged with resentment. He turned away from mother and child, stamped out of the bedroom and through the kitchen where a little group of women — neighbours, in dresses from neck to ankles and beshawled — sat around the fire. His two older daughters, Ursula and Lotte, aged four and three, slept on a couch as they always did. The neighbours avoided his eye and he passed them without acknowledgment. They listened to the tramp of his boots as he strode down the uncarpeted passage, then the slam of the front door that reverberated through the house. Only when the echoes of that had faded away did they relax and grin wrily at each other.

One jabbed the poker into the fire to prod the smouldering coals into flame, and said, 'It sounds like he's got another lass.'

Another answered, 'And he's not pleased.'

They were able to chuckle because Barney was not their husband.

Next door, in the bedroom at the front of the house, his wife could only smile. The child lay in her arms now and was quiet, while Betty was tidying up. Winnie Teasdale, plump and red-cheeked and Ethel's friend from schooldays, sat on the edge of the bed and leaned forward to

2

peep in at the little girl's fat and crumpled face. Winnie tried to cheer Ethel: 'Don't worry, pet, Barney will come round.'

'Oh, aye,' Ethel agreed, but neither believed it. She said reluctantly, 'You'll have to be getting home.' Because Winnie lived a mile away. 'It's after nine o'clock and pitch dark out there.'

'Fred knows where I am.' Fred was Winnie's husband. But she went on, 'Still, I'd better be getting back home. Mind, I'm glad I've seen her.' She bent to plant a light kiss on the child's brow and then another on Ethel's cheek. 'She's a bonny little lass. What are you going to call her?'

Ethel answered, 'Katy.'

* * *

Barney strode down the street towards the Tyne. The shipyard cranes standing stork-like by the river seemed to hang over the houses. The slate roofs glistened black from the recent rain and the sky above was a thick ceiling of low cloud and hanging smoke. Every little terraced house had its chimneys and from most of them the coal smoke trailed acridly. Barney did not notice it, was used to the smell of it as he was to the salt tang that came in on the wind from the sea. That bitterly cold, winter wind was now bringing in a fine drizzle on the heels of the rain but Barney was used to that as well.

He turned into the Geordie Lad, the public house at the end of the street, with its brass-handled front door. Inside there was more

3

smoke drifting around the yellow gaslights. One jet burned a naked flame so men could light their pipes and cigarettes. This time the smoke was only partly from the fire glowing in the hearth and most from the tobacco in the pipes of the thin line of men standing at the bar. Barney shoved through them and banged a fist down on the scrubbed but beer-stained surface: 'Give me a pint.' The barmaid was neat in high-collared white blouse and a white apron over her skirt that brushed on the sawdust covering the floor. She pulled the pint, set it before Barney and he thrust the coppers at her in payment.

The girl was a neighbour and now asked, 'How's Mrs Merrick?'

Barney answered curtly, 'All right.' And then told her what she really wanted to know: 'A little lass.'

'She's had a little lass!' The girl beamed. She called to the publican at the other end of the bar, 'Barney's wife has had a little lass!'

The man standing next to Barney, a neighbour living a few doors away, said, 'Another one? So, that's three!'

Barney's hard little blue eyes swivelled around towards him. 'What about it?'

The neighbour picked up his glass and moved further down the bar but he revealed another man, a stranger and taller, broader who grinned down, amused, at Barney. 'You've got three lasses. No lads?'

The publican came hurrying, scenting trouble. 'Now then, lads, I want no bother.'

Barney demanded, 'Who's this?' He cocked a

thumb at the big man, who was still grinning mockingly.

The publican replied, 'Joe Feeny. He's from over the river.' He meant from the south side of the Tyne.

Barney said, 'He wants to mind his own business.'

'Now Barney — '

Joe Feeny's grin had flickered at Barney's curt, slap-in-the-face tone but it widened now. He taunted, 'Three lasses. I reckon you're not man enough to get owt else.'

Barney's clenched fist took Feeny square in the mouth and he staggered back along the bar, scattering the drinkers. Then he steadied and wiped blood from his chin on the back of his hand. He swore and told Barney, 'You cheeky little bugger! I'll give you a hiding for that!' He knew he could. He had height, reach and weight in his favour and at twenty-eight was ten years younger. And he did. In the street outside he knocked Barney down time and time again. But Barney always got up. And in the bitter, bloody end it was Barney who stayed on his feet and Joe Feeny who lay stunned and defeated.

Barney looked around the crowd, glaring out of the one eye still open, and challenged, 'Anybody else?' Then he pulled on his jacket and stumbled unsteadily up the street and in at his own front door. The crowd, silenced, lifted the dazed Feeny and carried him, legs trailing, into the pub. There they revived him and saw him fit enough to get home before they sent him on his way.

Barney washed, wincing at the water on his cuts and bruises, then went to his bed, but first he paused to look into the cradle that stood on his wife's side of the bed. The child was sleeping but her small face was set, it seemed in determination. He thought in that, at least, she took after him. And her little fists were clenched. He muttered, 'She's going to be a fighter, then.' He found some satisfaction in that. Then he wondered, 'We'll see if that rich auntie of your mother comes up with anything.' But experience replaced hope as he turned away and he said sourly, 'She never gave owt towards the others, though, not even the price of a drink.'

A month later he had confirmation of that. He came home from his work in Swan Hunter's shipyard and found his wife and Winnie Teasdale sitting by the fire, which was half-hidden behind a clothes horse draped with damp washing. He nodded to Winnie curtly and demanded of Ethel, 'Where's my dinner?'

Ethel rose hastily to her feet. 'I'm just going to put it on the table.'

Winnie was holding the baby on her knee while the other two girls, Ursula and Lotte, played in a corner. But now Winnie said tactfully, 'I'd better be getting back to give Fred his dinner.' She had no liking for Barney. Minutes later the front door closed behind her and Ethel held little Katy in the crook of one arm as she served up the dinner, first to Barney then to the two little girls and lastly herself.

As Barney ate, Ethel said, 'Winnie came with me today when I went to see Aunt Augusta.'

Barney paused with loaded fork lifted to his mouth. 'Did she give you anything?'

Ethel managed a smile. 'She said all she had would be mine when she went, but she was hard-pressed to pay her bills at the moment. I thought she was going to ask me for help.'

Barney snapped at the food and chewed moodily. 'She made a mint in her time on the halls and that husband of hers left her well provided for. She can't have spent the lot. But I wouldn't be surprised if she did, just to spite us.' He pointed his knife at Ethel, 'Just remember, when she goes, I want to be there first.'

Ethel looked down at her plate. 'I'll remember.'

When Barney had finished his meal and pulled up his armchair to the fire, he spared a glance at his daughter, Katy. She lay in her pram while Ethel washed up in a bowl of water set on the table. He stared down into the pale blue eyes, so oddly like his own under the black hair, and saw her little fists were clenched. He muttered, 'Aye, you'll need to fight for anything you want in this life.'

★　★　★

'That's mine!' Matthew Ballard pushed away the other boy. At four years old he had already discovered the truth of Barney Merrick's remark. The broad waters of the Tyne flowed between them but they shared one trait of character — Matthew was as ready to fight as was Barney. Because his father was unemployed, Matt and

7

his younger brother were fed daily by the guardians of the parish. Forty or fifty children crowded into a bare hall, the boys in shorts or knickerbockers and woollen jerseys or jackets, the girls in dresses and white pinnies, but all their clothes were ragged or patched. They were given bowls of broth and hunks of bread to be eaten at the trestle tables ranked down the room.

'Gerroff!' the boy snarled at Matt. He was seated next to Matt on the wooden form, was a year or two older — and bigger. He reached out to grab the crust of bread by Matt's bowl. 'Or I'll punch you!' He received no warning or threat to prepare him. Matt had lost part of his dinner before in this fashion and was not going to suffer it again, but his reaction was wholly automatic. He lashed out, a wild swing, but his small fist landed on the dirty nose of the other boy, who yelled and pulled back. He still held the bread but now Matt tore it from him. He yelled again and put a hand to his bloody nose and Matt's next swing took him on the ear.

'Stop that, the pair o' yer!' One of the women serving out the meal came hurrying, a ladle still in her hand, to elbow them apart. 'Fighting like cat and dog! Away you go!' And she ran them out of the door into the street. 'Behave yourselves tomorrow or you're out for good!'

The bigger boy clasped his nose and looked hatred out of his watering eyes but Matt held onto his bread and his fist was still balled and held ready. His dark hair had been cut short with clippers so it stuck on end and his thin face, when wearing his usual happy grin, made him an

8

engaging if dirty child. But now he scowled determination and the other boy shambled away. Matt set off for home, chewing on his bread, and was soon smiling again.

The woman who had put him into the street returned to her task in the hall. Another, sawing up loaves of bread, asked, 'What was all that?'

'Little Matty Ballard. I think the other lad tried to steal his bread but Matty will have a go at anybody.'

'Aye? He always seems a bonny little lad and well-mannered.'

'He is,' her friend said grimly, 'but he's a scrapper.'

The other smiled fondly. 'I think he'll have a few lasses after him when he's grown.'

Her friend dug her ladle into the steaming cauldron of broth and predicted, 'Whatever lass gets him will be lucky.'

2

WALLSEND-ON-TYNE. JUNE 1896.

'Katy! Are you looking after those bairns?' Ethel
Merrick shouted it from her front door, head
turning as she scanned the children who
swarmed, playing, in the street. There were
makeshift swings, fashioned from a rope tied
around a lamppost, little girls sitting in loops of
the ropes and swinging as if around a maypole.
Hoops raced and leapt, pursued and driven by
boys with hooked sticks. Games of marbles were
scattered among holes in the interstices of the
kerbstones with boys getting their knees dirty.
Girls bounced balls against walls chanting, 'Salt,
mustard, vinegar, pepper . . . ' It was a fine
morning with a blazing sun overhead and all the
children too small for school were out on the
cobbles between the houses. Some were smaller
than others and these were 'looked after' by their
bigger and older siblings.

'Aye, Mam!' Katy called back to her mother,
and now Ethel saw her, on the opposite side of
the street. She was dressed like all the other girls
in a white pinny over a dark dress that came
down to her calves, black stockings and buttoned
boots on her feet. Her mane of black hair was
tied back with a ribbon — and there were those
pale blue eyes. They were the same colour as
those of Barney, but wide and innocent in her

10

thin face. It was mock serious now. A half-dozen tots sat on a doorstep, supposedly 'in school', while Katy stood in front as teacher. She held a piece of chalk, and a board 'borrowed' from someone's coalhouse made a grubby but effective blackboard.

Ethel craned her neck, peering. There was Ted, sitting with the others, but — 'Where's Robbie?' she demanded.

'Standing in the corner because he wouldn't learn his numbers.' Katy pointed to where the elder of her two brothers, four-year-old Robbie, stood in the doorway, grinning out at them all.

Ethel warned, 'Don't go wandering off. We're going to see your auntie today.' She had kept Katy off school for that reason.

'No, Mam, I won't.'

Satisfied, Ethel turned back into the house. She had aged more than just the six years that had passed since Katy's birth. Barney had got his wish with two sons, Robbie and Ted, but there had also been two miscarriages and Ethel had paid the price. At thirty she looked to be well into her forties. But today the prospect of an outing of sorts, albeit only to nearby Gosforth, cheered her and gave some colour to her cheeks.

When Winnie Teasdale arrived, flushed and jolly, Ethel greeted her with a smile: 'We've got a good day for it.'

'A bit too warm, if you ask me,' replied her old friend. She flapped a handkerchief before her face to cool it, but she also smiled, glad to see Ethel in such an unusually cheerful mood.

Ethel went to the front door again and called

11

across the street, 'Come in, our Katy, and bring those bairns. You've got to get ready.' Katy brought in the two boys; the two elder girls, Ursula and Lotte, were at school. Ethel and Winnie washed the children's faces, hands and knees and dressed them in their best. Any visit to Ethel's Aunt Augusta, also known as Katy's aunt for convenience, was special.

Augusta's house was a small one but in a good part of Gosforth, its rooms dark behind velvet curtains drawn to almost cover the window, and lace curtains that did. A maid let them in, a pale young girl in black dress, white apron and cap. She led them into the kitchen at the back of the house because the parlour at the front was used only on Sunday. The kitchen was the living-room of the house with table and chairs, an armchair either side of the fireplace and a couch between them. Various small tables were dotted about, their surfaces crowded with sepia photographs and souvenirs of Torquay. Winnie, Ethel and her brood had to edge their way through to sit where Aunt Augusta pointed. Then she ordered, 'Tea, please.' The maid rustled out.

Augusta Fleming was a straight-backed old lady whose formerly slender beauty was now skin and bone. Her skin was like paper where it stretched over her fine bones and it had a yellow tinge. Katy had seen her before but that had been a year ago and she found this a different woman. She heard her mother's quick intake of breath, to be followed by her enquiry, 'Are you keeping well, Aunt Augusta?'

'Don't talk such rubbish!' The reply came

tartly. 'You can see how I am. I only have to look in a mirror to see how I feel.'

'So Torquay didn't suit you this year?' Winnie put that in sympathetically. Augusta had spent the winter in a boarding house in Torquay as she always did. It was a totally alien lifestyle to that of the women and children sitting meekly opposite her now. They counted themselves lucky if they enjoyed an occasional day at the seaside in summer.

Augusta knew this and replied drily, 'There's some things money can't buy.' She had come from their world but had fought her way out of it by way of the stage. She had started, as a child, singing and dancing for coppers in and around the pubs of Tyneside and ended up as a top-of-the-bill act in music halls. Now she finished, 'And youth is one of them.' She inspected the children, her eyes flicking over the two boys without interest, but they settled on Katy for some seconds. Then she nodded slowly. 'Katy, isn't it?'

Katy had become uneasy under the stare from the old woman's dark eyes, which had a glassy look to them now, like the marbles the boys played with in the street. But she felt her mother's elbow in her ribs and answered, 'Yes, Auntie Augusta.'

'I remember. I saw you last summer. This last year has made a change in both of us.' The glassy stare shifted to Ethel: 'This one's going to be a beauty.' And when Ethel smiled complacently: 'It's nothing to be pleased about. She'll have plenty of trouble in her life if she isn't careful.

13

She'll have to fight. The men will be her downfall if she doesn't. I know. They'd ha' been the finish of me if I'd let them have their way.' She nodded several times in emphasis, but then dismissed Katy and the subject with a wave of her skinny hand.

The maid brought the tea now and there was lemonade and biscuits for the children. They said 'Thank you' to the maid, who finally smiled wanly as she left. The adults drank their tea while Katy and the boys devoured their biscuits and gulped down the lemonade. After that the women talked of families and scandals, present and past. Katy sat at the table with the two boys, turning the pages of a book showing pictures of Queen Victoria and her family.

The boys were becoming restive when Augusta said, 'That maid only comes in each day but she's been told she has to tell you when anything happens.' She eyed Winnie but addressed Ethel: 'You're sure this lass can keep her mouth shut?'

The two friends flushed in unison but Ethel confirmed firmly, 'Winnie won't repeat anything she hears. I've told you that before.'

'Aye. I just wanted to be sure.' Augusta cast that cold eye over the children: 'The bairns are too young to understand. Except that one.' The thin finger pointed at Katy.

Again Ethel assured her: 'She won't tell anyone.'

The old woman stared into Katy's light blue eyes, open and honest, and nodded, satisfied. She turned to Ethel and asked, 'You know where to look?'

14

Ethel replied soothingly, 'Yes, Aunt Augusta, but you mustn't talk as if — '

'Don't be damned silly!' Augusta's cup rattled in its saucer. 'It's not a matter of 'if' but 'when'!' She laughed, a dry rattle. 'I never gave you much money, only a few shillings now and then, partly because I wanted to be certain I'd have sufficient to see me out because I saw enough of poverty when I was young. I'll make damned sure I won't die a pauper. But on top of that I knew that if Barney found you had money he would drink it. He'll drink whatever I leave you now if you let him get his hands on it. Not that there will be much. They say you bring nothing into this world and you can't take anything out. True enough. But *I* made my money and *I've* spent it. As I said, it'll see me out. You'll get what's left.'

She lay back in the chair now, weary, and said, 'Those bairns are getting restless. You'd better be getting away.' So they made their farewells, the children kissing her dry cheek, then Winnie and last of all, Ethel. Augusta held her hand tightly for a moment. 'Take care now. Remember what I've told you.' And then with a nod of the head towards Katy, 'And watch out for her.'

'I will,' answered Ethel. Then the maid let them out. In the street Ethel opened her hand and saw a sovereign. She never mentioned it but closed her fingers again and they made their way home across Newcastle.

The maid came some six months later, early on a bitterly cold winter's morning. She wore a shawl wrapped over her head and around her shoulders to supplement her threadbare coat but her pale face was tinged with blue by the cold. Ethel opened the kitchen door to her knock and the girl standing in the passage outside held out the scrap of paper on which Aunt Augusta had written Ethel's name and address. Shivering, she said, 'Missus Fleming told me to tell you as soon as it happened. 'Fetch the doctor and the undertaker,' she said, 'and then tell Mrs Merrick.' ' Katy heard all of this, standing by her mother's side, dressed and ready for school. The two elder girls had preceded her by a few minutes while the boys were still eating their breakfast and had not heard a word.

Katy heard her mother's quick intake of breath, then Ethel said, 'Come in and get warm, lass.' Ethel held the door wide to admit her. Then she turned to Katy and told her, 'You can't go to school today, pet. I want you to look after the two bairns for a bit. I have to go out — ' she glanced at the boys and finished ' — shopping, but I'll be back in an hour or so.' She left shortly afterwards, accompanied by the maid, and Katy played with the two boys.

Ethel returned before noon. She was flushed despite the cold, and breathless as if from running — or excitement. She took Katy aside and said, 'Don't say a word to your dad about that girl coming.'

'No, Mam.'

So Katy listened in silence when Ethel told Barney that evening, 'I had a message today that Aunt Augusta died last night.'

'Aye? Well, we'll get over there and quick!' Barney washed hastily and changed out of his

16

dirty work clothes, then they all set off. The house in Gosforth was empty but Ethel had a key which she said the maid had brought her. The children sat in the chill, fireless kitchen, talking in whispers because of the body in the bedroom upstairs. Meanwhile Barney searched the house while Ethel followed in his wake. It proved fruitless.

Barney gave up in anger and despair at last. 'Nothing but her purse wi' fifteen shilling in it! There's a will, right enough, leaving all to you, including her bloody brooch, but this place was rented and there's nothing but what the furniture will fetch!' He glared up at the ceiling as if at the dead woman above. 'The tight-fisted old hag!' He cursed or maintained a brooding silence all the way home.

Ethel kept quiet except to say once, 'I'm glad she died in some comfort, not a workhouse bed.'

Barney snarled in disappointment, 'Aye, she blew it all on herself!'

Ethel did not argue with that and said nothing more, not wanting him to transfer his anger to her. But now and again she smiled.

★ ★ ★

Matt Ballard ran home from school, partly to keep warm because he had no winter coat, only one old and ragged jersey pulled on over another. He was already tall and sturdy for his ten years, face red with exertion and the cold. He made little noise as he ran along the bare boards of the passage because he only wore

17

plimsolls with his big toes poking out of them. He had no winter boots, either.

He pushed open the door of the kitchen and saw his father sitting on a cracket by the small fire in the grate. Matt knew what that meant, and asked with a sinking heart, 'No work today, Dad?'

'No, but I've got a job.'

'That's great!' Matt burst out excitedly. This news meant there would be enough to eat. Then he saw his father was not smiling, and his mother sat on the other side of the fire, her hands to her face and the big tears oozing out between her fingers. Matt's father got up from the stool and went to put his arm around her. Matt asked, voice hushed, 'What's the matter with me mam?'

'I've signed on in the Durhams,' Davy Ballard explained. 'There's never any regular work around here for a labourer like me. So I've joined the Army. At least you'll all have a roof over your heads and full bellies.'

Matt's mother wiped at her eyes with a corner of her apron and tried to smile. 'Your dad will have to live in barracks for a bit but later on we'll all be in a married quarter, probably down south in Colchester.' A battalion of the Durham Light Infantry was stationed there. It was a foreign country to her. Her man would go and she would be left on her own and later would be cast among strangers. But she hugged Matt and told him, 'So we'll all be fine now. And here's the rest.' The trampling in the passage signalled the arrival of Matt's four brothers and sisters. His mother stood up. 'I've got some bread and dripping for your teas.' She started to lay out the meal as the other children charged in.

Matt tried to come to terms with what he had been told. His father was going to be a soldier. Matt would be living in a strange place with a new school and none of his friends, just boys he did not know. He was not sure whether he was frightened or excited.

3

WALLSEND-ON-TYNE. DECEMBER 1903.

'*Listen* to me, Katy. Listen to what I tell you.' Ethel Merrick was propped up by pillows in the bed where she lay. It seemed the flesh had run from her frame in these last weeks. Her thin hand held feebly to that of her thirteen-year-old daughter.

'Yes, Mam.' Katy was frightened because she knew she was looking at death though she tried to deny it to herself. 'I'm listening.'

Ethel paused to get her breath. She thought with pride, She's nearly a woman, a fine young woman — but still too young to be left. She said, 'I want you to have the brooch, the one your Aunt Augusta left to me. It's in the bottom of the chest of drawers. I want you to think well of her. I know what your dad's told you, but she thought well of you.'

Barney Merrick still remembered Aunt Augusta at intervals, when he cursed her for bequeathing him: 'Not the price of a bloody drink!'

Ethel went on, 'And she wanted you to have some advice. She saw when you were just little that you were going to turn out a bonny lass. She said the men would be after you and you had to look out for yourself, that they'd ruin you if you let them. I want you to remember that, always.

You hear now?' The grip on Katy's arm tightened.

'Yes, Mam.' Katy knew that, of late, some men had looked at her — differently. Sometimes it had instilled in her a vague fear. Her mother had taught her the basic facts of life but that had been just talk. Experience was something else.

Ethel fumbled with the fingers of one hand with those of the other, took off a plain, gold ring and held it out to Katy: 'My mother gave me this. Put it away until you're older.' And as Katy took the ring, Ethel went on, 'I've got some things for your sisters. I'll treat you all alike, as I've always done.' But Ursula and Lotte had always taken their father's side while it was Katy who cared for her mother. The two older girls respected and feared his strength and power. They had some affection for their mother but he came first in their thoughts because he made the rules. Now Ethel pushed up from the pillows and urged her, 'Be a good girl. Try not to get across your father. I'm only trying to save you from a lot of grief. He can have a terrible temper.'

Katy knew what was meant by this warning. Over the last few months she had taken over a lot of the work of the house because of her mother's illness. The two elder girls had been excused because they were at work and putting money in Barney's pocket — and Ursula, the eldest, was his favourite among the girls. So Katy had been working with or for her father and had begun to question his orders and argue against his judgments when she thought them wrong or unfair. She had been browbeaten and shouted

21

down by him but had not given up. Her mouth had set in a stubborn line now at thought of him, but softened with her mother's eyes on her. 'I will, Mam.'

Ethel sank back on the pillows, satisfied with that assurance. 'You'll be finished with school before long. Your teachers said you were a good scholar and there's a job waiting for you in Mrs Turnbull's shop. Your dad has arranged it.'

Katy knew this and was not enthusiastic. She did not know what she wanted to do when she left school but hated the idea of serving behind a counter in a small corner shop. But at that moment she did not care. 'Thanks, Mam.'

Her mother smiled at her weakly. 'I didn't want to keep on at you, but I worry about you. You're such a bonny little thing.' She reached out to stroke Katy's hair then let her hand fall. 'Give me a kiss now and let me have a word with Winnie.' So Katy left and cried in the kitchen.

Ethel asked Winnie, 'You've done what I asked? You'll not let me down?'

Winnie, not jolly now but close to tears herself, held Ethel's hand, soothing: 'I'll see they get their rights. Just as you want.'

Ethel said, 'You don't need to worry about Barney.'

Winnie agreed, ironically, 'No.'

Ethel smiled faintly, 'He cares for me, you know. He hasn't — been near me for months — close on two years, in fact. Because the doctor said, you know, I couldn't . . . ' She paused, embarrassed.

Winnie said quickly, to save her from it, 'You told me.'

'Aye.' And then after a time: 'There's somebody else.'

Winnie protested, 'No, Ethel.'

'There is,' Ethel insisted gently. 'I know. I can tell from the way he walks out of here some nights, and then he doesn't come home till late. But he can't help it. It's just the way he is. He's hidden it from me — or thinks he has — because he doesn't want to hurt me. So don't blame him. Promise me?'

Winnie had to agree, 'I promise.'

Ethel managed to laugh softly. 'Promises! It's like we were two little lasses again. We had some fun in those days, didn't we?' And they talked of the old days and old friends, of when they were children playing in the street, until it was time for Winnie to go home and Ethel was exhausted.

Winnie saw that and said, 'I'll come round tomorrow.'

Ethel sighed, 'Aye. Tomorrow.'

But there was no tomorrow for Ethel because she died in the early hours of the morning.

Ursula and Lotte had a day off work for the funeral while Katy and the two boys stayed home from school. They stood around the grave, shivering in the bitter cold. The freshly turned earth, dug only the previous day, was silvered with the frost. Katy saw her father grieving for the first time in her life, tears leaking from the corners of his eyes and wiped away on the back of his thick-fingered hand, scarred from a lifetime of fighting. She felt close to him then

23

but it was not to last.

Some days later, after they had all eaten the tea which Katy had set out, and when they were trying to get back to normal living, Katy asked, 'Dad, can I have my mam's brooch, the one she promised me, please?'

Barney put down his cup and said shortly, 'Anything your mother left comes to me. I'll decide who gets what.'

The others were listening. Ursula, stolid and unimaginative, her dark hair crinkled like that of her father, nodded at Lotte, the other girl who always sided with her father: 'We should have first choice.'

'Aye, that's right.' Lotte, sallow and plain, agreed as always.

Katy protested, 'But Mam said I was to have it, that Aunt Augusta wanted me to have it.'

Barney declared, 'Nobody said owt to me. Anyway, what does a young lass like you want with a thing like that? It's more suited to a grown woman.'

Ursula put in, with a jealous glance at Katy, 'You were always a favourite of that old Aunt Augusta.'

Katy persisted, partly because she liked the brooch. It was of little value, a piece of costume jewellery Aunt Augusta had worn on stage, but it was pretty, with blue and white stones which sparkled in the light. But Katy also wanted it because it was hers by right. 'It was Mam's brooch and she said — '

Barney shouted over her, 'I've told you and I've had enough! Now shut up!'

24

Katy was chalk white but for two splashes of red colour high on her cheeks. She refused to give in: 'No, I'll not! It should be mine! That was the last thing Mam said to me. She said — '

'Never mind what she said!' Barney kicked back his chair and started round the table towards her. 'I've told you to shut up! You've got too much lip — a trouble-maker!' He had his hand lifted for the blow and Katy saw the others either ducking away from him or, like Ursula, waiting eagerly for punishment to be meted out. Katy ran. Barney shouted, 'Come back! Damn you! Come back!'

Katy did not. She fled in terror down the passage and out into the street, then wept as she walked around and around the streets. She was bitterly glad she had hidden away the ring her mother had given her. She had, at least, kept that. Fear kept her walking but the cold and lateness of the hour finally drove her home. As she entered, shivering and frightened, anticipating a beating, Ursula gloated, 'Serves you right. Dad's got dressed up and gone out. But he said he'd deal with you tomorrow.'

Ursula was to be disappointed. The next day Barney was in high spirits, grinning as he left for work and when he returned. It was a week later when Katy learned the reason. A letter arrived at the house, in a thick, white envelope addressed to Barney in copperplate. He opened it when he came in from work and nodded with satisfaction. When tea had been eaten he flourished the letter and fixed Katy with a grim stare. 'You were supposed to have another two or three weeks at school but I've seen the headmaster and he's letting you off that. He thinks you're bloody marvellous but he hasn't seen you around here like I have. Anyway, you'll finish at the end of this week. I've got you a position through an aunt on *my* side of the family, never mind your Aunt Augusta. That's Jinny Merrick as was. She married that Jim Tucker in North Shields and she's been dead and buried these last ten years, but before she was wed she was a maid with the Barracloughs. I went up to see them the other night and it turned out they're wanting a lass.' He wagged the letter again. 'Aunt Jinny was well-thought-of by them so they're taking you on.'

Katy whispered, 'But I've got a job waiting for me at Mrs Turnbull's shop.' That seemed attractive now.

'You can forget that,' said Barney brutally. 'I've told that Winnie Teasdale and she's going to take you shopping for a box for your clothes and get you fitted out with black dresses, white caps and aprons. It's costing me a pretty penny but you've been making too much trouble for me so you're going to work at the Barracloughs' house. They'll pay you a pound a month but they'll send ten shillings to me. Ten bob a month is enough for a lass like you.'

Katy listened, shocked into silence, as her sentence was pronounced. At thirteen years old she was going into service! A lot of girls went into the big houses of the wealthy to work as maids or in the kitchens. She did not want to do that any more than she had wanted to serve the

26

customers in Mrs Turnbull's shop, but it seemed her fate was determined for her and there was nothing she could do. She saw Ursula grinning and her father's air of 'That'll straighten you out, my lass!' Katy would not give them any further satisfaction. She would not beg for reprieve. She kept her face expressionless and said calmly, 'All right.' She saw her father's look of righteous confidence replaced by one of baffled anger and Ursula's smirk slipped away. Katy could have wept but instead she made herself smile at them. She would not let them get any change out of her.

The next morning she saw her father and the two girls off to work then accompanied the boys as far as the school gates. Katy was fond of them, and they of her; she had taken the place of their mother. She blinked away tears as they moved away from her but then she turned around. Back in the family home, she packed a small case with all she owned. Then she searched for her mother's brooch but could not find it. She hesitated a long time then, sitting by the fire, reluctant to take this awful step, but finally sighed and rose to her feet. Katy told herself there was nothing else for it. She left the house carrying her case and made her way through the streets lining the Tyne to the rooms a mile or so away. They were upstairs rooms in a terraced house like that she had left. She walked along the passage, that had a strip of thin carpet running from front door to back, climbed the stairs and knocked on the kitchen door. Winnie Teasdale opened it, stared at her and asked, 'What are you doing here? We're not going shopping for your things until the weekend.'

Katy said, 'I've left home.' And burst into tears.

Winnie breathed, 'Oh, my God! Come in.' She put her arms around the girl and comforted her. After a time Katy dried her tears and Winnie said softly, not wanting to frighten her, but warning: 'He'll know where to look for you, and you know what his temper is like.'

'I don't care.' Katy looked at Winnie, pleading. 'Will you take me in? I'll get a job and pay board.'

'Aye, you can live here.' Winnie had no need to remember the promise she had made to Ethel Merrick because she was fond of this girl, but also afraid for her. She thought, If Barney will let you stay. But she said, 'You can have the little bedroom over the passage.' That room had always been intended for her children but she had none.

Barney came that evening. Winnie answered his knock to find him standing on the landing outside the kitchen door. He was still in his work clothes of old suit and cap and unwashed. He craned his neck to look past her as Winnie said, 'Hello, Barney.' Behind her, Fred Teasdale, her husband, stood up from his seat at the table, scenting trouble.

Barney saw Katy sitting by the fire and beckoned her: 'I want to see you, miss. Outside.'

Winnie answered, 'She's not going anywhere. You can talk to her here.'

But Katy was already on her feet. She would

not have Winnie upset by a scene. 'I'm coming.' She walked past Winnie and followed her father down the stairs and along the passage to the front door. She halted on the step and he turned to face her. His pale blue eyes were like chips of ice flecked with the red of blood. She could see his mouth working with his suppressed rage and was frightened, but she had spent some hours anticipating this meeting and was ready for it.

Barney said tightly, 'I got home to find there was no dinner for anybody and no sign o' you. Not a note, nothing! I only guessed that you'd run off when I saw your clothes had gone. What the *hell* d'you think you're doing?' He paused for breath but not an answer. 'Get your things. You're coming back wi' me.'

Katy said, 'No.'

'*What?*' He glared at her, disbelieving what he had heard. 'What did you say?' He was used to the gentle Ethel giving in at this point. But this was not Ethel.

'I'm not going with you.' Despite her fear, Katy made herself stand face to face with him, eye to eye because she stood on the step and he below it. She stated it as a fact. 'I'm staying here with Winnie.' And as he lifted his hand, 'If you hit me I'll scream loud enough to fetch the street out.' He hesitated but saw she meant it. Instead of striking her he seized her ear and twisted it. 'I could take you home like this!'

Her face twisted in pain, Katy still resisted: 'I'd scream all the way and run off again tomorrow. I'll keep on running away until you're sick of it.'

Barney cursed her, gave one final twist to her ear then let it go. 'To hell with you! I'm sick of you now! But one of these days you'll come back to me, and I give you warning: I'm getting married again.' Katy finally flinched at that. Now she realised why he had been so cheerful after her last row with him: he had proposed that night and been accepted. She also guessed that her mother's brooch would be adorning another woman. Barney was going on, 'So if you show your face in my house again, you watch your tongue.' He waited again, watching for her reaction, for signs of weakening. But Katy turned her back on him and with one hand she slammed the door in his face.

She heard him bellow, 'You'll come crawling, one day!' But she was running along the passage and up the stairs. She went straight to her little room and fell on the bed, her face in her pillow. Winnie tactfully left her in peace. Katy grieved for the loss of her mother and the parting from her siblings, no matter that they had fought among themselves. Her father was marrying again. Now she knew that there was no home for her. When she had turned her back on her father she had turned away from one life and was now embarking on another. She would never go back.

There she was wrong.

4

Katy was sixteen when Charles Ashleigh came into her life and he meant her no harm — far from it.

Winnie Teasdale had found a job for her within a week of her moving in. Katy started work as an assistant to Annie Scanlon at Ashleigh's, an import and export warehouse down by the river. Annie was a bookkeeper and clerk, a cheerful, buxom, ruddy-faced spinster in her fifties. She lived in Sunderland and travelled to work on the train every day. Annie taught Katy her job and also something of life, while Katy worked hard and was quick to learn. Annie was pleased with her and they became friends. Katy enjoyed her work and loved the warehouse with its mingled smells of manilla rope and soap, tobacco and molasses, paint and lamp oil. She sat on a high stool at a desk beside Annie and returned to Winnie's house and her little room in the evening.

After two years Winnie's husband, Fred, had been offered a job in the dockyard at Malta. It meant he would be there for the rest of his working life but also that he would be making a great deal more money. And then there would be a pension and a nest egg that would keep Winnie and himself in comfortable retirement. It was an

31

opportunity he had to grasp at his age; he was well into his forties. Before she and her husband sailed, Winnie found lodgings for Katy in the house of Mrs Connelly, a widow without a pension who took in young girls as boarders. She was a righteous, sharp-featured, acid-tongued woman but her house was comfortable and Katy was happy enough for the next year. Winnie had insisted, 'We must keep in touch. I'll write and I want to know how you are, where you are and what you are doing.' She was as good as her word and wrote every two or three weeks. Katy always replied.

In April 1907 Katy was just a few months past her sixteenth birthday. She and Annie sat on high stools at their desks on a blustery day left over from March, with the wind off the river driving the wheeling, squalling gulls inland and rattling the doors of the warehouse. Mr Tomlinson, the energetic young manager, emerged from his office to ask, 'Can you spare Katy for an hour or so, Annie?' That was a courtesy question that was tantamount to an order and Annie murmured her agreement. Tomlinson told Katy, 'I just want you to take these papers up to Mr Ashleigh for his signature. He telephoned to say he wouldn't be in today. He's got his son at home — he's a sub-lieutenant in the Navy. His ship was in the Mediterranean Fleet and she's just paid off at Chatham.'

So Katy put on her coat and hat and set off for the Ashleigh house in the suburbs of Newcastle. She knew her way because she had been sent on these errands many times since starting to work at Ashleigh's. So she walked past the big wrought-iron gates and the wide drive which led up to the front of the house. Instead she turned in at the wooden gates marked 'Tradesmen' and followed the winding track round the side of the house to the kitchen door at the rear. A maid let her in and Katy explained, 'Hello, Jane! I've got some papers for Mr Ashleigh to sign.'

Jane led her through the kitchen and the green-baize-covered door which separated the servants' quarters and kitchen from the main house. In the hall running up to the front entrance Jane tapped at a door from behind which came a burst of male laughter. Then a voice called deeply, 'Come in!'

Jane pushed the door wide and ushered in Katy: 'Miss Merrick to see you, sir.'

The room was a study, office and library. Books lined the walls from floor to ceiling, a large desk stood in the bay window and two leather armchairs before the fire crackling in the grate. The men sat in the armchairs, heads turned towards her. Katy paused just inside the room to curtsy and explain, 'Mr Tomlinson sent me with some papers for you to sign, please, sir.'

Vincent Ashleigh, tall, greying and urbane, levered himself out of his chair and smiled down at her. 'Right you are. Let me have them, please.' He took the papers and crossed to the desk, seated himself at it and scanned the first letter. As he was facing the window, his back was to the room. Katy waited. While she had addressed Vincent Ashleigh she had been aware of the younger man. He was possibly three or four

33

years older than she. He had stood up in time with his father and proved to be as tall. His teeth showed white against a face burned brown by the sun under hair the colour of toffee. All this Katy saw only from the corner of her eye, not daring to face him. Nevertheless, she knew he was watching her and tried not to blush — but failed.

She started as Charles Ashleigh said, 'I take it you're working in the office.'

'Yes, sir.' Now Katy had to face him but kept her eyes cast down.

'D'you like it?'

'Yes, sir.' Now she looked up at him and saw his smile waver then return. She realised she was returning that smile and tried to straighten her face lest she should appear forward, but could not.

Charles knew he had to say something. He could not simply stand gawking at the girl. 'How long have you been there?'

'Three years, sir.'

He thought vaguely that confirmed his first impression, that she was about eighteen. And they were still staring at each other.

'There you are.' Vincent Ashleigh got up from the desk and gave the papers to Katy. 'Tell Mr Tomlinson I won't be in tomorrow.' He glanced across at his son and chuckled, 'We're going walking in the hills. But I'll be there the day after.'

'Yes, sir,' said Katy. She curtsied again and left the room. As she turned to close the door she saw Charles Ashleigh still watching her. She walked out of the house and back to the office in a dream. But when she handed the papers back to Mr Tomlinson in his office she had recovered her outward calm and was able to tell him, without blushing, 'Mr Ashleigh said he's going walking with his son tomorrow but he'll be in the day after.'

'Fine.' Tomlinson grinned at her. 'It looks like you'll have another walk, then.'

'I don't mind.' And Katy tried to sound as if she did not care either way. But supposing Charles Ashleigh did not go walking after all?

Next day she waited and worked at her desk, with Annie Scanlon, sniffing and watery-eyed with a cold, beside her. The morning passed but Tomlinson did not appear with a bunch of letters to sign. It wasn't until the afternoon that he came out of his office, on his way into the warehouse, and mentioned in passing, 'You won't get wet today, Katy.' He nodded at the windows where the rain beat at the glass and ran down in rivulets. 'There's nothing for the old man to sign.'

Katy smiled but her spirits sank, her mood changed to match the gloom of the day. But then she told herself not to be silly and bent to her work again.

Sub-Lieutenant Charles Ashleigh spent the day striding over the windswept hills of Northumberland revelling in the rain beating into his face and the occasional shaft of sunlight. He talked to his father, sometimes about the Navy but also enquiring about the warehouse and the family business. Vincent Ashleigh was delighted, because the firm would go to Charles one day, and he was quite ready to talk about all the staff, including Katy Merrick. At the end of the day they strode downhill by the side of a brawling stream to the inn where the chauffeur met them with the motor car, a Lanchester with a big, boxy cab which he steered with a tiller. Vincent Ashleigh had paid six hundred pounds for it. Many a working man toiled for ten years to earn that amount.

Charles said casually, 'I might look in at the place tomorrow.'

'Why not?' Vincent encouraged him, 'You'll find it interesting.'

He hosted a dinner party that evening at which his son was guest of honour and where there were a number of young women selected by his wife, girls she thought suitable for her son. Charles was pleasant to all of them. That was easy because they were pretty, fashionably and expensively dressed, and intelligent. But all the while he was picturing someone else. He knew the girl from the office was outside his circle and his class, that he should not start an affair. He told himself he was being stupid but — where was the harm in seeing the girl, talking to her, maybe flirting a little?

He made some plans for the next day but in the event they were not needed. It was a fine spring morning when he walked into the office at Ashleigh's. He found Katy sitting at her desk but she was alone. He had been prepared to find Annie Scanlon there and maybe Tomlinson as well. Katy had not expected to see Charles at all.

They stared at each other again and then smiled together. Katy got down from her stool and Charles said awkwardly, remembering his lines, 'I've come to look around. I thought I'd ask Mr Tomlinson to show me the ropes because I haven't been in the place for over three years, since before I went to the Med.'

'Mr Tomlinson is in with Mr Ashleigh,' Katy explained, 'but I'm sure it would be all right if you went in.'

'No, I won't disturb them.' He wore a well-cut tweed suit with narrow trousers and carried his cap in his hand. Katy was in her working dress of black skirt and high-necked white blouse with puff sleeves. He thought she was much prettier than the girls of the previous evening. 'Tell you what: you can show me around.'

'Well . . .' Katy hesitated, caught off-balance by the request, uncertain what she should do. She glanced at the work on her desk.

Charles put in quickly, 'I'll make it right with Annie.'

Katy admitted, 'Miss Scanlon hasn't come in today. I think she's poorly with a cold.'

Charles grinned at her, a conspirator: 'Who's to know, then? Come on. Please?'

Katy told herself she could not refuse her employer's son. She conducted him around the warehouse and Charles tried to take some notice of what he was shown, but most of his attention was on her. At the end he asked her, 'Where do you go for lunch?' He had not asked his father about the eating habits of his employees.

Katy blinked at the question. Go somewhere

for lunch? She explained, 'I bring a sandwich and eat it here.'

Charles realised he had almost made a mistake. If he asked this young girl to lunch with him in a restaurant she would take fright. He said, 'What about a stroll afterwards? I'll meet you outside at half past twelve.' And then he was able to turn to Tomlinson as the manager returned to the office, saying, 'Miss Merrick has just been showing me around. I asked her as you were closeted with Father.' Then he went in to see Vincent Ashleigh, so Katy wasn't given the chance to refuse him as she knew she should — though she did not want to.

For the rest of the morning she worked with her thoughts elsewhere. She was nervous and a little bit frightened, very much out of her depth. She was young and while boys had made advances they had been of her own class and background. Charles Ashleigh came from a different world. His kind employed and ordered the workers and servants — and she was one of them. But she was excited, too. She could not get him out of her mind.

Charles, walking the busy streets, crowded with horse-drawn carriages and carts, hooting cars winding between them, was uncertain now. Since seeing her again that morning he was aware that this affair might not be as simple as just talking and flirting. He was sure it was not when he saw her again at twelve-forty. She ran out of the tall building with its legend of 'Ashleigh's' above the gates and on a brass plate in the wall. Her face was flushed and she

38

apologised, 'I'm sorry, sir. I'm late because Mr Tomlinson asked me for some figures.'

All Charles could find to say, suddenly tongue-tied, was the truth: 'All right. I'm just glad to see you.'

That was how it started, with a fifteen-minute stroll and shy conversation.

They agreed that it would be better not to meet at Ashleigh's again. Both were uneasily aware that there could be trouble, and while they never discussed it, both preferred to put off the day of reckoning. They progressed to walking longer and in the evenings as the days lengthened, though in the beginning they still observed the niceties and strolled a foot apart. They ventured to Whitley Bay and wandered arm in arm by the seashore and by then it was 'Charles' and 'Katy'. And sometimes he hired a cab pulled by a lackadaisical old horse that clip-clopped along slowly and they rode out in that, holding hands, and kissing when the darkness hid them. Their joy in each other was only increased by the clandestine nature of their love. Occasionally he remembered that he was on leave and at some point would be recalled, and he mentioned this in casual conversation. But that was somewhere in the future and it did not trouble them.

Inevitably, the affair did not remain secret for long. Annie Scanlon did not probe, but watching the girl, seeing her excitement and happiness, Annie guessed in the first week that there was a man, was sure at the end of the second. Then she saw them at their lunchtime strolling one day.

Tomlinson saw them meet when Charles, recklessly eager and casting aside secrecy, waited for her across the street from the office. And one of the labourers at Ashleigh's glanced out of the window of a public house as they passed and next day the entire warehouse knew — except Vincent Ashleigh. All those who knew kept the knowledge to themselves as if participating in some unspoken conspiracy, but the one who found out and who really mattered was not one of them.

On a Saturday afternoon Charles handed Katy down from a cab in the middle of Newcastle, both of them laughing. He turned to come face to face with a tall lady in a stylish gown with a flowered bodice and narrow skirt that reached down to touch her neat little shoes. She wore a befeathered hat with a wide, shady brim and Katy knew dress and hat must have cost well over a sovereign — probably four or five times what she was paid for a week's work. She saw the smile of amusement on Charles's face turn to one of surprise and he said, 'Good Lord, Mother. I didn't expect to see you in town today.'

Eleanor Ashleigh's eyes were sharp, her smile thin-lipped and put on like the hat. 'Your father wanted me to go with him to the country but I changed my mind. I decided to go shopping instead.' She gestured with a gloved hand to where a liveried boy stood, half hidden by an armload of parcels. But her gaze had never left Katy and now she asked, 'Aren't you going to introduce me, Charles?' He did and Eleanor

Ashleigh nodded and smiled, then murmured, 'Merrick? I don't recall the name. Is your father in business in Newcastle?'

Katy answered, 'He works in Swan Hunter's yard at Wallsend.'

Eleanor kept her smile in place and pressed her: 'Are you at finishing school?'

Katy did not know what she meant, had no experience of a life spent learning the social graces and practising them at balls and other glittering functions. Charles tried to come to her rescue but was no good at manufacturing excuses on the spur of the moment. He could only speak the truth: 'Katy works in the office — at Ashleigh's.'

'I . . . see,' said Eleanor slowly. The smile was brittle now. 'Well, I must go. Good day, Miss Merrick.' And to her son, 'I expect I will see you at dinner.'

Charles warned, 'I may be late this evening.'

His mother's glance flicked from him to Katy and back again. 'Your father and I will wait up for you.' All this time the cab Charles and Katy had left, with its head-hanging horse, had stood at the kerb, the driver hoping for another fare. His foresight and patience were now rewarded as Eleanor told the boy, 'Put those in the cab.' And when the parcels were loaded Charles tipped the lad and handed his mother into the cab. She did not look back or wave as the cab wheeled away.

Charles said, 'That's torn it.' And then, philosophically, 'Still, they would have to find out some day.'

Katy, mouth drooping, whispered, as many a

41

girl had done, 'Your mother didn't like me.'

For once Charles lied, or possibly he hoped against hope: 'Of course, she does. She's bound to!' He believed that. 'I expect she was taken by surprise, that's all.' He put his hands on her shoulders and turned her to face him. 'Cheer up. This isn't going to make any difference to us.' And he meant it.

He took her to a music hall that night, and afterwards to supper, but he failed to lift her spirits. Katy sensed impending doom. He walked with her to the corner of her street and kissed her. 'Don't worry. I'll see you tomorrow.' And she smiled wanly and left him.

He hailed the first cab he saw and it took him to his home. True to her word, Eleanor Ashleigh waited for him with her husband. They sat in armchairs on either side of the big fireplace in the drawing-room. Vincent Ashleigh was falsely jovial and challenged, 'What's this about you walking out with the girl in our office?'

Charles sat down on the chesterfield between them and smiled at his father. 'I'm very fond of Katy.'

His mother said impatiently, 'Oh, don't be silly, a girl of that sort. She said her father works at Swan Hunter's yard, but did not elaborate. I expect he's a common labourer, or a — ' She stopped to search for the name of some trade she had heard mentioned, and found: 'A riveter or something like that!'

Charles shrugged, 'I don't know what her father does. To tell you the truth, I don't think she gets on with him.' Charles had gathered that from odd comments made by Katy and the way she dismissed Barney in a few words. She had not run him down, would not wash the family's dirty linen in public.

'I expect he's thrown her out,' put in Eleanor. 'And I can guess why: staying out to all hours with young men.'

'That's not so!' Charles defended Katy indignantly.

'How do you know? *I* know what trouble I have with the maids here. They're forbidden followers but given half a chance they will have some young man hanging around the kitchen door — and inside it and worse, I shouldn't wonder. You must give her up.'

'I will not.' Charles jerked to his feet, flushed and angry.

'Of course you must!' Eleanor flared at him, 'That sort of girl will wind up in the family way and blame you!'

'No!' Charles swung on his heel.

His father rose now and put an arm around his shoulders. 'Steady on, old boy. I think we're all getting too worked up about this. I can't see any harm in two young people keeping company but you're both too young to think of being serious. Let's think it over for a week or two and then we'll talk again.' He caught a furious glance from his wife at this treachery, but ignored it except to frown at her, the message clear: Leave this to me.

Charles was mollified by his father's attitude and answered, 'That's fine by me.' He believed his father hoped the affair would blow over but he was sure of his feelings about Katy. He would not, could not, give her up.

He reported as much to her next day. 'And in a week or two I'll be taking you home to meet Father — formally, I mean — and have tea.' Katy was not so sure but he insisted, 'You'll see. Just wait a week or two.'

It took just a week for Vincent Ashleigh to resolve the problem. At the end of that time Charles received a telegram from Admiralty ordering him to join a cruiser lying at Portsmouth at once; she was about to sail for the China Station.

He waited for Katy to come out of the office at noon, not caring who saw them now. When she came running he showed her the telegram glumly. At first she did not understand, or did not want to, and asked, 'Does this mean you have to go?'

He explained to her patiently that it did, and straightaway: 'When the Navy says 'now' that's what it means, not tomorrow or next week. I'll pack my kit and take a train south tonight.' He went on quickly, 'This doesn't mean we're finished. Lots of chaps have to leave their girls at home for three years or so. It's just one of the things about the Service. I'll write to you. Will you wait for me?'

'Yes.' Katy wanted to cling to him but that would not be seemly. She had to hold his hand and look up at him. 'I'll wait. I'll write.'

She was at the station that night. He had told his parents, 'We'll say goodbye here,' and he had left them standing on the steps leading up to their front door as the Lanchester and its chauffeur carried him away down the carriage drive. So he and Katy had a few minutes alone in the dimness of the station and they clung to each other, kissed and repeated their promises. Then the train came in and pulled out again a few minutes later, bound for King's Cross and carrying Charles. Katy was left alone, to cry herself to sleep that night.

It was a day or two later that she had to take a sheaf of letters into Vincent Ashleigh's office. He was not there, had been called away in a hurry to some minor emergency in the warehouse, so she left them on his desk. As she did so she saw a handwritten letter already on the blotter, its ripped open envelope lying alongside. She could not help seeing that it was headed, 'Re: Sub-Lt Ashleigh.' From that name her eyes were drawn to the rest of it, which read:

Dear Vincent,
It was good to hear from you again. Of course, the Service cannot give weight to one person's wishes rather than another's, but in this case the interest of the Service will be served. I have found a berth for your boy, as you requested. He is a promising young officer and I'm sure he will do well on the China Station. Thank you for your invitation. I will take you up on the fishing when I am next in your part of the world.'

Katy went back to her desk and sat staring unseeingly in front of her. She saw what had

45

been done to Charles and herself and knew why. After a time the hurt became anger and she slid off the high stool and made for the door. Annie Scanlon called, 'Here! Where are you off to? I've just asked you twice for that Wilkinson invoice and you've taken no notice!'

Katy paused just long enough to say, 'I'm sorry, Annie, but I'm finished.' Then she walked out of there and into Vincent Ashleigh's office. He looked up as she entered and frowned when he saw who it was. And she had not knocked before entering. Was the girl presuming on her acquaintance with Charles? He asked coldly, 'Yes, Miss Merrick?'

'I'm giving notice.' Katy was icily calm herself on the surface, though raging inside. All through the ensuing conversation she did not raise her voice and Vincent remembered this later, but the bitterness and hurt came through. 'I'm leaving today. Now. I don't want to work here any more. I don't want to work for you, or see you every day.'

'What?' Vincent gaped at her for a moment then pointed his pen at her: 'You're at liberty to go because I've had too much of your damned impudence!'

'And I've had too much of your sly tricks. I saw that letter when I came in a few minutes ago.'

She did not say which letter but Vincent knew. He reddened and blustered, 'Eavesdroppers don't learn any good of themselves.'

Katy agreed, 'I didn't learn anything good. I found out what you had done to Charles and

46

me. I know why you did it. I can guess what his mother thinks but this just — happened. I never set out to get him. He came here looking for me. I expect he can do better for a wife, I hope he will, and I expect she'll be a fine lady, but she won't care for him as I did.' The tears were ready to come but Katy would never let him see them. She slammed out of the office, the first visible sign of her anger, and out of the building.

Vincent Ashleigh was left to fiddle with his pen and to come to the uncomfortable realisation that he had been rebuked by a quiet-voiced girl — and he felt guilty despite himself.

Katy did not return to her lodgings because she knew Mrs Connelly would be curious as to why she was not at work. Instead she wandered about the streets, unthinkingly following the routes she had taken so often with Charles, and that caused more pain. She fed her sandwiches to the shrieking, diving gulls down by the river, because she was not hungry. At one point in the afternoon she whiled away an hour in a teashop. But she had been there, also, with Charles. She was relieved when she could go back to Mrs Connelly's and hide in her room.

The next day she sought work but was unlucky. She saw that there was a vacancy for a girl advertised at Ashleigh's but thought no more about it. But unknown to her, one of the other girls at Mrs Connelly's, seeking a better job, applied for the post at Ashleigh's and was accepted. On her first day in the job she had to go down into the warehouse and there the men told her about her predecessor. Mrs Connelly came on her that evening when she was excitedly recounting this scandal as she understood it: 'Katy was going out wi' this young toff that was the boss's son so they got rid of her. I don't know what she'd been up to but, you know . . . ' She pointed up the hint with a nod and a sly wink.

Mrs Connelly demanded, 'What was that?' She listened and turned Katy out instantly. 'I'll not have your sort in the house, giving it a bad name!'

Katy was more bewildered and depressed than angry. When the girls came to her to commiserate — or fish for information — she told them nothing of Charles or the reason for her leaving Ashleigh's. She only said defiantly, 'I'm off to — to Scotland. There are plenty of jobs there.' That was a bluff, a destination plucked out of the air, distant but having the sound of reality. It was another country but one she could go to — in theory. As she walked away with her cheap suitcase she knew there was only one place she could go. She had spent almost all of her small savings on new clothes. She had bought them when Charles started to take her out because she would not let him dress her but she did not want to embarrass him, either. Now she had what would pay her board for a week or so and that was all. She had to save that as a last resort. She had to find work.

Barney opened the door to her, stared open-mouthed at her for a moment as she stood with her case, then recovered to jeer, 'I told you that would come crawling back one day!'

Katy gave back to him, eye to eye, 'I'm not crawling. I'll work for my bed and board and I'll be out of here again as soon as I can. If you don't like that, I'll walk out now!'

Barney hesitated. He looked around at his two sons, now adolescents, and at Lotte, the daughter still at home. Her sister, Ursula, had married a year ago and moved away. He appeared to be canvassing their opinion but in fact he was seizing a chance to think. His wife now and for the last three years was ill with bronchitis and confined to bed. Lotte was having to stay off work to care for her, was tired of the job and continually complaining. He saw her nod eagerly now. Barney was tired of coming home to her whining, badly cooked meals and a house in disorder.

He turned back to Katy. 'Right y'are. But you're outa here afore long. I'll see to that!'

5

'So you can pack your gear and get out.' Barney Merrick bawled it, getting gloating enjoyment from it.

Katy had worked from dawn to dusk during the illness of her stepmother. Lotte had thankfully laid down the burden and gone back to her job and spending her evenings hunting for a husband. She had not expressed any gratitude to Katy, however. 'Serves you right,' she said. 'You shouldn't have given so much lip to our dad.' She smirked with self-satisfaction but Katy had never expected any thanks and ignored her.

She cooked, shopped, cleaned, washed, mended. She tended Marina, Barney's new wife, all day long, ran errands for her and rubbed her with camphorated oil until she reeked of it. All the while Marina pointed out the shortcomings, to her eyes, in Katy's running of the household. She wailed, 'I'll be glad when I can get out of my bed and put this house to rights.'

Katy never complained. So that Barney jeered, 'Are you hoping I'll keep you on here if you behave yourself?'

'God forbid!' answered Katy. She had entered into a bargain with her father and would stick to her side of it, was sure he would stick to his. Her grief at losing Charles and her anger at the way

50

of her losing him, ebbed away, but she remained heartsore. She hugged that sorrow to her breast. There was no one she could confide in. She would not write to Charles Ashleigh. That episode in her life was closed, a mistake she would prefer to forget. She never received a a letter from him so it was obvious to her that he had forsaken and forgotten her.

Katy was terribly wrong in that because he wrote several times, marking the letters 'Please Forward'. Mrs Connelly burned them all: 'I'll not encourage her to practise her profession through my house!'

Marina finally rose from her bed out of boredom because her only intellectual activity was to stand at the front door to gossip with her neighbours and she was missing that sorely. On the day Marina pronounced herself fit enough for that, Barney announced to Katy, 'I've been looking for a job for you and found just the place. You're going to work as a maid for the Spargos in Sunderland. You've got aprons and dresses that will have to do. You'll get no more money outa me but I'll buy your ticket — one way.' Then he issued his ultimatum: 'Pack your gear . . . '

Katy obeyed. She would miss the two boys who were awkwardly fond of her, but she could see trouble ahead between her and Marina. And she would be getting out of this, to a new job, a new start. She thought it would be better than her present situation — wouldn't it?

Barney put her on the train for Sunderland. Katy wore her best dark grey dress and buttoned

51

boots. On the way to Newcastle Central Station she caught a fleeting glimpse of the *Mauretania*, the huge, 32,000-ton liner, lying at her fitting out quay. Barney, who worked on her, said with pride, 'She sails on her maiden voyage in November.' Katy reflected that he thought more of the ship than he did of her. But that was nothing new; she was used to it.

Arrived in Newcastle, Barney strode along the platform ahead of Katy. She laboured after him with her cheap suitcase dragging at her arm, until Barney halted, threw open a door and gestured for her to climb in. He shouted above the hissing of steam and the clanking of shunting: 'The Spargos will have somebody waiting for you at the station so you won't have to carry that case far. They'll be sending me ten bob of your money every month.' That was half her pay. Katy did not answer, looked past him and he saw the contempt in her expression. So as the train started to move he warned her, 'Behave yourself. Don't expect me to support you again. If you get the sack I'll report you to the pollis as a vagrant!'

That was meant to break through her uncaring mask and it succeeded. Katy had heard, vaguely, of vagrants and how the police could arrest them. She did not know what was the truth of the matter but feared the unknown. Barney saw the flicker of apprehension in the quiver of the young girl's lip and nodded with grim satisfaction. Katy still stood at the window of the carriage, twenty yards away now, and he shouted across the widening gap, 'Just remember!'

The train was not full and Katy had secured a seat by the window. She stared out at the scenery sliding by as the train trundled along, stopping at one small station after another, each with its little garden bright with flowers. She began in dejection but she was still not seventeen and soon became more cheerful. The day was bright and she was starting again in a strange place — and the flowers helped. The train halted at Monkwearmouth station to set down a number of passengers and then rolled on across a bridge. She opened the window and leaned out, caught a glimpse of the river below and saw this new place had a familiar look to it. There were the shipyards lining the banks of the River Wear as they did along the Tyne. Ships were tied up to the quays or lying to their buoys. She sniffed the salt sea smell and the reek of coal smoke from thousands of chimneys. There was bright sunlight sparking off the black water of the river, and a stiff breeze whipped at her hair and brought a flush to her cheeks. Her father and his threat were forgotten. He was miles away and she was free now. She laughed with delight, a young girl's glee.

Sunderland Central Station was an echoing cavern with a sooty glass roof and filled with the frequent thunder of trains pounding through or sighing to a halt. Katy struggled up the stairs to the concourse with her case a deadweight on her arm. Outside the station, in the sunlight, a cab stood at the kerb, the horse in its shafts with its head in a nosebag. The cabman on his seat was in his fifties, a stocky little man with a stubby clay pipe in his mouth under a walrus moustache. He lifted his whip to touch his bowler hat in salute: 'Cab, miss?'

'No, thank you,' Katy replied politely. She set down her case, stood at the horse's head and rubbed his nose. 'Good boy.'

A cart passed in a clashing of steel shoes on cobbles and halted in the middle of the road, but beyond the cab and opposite a space between the cab and a wall. The driver of the cart jumped down, a tall, thin, gangling young man, sallow and his hair dressed with brilliantine and parted in the middle. A cigarette dangled from his lower lip and a thin moustache ran across the upper. He seized the head of his horse and backed it, cursing as it skittered, into the space. But he backed it too far and the cab shook as the tail of the cart slammed into its ironshod wheel.

The young man spat out the cigarette and shouted querulously, 'What're you doing, backing into me?'

'Me?' The cabman rejected the claim, bewildered. 'I never backed up!'

'Yes, you did.'

'No, I didn't.' The cabman started to get down from his seat.

The young man seized a length of wood from where it lay on the cart and brandished it like a club. 'Come on! I'll brain you!'

It was then that a policeman came stalking with measured pace and demanded, 'What's going on here?'

The driver of the cart whined, 'This bloody old fool backed into me!'

54

The cabbie stoutly denied this: 'No, I didn't.' He inspected the rear of his cab and said placatingly, 'No harm done, anyway.'

But the young man retorted, 'Yes, there is! Look at my paint!' He pointed to the fresh scratches on the tailboard.

The policeman hesitated, head turning from one to the other, his hand feeling for his notebook. But then Katy left the horse's head and approached him: 'Please, sir, the cab didn't back.'

He turned to her, pencil in hand. 'You saw it, then?'

'I was standing at the horse's head. The cab never moved.' Katy said that firmly.

'Ah!' The policeman pointed his pencil at the young man. 'It seems to me that you're the one at fault. What are you doing with that lump o' wood?'

'Defending myself.' The answer came sullenly, with a scowl for Katy.

'What?' The policeman was contemptuous. 'Against a chap twice your age? Put it down and get on about your business before you get into more trouble. What is your business, anyway?'

'I'm here to meet a new serving lass, come to work at our house.' He jerked his head to indicate the cart: 'Spargo and Son, that's us. Hauliers.' Then he tapped his chest: 'I'm Ivor Spargo.'

The policeman was not impressed. 'You behave yourself. If I have trouble wi' you again, I'll charge you.'

Now Katy, from her new position near the

policeman, could see the legend on the tailboard of the cart: Spargo & Son. Her heart sank and she stepped back to stand beside her case. Just then a middle-aged, portly man in a check suit and carrying a suitcase, bustled out of the station: 'Cabbie?'

'Aye, here y'are, sir!' The cabman hurried to take the suitcase from him and stow it aboard. Then he took the nosebag off the horse before climbing up onto his seat. But as he swung the cab away from the kerb he called to Katy, 'Thanks, bonny lass!'

Now the policeman went on his steady way and Katy was left with the young man, who was moodily lighting another cigarette. She said miserably, 'Please, sir, I think you might be waiting for me. I'm Katy Merrick, come to work for the Spargos.'

He glared at her as if he could not believe it. Then he said bitterly, 'You've made a bloody fine start! What did you take his part for?' Katy could only answer, Because it was right. But she wisely kept her mouth shut. He went on, 'I've half a mind to send you back where you came from.' Katy swallowed, frightened. What would her father say — and do? Ivor saw or guessed at her fear and it put him in a better humour. He smiled unpleasantly, 'You'd just better behave yourself from now on. Is that your case? Shove it on the cart then get up there.'

Katy obeyed. The cart seemed to have been used recently for carrying coal. While its flat bed had been roughly swept out there was a pocket of black dust in one corner. A seat was fixed on the front of the cart and she sat on that. She knew Ivor had watched her for a glimpse of her legs as she scrambled up. Now he followed to sit beside her. He laid the whip across the horse's rump and as it whinnied and jerked into life he wheeled the cart out into the traffic. 'I'm Ivor Spargo. You call me dad Mr Spargo and me, Mr Ivor. I'll call you Katy.' He glanced round at her and demanded, 'Well? Got a tongue in your head?'

'Yes, Mr Ivor.'

'That's better. You'll have to answer quicker than that with Ma or you'll get a flea in your ear. You call her ma'am or Mrs Spargo.' He smoothed his narrow moustache with one finger. 'But when you and me know each other better and we're on our own, maybe you can call me Ivor.'

He glanced at her again and Katy answered quickly, 'Yes, Mr Ivor.'

'That's the way.' Ivor showed his teeth in a smile then steered the cart close in to the kerb so a clanging tram could pass. He cursed its driver and then pointed with the whip. 'This is Fawcett Street and that's High Street East down there . . . ' He charted their route for her as the horse walked on. And bragged, 'Us Spargos are one of the biggest hauliers around. We've got another big yard full o' carts and lorries, down in Yorkshire and there's a manager looks after that. Ma likes it here and she won't leave to go down there. We shift people's furniture all over, and anything else for that matter. A lot o' them take their coal with them when they move . . . ' Katy listened, and saw that they were heading away from the bridge and the river, staying on its southern bank. The streets were crowded and busy and the people cheerful. After a time she thought that she could like this new place — except for Ivor. And what about Ma — and Mr Spargo?

He proved to be in his late forties, with a pot belly swelling out the waistcoat of his shiny suit and a jowly face. The waistcoat hid the braces which held up his trousers, but they had to be there because the wide leather belt with brass buckle hung loose below his belly like a decoration. He stood in the centre of the cobbled yard as Ivor turned the cart in through the double gates marked: Spargo & Son, Hauliers. The house lay at the back of the yard while a shed which served as office was on one side of the gateway. Katy could see a clerk in there, bent over books, and a telephone standing on a desk. On the other side was a ramshackle wooden workshop of some sort holding benches scattered with tools. The rest of the yard was empty save for two carts standing idle, their shafts upended. There was a general air of untidiness with litter lying about and harness tossed carelessly aside.

Ivor reined in the cart beside his father. 'Here's the lass, Da: Katy.'

Arthur Spargo inspected her as his son had done, then said approvingly, 'Work hard, do as you're told and you'll be all right.'

Katy needed no prompting now: 'Yes, Mr Spargo.'

'That's right.' Arthur turned away but told

Ivor, 'Take her up to your ma.'

Ivor drove the cart up to the front door of the house, which was three-storied and brickbuilt. No untidiness there. The windows were clean, the curtains hung straight, the paintwork was without a mark or blister. Yet Katy found it oppressive because there was a harsh coldness about the place. Ivor pushed open the front door and bawled, 'Ma! *Ma!*' And then, stepping back into the yard, 'Here's the new lass, Ma.'

Vera Spargo loomed in the doorway, tall and rake-thin, with a pointed nose and beady black button eyes that ran over Katy from head to toe. Then that sharp gaze flicked to Ivor instead and she ordered him, 'You behave yourself. Do you hear?'

He muttered, 'Yes, Ma.' He was no longer swaggering but submissive and wary. When his mother jerked her head at him in dismissal, he dropped Katy's case at her feet and slouched away. Vera said contemptuously, 'Him and his father, both the same — slipshod. But you'll find things different in here. I run the house.' Katy was to learn that Vera ran the business as well. But now the little eyes swept Katy again: 'You'll need to tidy yourself up, lass. I'll stand for no scruffiness in here. That's one of the reasons I sacked the last girl. But you'll dress plain, nothing to catch the men's eyes.' Her own dress which brushed the floor was unrelieved black and the white apron over it was starched and crisp, sterile. She went on, 'You'll have no trouble of that sort in the house, though. Speak a word to me and I'll stop it. And if I catch *you* at it, I'll put you out on the street where you belong.' The black eyes glittered with menace.

Katy answered, 'Yes, ma'am.'

'Fetch your case.' Then Vera warned, 'But after this you use the kitchen door and the back stairs.' The hall inside the door held a coatstand with one lady's coat, an umbrella and a walking stick. A wide carpet ran from the front door to the back of the house and also up the stairs. The floor on either side of the carpet gleamed with polish.

Vera led the way up the stairs. The bedrooms of the family were on the first floor but Vera went on to the landing at the top of the house and Katy followed, carrying the case. The house appeared immaculate to Katy's eyes, so far as she could see. But Vera sniffed and complained, 'There's plenty needs doing. I've only had dailies in to help Rita and after a day or two they don't come back.' Four rooms opened out of the landing and these were the servants' quarters. Vera pointed at one: 'That's Rita's, and Cook is next door to her. They're both working in the kitchen at the moment. You're the youngest so you'll do as they say if I'm not about. Otherwise, I give the orders and set out the duties.' She threw open one of the other doors. 'You're in here. Put on your working clothes and be down in the kitchen in ten minutes. As I said, there's plenty to do.' And she swept off down the stairs like a black shadow.

The room held a bed and a small chest of drawers. A string stretched across one corner, so clothes could be hung on it, served as a wardrobe. The narrow bed had a strip of threadbare carpet alongside it, otherwise the floor was bare, but scrubbed white. Katy guessed who would do the scrubbing. She laid her case on the foot of her bed, opened it and got out an old dress for work. She changed quickly then paused for a second or two to peer out of the window. She looked out over the smoking chimneys of the town and the cranes of the shipyards and thought that there was some advantage in living on the top floor. But it would be icy cold in the winter. Then she remembered Vera Spargo was waiting for her and hurried downstairs.

Vera greeted her at the foot of them, 'Come on!' She beckoned with a finger like a claw and Katy followed her as she started back through the house, pointing to her right then left, 'Drawing-room, dining-room, master's study, my *boodwar.*' She pushed open the door at the end of the passage and they entered the kitchen. Scullery and kitchen ran the width of the house. 'Cook' was Mrs Cullen, round-faced, with flyaway grey hair and beaming vaguely. The 'Mrs' was a courtesy title which went with the office of cook; in fact she was a spinster. Rita might have been forty or sixty and was sullen and pouting. Vera said, 'This is Katy. Start her on the vegetables.' And left.

Cook said, with an absent smile, 'Show her, Rita, there's a good lass.'

Rita threw aside the mop she was using to wash the floor and muttered bad-temperedly, 'In here.' Katy found herself in the scullery with a

61

sink, knife and sacks of potatoes and greens.

In the next hour or so she worked under Cook or Rita and learned from both — separately. Cook complained, 'You're just the latest. None o' the lasses stay for long. That Rita, she only keeps on 'cause she's frightened she'll never get another job.'

Rita whined that: 'Cook, she's been sacked from most o' the houses in the town. The bottle, y'know.' She mimed drinking. 'Rum when she can get it, owt else when she can't. Vera keeps her on because she's cheap and the men won't touch her. They won't touch me, neither.' She sniggered, 'Wish they would.'

Both said that Vera ran the house — and the two men: 'She wears the trousers and they do as they're told. Like us. And that stick she keeps by the front door, she uses it on anybody that gets on the wrong side of her.' Rita hoisted up her skirts to show the leg above her black stocking marked by a livid bruise: 'That was done by her and her stick!'

At six Cook looked up at the kitchen clock. 'Katy, you tell Mrs Spargo that dinner is just about ready.' So Katy walked through the hall and found Vera standing at the front door. She delivered her message and Vera nodded without turning. Katy could see past her into the yard and now it was full of vehicles. There were another three carts lined up beside those previously there and outside the workshop stood two steam lorries with their huge iron wheels, and tall chimneys giving off a drift of smoke from their coal-fired engines. As Katy watched a third turned in at the gate, its driver sitting behind the big locomotive boiler which ran across the front of it. There was a smell of smoke and oil and hot metal mingling with the ammoniac odour of manure coming from the stables.

Vera said with gloating satisfaction, 'That's a Yorkshire steam wagon coming in and that's the last of them. They're all ours and they're all home now. Sometimes the lorries aren't back till long after dark, if they're carrying a load to Shields or Durham.' Then she repeated what Ivor had told Katy: '*And* we've got a bigger yard than this in Yorkshire. But I grew up here, and here I'm staying.' She continued to watch as the drivers shut down their charges and dismounted, called to each other across the yard. One by one they reported to Arthur Spargo where he stood by the office, then walked out between the gates on their way home. As the last of them left, Vera turned away, but sneered, 'He's standing there like the boss but if it hadn't been for me pushing him he'd still be working out of a back lane with one horse and cart! Him and Ivor, they're stick-in-the-muds, the pair of them.'

Katy helped Rita to serve the dinner to the Spargos in the dining-room, then cleared up after it. By now Cook was sprawled in a chair before the kitchen stove with a glass in her hand, her speech thickened and face sweating. The work was left to the two maids and it was close to midnight when Katy locked her door and crept into her bed by the light of a candle. Nervous and physical exhaustion brought sleep soon, but in the few minutes before it claimed her images flickered through her brain like those she had seen in the silent films: her father sending her away, the Spargos, Cook and Rita. But she was determined she would not break and run. She would never go back to her father again, nor fall into vagrancy, whatever dreadful fate that might mean — or go to the workhouse. She would make a better life for herself, somehow.

It was a determination difficult to hold to. Rita was a hard-working maid under Vera's eye but idle out of it — and no cook. So Katy had to cook when Mrs Cullen was unfit for duty, drunk and insensible. This was on top of her other duties. Then the Spargo men both attempted to fondle her but she immediately threatened, 'I'll tell Mrs Spargo!' Somewhat to her surprise, they always retreated, grumbling, 'No harm in a bit o' fun!' Or some similar complaint. It proved they were afraid of Vera, but they always tried again and the threat was always there. So Katy often went to her bed afraid, despite the lock on the door, and despairing of any improvement in her life. She slept in spite of her misery, the sleep of exhaustion, falling into bed every night, worn out, and was unconscious in seconds. Relief came only after three hard months which seemed like three years.

'To hell with him! He'll not tell me how to run my business!' Arthur Spargo fumed as he sat down to the mid-day meal. He had just sacked his clerk after an exchange of insults.

Vera Spargo said acidly, 'Somebody has to. You'll have to replace him.'

Arthur grumbled, 'That won't be easy, the money they're wanting these days. It could take me weeks to find the right feller.'

Katy was leaning between Vera and Ivor to set a dish of potatoes on the table and she skipped away as she felt his hand on her leg. She said, 'Mrs Spargo?' And Ivor looked scared for a moment.

Vera glared at her, outraged. 'How dare you! Speak when you're spoken to — and till then you keep your mouth shut! Have you got that into your thick head?'

Katy swallowed her anger. 'Yes, Mrs Spargo.'

'I should hope so. I don't know what the world's coming to, with lasses like you putting your oar in.'

Katy said, 'I'm sorry, Mrs Spargo.' But she did not retreat.

Vera, mollified, said, 'That's better.' Then remembering: 'What did you want, anyway?'

Katy ventured, 'I think I could do the books for Mr Spargo. I worked in an office for three years before I came here.'

'Did you now?' Vera raised her eyebrows. 'I wonder why you left?' But she did not press the matter when Katy remained silent, but glanced at Arthur and told him, 'You might as well give her a try.'

He protested, jowls wobbling, 'What — a lass?'

'Why not?' demanded Vera. 'If I can run this business better than you, the lass could well manage better than the feller you sacked.

Besides, she's on the doorstep and she'll be cheaper.'

That appealed to Arthur. 'Aye, all right.'

So the next morning Katy carried out her normal duties of cleaning out grates and lighting fires, sweeping and dusting. But before the men arrived for work she was seated at the desk under the window in the office. She found that all she had to do was follow the ways of her predecessor. Inside of a week, Arthur was satisfied. 'Right, I'll keep you on. You can work for me instead o' the missus.'

There was a brief argument when Katy insisted she should give up all her housework. Rita wanted her to continue with some of it but Katy found an unusual ally in Vera, who ruled, 'The business comes first. We'll be taking on another lass as a maid and she will do the housework. Until she arrives, Rita will have to cope.'

Katy was closer to happiness than she had ever been since Charles Ashleigh had left her. It was as well she could not see into the future.

6

Corporal Matthew Ballard, Army Service Corps, stepped out of the barrack room onto the verandah and paused to look out over the bare expanse of the square. He squinted into the evening sunshine, watching the mounting of the guard with a bawling of orders and rattle of rifle drill. To one side of the square lay the vehicle park and the big sheds which housed the tractors and lorries . . . There were a lot of them because it was the job of his company to evaluate them for use by the Army.

The file of men that was the guard marched off the square, heading for the guardroom and their duty. Matt started down the stairs, a tall, wide-shouldered young man now, with dark eyes and a thatch of black hair cut short by the Army's barber. His parents had died of cholera in India and he had been raised by the Army in the Duke of York's School at Dover. From there he had entered the Army Service Corps and worked on and with tractors, for some years in South Africa. He had returned to join this company when it was formed in 1903.

He carried himself like the soldier he was as he marched round the square and out of the barracks. In the married quarters he saw Eunice

67

Taylor, the pretty daughter of a sergeant-major, passing on the opposite pavement. He swung his hand up to his cap in a salute and smiled. Eunice blushed and returned the smile but Matt marched on.

He found his friend in the married quarters. Corporal Joe Docherty, thin, leathery brown and a head shorter than Matt, stood by the horse-drawn cab at his front door. He grinned as Matt came up and said, 'Off in a minute. Just waiting for the missus.'

Matt nodded, 'Aye.'

Joe was an older man by ten years or more. He had taken Matt under his wing when the boy moved up to man's service, and had been like a father to him. Joe was leaving the service partly because he had finished his engagement, partly because he had amassed a comfortable sum running a crown and anchor board, which was illegal in the eyes of the Army, but Joe had not been caught. Mainly he was leaving because his wife had said she was tired of living in a succession of married quarters and wanted to settle down. Now he said, 'If you ever want a job, just drop me a line.' Joe was going to buy a lorry and start his own business. As he put it, unconsciously repeating Ivor Spargo some three hundred miles away, 'Shifting furniture or anything else, anywhere.'

Matt grinned, 'I'll think about it.'

Joe's wife came out then, a pretty but faded woman. She had a smile for Matt and they all said their farewells, the two men monosyllabic, with nothing to say now because they had said it all before. They shook hands, then Joe and his wife rolled away in the cab and Matt strode away. He had a good idea where he would find Eunice.

7

SUNDERLAND. SUMMER 1909.

Howard Ross was tall and strong, blond, blue-eyed and handsome and he came as Katy's saviour on a fine morning.

'What have we got today, Katy?' demanded Arthur Spargo as he entered the office. Outside in the yard the men were harnessing the horses and starting up the other vehicles. There was a throbbing of engines, clatter of horses' hooves and the rumble of ironshod wheels of the carts on the cobbles of the yard. Katy could sniff the mingled smells of the petrol driven lorries, the hot metal odour of the coal burning steam tractors with their little ashpans slung beneath the engines, and behind all the ammoniac reek of the stables.

Katy turned to Arthur from her desk under the window, 'Here are the job chits. It's a full turnout today, everything out on the road.' She handed him the slips of paper, each one detailing the job to be carried out by either a cart, a steam wagon or a petrol-engined lorry. Spargos now had two of the latter, bought at Vera Spargo's urging.

Arthur barely glanced at the papers because during the past two years he had grown to rely on Katy, though she was still only eighteen. She kept the books and correspondence neat and tidy and could always find whatever figure or document Arthur wanted. She read the trade magazine, *Motor Traction*, which the Spargo men barely glanced at but Katy learned thereby. She was brisk and efficient on the telephone and had even learned how to price a job so as to get the business but still make a profit. Now Arthur asked, 'What about bills?'

Katy pointed her pen at one of two neat piles of invoices. 'I've done those — and I'll have finished the others before long and then I'll take them to the post.'

Arthur grunted acknowledgment and waddled out of the office — he had put on a lot of weight in the past two years. Katy got on with her work, glancing up occasionally to peer out of the window when the carts, steam wagons and lorries rolled out through the gates, on their way to their work for the day. All the drivers waved to her as they went by. Katy was popular with them, and not only because she worked out their pay and overtime correctly, but because she always had a smile for them at the start and end of the day.

Because of her involvement in working out their pay, she had made a claim for better pay for herself and had it granted, in part at least. Katy had pointed out that young male clerks were being paid fifteen shillings a week. Vera Spargo had reluctantly agreed to pay Katy ten shillings a week because she was being fed. That was twice what she had earned as a maid. She knew she was still underpaid and so did the Spargos, but for the moment she was content. While her father still got his ten shillings a month, Katy was able to live frugally but also to save a little. That was important because she planned to escape from the Spargos. To do that she needed enough money to pay for lodgings until she found work elsewhere and there was no knowing how long that might take. She was still fearful of the charge of vagrancy — and the workhouse.

At mid-morning Vera Spargo came to the office, as she did each day, to ask, 'What's going on?'

And Katy told her what work was being done and where: 'Vic is shifting some furniture for a couple in Hendon moving to Bishopwearmouth, Jim's lorry is taking a load to Durham . . . '

Vera listened intently to the list of jobs and their prices and at the end nodded grudging satisfaction: 'That sounds all right. Now, I've got a carpenter coming to do some work on the house, a feller called Howard Ross. He's not been here before, so when he comes you direct him round to the kitchen door.'

'Yes, Mrs Spargo.'

So Vera went off with a curt nod and Katy returned to her work. She still had respect for, and fear of, Vera and acknowledged that she ran the business, rather than Arthur. But Katy also knew, from her reading of *Motor Traction*, how a yard like that of the Spargos should be run. Vera was better at it than Arthur but was still far from perfect. The general untidiness was just an example of the sloppiness. Poor and infrequent servicing of the vehicles was another . . .

An hour later Katy heard the *clip-clop!* of

trotting hooves and a pony pulling a smartly varnished trap passed between the entrance gates and was reined to a halt outside the office. Its driver jumped down and came to stand tall at the open window. With his blond hair that crinkled and his blue eyes smiling he reminded Katy, with a pang, of Charles Ashleigh. But it was a very slight pang; time had healed. And this was not Charles but a young man called Howard Ross. He wore overalls and carried his tools in a brown canvas bag. 'I've come to do a job for Mrs Spargo.'

Katy returned the smile and leaned over her desk to point a slim finger: 'You'll find her up at the house. She's expecting you, but go round to the back and use the kitchen door.'

He asked, 'Are you Mrs Spargo's daughter?'

Katy kept the smile in place while thinking, No, thank God! She said, 'I'm just the clerk. There is a son but no daughter.'

'Ah!' There was an involuntary hint of disappointment in that exclamation, but he stood there another second or two, appraising, then said, 'I'll see you again.' He waved and vaulted easily into the trap and the pony walked on up to the house.

Katy watched him go. She was used to young men eyeing her appreciatively, and cautious. Ivor was still a lurking presence but he was now involved with the latest maid, Betsy, a buxom, giggling girl — as he had been with the succession of maids who preceded her. There was no young man in Katy's life, nor had there been since Charles Ashleigh. There had been

73

offers but she had declined them all. Quite apart from Vera's ruling against 'followers', none had attracted her. But now she thought this tall, blond stranger was good-looking . . . And he had said he would see her again . . . She was smiling as she turned back to her work.

Howard Ross, as he skirted the house, thought dispassionately that it was a pity there was no young girl of Spargo's with money to add to her attractions. He combined his work with profitable philandering, seeking work in houses where the plain but wealthy daughters — or wives — could be persuaded to buy him handsome presents. But business wasn't everything, and one day when he was in the mood he would come back here for the girl in the office. Besides, in the past year he had built up a sideline which paid much better than an occasional silver watch or cigarette case.

* * *

Matthew Ballard, now a sergeant, stood in his colonel's office in the barracks at Aldershot and refused to be persuaded or tempted. 'No, thank you, sir.'

The colonel urged, 'You have an excellent record and have done sterling work in this unit evaluating vehicles for the Army's use. I can assure you that you would soon be promoted to warrant officer if you signed on for a further engagement. You would have an excellent future in the Corps.'

'I understand that, sir, and I'm grateful. But I

74

have already committed myself.'

His commanding officer sighed, 'Very well. I respect your loyalty to an old friend and wish the pair of you all good fortune.'

'Thank you, sir.' And Matt saluted and marched out.

Joe Docherty had written, 'I know your time finishes about now. My offer of a job is still open but now I need you. Betty passed away a month ago and I'm left with little Beatrice. On top of that I haven't been too well lately and can't cope with the work on my own. So if you want to do yourself and me a good turn, now's your chance.' Matt had seen a lot of service with Joe Docherty and could not resist this appeal.

He got down from the train in Sunderland on a wet evening and found Joe renting a comfortable house in Monkwearmouth. It was one of a terrace but each had its own front garden and all were well cared for, with clean lace curtains at the windows and smart paintwork. Matt rapped with the shining brass knocker and the door was opened by Joe. He had a wide grin for Matt, shook his hand and pulled him inside then took his suitcase from him. 'Matt! It's great to see you! Come on in.' He led the way into a sitting-room filled with furniture and edged through it to the armchairs set either side of the fireplace. 'Make yourself comfortable. I'll just tell Alice that you're here — '

He broke off there because a young woman in a worn, dark brown dress and white apron appeared in the doorway. Her hair was drawn back tightly into a bun and she snapped

75

impatiently, 'I heard the knock and came as quick as I could! I haven't got two pairs of hands and I was in the kitchen getting the supper.'

Matt saw a flicker of exasperation cross Joe's face but then it was gone. He said, 'I was in the hall when he knocked. This is Mr Ballard. Matt, this is Alice. She's mainly here to look after Bea but she cooks as well and she's got a meal ready for you.' He smiled stiffly at Alice, 'That's right?'

Her lips twitched in reply, 'I'll be ready to serve in ten minutes.' Her thin smile moved to Matt, assessing, taking in the tall strength of him, the dark good looks. Her eyes widened.

Joe laughed, 'So we'll have a quick one while we're waiting. How about a scotch and ginger ale, Matt?'

'Fine.' Matt thought that he and Joe had always drunk beer before because it was all they could afford. As Alice left the room he also thought that Joe had done very well for himself: a nice house, business of his own that was flourishing and a cook/nursemaid. But Joe himself was not doing so well. To Matt's eyes he looked to have a yellowish tinge and to have lost weight.

They sat down by the fire and Joe leaned forward to say eagerly, 'I'm really glad to see you, Matt. I've been doing the best I can but I can't work like I used to. There's lots of jobs I could pick up but I've had to let them go. Now you're here — but I'll take you down to the yard in the morning and you can see the business.'

They chatted about old friends and places while they waited for their meal and it was all of twenty minutes before Alice entered, simpering, and announced, 'I'm ready to serve now.' The drab brown dress had been replaced by a newer, smarter affair in pale blue with a noticeable décolletage and her hair was now piled on the top of her head. Her smile never faltered all the way through dinner.

The next morning Matt went with Joe to see the yard. It lay down by the river and was reached after walking through long streets of terraced houses built for the shipyard workers. The shipyards were close by with their towering cranes and the battering noise of the riveting hammers. The children running in the streets were ragged or wore patched clothes and some were barefoot in the summer weather. Joe muttered, 'We were brought up like this but I want something better for my daughter.'

They came to padlocked gates set in a high wall and painted with the words: J. Docherty. Haulier. Joe used a key to unlock the gates and then swung them open. The yard inside was square, cobbled and half the size of a football pitch. Matt saw, on the left-hand side of the yard, a stable and a shed or garage. A cart and a lorry stood before these buildings on a square of concreted hard-standing. Joe pointed to the lorry: 'Dennis three-ton flatbed — ' He broke off and laughed, 'But you can see that! I can't tell you anything about lorries!' Matt shrugged modestly and Joe went on, 'I've got a canvas housing I can rig on it if I'm carrying furniture. I just use the horse and cart for local, small stuff.' The horse hung its head over the stable door, watching them. Joe explained, 'The garage is big enough for both the Dennis and the cart and I put them inside during the winter. I don't bother this time o' year, though.'

Matt stroked the horse's nose but his eyes were on the Dennis. It could have been cleaner. He asked, 'What about maintenance?'

Joe flapped a hand, 'She's due for a service but I haven't been too good these last few days.'

Matt thought this was not like the old Joe Docherty. His gaze shifted to the building on the right side of the yard, opposite the garage and back from the gate. It had two floors, with windows and a door facing him. While curtains sagged at the upstairs windows, those on the ground floor were uncurtained and Matt could see a desk inside. He nodded at it: 'Is that the office?'

Joe agreed, 'Right. Come and have a look.' They crossed the yard and Joe slid his hand into a crack between doorstep and door sill and took out a key. He grinned, 'Always keep it there.' He turned the key in the lock and pushed open the door, then apologised, embarrassed, 'Sorry, it's a bit scruffy in here. I haven't had time to clear it up lately.'

The desk was littered with papers, the old swivel chair was dirty and the bare floorboards needed sweeping. There was a thin layer of dust over everything and a cobweb hung in one corner. The office ran back for some twenty feet but a counter bestrode it halfway. There was a flap that could be lifted up to let people pass behind it. The walls past the counter held shelves, empty and dusty. Joe explained, 'I think the place was used as a store of some sort at one time.' He nodded at the stairs which ran up one wall to the floor above: 'There's a couple of rooms up there. Not a stick of furniture, but they *could* be a bedroom and kitchen — there's water and gas laid on and a kitchen range. Not that I'm suggesting you live up there. You'll bed and board with us — if you're taking the job?' He stopped then, racked by a fit of coughing. When he got his breath back he muttered, 'I'll have to have a drink.'

'I'll take the job.' Matt grinned and shook Joe's outstretched hand.

Joe grinned back at him. 'I knew you wouldn't let me down. Come round to the Frigate and we'll drink to it.'

It was early in the day so when they got to the Frigate Matt settled for a cup of coffee, but Joe had a stiff rum with his and stayed on when Matt left. He started work that day by cleaning up the office, but soon he was out on the road every day, driving the Dennis. Meanwhile Joe handled smaller jobs with the horse and cart, or more often sat in the office and dealt with the paperwork. He was incapable of physical effort for very long.

Matt did not stay long in the Docherty house. His bed was comfortable and the food was good, but little Beatrice, Joe's three-year-old daughter, was spoilt by her father out of over-affection and Alice because of laziness — she let the child do as she wished. Added to this, Alice became more and more attentive to Matt. Joe grinned amiably, seeing nothing wrong with the match, but Matt was not ready for marriage at that time — or to Alice at any time. Nevertheless, he did not want to hurt her, so he left and moved into lodgings, making the excuse that he wanted to live nearer the yard. It was a poor excuse as the new lodgings only saved him another five minutes' walk, but he was not good at contriving excuses.

It did not fool Alice. She knew why he had left and cried into her pillow.

Matt's fate lay elsewhere. He had only jumped out of the frying pan.

★　★　★

'Have you reserved a table, sir?' The head waiter in the restaurant of the Palace Hotel was respectful because Matt wore his dark grey suit with narrow lapels to the jacket and narrow trousers. His starched collar was high, his silk tie neatly knotted and his shoes gleamed with polishing. He looked a picture of a young gentleman. The head waiter was not to know that Matt had worked very hard for weeks and was in the mood to blow some of his savings on a meal and a visit to a theatre. Nor that the suit was the only one Matt possessed and the polish on the shoes was the result of his own efforts and not those of some valet.

Matt answered, 'I'm afraid not,' and thought that he should have booked a table because he knew the rules. As a young soldier he had sometimes helped in the officers' mess on the occasion of a mess dinner, and he had heard the young subalterns talking about booking a table for dinner at a restaurant. He had learned the etiquette, and that he was as good a soldier and a man as they. He was not overawed by the Palace or the head waiter.

'There is one table free, sir.' The head waiter inclined stiffly in a little bow, then the young woman appeared at Matt's side. He asked, 'Will you and the lady come this way, sir?'

The young woman said coolly, without a glance at Matt, 'We are not together.'

'I'm sorry, miss.' Her tone rankled with him. Besides, he wasn't sure that it was a good idea to allow young women in unescorted. 'Do you have a reservation?'

'No.' That was curt. She was angry because she had only wheedled the money from her mother at the last moment. If she had got it sooner she would have booked a table. The Palace was always full on a Saturday evening.

'I'm sorry, miss, but this gentleman has the last vacant table.' And he thought, And serve you right.

Now she looked at Matt and saw what the head waiter had seen and came to the same conclusion: this was a young gentleman of means. She smiled and said bravely, 'Oh, well, it can't be helped.' Her blonde hair was piled high and her blue eyes were wide and long-lashed. Her dress of taffeta reached down to her neat shoes of black patent leather and covered her bosom without concealing it.

Matt looked into those eyes and volunteered, 'You must have it.'

81

'Oh, no, I couldn't possibly deprive you. But you are extremely kind.'

Matt ventured, risking a snub, 'Perhaps we could share?'

'Well . . . ' She pretended to be unsure. 'If you wouldn't mind.'

'I'd be delighted.' Then he introduced himself, 'I'm Matthew Ballard.'

She held out her gloved hand, 'Fleur Ecclestone.' Her birth certificate showed Fanny but she had early discarded that, before she became a pupil at her private school. Matt shook the gloved hand she extended then gestured to her to precede him. 'Thank you.' She followed the head waiter, who thought, I was afraid we were going to be all bloody night! Matt followed her and was conscious of the movement of her lithe body inside the thin dress.

Seated at the table, Fleur set out to enchant him and succeeded. She was shy and soft-voiced, graceful and smiling, ate like a bird and took one glass of wine and no more. When dinner was over he suggested, hopefully, 'I was going on to a theatre. Would you care to join me?'

Fleur hesitated, looking up at him from under those long lashes. 'We've only just met.'

Matt coaxed, 'Does that matter?'

Fleur yielded as she had always intended to, and laughed, 'I suppose not. Very well, I'd love to go.'

They drove to the Empire in a cab and afterwards he took her home in another. She lived with her mother in a good class rented apartment near Mowbray Park. Matt was not surprised because he had concluded that she came from a monied background. Nor was he put off: 'Faint heart never won fair lady.' They parted with an agreement that he should pay his respects to her and he strode back to his digs humming the tunes from the show.

'Did you enjoy your evening, dear?' Fleur's mother had been dozing by the fire and woke as her daughter entered.

'I'd have enjoyed it more if you'd given me the money sooner,' Fleur replied curtly. She was remembering the embarrassing scene when the head waiter told her there was no table for her — and blaming her mother for it.

Mrs Ecclestone said anxiously, trying to ward off the tantrum she could see was coming, 'Did you meet any nice people?'

'Yes. Just as well I did. I can't face my old friends as a pauper.'

Her mother winced, 'We're not paupers, dear. Your father left us provided for, as best he could. We can manage if we're careful.'

'Careful!' Fleur shouted in rage and frustration. 'Scrimping and scraping! And he left you a pension but nothing for me!'

'It was all your poor father had,' wailed her mother.

'What did he expect me to do? Get a job in a factory?' Her father had sent Fleur to a private school when his business had been doing well. The friends she had made there now spent their days in wealthy idleness and pastimes she could not afford. When her father's business failed he had scraped together enough to buy an annuity for his wife in the event of his death. That came soon afterwards, from overwork and stress.

Mrs Ecclestone tremulously suggested, 'It need not be in a factory. Possibly in an office — '

'And have one of those friends find me banging away at a typewriter? I have my pride! Oh! You just don't *understand!*' And Fleur stormed out of the room, slamming the door behind her.

Matt paid his respects with flowers and walks in the park. They sometimes repeated that evening at the Palace Hotel and then a show, but not often because Matt could not afford it and said so. Fleur was only slightly disappointed. She wanted a man who would give her a home, income and a place in society and was sure Matt would do. She easily got him to talk about his work, listened to his eager talk and deduced, rightly, that he did most of the work at Docherty's. He was a young man who was going somewhere. She would trust her instinct and there was no hurry. She calculated cold-bloodedly that her mother would not make old bones, but believed she would live long enough. That was important, because when Mrs Ecclestone died her annuity would cease and Fleur would be penniless.

8

'Take your baggage and get out!' Vera Spargo squawled and it echoed round the yard. Katy winced, remembering her father bawling a similar order at her. She looked up from her work and out of the window of the office and saw Vera standing in the doorway of the house. In the early dusk of autumn she was silhouetted against the gaslights in the hall. The men had mostly returned from their day's work and were putting away the carts, steam wagons and lorries, feeding and watering the horses. They stopped work and turned at the eldritch screech. Vera held Betsy, the young maid, by the hair at the back of her head and now thrust her out of the house and down the steps so she sprawled in the dirt of the yard.

Betsy shrieked and got up onto her knees. She cried out, 'It was your Ivor made me do it! Always after me, he is!'

Vera said contemptuously, 'It takes two, and from what I saw when I caught you at it, you were as much to blame as him!' Rita appeared beside her now, carrying a suitcase, obviously hastily packed; it bulged and scraps of garments stuck out here and there. Vera snapped, 'All there?'

Rita nodded, 'Yes, ma'am.'

85

Vera snatched the case from her and threw it after Betsy. She followed it with a handful of coins. 'There's what's owing you! Now take yourself off!' She reached behind the front door and brought out the walking stick. Betsy shrieked again, but scrabbled for the coins, picked up the case and ran. The men working in the yard guffawed and their hooting laughter followed her out of the gate. Katy saw her tear-streaked face as she stumbled past with the case clasped against her body.

Katy was sorry for her and sorry to see her go, though not surprised. She had guessed long ago at the affair with Ivor; Betsy had dropped some coy hints. But the giggly girl had been about Katy's own age, and though silly, she was nevertheless someone to talk to and laugh with. Katy was lonely in this house and hungry for companionship.

She saw Ivor come skulking around the corner of the house. He had run out of the back door to escape from his mother's rage. That would not be directed at him for any immorality but because of his dallying with a servant, someone beneath him in Vera's opinion. Now he waited by the side of the house, hidden from her there, until she swept back into the hall. She slammed the door behind her, probably gone to seek him. Ivor saw his chance then and ran to the gates. The men did not laugh at him, only grinned and that behind their hands, because a word of complaint from Ivor could get them the sack. Vera would castigate him but woe betide any worker who dared deride him. As he fled through the gateway he shot a look at the office before running away down the road. Katy did not laugh at him, either, but kept her head bent over her books. She was not sorry for him and did not see how the affair could affect her. She would learn in time.

Ivor returned late in the evening when his mother's wrath had abated but Katy still heard her shouting at him while she lay in her cold bed two floors above them, with a chill wind moaning about the house. Vera finished: 'You'd do well to think less about lasses and more about this business! You take no interest in it! I've a mind to tell your father to sell up and let you make your own way . . . ' Her voice tailed away into grumbling then, but that went on for some time. Katy fell asleep to the distant mutter of it.

'Don't you dare touch me!' Katy hissed the words a few days later. Vera's tirade and threat had borne fruit in that Ivor was more busy in the yard and working out of it for longer, but now that he had lost Betsy he returned to loitering around Katy. This morning, with its gas-lit grey dawn light, he had sidled into the office where Katy sat alone and attempted to fondle her. He backed off now when she warned, 'I'll tell your mother!'

'Just a bit o' fun.' He licked his lips and smirked at her. 'I'll see you later.'

'Talk to me through the window.' Katy pointed to the door and Ivor shrugged and walked out of it, into the yard. A few minutes later he drove off with his horse and cart; Arthur would not trust him to drive a lorry as yet.

When he returned that evening he reported to his father. Arthur stood just outside the office, so Katy heard all of the exchange. Ivor complained, 'That feller in Monkwearmouth — Docherty — he's started working on our side of the river, taking trade away from us.'

Arthur scowled at the idea: 'What trade?'

'Shifting some woman's furniture from Bishop-wearmouth to Millfield.'

Arthur's frown was now more puzzled than annoyed. 'I didn't know we had a job like that booked.'

'We didn't.' Then Ivor pointed out, 'But if he'd stayed his side of the river we might ha' done.'

Arthur shrugged, 'We might, but we're not the only hauliers this side of the river. One o' the others could ha' got the job. And what he's done, well, that's competition and you can't do owt about it.' He turned and waddled away.

Ivor called after him, 'I'll do something!' But Arthur either did not hear him, or ignored him. Ivor, disgruntled, saw Katy sitting in the office and snapped, 'What are you laughing about?'

Katy responded truthfully, 'I'm not laughing.' Though she had just stopped herself from grinning at his dismissal by Arthur. Now she bent over her books again.

Ivor scowled at her bent head, but then muttered, 'I will do something, you'll see.'

A week later Ivor bounced into the office late in the afternoon and boasted, 'I told you I'd fix that feller from across the river.' Katy had seen him rattle past the window sitting on his cart. His head had turned this way and that, presumably seeking someone to impress, but his father was out on a job and none of the men had returned at that time. So he had come to the office, and Katy.

She looked up at him, saying nothing, and this spurred him into going on, 'I saw him this morning, the feller driving a lorry for Docherty. He went into this house at the back of the High Street and came out a few minutes later and drove off. So I went in, saw the old woman in there, and said, 'Have you asked Docherty's to move some furniture for you? When is he going to do it and what is he charging?' And when she told me how much, and that he was coming back that afternoon after finishing a job, I said I'd do it right off for half the price. I told her Docherty was notorious for booking more work than he could handle and he might not be back for a week.' Ivor grinned, 'I got the business. I'd like to have seen his face when he found out.'

It was at that moment that a lorry pulled into the yard. As it rumbled through the gateway the name on its side slid past the window of the office: J. Docherty. Haulier.

Katy asked, 'Is that the one you saw?'

'Aye, it is,' Ivor breathed. 'Oh, Lord!'

The lorry had stopped and a young man got down from the driving seat and strode towards the office. For a second or two he disappeared from Katy's sight where she sat at the window, then he shoved open the door and stepped in. He was a very tall young man and broad-shouldered, seeming to fill the rectangle of the doorway, his thatch of black hair brushing the top of it. He paused there to look around and his dark eyes held a hard stare. They flicked over Katy and passed on, then settled on Ivor, but Katy found she had risen to her feet under that stare and backed away from the desk. She was angered that she had taken fright that way and now she challenged, 'Who are you? What do you want in here?'

The young giant answered, eyes still on Ivor, 'I'm Matt Ballard and I work for Joe Docherty. I'm looking for Ivor Spargo.'

Katy demanded, 'What for?'

Matt's gaze shifted briefly to the girl, irritated by her interruption. 'He played a dirty trick on me and I've come to square it up.' He saw her staring back at him defiantly, but he also saw the swift glance she shot at the other man in the room. Matt pointed a finger at him and charged, 'You're Ivor Spargo! You fiddled me out of a job! The old girl described you to a T. Long and thin and that 'tache.' He started forward and Ivor ducked behind Katy. Matt found himself face to face with the girl and ordered her, 'Get out of the way.'

'No! Don't come in here giving me orders!' This was not one of the Spargos who could sack her and put her on the street. 'And you'd better not lay a finger on me!'

Matt glowered at her and knew she was right, that he would not lay a hand on her. He looked over her head and his eyes bored into Ivor. 'You pull that trick again and I'll settle your hash for good.'

He turned and walked towards the door. Ivor

whined, 'If you touch me I'll have the law on you!'

Matt turned his head and eyed him sardonically. 'The law won't put you together again.' The door slammed behind him, then he swung up into the cab of his lorry and drove it out of the yard.

Katy, her knees suddenly weak, sat down at her desk with a bump.

Ivor mumbled nervously, 'He doesn't frighten me.'

Katy remembered the tall young man's outrage and anger, the look in his eye as he left. She warned, 'I wouldn't cross him again, if I were you.' She did not want to face him again, either. He had included her among the guilty because of her presence here with Ivor. She had been breathless and frightened when he loomed over her. At the same time she had somehow known that he would not hurt her.

Katy kept recalling the young giant over the next few days but Ivor soon forgot, or tried to. In a day or two he was as brash and leering as ever. There came a day when Vera Spargo addressed them all at the dinner table: 'That carpenter — Howard Ross — he's coming tomorrow to do some work to the floor in the hall, a few loose boards needing nailing down. It's an easy enough job but I've been asking for it to be done for weeks and people are always busy.' She glanced coldly at Arthur and his son but they kept their eyes on their plates, so she continued, 'I don't want to be here while he's hammering so I'm going out for the day. Cook's been given her instructions so you'll eat all right.' Now Ivor's gaze flicked to Katy and she was suddenly uneasy. She remembered that Betsy was no longer there to engage Ivor's attentions.

Vera went off the next morning, dressed in her best of funereal black dress with choker collar and leg-of-mutton sleeves under a black raincoat, and topped with a black straw hat like a plant pot, held in place by a pin a foot long. She picked her way in her buttoned boots around the puddles in the empty yard — all the men had gone out to work by that time. She nodded curtly to Katy, a bob of the black straw, as she passed the office, a gesture that said plainly, 'Don't sit idle because I'm away.' Then she was gone.

Katy continued working but she did relax, knowing that there was no one watching her. But only a few minutes later she heard the rattle and clatter of a horse and cart and looked up to see it entering the yard. Ivor sat on the front of the cart and he reined in the horse, jumped down and sauntered into the office. He closed the door behind him and shot the bolt before advancing to stand behind Katy. He leaned over her and murmured, 'I watched Ma until she got on her tram and it drove off.' He had his hands on her shoulders and now he slid one forwards and downwards.

Katy warned or pleaded, 'I'll tell your mother!'

But Ivor was bolder, or hungrier for her, than he had ever been before. He fumbled at the buttons of her blouse while her fingers strove to hold him off. He said hoarsely, 'You can tell her what you like and she can do what she likes. She'll play hell but she won't throw me out. And she can't expect me to sit on my hands with a prime piece like you here.'

Katy had sat with heart thumping, not wanting to face up to this threat and hoping to talk him out of it, as she had always done before. But now she fought, shoving back the chair so it rammed into his middle. He yelped and swore and stepped back a half-pace. It was enough for Katy to squirm out of the chair and make for the door but he caught her before she reached it, his hands clamping on her shoulders. Her stretching fingers managed to slide back the bolt but then he spun her around and slammed her back against the wall. He pinned her there with one hand at her throat while the other pawed at her clothes again. She tried to reach his face with clawed fingers but could not and kicked out at him instead. He yelped again but his grip did not relax. Then the door was flung open and a hand came between Ivor and Katy to cover his face. The hand yanked him backwards, tottering on his heels, and now Katy saw it belonged to the carpenter. Howard Ross was grinning as he gripped Ivor by the throat. He still grinned as he beat Ivor mercilessly.

Until Katy cried, 'No! Please stop!' She hated Ivor now but this was too much for her, certainly too much for Ivor. She sat down shakily, picked up her shawl from the back of the chair and used it to cover her torn blouse. She pushed at her hair that had fallen down under Ivor's attack and wiped at her face with a scrap of handkerchief.

Howard, big and blond, looked round at her. 'Stop? I saw what he was trying to do. He deserves a hiding.'

'That's enough.' Katy averted her eyes from Ivor.

Howard shrugged, 'If you say so.' He dragged Ivor out of the office and dropped him to sit on the ground with his back to the wall of the office. Katy saw from the window that Howard's little trap, varnish gleaming, stood outside with his pony waiting patiently between the shafts. Howard re-entered the office and glanced at Katy: 'You'd better go and tidy yourself.'

Katy realised her hair had come down and her blouse was torn. She was shaking.

She nodded and started towards the house, putting up her hair with trembling hands. Howard took his bag of tools from the trap and followed her round to the kitchen door. Cook and Rita were working in the kitchen and Katy explained to them, 'It's the carpenter.' She contrived to conceal the tear in her blouse and kept her voice under control. But the two women were more interested in the man. Katy led Howard through to the hall then she paused to say, grateful but embarrassed, 'Thank you.' Because if he had not come along . . .

He dropped his toolbag and smiled at her, 'Glad to be able to help you, miss.'

Katy climbed the back stairs to her bleak little room. After washing and changing she sat in her room, trying to put thoughts of her ordeal out of her mind. When she had regained her composure to some extent she went back to her desk, though not without first looking for Ivor, by or in the office, but he was not to be seen. She started work but worried at his absence. When Howard came out of the house and put his tools back in the trap she called to him, 'I haven't seen Ivor. I'm wondering if he is all right.'

Howard grinned at her, 'Don't worry about him. He came through the hall a while back, just a few minutes after us. He didn't look at me and crawled up the stairs.'

'Oh! Thank you,' said Katy, relieved. She was grateful to him, thought he had a nice smile and was good-looking.

Howard lounged in the doorway of the office and asked, 'When do you have an evening free?'

Katy was unprepared for the question and stumbled over her reply: 'Well, any — well, it depends, sometimes I have to work . . . ' That was when the men were paid; Katy worked out what was due to each man.

Howard prompted, 'What about tomorrow? There's some new pictures on at the Pavilion.'

Katy thought excitedly, Pictures! The Pavilion was the theatre in Sans Street which showed silent films. Katy had seen an advertisement in the *Echo* that said it was screening *A Child's Faith* and other films plus a succession of comics. Seats were priced at twopence, threepence and fourpence. Katy, blushing and confused, breathed, 'Yes, thank you.' So it was arranged.

When Ivor appeared at dinner that evening his face was swollen and bruised. Vera demanded,

'What happened to you?'

Ivor mumbled, 'I got into a fight. I won but he was bigger than me and it took me all my time.' He did not look at Katy then and she said nothing, but later he shot her a glance of hatred. And afterwards he managed to mutter to her, so no one else could hear, 'I'll pay you back one day.'

But Katy only put that down as his usual bluster. Besides, she was filled with excitement at this new love affair, because it was already that to her. She had been lonely too long and now she snatched at this chance of affection. She watched the moving pictures with Howard, stemmed tears at *A Child's Faith* and laughed at the comics. Afterwards they went to a public house, a new experience for Katy and one she was unsure of, but she trusted Howard. They sat in the saloon bar and it was warm and cheerful. The people in there were shopkeepers or shipyard foremen and the like and they spent lavishly to Katy's mind. She thought that Howard must make a lot more money than the usual carpenter. And at the end of the evening he asked, 'Can I see you again?'

Katy answered, simply and happily, 'Yes, please.'

Vera soon challenged Katy: 'You're going out a lot, Miss. What are you up to?'

'Just walking, after sitting in that office all day. Or going to the pictures.' Katy met Vera's gaze defiantly. That was not the whole truth but it was not a lie, either.

'It's more likely you're meeting some feller.'

And Vera warned, 'I won't stand for followers, remember.'

'I remember, Mrs Spargo.'

Vera left it there. She did not want to catch Katy breaking her rules and have to sack her because the girl would be hard to replace — and expensive.

Katy cannily avoided trouble by always meeting Howard a block or two away from Spargo's yard. He took her out several times before he kissed her and then she was agreeable. She was happy to stroll with her arm through his and on a fine weekend they would walk in Mowbray Park. One night they went to a music hall and there was a German band playing. During an interval Howard fell into conversation with two of the bandsmen, portly men in their fifties with big, upswept moustaches and frogged jackets. Afterwards Katy said, 'You seemed to speak their language as well as they did.'

He laughed at her, 'I do. My father is English but my mother is German. They haven't lived together for twenty years. Mother went back to Bremen and brought me up there but I came here a lot for holidays with my father. I'm as English as they come.'

Katy asked, trying not to sound afraid, 'Will you be going back to Germany soon?'

'No,' Howard shook his head definitely. 'I came over about five years ago and haven't been back since. I like it over here.' And the police in Bremen were becoming too attentive, but he would not tell her that.

On another evening, when he was without

Katy, he sat in a very different pub down by the river. The drinkers were shabby or ragged and unwashed, shifty-eyed, or coldly staring. Howard sat alone and unworried because he knew the place, and its customers knew him too well to cross him. Three times during the evening a girl came to sit beside him, a different one each time but all were flashily dressed and heavily made up. They all slipped money into his palm and he went back to his rooms, which were decidedly lavish for a carpenter, a richer man than he had left them. The girls went on to ply their trade, knowing they had his protection.

He had plans for Katy.

9

SUNDERLAND. MARCH 1910.

'I don't think that would be right.' Katy blushed and lowered her gaze. Howard had courted her ardently over Christmas and into the New Year. Now, for the first time, he had invited her to his rooms.

He laughed at her, 'You're one of those old-fashioned girls!' But then he squeezed her hand: 'I love you for it.'

Katy loved him. It was three years since Charles Ashleigh had gone out of her life. Remembering him now brought no pain and there was only a faint residue of bitterness at the way she had been treated by his family.

A week or so later, as she and Howard sat over tea in a café on a Sunday afternoon, he proposed and Katy accepted him and the ring he gave her. As he walked her home towards Spargo's yard she asked, her head full of dreams, 'When shall we get married?'

'Next year, I think,' Howard answered. 'I want to save some more money, enough to rent a decent house and furnish it. We don't want to start our married life in furnished rooms. That's all very well for a bachelor but not as a home for a married couple.'

A home — for a married couple. Katy shed tears of happiness as she lay in her little room that was cold and cheerless. Howard was content that his plans were coming to fruition.

The next time he invited her to his rooms she hesitated but agreed, because wasn't she his fiancée now? She found he lived in a big house near West Park, renting a whole floor of it. He first took her in one evening after they had been to a matinée at the Empire theatre. The rooms were comfortably furnished and they settled down on a chesterfield before a good fire burning in the grate. It was then he seduced her. Katy was shy and reluctant at first but then yielded to him and to her passion, abandoned and trusting in him.

That was the only time. Alone in her own bed that night, away from temptation, she remembered her mother's advice, that men would pursue her, and the warning: 'Look out for yourself'. She wondered now if she had been reckless, had cheapened herself. She decided to be more careful in future, but that was not easy. When Howard demanded her body she soon ran out of excuses and was a poor liar anyway. She had to tell him, pleading, 'I don't want to, not until we're married.' He wheedled and cajoled but she would not go back to his rooms again. This had never happened to Howard before, so it took him some time to realise he had made a mistake and this girl would go no further down the path he had planned for her. She would never sell herself for money and so was useless to him.

His attentions faded as spring came and then gave way to summer. Whereas he had taken her out two or three times a week, now it was only once, on a Saturday or Sunday. It was on such a sunny day in June, as they walked in the park, that she told him she was pregnant.

He stopped dead in his tracks and swore, 'Aw, bloody hell!' He glared at her. Katy's arm had been through his but now he disengaged it. 'Are you saying it's mine?'

Katy flinched as if slapped, shocked by the implication. 'There's never been anyone but you.'

He saw the tears brimming in her eyes and noticed now that she was pale, her mouth drooping. Strollers were passing by all the time and he did not want a scene there. He took her arm again, walked her on and soothed her with his head close to hers, murmuring, 'I'm sorry. Of course I'm the father.'

Katy said, 'We'll have to get married soon, now. So people won't talk when the baby comes.'

'I'll get a ring next week and make the arrangements on Saturday.' He escorted her back to a street corner out of sight of Spargo's yard, where he repeated the assurance and promised, 'I'll meet you on the corner here.' Then he kissed her and left her.

On the Saturday Katy waited for him in vain. She sought him at his rooms but only found his landlady, a sour spinster who eyed Katy with disapproval. 'Mr Ross? I don't know where he's gone. He gave me notice and there was no rent owing because he was a very good payer. He didn't leave an address, just packed up and went. That would be on Wednesday.'

Howard had boarded a train then and taken his girls with him.

Katy walked dazedly back to her little room in the Spargo house. Only now did she see how little she really knew about Howard. While he had told her about his background in general terms and she knew his mother lived in Bremen, she did not know where he had lived in England, apart from the rooms in Sunderland. She assumed he had been at home with his father, but where? On several occasions, when Katy had talked of her years in Newcastle, he had shown a familiar knowledge of the city and said that he hailed from there, but he had not been specific. Katy would not find him there without an address. The police would not help because he had broken no law. It seemed that, after all the time they had spent together and their love-making, she only knew his name. In truth, she did not know that either. He had taken the name Howard Ross from a newspaper.

Katy asked herself despairingly, what was she to do now? She was to have a child, unless — She had heard of abortions, carried out bloodily in backstreet rooms by boozy, dirty old women. She shrank from that. She would bear the child. Without a husband she would be regarded as a woman of loose morals, and her child would be labelled a bastard. She shuddered at the thought. She would not allow that to happen, would find a way round it, somehow.

But now she could think of nothing, save to go on and see what the morrow might bring. She sat in the darkness at the window of her room close under the roof, unable to sleep for thoughts of what might lie ahead for her.

Heartbroken, she knew she would never trust a man again.

★   ★   ★

It was on that same Saturday that Matt escorted Fleur Ecclestone to a summer ball. As they whirled around the floor in a waltz he was conscious that a number of male eyes followed Fleur. She wore a ball-gown with lace insertions so that it floated about her. Her gloves were long and white, she carried a fan and flashed a brilliant smile at Matt from behind it, 'Are you enjoying yourself?'

He responded gallantly, 'Why shouldn't I, with the prettiest girl in the room?' He meant it, was not one to pay empty compliments.

'Oh, really, Matt, you do say the nicest things,' Fleur replied coyly. She was encouraging him as much as she could but in fact it was not needed, because Matt had made up his mind.

They were at the ball as a celebration. Only that week, Joe Docherty had called Matt into his office at the yard and told him, 'I'm going to make you a partner. It seems to me to be only fair. You're doing nearly all the outside work and there's no sign of me getting well enough to help you.' That was true; Joe was even thinner and spent more time in his bed than before. He said, 'You'll still draw your wage as usual, but after the end of the year you'll share in the profits.'

Matt could hardly believe his good luck. To be

a partner in a firm like this while still only in his twenties! 'Thanks, Joe. That's generous of you because I still don't know much about this business.' He pointed to the books on the desk.

'Oh, that!' Joe waved a careless hand. 'Mebbe you don't but you know plenty about running lorries. I'll teach you the office side later on.' Joe laughed, coughed and took a bottle and glasses from a cupboard as he was still coughing. 'Let's have a drink to celebrate.'

Matt grinned, 'For your chest.'

Because that was what Joe said when he drank during the day: 'It's good for my chest.'

Now he coughed, laughed and coughed again, then wheezed, 'Aye.' They clinked glasses and he swallowed a mouthful of Scotch whisky. 'That's better, see?'

They grinned at each other, old friends.

Matt had told Fleur that he was now a partner and she had been delighted. She had also decided that it was time to secure her advantage with him and so she had set out to charm him. But she did not have to try hard or long. As they sat out one dance in the garden under Chinese lanterns, he proposed. After simulated surprise and confusion Fleur accepted him. As they drove home in a cab she teased, 'I've never seen this yard of yours. It's over the bridge, on the other side of the river, in Monkwearmouth, isn't it?'

'I'll take you to see it,' Matt promised, and on the Sunday a week later he did so.

He fetched her in a cab and it rattled through the streets of terraced houses down to the river, with children running barefoot alongside. Fleur looked askance at the yard under the looming shipyard cranes as he unlocked the gates with their lettering: J. Docherty. Haulier. Fleur read the legend and asked, 'Shouldn't it be Ballard and Docherty?'

Matt shrugged, 'There's plenty of time to get that changed. It should be Docherty and Ballard, really. This was Joe's business to start with.'

'Ballard and Docherty sounds better.' And Fleur decided that was what she would call the firm when she was asked: 'My husband? He's a partner in Ballard and Docherty.'

She looked at the yard and the office, dusty and untidy, then pointed to the stairs. 'And what lies up there?'

'An empty flat.' Matt shrugged, 'It hasn't been used for years.'

It would not be used by Fleur, she was sure of that. She stared uncomprehendingly at the Dennis and said vaguely, 'It looks nice and clean.'

Matt said with pride, 'I wash her off and service her every week. She runs beautifully.'

Fleur smiled brightly, 'I'm sure it does.' And asked, 'Why do you call it 'she'? It sounds silly. It's not a person, just a lorry.'

Matt shrugged, irritated. He could not tell her he was fond of the Dennis. Instead he said, 'Just habit.'

Fleur had seen enough. She was sure this man was on his way up and she would marry him when it suited her. But this place where he made his fortune could remain his domain; she wanted none of it. She said faintly, 'I've got a headache.

Do you think you could take me somewhere for tea?'

When the gates were repainted the name that was shown on invoices and receipts: Docherty and Ballard. Fleur did not know that and called the partnership Ballard and Docherty anyway. She was happy that her problems were over; she had secured her financial future. She was convinced of this when Matt rented a small house, bought some furniture and moved out of his lodgings. Fleur congratulated herself on making a good catch.

* * *

The morrow brought no solution to Katy's problems. The summer slid by and the fear grew as the child grew inside her. She knew that, sooner or later, she would be found out and it was Rita who came on her one morning when she was being ill.

Rita told Vera, vengefully, 'That Katy, she's throwing up.'

Vera sought out Katy, in the office by then, though pale and apprehensive. The old woman's beady eyes roamed over Katy where she sat at her desk and she ordered, 'Come here, my girl!' When Katy stepped up to her the crone shot out a hand to feel at the girl's body and crowed, 'He's bairned yer! Your fancy man's bairned yer!' And as Katy shrank away from her, 'You can pack your duds and leave! Now, this minute!' Because Katy had committed the unforgivable sin. Vera could turn a blind eye to 'followers' when it suited her, to keep this girl who worked so well — and so cheaply. But pregnancy offended Vera's sense of proprieties, and Katy's presence in this house would besmirch the reputations of the Spargos. Vera put her head out of the door and shrieked, 'Arthur!'

He came waddling across the yard and demanded testily, 'What's the matter now? I'm sending the men off to their jobs.' They were all busy in the yard, starting up engines and harnessing horses, but their heads were turned towards the office now, curious.

Vera shouted, 'You'll have to stay back and do the books yourself!' She grabbed Katy's wrist and shoved her out of the office into the yard. 'This one's got herself into trouble and she's leaving.'

Startled and caught off-balance, Arthur said the first thing to come into his mind: 'Not Ivor!'

Katy had lived through these last months in worry and misery — heartbreak. She had loved again and been cheated again. Now she was being humiliated, held up before the men in the yard as a figure of shame. She saw Ivor standing across the yard, a gloating smile on his face, and she called out so they could all hear, 'Not Ivor! Never! Though he's tried often enough and once tore the blouse off me! And his father tried until I threatened to tell you.'

Some of the men grinned at Ivor's and Arthur's embarrassment, but others among them who had daughters eyed their employers with distaste. Vera was enraged at this rebellion, tried to drag Katy back into the office and hissed at

107

her, 'Shut your dirty mouth!'

'I've kept my mouth shut too long.' Katy dug in her heels and refused to leave the yard. 'I'm going but I want my money, what's due to me.' Then, remembering Betsy's departure, 'And I want it in my hand, not thrown in the dirt for me to grub for! And a cab to take me to the station and you can pay for that.'

'I will not!' Vera was now red with rage and brandished her fist at Katy, who looked back at her with contempt. Vera threatened, 'You'll get nothing now!'

Katy did not yield, but lowered her voice so only Vera could hear: 'You'll give me what I ask, mine by right, or I'll go to the justices and tell them the father is Arthur or Ivor and I don't know which.'

Vera gaped at her then countered, 'They'd never believe you! You might perjure yourself but you couldn't prove it was either of them.'

Katy pointed out grimly, 'Arthur and Ivor couldn't prove it wasn't.'

Vera said, uncertain now, 'You wouldn't dare.'

'Yes, I would,' replied Katy, chin set determinedly. 'I've got nothing to lose.'

Vera hesitated for some seconds but Katy's gaze did not waver and finally she muttered, 'Keep your mouth shut and pack your bags. I'll get your money.'

Katy insisted, 'And a cab.'

'And a cab.' Vera spat that out like something sour.

Katy did not care. In less than an hour she descended the back stairs, leaning under the weight of her cheap, old suitcase. The cabman waited in the hall, took the case from her and shoved it into the cab. He looked vaguely familiar to Katy, a stocky man with a walrus moustache. But Vera was waiting by the kitchen door and glared as Cook, tearful and fortified by gin, ventured, 'Good luck, lass!'

'Thank you,' Katy replied. Then again, when Vera handed her the pay due to her: 'Thank you.' She would not abandon her manners. Vera said nothing, fearful of provoking the girl into the action she had threatened, but her little eyes followed Katy venomously as the cab rolled away. When it had passed from sight, Vera swore, 'I'll get my own back on you, trollop! You'll weep for this one of these days!'

Katy was ready to weep there and then, from reaction after the row and fear of what lay ahead. Her bold defiance had hidden a core of fear and the threat to go to the justices had been a huge bluff. She could never have shamed herself in that way, never have lied in that way, no matter how wronged. But she sat dry-eyed, her lip caught between her teeth as the cab rattled and swayed down the road to the Central Station. There she climbed down but did not seek a ticket for a train.

She did not know where to go. She would not return home to be humiliated again by her father, and that was the best she could hope for. Realistically, she was certain Barney Merrick would turn her away from the door, refusing to harbour her, a fallen woman. So she had to find lodgings, and cheap ones at that.

The cabman climbed down from his seat, hauled her suitcase out of the cab and asked, 'Do you want a porter to put this on the train, lass?'

'No.' Katy looked around her, wondering what to do, and said, 'Put it down there by the wall for now, please.'

The cabbie blinked but set the case down. Straightening, he said, 'It's just that the old girl said to take you to the station to get a train. Mind, she sounded as though she'd be better pleased if I had to take you to the infirmary.'

Katy smiled faintly, 'We didn't part as friends.' Encouraged by his sympathy she admitted, 'She threw me out.' Then she added hastily, 'But I was ready to go and have been for some time.' She stopped there because she did not want to go into further details as to why she had left now.

'Ah!' said the cabbie, astutely, 'you're wanting some digs.' He was looking at her with his head on one side now, puzzled. He asked, 'Have you been one o' my fares before? It seems like I've seen you . . . ' He fumbled a short clay pipe out of his pocket and jammed it into his mouth under the walrus moustache. Now he pointed a finger at Katy and spoke round the pipe: 'Got it! Weren't you the lass — years ago now — that said I wasn't to blame for a feller taking the paint off his cart? He said I backed into him and you told the pollis I didn't.'

Now it was Katy's turn to eye him, and she recollected the incident. 'I remember.'

'Ah!' He pointed the pipe triumphantly. 'I have a good memory for faces. And am I right, are ye wanting digs now?'

Katy admitted hesitantly, 'Well, yes.'

'I thought so.' The cabbie took up the suitcase again and put it back in the cab. 'One good turn deserves another so just you come with me.'

Katy hung back, wondering if she could trust this stranger. 'I can't afford anything too expensive.'

'It won't be that.' The cabman tamped down the tobacco in his pipe with his thick thumb. 'Not flash, either, just one room. It's with a respectable auld woman that takes in a lodger to make ends meet. Anyway, seeing's believing. You come wi' me and if you aren't satisfied I'll bring you back here without charge.'

Katy took a breath and said, 'I'll come.' She climbed back into the cab and when it set off again she turned her mind to concocting a story. Ever since she had left home, and knew she was safe from her father stealing it, she had taken to wearing the ring her mother had given her. Now she took it from her index finger and placed it on the third.

The house was in a quiet street in Bishopwearmouth, not far from the centre of Sunderland. The cabman said, 'This is Mrs Gates.' And to the old woman standing at her front door, 'This is a decent lass wanting a room, nothing fancy nor expensive.'

Mrs Gates was stooped and frail. She had a smile for Katy and stood back to allow her into the house then showed off the room, small but comfortable. Katy performed some mental arithmetic and decided she could just afford it. 'I'll take it, please.'

The old woman eyed her and warned in a quavering voice, 'I'll tell you now, this is a respectable house. I don't allow any shenanigans with young chaps, Miss — ?' She let the question hang.

'Mrs,' corrected Katy, 'Mrs Katy Merrick. And there won't be any shenanigans.'

Mrs Gates peered short-sightedly at Katy's hand and her mother's ring. 'Oh, you're married. I took you for a single lass. But I'm sorry, I don't have any men in here, not husbands either. Men make for trouble.'

Katy could agree with that, but only said, 'You won't need to worry about my husband.' She produced her rapidly manufactured story, shyly, 'I'm not long married, and he's at sea, on a ship gone to China and he won't be back for nearly a year. We had some bigger rooms but with him away and me having to be careful with money because of the little one to come, and I don't get on with his mother . . . ' She let the explanation trail off so Mrs Gates could fill in the gaps for herself, of the young bride left to manage alone, with a child on the way and a dragon of a mother-in-law.

Mrs Gates did that, noting the mention of the 'little one', and became solicitous: 'Don't you worry, I'll do all I can to make you comfortable.'

So Katy settled in, ate plain but nourishing meals cooked by Mrs Gates and went for walks. She saw a doctor and prepared for her child to be born, relying on what she remembered of her mother's pregnancies and the hazier recollections of Mrs Gates. Once a month she drew from the savings bank just enough to pay her way. At these times she told Mrs Gates she had been to the shipping office in Tatham Street to collect the wages from her sailor husband's employers. Sometimes she brought back letters supposed to have been written by him and read them out to Mrs Gates.

Katy did not like practising this deception but was forced to it. Nor was she happy. Added to the slowly subsiding pain of Howard's betrayal was her fear of the future, for her and the child. She could not stay where she was for ever because some day the mythical sailor would be expected to return, nor could she confess the truth to Mrs Gates. Where would she go? How would she earn her living?

Who would help her now?

* * *

Charles Ashleigh had come home from the China station in July. In Newcastle Mrs Connelly, sour-faced and in rustling funereal black from head to toe, opened to his knock on her front door and peered at the young man standing outside. He was dressed in well-cut tweeds from Gieves with polished brogues and doffed his cap on sight of her. That showed his butter-coloured hair which contrasted with his bronzed features. His teeth showed even and white when he smiled and asked, 'Mrs Connelly?'

Katy's erstwhile landlady eyed him with suspicion, distrusting all toffs, and asked in her turn, 'Who wants to know?'

He introduced himself: 'Charles Ashleigh. I have a card here, somewhere.' He produced one from a leather card case, a rectangle of pasteboard which stated he was Lieutenant Charles Ashleigh, RN.

Mrs Connelly scanned it and handed it back, unimpressed; sailors were the worst. But the name of Ashleigh was familiar to her and she admitted, 'I'm Mrs Connelly, but if you're looking for digs you're wasting your time. I only take young ladies.'

Charles said hastily, 'No! I'm not seeking lodgings. But I am looking for a young lady.' He saw her brows come together and hurried on: 'A young lady who boarded with you about three years ago, a friend of mine. Her name is Katy Merrick. I wrote to her several times but haven't had a reply. Is she still with you? Or do you know where she is?'

Mrs Connelly's scowl had become fixed at the mention of Katy Merrick: 'No.'

Charles probed patiently, 'She's not here?' And when she shook her head, 'But didn't she leave a forwarding address?'

'No.' Flatly, again.

The door was closing and Charles pressed desperately, 'But you do remember her.'

He received only the reiterated, 'No.' The door slammed shut in his face. Inside the house Mrs Connelly rustled into that holy of holies, the front parlour, sacred to Sunday. Through the lace curtains she watched the young man slowly turn from the front door and walk away.

She muttered, 'Good riddance, to him and her. She deserves all that's coming to her, little hussy.'

Charles only retired as far as the corner of the street, where he would not be seen from the house. He waited there for an hour or more, until the shipyard hooters warned of the end of the working day, waited still until the girls came back to Mrs Connelly's house from the shops and offices where they were employed. He cherished a faint hope that Katy might be one of them, but they all returned in the space of a half-hour, six of them, and Katy was not among them.

When he was sure there could be no more girls to come, and that Katy was not going to walk around the corner into his arms, only then did he give up his vigil and go back to the Ashleigh house to eat a late dinner with his parents. He told them, morosely, 'Katy wasn't there. Her landlady denies all knowledge of her but she's lying, of course.'

Eleanor Ashleigh's judgment was brusque and sure: 'That girl was a fortune hunter. Once you had gone she left her lodgings and her place at Ashleigh's to seek it elsewhere.'

Charles was equally sure: 'You're wrong, Mother. Katy was not like that. I can't understand why she left Ashleigh's. She always said she liked the work.'

His mother started, 'I told you — '

Charles broke in, 'Yes, Mother, I know you did and I answered you.' He was silent a moment, brooding, then finished, closing the conversation as far as he was concerned, 'I'll try again tomorrow.'

Eleanor opened her mouth to remonstrate but caught her husband's eye on her, warning — or pleading? She held her tongue but later, when they were alone, she protested, 'Why do you let him pursue this ridiculous affair?'

Vincent pointed out, 'We can't stop him.' And then, uneasily, 'I wonder if we were right to act as we did? If he ever finds out how I got him the draft to China . . . ' He shook his head unhappily.

Eleanor brushed his worries aside: 'He won't find out, unless he meets that girl again, and then it would only be her word against ours. And we acted in his best interests. He was very young. The girl was quite unsuitable and he will be far happier with one of his own kind. I'll do something about it tomorrow.'

Charles was at his post at the end of the street when Mrs Connelly's girls left the house, one at a time, next day. He let the first two go by because he judged them to be too young, would still have been at school when he sailed for China. He stepped into the path of the third, a tall, dark girl in her early twenties, and lifted his cap. 'Good morning. I'm Charles Ashleigh. I wonder if you could help me? I'm trying to find a young lady called Katy Merrick. She boarded with Mrs Connelly about three years ago. Were you here then?'

The girl had been trying to sidle nervously around him but now she paused. 'Katy Merrick? Dark lass, pretty, must have been about

116

seventeen or eighteen then?'

Charles answered eagerly, 'That's right!'

The girl nodded, 'I remember her. She left years ago. There was a rumour she'd been carrying on wi' some young toff — ' She broke off there, realising who she was talking to, then apologised hurriedly, 'Beg your pardon, sir, but that's how it was told to me and that's how it got to Ma Connelly and she threw Katy out.'

Charles asked tensely, 'Do you know where she went? Have you an address?'

That brought a shake of the head and: 'No. She said she was going to Scotland but that's all; there was no address. She went off with her case and that was the last we saw of her.' The girl waited now, no longer in any hurry to go to her work.

But Charles only said heavily, 'Thank you.' He turned and walked away. The girl watched him go and sighed.

Charles returned home despondently. Over the next few weeks he placed advertisements in newspapers in the north-east of England and Scotland but without result. Then his mother announced brightly, 'Your father has taken a house in Town for the Season! We'll all have a marvellous time!' And, she thought, Charles could meet some girls of his own class and put this affair behind him.

They travelled down to London on the express, with a mountain of luggage, a few days later.

★ ★ ★

117

Louise was born at the beginning of December, on Katy's own birthday. On that one day Katy was wholly, supremely happy, filled with joy and confidence. Only later did her fears return.

And on that day Matt Ballard witnessed death and stared ruin in the face.

10

Matt Ballard sat at Joe Docherty's bedside and watched him die. The doctor had already given his verdict: 'There's nothing I can do for him now. The root of the problem is his heart. It's enlarged and feeble, struggling to do its job and failing. On top of that he's been drinking very heavily when he should not have been drinking at all. And now that pneumonia has set in . . . ' He had shaken his head and gone away.

Joe slept, or was unconscious, most of the time, but late that night he roused and saw Matt sitting haggardly watching him. 'Matt? I feel bad.' His breath rasped.

Matt murmured softly, 'Just try to rest.'

But Joe could not: 'I made you a partner because I knew this was coming and I wanted you to have something, but I think you're going to find I've let it all go to hell. I just couldn't cope without a drink, and then not for long.'

Matt gripped the thin, bony hand with his big one: 'Don't worry about it.'

'I'm sorry, really sorry, Matt.' Joe was silent for a minute or two, just the sound of his laboured breathing filling the room, his eyes closed. Matt wondered if he was sleeping again but then Joe's eyes opened once more and he wheezed, 'We had some good times together, didn't we, Matt?'

119

'Great times.' Matt remembered wryly that a lot of the time when they were in the Army they were cold, hungry or frightened — or all three. But he added with sincerity, 'I wouldn't have missed them for a fortune.' Because the older man had been like a father to him.

'Matt,' said Joe, 'will you promise me one thing, do me a last favour.'

'Don't talk like that, Joe.'

'I've got to.' His hand trembled in Matt's. 'Will you look after Bea for me? She's all I've got and I've let her down as well. There's nobody else who can take her because I've no relatives. Will you?'

'I'll do that, Joe,' Matt assured him. 'Put your mind at rest.'

'Thanks.' Joe sighed and lay quiet then, and after a time the hand lying in Matt's stopped shaking. Joe slept. He woke twice more but said little, just a few murmured memories of old times, his young days. Mostly he lay fighting to draw breath, and in the night he died.

Matt arranged the funeral. He found an insurance policy in Joe's papers that just covered the cost but that was the only good news. He found books not kept up to date and bills unpaid for months. All bore the names Docherty and Ballard. There was also evidence of Joe's drinking in the form of empty bottles — a lot of them. Matt drew up a rough balance sheet that showed the profit from the business had been eaten up by Joe's living expenses, the house, the nurse — and the drinking.

Matt gave up the house he had rented some

120

months before and sold the furniture. Fleur was furious and reviewed her position. Had she made a mistake and should she cut loose from Matt? But then she remembered that the business was now all his — such as it was. She decided it would be wise not to act hastily. She wanted to wait and see if he recovered.

Matt also sold most of the furniture left in Joe's house, keeping just enough to furnish the flat above the office. He paid off the nurse and Alice left weeping. Last of all, he sold off the lorry to a man out on the Newcastle road. Most of the bills were paid but a pile remained outstanding. Matt promised those creditors, 'You'll get your money, every penny of it.' He was left almost penniless with five-year-old little Beatrice, and only the horse and cart to earn a living for them.

He sat in the swivel chair in the office on the night they moved into the yard, his rough statement of account on the desk before him. Matt stared into the future and found it bleak. The child was fractious, blonde and blue-eyed and spoiled by Joe and Alice. She complained, 'I want to go home. I don't like it here. It smells.'

Matt explained wearily, 'That's only petrol and oil — and the horse — that you can smell. They won't hurt you. And we'll be living upstairs, not down here. It's nice, you'll see.'

'I don't care!' Beatrice stamped her foot, 'Take me home!'

'You can't go back there because we've given up that house.'

The child stared at him a moment, taking this

in but refusing to believe him. 'Why?'

'Because we haven't any money to pay for it.'

Beatrice did not understand this either. Her daddy had always had money when she wanted it. She fell back on the tactic which had served her so well in the past and screamed in rage and frustration.

Matt lifted her and carried her up the stairs to bed, shrieking all the way. He wondered how the hell could he cope with this?

★　★　★

As soon as Katy was well enough to go out she took Louise in her arms and looked for work. She knew it would be hard because employers were unused to a mother taking her child into the office, but she hoped she could persuade them that Louise would not interfere with her work. She tramped the winter streets in the bitter cold and biting wind coming off the river. In the beginning she went to employment agencies but it was soon made clear to her that there was no work for a young woman accompanied by a child. Katy was advised, 'Leave her somewhere.' But she could not bring herself to do that.

In casual conversation, long before Louise was born, Mrs Gates had said, 'I'm not one for looking after other people's bairns. If they have them, then they should look after them.' But anyway, Mrs Gates was too old and infirm to care for a child all day. And Katy could not hand her child over to a stranger. Besides, she was grimly certain that whatever work she obtained

122

she would not earn enough to pay some respectable person to care for Louise and not some boozy crone seeking money for drink. But the advice was repeated more than once when she cast her net wider and carried Louise from one office to the next and then to a succession of factories: 'You can't bring the bairn with you. Get somebody to look after her.'

Her sight of the shipyards lining both banks of the Wear, and the vessels moored in the river and discharging their cargoes, gave her hope; here she would find work which she knew from her time at Ashleigh's on the Tyne. But the work in the shipyards was for men only, and in the warehouses she received the same reply as she had in the town: 'We'll want a reference . . . it's work for a single lass, not with a bairn. Can't you leave her wi' your granny?' That lack of a reference from the Spargos often resulted in her being turned away before the question of Louise was discussed.

There came a day when Mrs Gates, becoming suspicious, asked when Katy's sailor husband would be coming home. Katy had spent another week in her fruitless search — and her savings were running out. So in desperation she crossed the bridge over the River Wear into Monkwearmouth and began to search there. On that day of rain she walked the length and breadth of Monkwearmouth with Louise in her arms and her cold feet squelching in her buttoned boots, but she failed to find work. Katy faced the fact: there were plenty of girls as well qualified as herself and without the encumbrance of a child to put off potential employers.

Katy was frightened now. She turned for home in the early dusk because the yards had shut down for the night and the warehouses closed their doors. She did so reluctantly because she had to pay her rent the next day and did not have the money. All she had now was the ring her mother had given her and she could not sell or pawn that. It would have shamed her before the world, a woman with a child and no ring on her finger. That was her badge of respectability. She needed work and a sub — an advance of pay — this day, or she would have to throw herself on the mercy of Mrs Gates, admit her shame and that she had lied and invented a sailor husband. But that would be only a brief period of succour because the old woman could not afford to keep her for nothing. And after that — the workhouse?

Katy shuddered, and only partly because of the cold and the rain that were chilling her to the bone. Louise was wrapped warmly in a thick woollen shawl, Katy's arms shielding her from the dampness, as they walked along a terraced street close under the towering cranes of the shipyards. It was then she came to the gates that stood open. The legend on them was broken between the two leaves but she read it by the light of a street gaslight to be: Docherty and Ballard. Hauliers. Inside the gates was a yard and an office with a square of light that was a window.

Katy paused in the gateway. She told herself that she knew the work in the haulage business.

But she remembered the name Docherty and how Ivor had cheated the young man from that firm. She could picture him now, standing in the doorway of the office and announcing, 'I'm Matt Ballard.' Suppose he was in the office? And would Docherty's be any different from the other employers with whom she had pleaded for work? Then she reasoned that none of this mattered because she had to try. She had to put a roof over her child's head and care for her, *had* to. So she walked across the muddy yard and tapped at the door of the office.

'*Somebody knocking!*' A startled Katy heard the high voice of a child come from inside the office, then the swift patter of flying feet. The door was opened by a small girl, blue-eyed with blonde hair hanging down her back. She stared, thumb in mouth, at Katy.

Another voice, deep and male, demanded, 'Who is it?'

The thumb came out of the mouth and the child called, 'It's a lady.'

'Stand aside and let her in, then.'

The little girl obeyed, eyes still curious, and she said as Katy entered, 'You're all wet.'

'Yes. Thank you.' Katy was well aware of how she looked, knew the rain had soaked through her hat and her hair clung wetly to her neck, could feel the cold dampness inside her buttoned boots, her skirts sticking to her legs. She found a smile for the girl then confronted the young man who had risen from an ancient swivel chair behind a desk. With a sinking heart she recognised him. He had stormed into Spargo's

125

office in search of Ivor and frightened her: Matt Ballard. Did he remember her?

For a time he did not. Matt, hoping for business asked, 'Do you want something moving, ma'am?' He had spent the day shifting light furniture between several houses in Monkwearmouth, time-taking, poorly paid work as the owners only used him because they could not carry it on a hand barrow. Beatrice had gone with him and he had rigged the small tarpaulin shelter on the cart to keep her — and the furniture — dry. She had grizzled and whined because she wanted to play at home, repeatedly thrown her toys out of the cart and finally was rude to some of the customers. They told Matt, 'That bairn wants her backside warmed.' Beatrice had pulled a face and thrust out her tongue. Matt, patience exhausted, smacked her and drove back to the yard, with Beatrice in sullen silence and Matt grimly aware that he had barely made a profit on the day.

Now he looked at the girl holding the baby and thought there might be a removal job to be done. But then Katy asked, 'Are you needing any help, please? I've done a lot of this sort of work.'

Matt shook his head, 'Sorry, but I don't.'

Katy pressed him, 'I've three years experience of keeping books, pricing jobs, invoicing . . . ' Her voice trailed away then because Matt now looked at her sharply.

The mention of her experience had triggered a memory and now he accused her, 'You're one of the Spargos. You were there that day I was looking for Ivor and you shielded him.' Worry

126

and anger gave a harsh edge to his voice.

Katy winced but defended herself: 'I'm not a Spargo. I worked for them, that's all. And I didn't shield Ivor, he just hid behind me. The Spargos sacked me because I had a row with them.' She felt a pressure against her leg, looked down and saw the small girl craning her neck to peer at Louise. Katy whispered, 'Do you want to see the baby?' When Beatrice nodded, Katy lifted the shawl so Louise's face showed and stooped so the child could see it.

Matt's anger ebbed and he shrugged off the past, but he said, 'Anyway, I can't take anybody on.'

Katy persisted, 'Is Mr Docherty about?' She thought that, possibly, this young man had no authority to engage staff, so she would appeal to the senior partner.

Matt sighed, 'Mr Docherty died a couple of weeks back. I run the business now and I can't take you on.'

Katy felt a tug at her skirt and Beatrice asked, 'Can I hold her?'

Katy prompted automatically, 'Please.'

'Please.'

The baby was transferred to the arms of Beatrice but Katy maintained a steadying hand. She smiled down at the two children then up at Matt: 'Your little girl is quite taken by my daughter.'

'She's not my little girl,' Matt disclaimed. 'That's Joe Docherty's Beatrice. I promised him I'd look after her.' And he had found it trying.

Katy smoothed a hand over Beatrice's hair.

She noted that it needed brushing — badly — also that Beatrice's face had not been washed since her last meal. Remembering her own feelings when her mother died, she sympathised with the child: 'How awful for her. But she's lucky to have you.'

Matt replied drily, 'She doesn't think so.'

Katy heard the wry humour in his voice, could guess at his difficulty with Beatrice but also thought there was kindness. She pressed her case, because she had to: 'I need a job where I can keep the baby with me because I've no one I can leave her with. My husband is at sea and I don't know when he'll be home. I haven't had any money from him for a month now.' Matt shook his head unhappily but she went on, desperate now, 'I could look after the little girl, Beatrice, for you. As well as working in here.'

'One of the reasons I'm in this mess is because my partner was paying the wages of a nurse.' Matt could hide his poverty no longer and admitted, in a voice savage with anger and bitterness, 'It's no good! I'm sorry, but I can't afford to pay you. I haven't the cash. I was left this yard but it's on a long lease, I don't own it. I've sold everything I can and I'm still left with a pile of debts. So will you get out of here and leave me alone.'

Katy flinched but could not obey. Louise was there to remind her of that. For her sake . . . She said, 'You don't have to pay me.' She let the shawl fall from her shoulders and shook out her hair. 'Give us a roof over our heads, board and — and bed, and I'll — I'll do anything you want.'

Matt whispered, 'Dear God! You're not that sort o' lass.'

Katy whispered in her turn, '*Please!*'

He stared at her, then said, 'Come up here.' He started up the stairs leading to the floor above. Katy took the child from Beatrice and followed him.

11

MONKWEARMOUTH. DECEMBER 1910.

Katy numbly followed Matt's broad back up the
stairs and into the room at the head of them. She
saw, in the glow from a heap of embers in the
grate, that it was a small kitchen-cum-sitting-
room with space for just a table at its centre and
four straight-backed chairs set around it. Two
sagging armchairs stood either side of a black
kitchen range where the fire glowed. Katy did
not see more because Matt led on to the room
beyond. He pushed the door wide and gestured
to her to precede him. She entered and saw in
the dimness a room no bigger than the kitchen,
with two single beds and a chest of drawers. His
shoulders now framed in the doorway behind her
blocked out what little light spilled into the room
from the kitchen. She could sense his presence,
close to her.

He said, 'You can stay up here with the two
bairns. I'll be all right downstairs. When do you
want to move in?'

That was an easy decision to make, but first
Katy drew a deep breath of relief as she realised
she was grasping salvation not straws. She had
found a home of sorts for her child. She could
have shed tears of gratitude but she held them in
and said, 'Thank you.' She had not known what
to expect at the hands of this stranger, but just to

130

confirm what she believed now she asked: 'You only want me to work in the office?'

'No!' Matt stumbled over the words, embarrassed. 'I mean yes! I mean, I don't want you messing about in the office. I do all that. You just live up here.' He finished vaguely, 'You can keep the place tidy and maybe cook me some grub.'

Katy saw he did not trust her to 'mess about' in his precious office, but she only asked, 'Can I move in tonight?' Then she admitted, 'My rent is due to be paid tomorrow and I haven't the money. If I leave tonight I won't be owing anything.' And making light of the task: 'It will take me about an hour or so. I only have to fetch a pram and a suitcase from where I live now, in Bishopwearmouth.'

Matt stared at her and tried to picture her shoving the pram, probably with the baby inside and a suitcase balanced on top. Instinctively he offered, 'You can't cope with all that lot. Go back and pack your things. I'll get something to eat then come over with the cart and fetch you.'

So it was arranged and Katy set off for her lodgings. Matt heated up some broth left over from the previous day. As he and Bea ate and she complained he watched the rain rattling on the window panes. The meal over, he dumped the dirty dishes in a bowl of water and told Bea, 'Get your coat. We're going out.'

She pouted, 'I don't want to go out. It's raining. I want to stay in and play with my dollies.'

'We have to go out. Bring one of your dolls with you.'

131

'We'll get wet. My dollie will get wet.' Bea started to wail.

'No, you won't. Get your coat or I'll — ' Matt bit off the threat as he remembered Bea's absorption not so long ago. 'We're going to fetch that lady.' And he coaxed, 'Do you want to see the baby?'

'Can I?' The tears ceased and Bea moved to wipe her nose on the back of her hand.

Matt used his grubby handkerchief instead and promised, 'You will. Now get your coat — and the dollie.' As he led Bea through the rain across the muddy, pool-bespattered yard he cursed himself for his soft-heartedness. The strange woman was proving to be a bloody nuisance already.

Katy broke the news to Mrs Gates as soon as she entered the house. She had prevaricated too long and thought the old lady deserved the truth. 'I'm leaving tonight, Mrs Gates . . . ' She explained that she had lied about having a husband and had done so because of the child. Katy told the whole story, too tired to be ashamed or defiant, as she sat by the fire, her rain-soaked skirts steaming, and fed Louise.

Mrs Gates listened as she prepared a meal for Katy and herself. It was what she called 'Panacklety', bacon, onions and sliced potatoes, cooked in a frying pan on the fire. At the end of Katy's tale she said slowly, 'Well, you're not the first lass to be caught like that and you won't be the last. And that's a bonny little bairn you've got there, anyway. You're right that I couldn't cope with her all day long at my age, or afford to keep the pair o' you, but I wouldn't have turned you out because of the rent. We'd have managed somehow.'

Katy ate and packed her case. She had barely finished when someone knocked on the street door and she opened it to find a drenched Matt standing on the pavement. He loaded the pram and the case into the tarpaulin shelter on the cart where Bea sat clutching her dollie. She asked eagerly, 'Is the baby coming?'

'Aye, in a minute.' Matt wondered what the hell the woman was doing now.

Katy held the sleeping Louise in one arm while the other was around Mrs Gates and both of them were crying. Then Katy kissed her: 'Thank you.' She ran across the glistening wet pavement to climb up onto the cart. Matt's hand on her arm steadied her while half-lifting her into her seat.

The cry followed her, 'Come and see me sometimes!'

'I will,' Katy replied.

'Good luck!'

Matt thought, I'll need it. Then he twitched the reins and the horse set off, nodding his head and pulling the cart through the driving rain.

At the yard, Matt carried the pram and case upstairs to the flat, while Katy took off her coat and Bea's and hung them up to dry. Matt saw with relief that the little girl had attached herself to Katy. He also glanced at Louise, now lying in the pram, awake and watchful. From her his gaze shifted to the dark loveliness of this stranger and he said, 'With that blonde hair and those blue

133

eyes she must take after her father.'

That much resemblance was clear and Katy smiled, 'Yes.' But she could not believe her daughter could grow up like Howard Ross, not her child.

Matt said, 'I'm going to bed down the Sergeant.' And when Katy looked at him blankly, he explained, 'The horse.'

'Oh! I see.' But she did not. Why Sergeant?

Katy spent the rest of the evening unpacking and settling in. She expected Matt to return before long but while she soon heard him below in the office, he did not come up to the flat. At the end of two hours she had put Louise into her pram to sleep. Then she told a story to a chattering Bea until she had finally yielded and was silent in one of the two beds. Katy washed up all the dirty dishes and also investigated the cupboards, established her resources and made some plans.

She made a pot of tea and ran lightly down the stairs. Matt sat at the desk, head bowed over a small notebook and writing on a scrap of paper. Katy asked, 'I've made some tea. Would you like a cup?' And as he looked up fom his work, blinking, she offered, 'Shall I bring it down?'

'No, thanks.' He glanced down at the paper then closed the notebook and stowed it in his jacket pocket. 'I was just making up my route for tomorrow from the order book, but I've finished now. I'll come up.'

He followed her up the stairs and they sat on opposite sides of the table, sipping the tea from thick china mugs. Katy was aware of his eyes on her. Assessing? She was aware that she had not put up her hair again, that the dress she wore was a good one, donned that morning to impress potential employers but now damp and creased. She wished she could look at herself in a mirror — but then was glad she could not.

Matt was abstracted, wondering how this woman and this new arrangement would affect the business — and his life. He thought she might help a little in the office but was not impressed by her qualifications because he had a poor opinion of the Spargos — when he had seen their yard it had been a mess. Still, if she could care for Bea and take the little girl off his hands so he could get on with his work . . . He remembered then and asked, 'Where's Bea?'

'In bed and asleep, with Louise alongside in her pram,' Katy answered.

Matt stared in surprise. 'Already? She keeps on getting up when I put her to bed.' Katy smiled but made no answer to that. His gaze went to the bedroom door and he murmured absently, half to himself, 'I need to get some bedding out of the cupboard in there.'

Katy said quickly, 'I got some for you. It's hanging on the clothes horse, airing.' She pointed to where the horse stood by the fire.

'Then I'll go to bed.' Matt stood up from his chair.

Katy asked, 'Is there anything in particular that you want me to do tomorrow?'

Matt ran a hand through his hair and yawned, 'No, I don't think so. I've got the paperwork up to date.'

Katy thought, You did it during the last two hours. And: He doesn't trust me to do it. So when Matt picked up his bedding and made for the stairs she said only, 'Good night.'

As he replied he thought that she had sounded starchy. He made his bed under the counter in the office and turned off the gaslight. He wondered if he had made a terrible mistake, and thought that he was already in enough trouble before the woman came. Now he was committed to supporting her and her child, at least until she found a job and a place of her own. But he didn't see what else he could have done. And he had work to do the next day. He turned over and soon slept.

Katy lay in bed and listened to his movements in the office below. She sensed his antipathy and guessed he was uneasy about her being there. He was judging her when he did not know her and that angered her. But he had taken in her and Louise, when he was in dire straits himself. She could hardly blame him for having doubts. But tomorrow she would show him.

Louise woke her early the next morning, a hungry mewing. Katy saw the weather had changed dramatically in the night. In place of the rain there was a clear, hard blue sky and there was frost on the windows. She pulled her coat on over her nightdress against the cold; she had no dressing-gown. Then she took her daughter into the kitchen where it was warmer. The fire that Matt had banked up with coaldust the previous night was just burning itself through and out, a bed of glowing embers. Katy put on more coal then sat down in one of the armchairs, changed and fed the baby and put her back in the pram. Beatrice still slept but Katy could hear sounds of movement in the yard below. She rubbed frost from a window and looked out. Matt was harnessing the horse and Katy thought, Why Sergeant? But then she scurried to wash and dress.

She was just in time to answer Matt when he called from the foot of the stairs, 'Can I come up?' He kept his tone soft but there was an edge of impatience in it. He was eager to be on his way and it irked him to have to wait to climb the stairs because decorum had to be maintained. When he was on his own he could do as he liked . . .

Katy answered, 'Yes! I'm just cooking breakfast.' And in truth, the bacon was in the pan and that was set on the fire. She whisked about the kitchen while Matt blew on his hands and held them out to the blaze. Katy said, 'It's cold out there, this morning. Haven't you a pair of gloves?'

He shook his head. 'The old pair wore out and I haven't had the chance to buy another.'

Katy thought, Or the money? But she knew his pride would not let him admit that. And it must have been humiliating for him to have to confess his poverty to her the night before. She was getting to know this young man, so she dropped the subject. And at that point Beatrice emerged from the bedroom in her nightie, complaining, 'I don't want to go on the cart again.'

Katy wrapped her in her dressing-gown and

plumped her on an armchair. 'You're not going on the cart. You're staying with me and looking after Louise.' Then she served Matt his breakfast and started on that of Beatrice. She asked Matt, 'Will you be coming in at dinnertime?' By that she meant the main meal at mid-day.

He shook his head. 'I'll take a sandwich with me and have my dinner when I finish tonight.'

'I'll make some for you.' And she did so, with bread and some rather hard cheese, then wrapped them in a clean tea towel; she had found a supply of them in a drawer.

Matt noticed and said, 'They were in Joe Docherty's house. I brought them along to clean this place.'

Katy reflected that she had found them just in time. As he stood up she asked, 'Have you had enough?'

'Aye, I've fed well.'

Beatrice put in, 'We usually just have bread and jam.'

Matt scowled at her but admitted, 'What you've just cooked was for Sunday, but I can get some more.' This was Friday.

Katy said quickly, 'No, I'll see to that.'

He bit his lip then said, 'I think we need to buy some grub, for dinner and so on. I've been doing it when I could.' Katy knew food was needed from her investigation of the cupboards, but held her tongue. Matt dug in his pocket and came out with some silver and copper. He counted coins out onto the table, two shillings and sixpence, then asked, 'Will that be enough?'

Katy saw he had only a few coppers left, and

138

answered, 'Oh, yes.'

He glanced at the clock on the mantelpiece and said, 'I'll be back tonight.' Then he was gone, waving a hand as he ran down the stairs. Katy called after him, 'Goodbye.' Then she went on with her work, but thoughtfully. She knew she would have to earn her keep in this place. Matt could only support her and Louise if she put something in by way of exchange. She was determined she would. When Beatrice finished her breakfast Katy ate hers — but only bread and jam.

Katy spent the day in a whirlwind of work. She had spotted a clothes line strung, sagging, between two posts behind the office. Investigating further, with five-year-old Beatrice by her side asking questions, she found a little washhouse at the back of the office, with copper, mangle, poss stick and tub. Katy stooped to pull open the door under the boiler and peer inside.

Beatrice stooped beside her and asked 'Why are you looking in there?'

'To make sure it's empty. I'm going to light a fire in there and boil some water.' Katy stopped there to let Beatrice get her question in.

It came: 'Why?'

'It's a fine day so I'm going to do a load of washing.' Then anticipating as Beatrice opened her mouth, 'Because it needs doing.'

There was a tap on the outside wall of the washhouse and she used a bucket to fill the boiler from this. She started the fire by digging a shovelful of glowing coals from the fire in the kitchen and carrying them down to the boiler.

Then she topped them up with fresh coal. While she waited for the water to boil she tidied the flat and collected all the dirty clothes she could find. There was an old woollen cardigan of hers which now had holes in it. She decided it would serve a purpose and put it with the rest. At the end of a morning spent possing the clothes with the stick, scrubbing and mangling she had a line full of washing that flapped and cracked in a stiff breeze. And somehow on the way she had fed Louise and managed to keep Beatrice amused. She thought that, after a cup of tea, she would just have time to go to the shops.

Katy knew from her search for work that the nearest were in Dundas Street, five minutes walk away. She found them busy, with a butcher, grocer and greengrocer. She spent two shillings out of the money given her, the two largest items being a pound each of meat and bacon pieces — cheaper than the full rashers. As she moved from shop to shop, with Louise in her arms and Beatrice trailing along by her side, there was a succession of demands: 'I want some sweets . . . that dolly . . . chocolate . . . ' Katy refused them all, partly because the money was not hers to spend but also because she had a feeling Beatrice had been used to getting whatever caught her eye. The little girl was mutinous and sulking but Katy jollied her along as they walked back to the yard: 'Do you want to help feed Louise?'

That cheered Beatrice: 'Can I?'

'And then we'll have a game.'

'What game?'

'You'll see.'
'Tell me!'
'Guess.'
'Skipping?'
'That's one.'
'Is there another?'
'Lots.'

Beatrice said forlornly, 'I don't know any more.'

Katy paused, stricken, and looked down at her: 'Don't you?' And when Beatrice shook her head, 'Well, I'll teach you.'

So when Louise had been fed and put to bed in her pram, Katy prepared a thick stew and set it in the oven to cook, then led Beatrice out into the yard. There was a rectangle of concrete by the stable where the Dennis had stood. Katy swept it clean of straw, stones and oil then grinned at a watching Beatrice, 'We'll start with itchydobber.' She hitched up her skirts, and with an empty boot polish tin, demonstrated the art of hopscotch.

Katy had left a window open so she would hear if Louise woke and cried but she only returned to the flat in the dusk with a grubby, tired and quiet Beatrice by her side. Katy carried a basket filled with the washing from the line and told Beatrice, 'Now we're going to play: 'Helping with the ironing.' She did it on the table, using the smoothing iron heated on the fire, and with the pram close by so she could watch and talk to her tiny daughter.

With the ironing done she descended to the office and set about dusting and tidying the desk — the room itself, she decided, would be a full day's job. She glanced through the books and saw how they were made up and how the business was run. She also saw that a lot of work was done for very little payment. Matt's blankets lay under the counter as he had left them that morning. She made up his bed there again before climbing the stairs with Beatrice, replying absently to the child's chatter while deep in thought.

The thoughts were not cheering and all through what was left of that afternoon she wondered when Matt Ballard would return — and would he have changed his mind and decided he did not want to be bothered with her.

It was dark when he drove the horse and cart into the yard. Katy saw him from a window of the flat where she was keeping watch. She hurriedly dressed Beatrice in her coat then ran down the stairs as she pulled on her own. Matt found her, breathless, at his elbow as he lit a lantern to hang up at the stable door. Katy panted, 'I'll help you to finish out here.' Then she asked, 'Was it a good day?'

Matt nodded and replied, briefly as usual, 'Aye.'

Katy said brightly, 'Oh, grand.'

He watched her for a while as they both worked at the stabling of the horse. He saw that she was quick on her feet, deft with her fingers and knew what she was doing. He knew she would have learned at the Spargo yard. He listened to her seemingly light-hearted talk: ' . . . and we played itchydobber. Didn't we, Bea?

Then we got in the washing and ironed it . . . '

He made his monosyllabic replies, but then as she paused for a second, he asked, 'Are you trying to get round me?'

They were in the darkness of the stable now, talking over the back of the horse, their faces only half-lit by the lantern. Katy was silent for a moment, stroking the back of the horse. Then she looked up to meet Matt's gaze and answered honestly, 'I was trying to — please you.'

He said, 'You don't have to. I thought I made that clear.'

Katy winced at the rebuff. 'Yes, you did.'

'That's all right, then,' said Matt, relieved.

But it wasn't. They worked on in silence and when finished returned to the flat. Katy served the meal and Matt ate heartily, but she managed only half of her small helping. Afterwards he sat by the fire and immersed himself in the newspaper; he had brought home a copy of the *Sunderland Daily Echo*. Katy returned to her room and fed Louise then laid her down to sleep in the pram. Beatrice followed soon, after Katy had told her a story.

As Katy came out of the bedroom and closed the door, Matt lowered the paper and said, 'Bea seems a lot quieter — and more cheerful.'

Katy answered only, 'Yes.' She sat down and picked up some sewing she had seen needed doing when she was ironing. Her head bent over it.

Matt laid the paper aside. 'You're quiet tonight, too.'

'Yes.'

'I suppose that's because of what I said when we were putting the Sergeant to bed?'

Katy thought he cared more for the Sergeant than he did for her. She saw wry humour in that and almost smiled. But she also understood it. She had only been there for twenty-four hours while the Sergeant had been Matt's workmate and companion for months. She answered again, 'Yes.'

'Well, I don't mind you talking but I don't want you to think you have to.'

Katy laid down the sewing and faced him. 'I didn't talk because I thought I had to but because I wanted to please you. You've been good to us, me and my baby, giving us a place to live. I want to earn my keep and I know I can't, can I? If I cook and clean and care for Beatrice, I am still taking money out of your pocket, not bringing it in.' Matt stared at this summing up. Katy demanded, 'That's true, isn't it?'

Matt nodded.

Katy took a breath, then asked, 'Can I run the office for you? I still wouldn't be making money but at least it would leave you more time to work outside.' She could cope with Louise, who slept a lot of the time, and Beatrice would be back in school after the holidays.

There was an edge of exasperation in Matt's voice when he replied. This woman, though well-meaning, was wanting to interfere with his routine, change his organisation. 'You can try, but I won't be able to show you the ropes for a while.' He glanced at the clock on the mantelpiece, then returned to Katy. 'I have to go

144

out tonight. I expect I'll be back late so don't worry if you hear me downstairs.'

'Very well.' Katy's head was bent over her sewing again. Matt fetched his suit and other clothes from the bedroom, going on tiptoe so as not to wake the children, then washed and dressed downstairs in the washhouse.

He returned briefly to the head of the stairs to say, 'If Bea wakes and asks for me, tell her I've gone to see Fleur.'

Katy looked up, questioningly, 'Fleur?'

'That's right. The young lady I'm engaged to, Fleur Ecclestone.' Then he was gone, running down the stairs.

Katy thought, Fleur. Engaged. And: She's welcome to him. But then she thought that, when he married this Fleur, he would bring her to the flat and she would care for Beatrice. There would be no place for Katy and Louise. She tried to put that fear out of her mind, telling herself that there was no sign of a wedding yet. But thoughts of its consequences were to haunt her through the coming months.

Now she saw he had left his notebook on the table. It was his order book in which he kept a record of the jobs he had to do. Katy read through the entries, pencilled but neatly written, and at the end she had a good idea of the planned pattern of his work for the next week or two. And of the gaps when he would be seeking work. She made her own list of those then put the book back on the table.

★ ★ ★

145

'I thought you had gone for good.' Fleur's greeting was both acid and cool when she opened the door to Matt.

He paused on the threshold and reminded her, 'I told you I couldn't get out on account of young Beatrice.'

Fleur replied tartly, 'Neither can I. You should never have taken on the child. I said so at the beginning.'

'I had no choice. I'd promised Joe.' That edge of irritation was back in Matt's voice.

Fleur noted it and became cautious; she would not push this tall young man too far. She was still convinced he was headed for success. Hadn't he plenty of money before that stupid Joe Docherty lost it all — and saddled Matt with debts? Now he said, 'And I'm here to take you out now. It will only be a couple of seats at the Empire because that's all I can afford.' He still had debts to pay and was paying them. The seats at the Empire would consume his spending money for the week.

Fleur decided to settle for what she could get and smiled, 'I'll get my coat.' As he held it for her she asked, 'What has happened to that child tonight?'

'Mrs Merrick is looking after her.'

Fleur questioned sharply, 'Who?'

'Mrs Merrick. She's married to a sailor away at sea. She's got a baby daughter.'

Fleur relaxed, 'And it gives you some freedom. That sounds like a sensible arrangement.' Because it seemed to her advantage; Matt would be able to escort her again.

146

Matt was still not sure about the arrangement, but Fleur took his arm then, smiled up at him and they set out.

It was close to midnight when he returned to the yard. Katy had long since gone to bed but she heard him moving below. She thought that he was engaged but by his own admission still in debt. He was sheltering Katy and Louise when he needed all his money to marry one day. Katy had to make it up to him. Somehow . . .

12

Katy had been living above the office for a week when, glancing out of the kitchen window at mid-morning, she saw the stranger cross the yard to the office. He was burly, roughly dressed and unshaven. It was a grey, bitterly cold winter's day and there was not another soul to be seen, in the yard or the street outside. She told Beatrice, playing with her dolls, 'You stay here. I'll just be downstairs.' Then she looked to see that the fireguard was in place and ran down to the office. She was not taking fright at the man's appearance because she had seen many such when she was at the Spargo yard, honest men dressed for honest toil. But she was aware of her vulnerability, alone in the yard.

As she reached the foot of the stairs there came a hammering at the door. Katy smoothed down her apron and opened it, disclosing the stranger with his fist raised. He lowered it then and asked, 'Now then, lass, where's the boss?'

'Mr Ballard's out on a job.'

'Aw, blast it!' He started to turn away.

Katy asked quickly, 'What did you want? Something moving? Maybe I can help.'

He scowled at her over his shoulder, 'Don't be daft, lass. I can't see you shifting half-a-ton o' bricks.'

'When? Where?'

'What?' He turned back to her, the scowl still there but now he was puzzled.

'When do you want them moved?'

'Today. I'm doing a building job just round the corner in the next street and another in Fulwell. I want the bricks I've got left here over there for a start tomorrow morning. My cart's gone out Seaham Harbour way and won't be back till after dark.'

'We'll do it this afternoon.' Katy knew, from his order book, where Matt would be while she was speaking. She also had a good idea, from her own experience and studying his books, what he would usually charge. But this customer wanted the job done urgently . . . 'It'll be five shillings.'

'Five bob! That's near a day's work and it won't take him more than a couple of hours!'

'If he thinks it's too much he'll knock the price down. But I doubt if you'd get it cheaper from anywhere else. I think Spargos across the river would charge the same, but you could try them.' If memory served her correctly, Spargos would charge four shillings. She said, 'I'll tell you what, you keep us in mind for any work you want doing and I'll book the job at four and six.'

'This afternoon?' And when Katy nodded, he grinned. 'Thought I could knock you down a bit. I wasn't born yesterday. Done.'

'Done.' Katy had got the price she had wanted from the beginning. 'Now where are these bricks and where do they have to go, Mr . . . ?'

'Billy Nicholson.'

Katy got the addresses from him and before he

had reached the gates she was running up the stairs. She bundled Beatrice into her coat and pulled on her own.

Beatrice clasped her doll to her chest and asked, 'Where are we going?'

'To see Uncle Matt.' Katy picked up Louise, wrapped her in a shawl and preceded Beatrice down the stairs.

Out in the street she walked quickly and found Matt where she had calculated, a mile or so away, unloading furniture from the cart at a house in Southwick on the northern border of Sunderland. He turned from the cart with an armchair in his hands and paused, staring. Then he asked as she hurried up, 'What are you doing here?'

Katy caught her breath, smiling, 'I've booked a job for this afternoon.'

Matt set the armchair down carefully and straightened. He asked coldly, 'You've done — what?'

Katy heard the irritation in his voice again but replied patiently, 'A man called Billy Nicholson came to the yard. He wanted some bricks moved from just round the corner from the yard to Fulwell, today. I knew you only had the one job at the start of the afternoon so I said you'd do it.'

Matt asked, 'How did you know? And how did you know where to find me?'

Katy admitted, 'I saw your order book. I've been reading it so I knew what was going on — in case I could help. I didn't think it was private, just part of the business. Are you annoyed?'

150

Matt thought about this for a moment, while Katy changed Louise from one arm to another. He asked, 'Why are you carrying her? Why isn't she in the pram?'

Katy explained, 'It has a broken spring. Look, I wasn't prying. I just thought that if anyone came along wanting some job done I could deal with them rather than send them away.'

Matt shrugged. 'I don't mind you looking at the book. It seems it's just as well you did. But you say you booked the job. How much did you ask for?'

'Four and six.'

'*What!*' Matt shook his head in disbelief. 'You've got a nerve.'

'Did I do right?' asked Katy.

'You did — and better. I would have taken four bob and thought myself lucky.'

Katy smiled, 'I let him beat me down from five shillings because he promised to give us any carting jobs he has in the future.'

Matt burst out laughing. 'You cheeky — ' He stopped there, and asked instead, 'Righto, then, tell me where to find this job.'

He thanked her when he returned to the yard that night. Katy ran down with Beatrice to help him stable the horse and Matt dug in his pocket then opened his hand to show her a jumble of silver and copper. 'What I made this morning — and four and six from Billy Nicholson. You did well.' He passed the money to her: 'Put it in the cash box and book it.'

'Thank you.' Katy put it in the pocket of her apron, smiling. She had been accepted. And

151

before they left the stable, as she stroked the back of the gentle beast, she asked, 'Why do you call him 'Sergeant'?'

Matt laughed, 'It's Sergeant O'Malley if you give him his full title. Joe Docherty called him that because he reminded us of a sergeant we had once. He used to nod his head when he was drilling on the square, just like the Sergeant here.' Katy laughed with him.

Later, after they had eaten, Matt said, 'That was a good bit of business today.'

Katy ventured, 'We're going to need a lot more before we're rich.' And when he blinked at her, startled, she added, 'I mean, with a horse and cart you can only handle small loads and those from the cheaper end of the market, people who can't borrow a cart to shift their stuff themselves.' Katy knew this from her time at Spargos. She also knew the scarcity of loads Matt could handle meant that, to earn a few shillings, he sometimes had to buy coal or vegetables at the market and sell them off the cart around the streets.

Matt was impressed: 'Aye. You've got the right of it.' Now he went on, 'When Joe and me had the Dennis — the lorry, that is — we could get the jobs that paid better.' He was silent a moment, then sighed, 'Thinking back, I can see where Joe went wrong. He took a long lease on this yard and it's far too big, for me now and the pair of us when he was alive. He was planning to expand, had big ideas, but his illness put an end to that.'

Katy tried to cheer him: 'You can expand in

the future — when you've paid off the debts.'

Matt grimaced, 'A long way in the future. My profit at present won't allow me to clear them for months. And as for buying another lorry, that's wishing for the moon.' Then he looked at the clock and shoved back his chair. 'I'm off out to see Fleur. I'll be late back.' Then he turned at the head of the stairs and grinned at Katy, 'It was a good thing you got this job for me today. It will put food on the table for Beatrice and all of us.' And he thought that now he might use a few shillings from his meagre savings to buy a Christmas present for Fleur. He clumped down the stairs.

Talk of Fleur set Katy to clear up in silent bad temper, but then she told herself she didn't care. When she had put the children to bed and then retired herself, she was more cheerful. It was clear now that she would be running the office. Despite their poverty she felt that she and Louise would be safe there. She was more optimistic than she had been for nearly a year.

The next day dawned cold but bright with sunlight and a clear, blue sky. In the afternoon Katy took out the children, Louise in her arms and Beatrice dancing alongside. She walked through the ravine of Roker Park and so down to the beach. The big rollers came crashing in from the North Sea to pound the shore and Beatrice ran shrieking and laughing as they threatened to wash around her shoes. Katy showed her how to throw stones so they skipped across the waves.

Beatrice shouted a dozen times, 'I want to go plodging!'

Katy always refused to let her paddle, shouting back, 'It's too cold!'

They walked home in the dusk, Louise heavy on Katy's arm and Beatrice with dragging feet.

Katy was surprised to see the cart already in the shed and the Sergeant in his stable with his head poked enquiringly over the half-door. Matt was in the office, tossing a collection of tools back into their box. The pram stood beside him. Katy commented, 'You're early. Is anything wrong?'

Matt closed the lid on the box. 'No. I finished the day's jobs quicker than I expected and found another spring in a scrap yard so I've mended the pram.' He pushed it back and forth to show her: 'There you are, runs smooth as you like.'

'Oh, Matt, thank you!' That came from the heart. 'This child is breaking my arm. We've had a lovely afternoon, but if only I could have taken her in the pram.'

Matt laughed and took Louise from her: 'From now on, you can.'

That evening, Katy wrote to Winnie Teasdale in Malta, in her usual cheerful vein. She explained that she had not written recently because she had been on the move, but she was now settled. Katy paused for a moment then, to reflect wryly that she could not afford to go anywhere. But then she went on to write enthusiastically of her new home and work. She did not mention Louise, not wanting to shock Winnie. She described her new employer: He has a quick temper but he has been fair to me. He is certainly better than the Spargos.

Katy spent a lot of time in the office in the week that followed. Once she had it cleaned and organised to her liking — and Matt's — she sat in the swivel chair and knitted, with Beatrice and Louise for company. This paid dividends because three times in the first week there were callers looking for Matt to carry some load. Katy asked them, 'If I hadn't been here would you have come back later?' All replied that they would have looked elsewhere, two of them mentioning Spargos.

'That's good,' said Matt. 'Those orders will keep me busy until the New Year. I'm pleased.' So Katy was, too.

Christmas was frugal — dinner was a bacon joint cooked by Katy — but a cheerful occasion. Matt brought in a bunch of flowers on Christmas Eve and gave them to Katy, saying awkwardly, 'Happy Christmas.' She thanked him and next day gave him a pair of woollen gloves. He was taken aback: 'That's very good of you, to remember I needed them.' Then he added, embarrassed, 'But you shouldn't have spent your money.'

Katy laughed, 'I knitted them.' From the old cardigan she had washed and unravelled.

'Just the same . . . ' Matt rubbed the gloves gently between his big hands, feeling their softness. 'I think I can pay you some wages from now on. Not much, but something. You're earning it and I'm making a little more now.'

Katy was grateful, but for a moment was unsure whether to accept. She knew how much money he made and how little he spent on himself. After providing her with housekeeping and setting aside a sum towards settling the remaining debts, he was left with only a few shillings — and these he spent on Fleur. From casual comments he had made, Katy knew that when he went to see his fiancée at the weekend it was only to take her to the modestly priced seats at a theatre or picture palace. And if the weather was fine he took her strolling in Mowbray Park. Katy gathered that Fleur liked to be seen. Now she thought that she could find a use for these wages and said, 'Thank you.'

That was a happy day, at least until the evening, when Matt left with a carefully wrapped parcel under his arm, on his way to eat another Christmas dinner with Fleur and her mother in their apartment. Katy lay in bed listening to the breathing of the children with their occasional catch of breath and little sigh. Her thoughts drifted idly between Matt and the business. The latter because of the problem facing Matt — and therefore herself, because the sanctuary she had found there was fragile. If the business should fail . . . So she wondered how she could help and determined on certain lines of action. And she wondered if this Fleur was the right girl for him . . .

★　★　★

They were well into the New Year when Matt returned to the yard late on a wet evening. Katy helped him to stable the Sergeant, then as they entered the office she warned, 'Dinner is ready.'

156

'I'll just write up my book, then I'll be up.' Matt shrugged out of his wet jacket and went to hang it on the end of the counter. He paused, staring, then called after Katy who had run up the stairs, 'Hey! Where did this come from?'

Katy feigned ignorance: 'What?'

'The bed.' Because now there was a proper mattress under the counter with Matt's bedding laid on it.

'Oh, that!' Katy smiled to herself. 'That's just a 'thank you'. I bought it out of the money you paid me.'

Matt could not believe that. 'It must have cost all I paid you.'

'No, it didn't.' But she had spent all of it, one way or another. 'You need a decent bed and I'd taken yours so I'm just paying you back.' Then changing the subject, 'I have an idea that might help you find more business. I'll show you when you come up.'

The next day Katy went shopping in Dundas Street.

'Now then, bonny lass, what can I get you today?' The butcher, burly and florid, grinned across his counter at Katy. She was one of the regular customers at his shop. What she had left of the money Matt had paid her she had ploughed back into the housekeeping. She was intent on building up a reserve of food, rather than living from day to day as Matt had done. Then he had been struggling to survive on his own and at the same time caring for Beatrice. Now she was at the National School by St Peter's church while Louise lay in her pram

157

outside the shop door. Katy could see, from the corner of her eye, the back of a woman bending over the pram.

But the butcher was waiting so Katy asked, 'I'd like a piece of rib for roasting, please.' And when she had paid the shilling for her meat, she asked, 'Will you put this in your window, please?' She passed him the handbill she had carefully printed herself, advertising: 'MATT BALLARD. Removals and haulage.' And it showed the address of the yard.

The butcher wiped his hands on his apron and took it, eyebrows raised. 'Oh?'

Katy smiled at him, 'Mr Ballard will give you ten per cent discount on any work he does for you.'

'Aye?'

'Yes. Two shillings in the pound. And you don't have to do anything.'

He grinned at her. 'For you, bonny lass, why aye. Jimmy!' He called his boy and gave him the handbill: 'Get a bit o' stamp edging out o' the office and put that in the window.'

Katy left the shop. The woman was still stooped over the pram, cooing at the wide-eyed, gurgling Louise. She straightened when she became aware of Katy's presence and started to say, 'I was just admiring — ' Then she stopped with her mouth open, and gasped, 'Katy Merrick!'

Katy recognised her old friend from the days when she worked at Ashleigh's in Newcastle: 'Annie!'

Annie Scanlon was ruddy-faced as ever but

greyer now. She shook her head in disbelief, 'Where did you spring from? What are you doing here?'

'I'm working for Mr Ballard.' Katy nodded at the sign going up in the butcher's window.

Annie read it: 'Ballard — that's Docherty and Ballard as was, he's just round the corner from where I live.' She changed tack: 'I thought this was your baby.'

'It is.'

'She's lovely.' Annie's smile shifted from Louise to Katy, 'So it's not Katy Merrick any more.'

Katy said softly, 'It is.'

There was an awkward pause while Annie took this in. Then she put a hand on Katy's arm: 'It's been — what? About four years since I last saw you. Come on home with me and we'll have a cup of tea and you can tell me all about it.'

Annie lived in a neat terraced house in the next street from Ballard's yard. She settled Louise in one armchair and Katy in another, made tea then listened as Katy told her of her life after leaving Ashleigh's. She told the truth to Annie, that she had been seduced and abandoned by Louise's father, Howard Ross. 'But I've told other people, Mrs Gates and Matt, that my husband is a sailor at sea.'

Annie could understand that, and said, 'I don't blame you. Folks can be cruel to a lass that's been let down like you were. But don't worry, I won't tell anyone.'

Katy went on with her story and when she finished, Annie said softly, 'You've had a hard time, lass. And now you're working for this Matt Ballard. I've seen him about, a big, dark lad, driving the lorry him and Joe Docherty had, and nowadays with the horse and cart.' Her face turned a little redder as she asked, 'Don't be angry, but just so I know and don't put my foot in it — are you and him . . . '

Katy shook her head firmly, 'No. It's strictly a business arrangement. I don't feel anything for him except gratitude because he took in me and Louise. He didn't want to do it because he had enough trouble already, but he did. And he's engaged to a girl who lives over the bridge in the town and he's off there whenever he has some spare time — though that's not often. And after my experiences . . . ' She stopped there, not wanting to list them, to probe the wounds: Barney, Charles Ashleigh — though it had not been his fault but his mother's — Howard, Ivor Spargo. She finished, 'Never again.'

Annie sighed. 'Nobody could blame you. Well, I hope the pair of you get on and have better luck.' Then Annie added drily, 'Mind, my old granny had a saying I found was true: 'You spend your life in a bottle. You climb up as far as the cork then slide down again.' Still,' and here she looked around her at the cosy room, 'I can't complain. Ashleigh's paid me a fair wage and they've given me a pension which keeps me comfortable.' Then she realised she had brought up the name of the Ashleighs again, and apologised, 'I'm sorry, lass. I didn't want to bring back unhappy memories.'

Katy shook her head, smiling. 'It's all

forgotten now. I'm well over it.' She was sure of that now.

They talked for an hour or more and only stopped when Katy glanced up at the clock on Annie's sideboard and jumped to her feet: 'I have to get back; Bea will be in for something to eat.' Because all the pupils at the National School walked home for lunch every day.

Annie said with regret, 'I'm sorry you have to go. It's been lovely talking to you. Will you pop in again?'

Katy planted a kiss on her cheek. 'Of course I will. And you must come round to the yard and see us.'

So their friendship was revived. It was not long before Annie offered hopefully, 'I'll look after those two little lasses you've got if ever you're busy.'

And Katy took her up on that, though warning, 'You're not to spoil them, mind,' but guessing correctly that Annie would do just that. The two girls loved her.

Katy and Annie met and talked often — and later it did not stop at talk. Annie was a member of a dancing club. She told Katy, grinning, 'It's one way I can get my hands on a man.'

Katy asked, 'Is there one in particular?'

'No!' Annie laughed at that. 'I'm not sure whether they're after me or my pension. I think I'll stay single.'

So at the weekends, while Matt pursued Fleur, Annie taught Katy all the latest steps she had learned at the club: jazz, ragtime, foxtrot . . . They practised in the office where there was

161

more floor space, to the squeaky rhythm of Annie's wind-up gramophone with its big horn. She had bought it at Palmer's store for thirty-five shillings — in cash, because Annie said, 'I don't hold wi' this hire purchase.' She and Katy usually wound up convulsed with laughter, though Annie said approvingly, 'You're a natural dancer.'

Meanwhile, when Katy visited the shops in Dundas Street, she gently persuaded one or two to display her handbills. Eventually she had an advertisement for Matt's services in most of the shops. And it was as she left the last, the baker, that a voice said harshly, 'So that's where you are now.'

Katy turned and saw a horse and cart at the kerb and Ivor Spargo seated on the front of it. He was reading the handbill being put up in the window of the baker's shop. His gaze slid round to Katy and he jumped down from the cart and taunted her, 'I saw you passing that over and I wondered what you were up to now. You're dafter than I thought, working for Ballard. A one-man firm will get nowhere. Twenty years from now he'll still be working all hours, or scratching about looking for jobs with his horse and cart.'

Katy said nothing, but her gaze went from Ivor to dwell on his horse and cart. He saw the unspoken comment and flared, 'You needn't look like that! I'm only driving this for a few small jobs that we get. Most o' the time I'm in the office or out on one o' the lorries.'

Katy said coolly, 'Helping the driver.'

That stung because Katy had guessed correctly. Ivor blustered, 'I'll be driving meself before long! You'll see! And don't you answer me back! Any more of your lip and I'll tell Ballard and the people around here what sort you are!'

Katy returned him look for look: 'Two can play at that game. How long would you last here, or across the river in Sunderland, if I opened my mouth about you?'

Ivor glared his fury. He spat in frustration but said nothing, climbed back onto the cart and lashed the horse into a frightened canter. The cart careered off down the street and Katy drew a shuddering breath of relief. But the memory of the confrontation stayed with her and she lay wakeful that night, recalling not the happy times with Annie Scanlon but the meeting with Ivor. When she finally slept she threshed restlessly with bad dreams where she frantically climbed the inside of a glass bottle held by a jeering Ivor Spargo.

13

'*Oh, my God!*' A woman screamed. People passing by on both sides of the road scattered with shouts of: 'Look out! He's down!' The horse had skidded and now fell, hooves flailing, whinnying in panic.

Matt leapt down from his seat on the cart, instinctively certain that disaster had struck, not in the ice and snow of winter when such accidents to horses were commonplace, but in high summer. Not on a night of fog and rain but in the bright light of mid-morning. The sun was hot on his back and his shirtsleeves were rolled up above the elbows. He ran to the horse's head and knelt by him, stroking his neck, looking into his frightened eyes and speaking softly as if to a hurt child. 'There now, Sergeant. Good boy. You'll be all right.' But Matt knew Sergeant O'Malley would not be all right.

He was aware of the ring of curious but sympathetic spectators gathered around the cart and the fallen horse. He heard the murmurs of: 'What a shame.' And: 'Poor thing.' There was one face in the crowd which was familiar, one face which was smiling, gloating. Matt recognised Ivor Spargo.

Katy ran from the office to meet Matt as he strode up the yard from the gate. 'Matt! What's wrong?' The dust of summer rose up about his boots and he carried the Sergeant's collar and harness over his shoulder. He stepped past her into the office, threw his burden onto the counter then slumped down in the swivel chair. He looked up at her and said heavily, 'He's dead.' And when she put a hand to her mouth he added, 'He fell. We were coming off the bridge and down Charles Street when he slipped. We've been up and down there hundreds of times without any trouble. We've done it in the winter with the ice like a skating rink, but today his legs went from under him and he — I heard it break. I had to have him put down.'

'Oh, Matt!' Katy laid a hand on his shoulder, 'I'm so sorry.' She felt the tears on her face and wiped them away with the back of her hand. 'Poor old Sergeant O'Malley.'

They mourned him all that day, as a friend or one of the family. Beatrice was grief-stricken with big tears rolling down her pink cheeks. A coal merchant, eyes and mouth white and pink in his black face, brought back the cart, drawn by one of his horses. He refused payment: 'No, hinny, not after your bad luck.'

Katy helped Matt as he carefully cleaned the harness and hung it, gleaming, on a nail in the stable. They never mentioned the fear lurking at the backs of their minds.

It was the next morning when Matt put it into words: 'If I can't get another horse somehow, I'm done for.'

Katy corrected him: 'We're done for.' Because

165

this was her home now. Where would she go if Matt failed?

He nodded acceptance of that: 'True. I'm sorry. I expect that's what Spargo was thinking, that we were finished.'

'Spargo?' Katy questioned.

Matt nodded, 'Aye. He was there and enjoying it, laughing. He would have laughed on the other side of his face if I hadn't been busy with the Sergeant.' He grimaced, then turned it into a grin, 'But we're not finished yet. I'm going to go out and get a job, try to save enough to buy another horse.'

Katy smiled at him but knew it would not be easy. She remembered Annie's talk of living in a bottle. Matt had wanted to make a success of this business. Then she admitted to herself, So do I.

Matt pulled on his coat and started out. Katy sent Beatrice off to school and then set off for the shops with Louise in her pram. As she walked out between the gates Ivor Spargo said, 'There you are. I've been waiting for you.' Katy jerked around, startled, and saw his cart pulled up to one side of the gateway so it was out of sight of the office. Ivor sat on the front, smirking at her. She turned away and set off along the pavement, heading for Dundas Street. A moment later the horse walked past her, then Ivor, sitting on the cart on her side, so that he looked down on her set face.

He jeered, 'Off out to look for another job?' And when Katy did not answer: 'You'll be wanting one. Ballard's horse broke a leg yesterday.' Katy walked faster but he flipped the reins and the horse quickened its pace. A second or two later Ivor was abreast of her again. He boasted, 'I'll be driving a lorry before long. Me dad says he'll let me have one. I'll look you up any time I've got a job around here. You just remember, us Spargos have two yards, one here and another in Yorkshire and they'll both come to me one day. So when Ballard goes broke and gives you the sack, I might offer you something.' He laughed coarsely.

Katy let go of the pram with one hand and whacked the horse across its broad rump, yelling, '*Yarrh!*' It lunged forward and broke into a wild gallop. Ivor, caught unprepared, fell back over the seat into the cart, his legs in the air. Horse and cart careered down the road until he managed to get to his knees, haul on the reins and halt the equipage.

He was fifty yards away as Katy turned into Dundas Street, but he shook his fist and shouted, 'You'll be sorry for that!'

Ivor drove back to the Spargo yard, nursing his humiliation and raging. The idea came to him as he crossed the bridge and saw the train to Newcastle thundering across the railway bridge running parallel to that which carried the road. He found Arthur Spargo at the yard and demanded of him, 'That feller Barney Merrick, Katy's father, have you still got the letter he wrote to us?'

Arthur asked, 'What d'ye want with that?'

'His address.'

Arthur asked, 'What are you going to do with

it?' And when Ivor told him, agreed, 'Aye, it'll serve the bitch right.'

Katy had gone on her way, trembling with reaction, trying to soothe Louise, who had been frightened by her shout that had sent the horse galloping: 'There now, bonny lass. There, there. All over now.' But she did not think it was. She was sure Ivor would return, again and again. Thoughts of him haunted her through the ensuing days. She did not tell Matt of the encounter because she knew he would seek out Ivor as he had done before and this time Katy would not be there to come between them. That might mean trouble with the police. She did not want that for Matt, nor did she want him to fight her battles.

He had found a job, working for a builder as a labourer, but he was paid by the day and could be sacked at any time without notice. Jobs were hard to get because the shipyards were in depression and many of their workers were unemployed. Katy worried about Matt. Each day, when her shopping and housework were done, she would sit in the swivel chair in the office to sew or knit. It was as if, by being there, she was keeping some semblance of life in the business, though it was only a gesture of defiance. Her daughter crawled uncertainly about the office floor, a newly learned skill. Katy always talked to the babe, telling her all the problems of her days, large and small. One day, twisting her mother's ring on her finger, she said softly, 'I suppose I could sell this, bonny lass.' She had been down this road before, when she

168

had been driven to appeal to Matt for shelter. She was reluctant to part with the ring for several reasons. It was all she had of her mother — and she wanted it for Louise. In a way she regarded the ring as being held in trust for her daughter. 'I wonder — if I pawned it? I could reclaim it later on.'

Louise gazed up at her from solemn blue eyes and chewed at one of Beatrice's dolls. Katy worried, 'But suppose I never got the money to claim it back? And I'm living here as a married woman, a sort of housekeeper or nursemaid like Alice that Matt told me about, the one who worked for Joe Docherty. That's respectable. But I have a bairn of my own so I've got to have a ring, otherwise I'm — what? I don't want folks saying bad things about your mammy — and you. Besides, talk about Uncle Matt having that sort of woman in here — that would wreck his business.' And then, the clinching argument: 'Anyway, whatever I got for the ring, it wouldn't pay for another horse.' Katy sighed, 'So it looks like I'll just have to think of something else — and pray.' She scooped up Louise and held her tightly. She was very frightened that she and her child would be cast out into the streets again. The old fears of being arrested for vagrancy, or being sent to the workhouse, returned.

Matt strode into the yard at noon. Katy was watching for him and had the mid-day meal ready. He was not alone, being flanked on one side by Beatrice, holding his hand. The postman trudged on the other side, bag slung over his shoulder. Katy ran down the stairs to meet them at the office door. Matt said, 'I was passing the school and thought I might as well wait for Bea so we could walk home together.'

Beatrice announced, 'Miss Williams came out to see us.' Katy had met Miss Williams when she took Beatrice to school on her first day at the National. She had thought the teacher might be flighty out of school. Now Beatrice added, 'She was all tee-hee.' She simpered. 'And saying ' 'Yes, Mr Ballard,' and 'No, Mr Ballard.' I couldn't see anything funny about him, can you, Katy?'

Katy glanced at Matt who looked back at her blankly and said, 'I couldn't see what she was giggling about. I didn't say anything funny.' Katy replied straight-faced, 'No, I don't know what she was laughing at.' Miss Williams had obviously been taken by Matt. 'Now run upstairs, Bea. Your dinner will be on the table in a minute.'

The postman said, 'Will you sign for this, please, missus? It's a registered letter, all the way from Malta.'

Katy took it and felt the thickness of the linen envelope and its contents. She sat down at the desk, signed the postman's book and he went away, whistling as he crossed the yard. She knew the sender of the letter would be Winnie Teasdale, living in Malta. She had kept up her correspondence with Winnie Teasdale, though sometimes there had been gaps of several weeks, and had written to Winnie just a few weeks ago. But why registered?

Matt said, 'From your husband?'

Katy jerked out of her reverie and shook her

head. 'No, it's from an old friend in Malta — Winnie Teasdale.'

Matt was still curious: 'Does he write at all? I don't remember you having a letter all the time you've been here.'

'He writes, but I don't see that it's any of your business.' Katy reacted defensively, rapidly recalling the story she had manufactured. 'He's always written care of the General Post Office because of the way I moved around and now it's just a habit. I look in there every few days to see if there's a letter waiting for me.'

Matt's brows came together in anger. He said curtly, 'I wasn't idly poking my nose in. I wondered if there was any trouble, if he'd thrown you over. But you're right, it's your business, not mine.'

He started to turn away but Katy said quickly, 'Matt, I'm sorry. I didn't mean to snap at you. It's just that I'm still a bit upset over the Sergeant.'

Matt sighed and agreed, 'I can understand that. I miss him. I used to talk to the old feller. I sometimes think I'd rather not buy another horse, but it's the only way to get started again. Now if I could borrow the money to buy a lorry — but the banks would want security for that.'

Katy said tentatively. 'There's been a big drop in the number of licences taken out for horse-drawn vehicles over the past year. That sounds as though people are changing to lorries instead.'

Matt stared at her in surprise. 'How do you know that?'

Katy admitted, 'I read it in your magazine — *Motor Traction* — the other day.'

Matt said, 'Well, I'm damned!'

But then Beatrice called plaintively from above, 'Katy? Is dinner ready now, please?'

Katy laughed at Matt, 'I think somebody is hungry.' They climbed the stairs to their meal and Katy set the registered letter aside to read later — when she was alone.

When Beatrice had gone back to school, and Matt returned to his work, Katy cleared up after the meal and then sat down in the office to read the letter. It was then she found the linen envelope was addressed in a big, sprawling hand that was not Winnie's. She ripped it open and found it contained one sheet of paper in that same large hand and several covered with Winnie's careful copperplate, but shaky now. There was also a deposit book issued by the Grainger Building Society in Newcastle. Katy spread the sheets on her knee and read the top one:

Dear Katy,

I am writing on behalf of my late wife, Winnie, at her request. She had a nasty turn a week or two back and wrote the enclosed in case something happened and I think she knew something she did not tell me because she didn't want me to worry. I came home from the dockyard on Thursday and found her lying dead in her chair. She had told me she had to send this to you in December, when you will be twenty-one, or earlier if

172

anything happened to her, because that was your mother's wish.

Katy bit her lip and shook her head. Winnie Teasdale had been a dear friend of her mother and herself, had given her a home when she ran away from her father. She wept for sometime as Louise played around her feet unheeding. Katy finally wiped the tears from her eyes with a corner of her apron and read on. The rest was an outpouring of grief and hopes that she was well and settled now. He closed, 'Best wishes for the future. From, Fred Teasdale.'

Katy set that aside — then she realised the crawling Louise had found one of Matt's spanners lying on the floor behind the desk. It was big, too heavy for Louise to lift, but Katy took it from her and pushed Beatrice's doll into her arms instead. She put the spanner on a shelf by the door where Matt would see it and spread out the other sheets. Winnie had written:

I promised your mother I would give you the enclosed when you were twenty-one. That is why I insisted you write to me. I needed to keep track of you. She didn't want to give it to you while you were only young and at home because she was afraid your father would get hold of it. Ethel wanted you to have it because you were always her lass, the one she could rely on, while the others sided with their father. The building society knows all about you and that you are to have it when you turn up with the book. This money was left to your

173

mother by your Aunt Augusta. Do you remember, when your aunt died, your mother left you to look after the two boys? Well, she came to me and asked me to go to the house in Gosforth . . .

The maid had gone with them. She had a key and let them in but declined to go further into the house: 'Not with her dead upstairs. I found her and that's enough.' She pointed to a small table in the hall, 'That's the death certificate the doctor left. As soon as I've got my money, I'll be off.'

Ethel Merrick paid her out of her own purse, almost emptying it, and the girl scuttled away down the street. Ethel whispered to Winnie, 'It's upstairs. In her bedroom.' She led the way, the stairs creaking under them, up to and into the bedroom. The curtains were drawn but in the dim light they could make out the still form lying under the sheet. Ethel lay flat on the floor, face-down and wriggled under the bed. It appeared to have been regularly swept, probably with a long-handled brush, because there was little dust or fluff. She prised at a board and a section of it, some two feet long, lifted under her hands. She peered down into the hole between the rafters and saw a ladies' leather handbag. It chinked as she lifted it out, weighty in her hands. She turned her head to look back at Winnie, kneeling by the side of the bed, and breathed, 'Got it!'

Ethel replaced the floorboard and joined Winnie. They stood together at the foot of the bed and Ethel said aloud but shaking with emotion, 'Thank you, Aunt Augusta.' They followed that with a silent prayer.

The two friends left the house quietly and from there went to inform the undertaker. Then they moved on to the building society where they deposited the contents of the handbag — gold sovereigns — and instructions as to their disposal.

Winnie finished: 'Your mother left a letter with them to say the money was for you and I was to hold the book until you were twenty-one, or sooner if I thought fit. I think that time has come.'

She sent her best wishes: 'You've had a hard start in life through your father but I'm sure you will know happier days, as you deserve. I hope and trust, as your mother did, that the money will help towards this.'

Katy sat back, the letter left on her knees as she held the savings book and thought about the two women in that house of the dead. She could remember Aunt Augusta, who had left what money she had to Katy's mother — and who had no benefit from it because of Barney Merrick. Now it had come to her, Katy. She would be able to buy new clothes for Louise and Beatrice, possibly a new dress for herself — she needed one. There would be enough for that, surely? She opened the book and read the amount held on deposit: One hundred and twenty-seven pounds, fourteen shillings and eight pence.

The figures blurred before her eyes as her hands shook. Then eyes and hands steadied as she gripped the book tightly. New clothes faded into insignificance. She was rich! She was independent! This would keep her and Louise for two years! If Matt got a job driving a lorry he would be paid one pound, ten shillings per week, seventy-eight pounds a year. She had nearly twice that amount because the account would have incurred interest!

But she still mourned dear Winnie.

Matt. Thought of him brought her up short. In her excitement and grief she had forgotten him and her situation — and her past. She remembered her despair on the night when she had come here and thrown herself on his mercy. He had taken her in. He could have seized on that moment when she would have done anything for the sake of Louise, but he had not.

She sat in thought for some time and then determined on a course of action. At that point there came a pounding at the office door. Katy ran to answer it eagerly, thinking it might be someone come to offer work to Matt, forgetting that, without a horse to pull the cart, he could not take on work. She was in a buoyant, optimistic mood because of the letter. She opened the door and confronted Barney Merrick.

Katy's new-found hope turned to shock and dismay. Barney wore his suit, old, worn and shiny. His shirt was fastened at the neck with a collar stud but he wore no collar. He had not shaved for some days. He greeted Katy: 'Aye, there y'are.' Then he pushed past her into the office to sit on the swivel chair and gaze around him with his ice-blue, red-flecked eyes. 'So this is the whorehouse. I always knew you'd go to the bad.'

That shook Katy like a slap in the face. She was still too taken aback to say anything but, 'How did you get here.'

'On the train.' Barney laughed unpleasantly.

'I meant, how did you find out I was here?'

Barney answered piously, 'The Spargos. One o' them wrote to me, doing his duty, and doing right by me. It's my name you're dirtying here.'

Ivor. Katy knew it had to be him. He had written to Barney and told him where to find her. She was getting over her shock now, anger building inside her because he had come there at any time, let alone on this day of celebration, to try to spoil it for her. As he had spoilt everything. It was as if he had some evil second sight, to be able to choose the time he could cause most damage, most hurt.

Katy now framed the inevitable question, the key to this visit: 'What do you want?'

Barney answered with a note of surprise in his voice, as if it was obvious, 'I've come for what's mine, my share of what you've been paid since you left the Spargos. I've not had a penny since then and I'm entitled. I'm your father.'

It was as Katy had thought, he wanted money. Had that evil second sight told him that she would come into money that day? But it belonged to her — and Louise — a gift from Katy's mother. She replied flatly, 'You'll get nothing from me.'

Barney jerked forward in the chair, '*What!*'

Katy took an involuntary step backward then stopped. She would not let him intimidate her. He snapped, 'D'ye mean you've spent it?'

'No, I — '

'He must ha' paid you this last six months. You're not saying you let him bed you for nothing!'

'He doesn't bed me!' That charge enraged Katy. 'I'm a housekeeper and respectable!'

'Are ye?' Barney sneered. 'Then what about her?' He jabbed a pointing finger at Louise. 'Isn't that a child of sin? I see a ring on your finger but I know you're not married.'

Louise, frightened by his bawling, began to wail and Barney grumbled, 'Can't you shut that bairn up?'

'I could but I won't.' Katy's anger was at boiling point now. That he should talk of her daughter as he had enraged her more than had the other vile insults. She pointed to the door, 'Get out of here!'

'Don't give me lip!' Barney lifted his hand and Katy flinched instinctively, remembering how he had doled out punishment all her life, the word and the blow coming together, to leave her hurt, inside and out. That added fuel to her anger. He saw how she had reacted and he grinned, then let his hand fall to the desktop again. 'Now you just give me what you owe me.'

Katy now stood by the shelf alongside the door. She picked up the spanner she had set there and smashed it down on Barney's hand. He shrieked with the pain of it and clasped it to his chest with his free hand. 'You mad bitch!' His

178

face was contorted with agony. 'What the hell did you do that for?'

'You won't lay a hand on me again.' Katy held the spanner ready to strike again. 'Get out while you're still in one piece.'

Barney glared at her for a moment, refusing to believe her, but then saw she meant it. He said, his tone still disbelieving, 'You wouldn't dare.'

'What I did once I can do again,' Katy answered grimly. She wondered, could she? But she jerked her head to indicate the door.

Barney believed her now. He pulled himself out of the chair, cradling his throbbing hand, then sidled past Katy and out of the door. He halted then to accuse her, 'You're a child of the divil to do that to your own father.'

Katy was unmoved by that: 'I only know one devil and that's my father.'

'Was,' Barney corrected her. 'You're no bairn o' mine now and you can look for nothing from me. I'm disowning ye.'

Katy replied inflexibly, 'I've never looked for anything from you and never got anything.' She prayed, For God's sake, go!

Barney spat at her, 'Damn you to hell for an evil-tempered witch!' He walked away across the yard but halted again at the gate to shout back at her, 'Damn you!' Then he was gone from her sight before the echoes ceased reverberating around the yard.

Katy felt sick. She cuddled Louise and cried, until the child stopped wailing and struggled to be on the floor again. Katy set her down, washed Louise's face and her own then sat in the swivel chair, staring out at the yard. She examined her conscience and decided she regretted nothing she had done. Her father's threat to abandon her meant nothing because he had effectively done that years ago. That part of her life was over. She was done with him. Now she had to look forward.

She could not foresee that he had not done with her.

Katy thought again of the sum she now owned, the future it opened up for her, and this brought her back to a more cheerful mood by the time Beatrice and Matt came home. She said nothing to him about her father or the letter. Matt was also in good spirits: 'I've got another job, driving a cart for a feller with a greengrocer's shop. I looked in on him on the way home and he's taking me on. The money isn't good but it's regular and it'll keep us going until I can find something that pays more.'

'Oh, good!' Katy said delightedly. But she knew it was not good at all. He deserved better.

Katy saw him off to work the next day with a packet of sandwiches for his lunch. Then she put the letter and building society book in her bag and Louise in her pram. With Beatrice trotting alongside she walked to Monkwearmouth station. There she boarded a train to Newcastle with the pram in the guard's van. She was back in the flat in time to give Beatrice a late lunch, then sent her off to school with a note explaining her absence that morning, due to having to travel to Newcastle. She considered telling Beatrice not to mention the trip to Matt, but then decided that would only make the child more likely to blurt it out. As she did, greeting Matt when he came home from work with, 'We went on a train today.'

Matt looked questioningly at Katy and she explained casually, 'I had to go to Newcastle.'

Katy knew he must still be curious but said no more and he only commented, 'Oh?' He did not press for details.

Katy broached the subject that night when the children were abed and asleep, and she sat sewing on one side of the fire while Matt read the *Sunderland Daily Echo* on the other. 'Matt, could you buy a second-hand lorry for a hundred and fifty pounds?'

He lowered the paper to smile at her bent head: 'You could, and a good one at that, if you knew what you were doing.'

'No, I meant yourself; do you know where you could put your hands on one if — just suppose — you had a partner who could put up the money?'

Matt laughed, 'Fat chance of that!'

Katy smiled, 'But just supposing?'

Matt grinned, humouring her, 'I could find one, a decent one, easily enough. Not in five minutes, but give me a day or two to look around. Maybe in Newcastle if not here. So if you know of anybody wanting to get into a promising little business on the ground floor, let me know.' He raised the paper again.

'I do. I've got a hundred and fifty pounds.' Katy smiled up at him.

Matt slowly laid down the paper and asked,

disbelieving, 'You've — what? I thought — when you came here you said — '

'That I was broke?' Katy cut in, nodding. 'But I've had some money left to me. That was the news in the letter from Malta.' She recited the details in the letter, then finished, 'That's why I went to Newcastle. I want to keep a bit back as a sort of insurance, just so I have some money, but I'll put a hundred and fifty pounds into the business.'

Matt said, 'Good God!' He ran a hand through his hair, shook his head, then grinned at Katy, 'You're full of surprises, aren't you?' And then more seriously, getting down to business, 'And you want to be a partner?' Then when Katy nodded, he added wryly, 'Well, I don't have to tell you that it will be a gamble. At the moment we haven't even a barrow. How much of a share do you want for your money? Half?'

'No.' Katy bit off a cotton. 'I'll be helping in the office and any other way I can, but you will be driving and doing all the real work. I thought twenty per cent but I'll take whatever you think is fair. I think I owe you that for taking us in — Louise and me, I mean.'

Matt shifted uncomfortably. 'You don't owe me anything for that. It was the least I could do — and I wasn't very civil about it at the time, as I recall.' Katy saw his embarrassment and did not argue the point. He said, 'I think you should take twenty-five per cent. From what I've seen, you'll earn that.'

Next day Katy gave him the money and he set

182

off. She was too excited to wait patiently at the yard for his return. After Beatrice had gone to school she put Louise in the pram and hurried to Annie Scanlon's house. Seated before the fire with a cup of tea, she told Annie, 'You'll never believe what's happened to me.'

Annie asked, 'Something to do with that feller Ballard? Are you and him — '

'No!' Katy laughed at the idea. 'Nothing like that. Though it does involve him.' And she told Annie all about her inheritance and the partnership. 'And Matt's out looking for a lorry now.' Then she asked, 'But will you keep that to yourself, Annie? About the money and me paying for the lorry. I think it will be better for business if Matt looks to be running it.' She remembered how little respect was shown to Arthur Spargo by the men because it was known his wife ran his business.

'Aye, I think folks prefer to deal with a man as the boss. And you can rely on me to keep quiet. I'm that pleased for you,' Annie went on, holding Louise on her knee. 'And how is the other little lass — Beatrice?'

'She's at school and loving it.' Then Katy asked her, 'Why don't you call round when she comes home and have some tea?'

So that afternoon they met in the flat over the office and Annie was seated on the floor, playing with Beatrice and Louise, when the lorry trundled into the yard. Katy, busy cooking dinner for that evening, wiped her hands on her apron and ran down the stairs. Matt was climbing down from the cab of the lorry and he

183

grinned at her and called, 'Here she is, a three-ton Dennis. How do you like her?'

Katy stood beside him and looked over the Dennis. 'She looks all right to me.'

Matt rubbed at an oily mark on the wing with a cloth. 'She's been worked fairly hard, four or five hundred miles a week, and she's a bit dirty, but she's in first-class order and she goes well.' He winked at Katy, 'The feller was asking a hundred and forty but I knocked him down a fiver.' He started to walk around the lorry: 'I'll make a start on cleaning her up tonight and tomorrow I'll service her. Then we'll be back on the job.'

Katy could see his thoughts were already on what he had to do, and planning. She called, 'Matt! *Matt!*' And when he turned she told him, 'Annie Scanlon is upstairs. I asked her round for a bite and the dinner's just about ready, so can you put the lorry in the shed until tomorrow — please?'

He agreed, reluctantly. Katy smiled to herself and thought he was like a child told he could not play with his toy, but he greeted Annie pleasantly and they ate a cheerful meal. He talked a good deal about the lorry, and at one point stopped and grinned at Katy, 'I should say 'our lorry'.' And to Annie, 'I expect Katy told you about her bit o' luck?'

'Aye, she did. She told me about the partnership as well and I promised to keep it to myself.'

He stared, surprised, and Katy put in quickly, 'I think it would be better if the firm was still in your name and people were just dealing with you.'

Matt shrugged, 'If that's what you want.'

'It is.' Katy hesitated, then said, 'I think it might be better if you didn't mention it to your fiancée, either.'

Matt's brows came together. 'What are you suggesting? I trust Fleur.'

Katy stepped in quickly again, 'Of course, but I think if we keep this just among the people involved . . . ' She let the suggestion hang there.

Matt thought about it. He admitted to himself that Fleur was not interested in the firm but he argued, Why should she be? It might well be best to act as Katy suggested, and there would be no question of the yard being 'under new management'. He grinned, 'We wouldn't have to paint those gates, changing the name to Ballard and Merrick.'

Katy laughed, relieved that he had agreed. She had a shrewd idea how Fleur might regard the partnership. Matt ran down the stairs to the office and returned a few minutes later with a sheet of paper, a pen and bottle of ink. He laid the paper on the table before Katy: 'There you are. A written agreement. You take twenty-five per cent of the profits and assets.' He grinned at Annie: 'You can witness our signatures.'

So it was done.

Katy was relieved that she had got her way, glad that Matt was happy, and happy herself that she had secured this home for her and Louise. Only the spectre of Ivor Spargo haunted her.

A day or two later, Matt told Fleur, 'I've

bought a lorry. I'll be able to branch out into bigger loads, longer distances.'

Fleur smiled delightedly, 'I'm so pleased for you. You work so hard.' For a time she had doubted him. When his business had slumped and he had been reduced to driving a horse and cart, and even worse, working as a labourer, she had cold-bloodedly decided to ditch him. She had only delayed while she sought another escort with better prospects — though without success. She decided now that she had been right all along, and Matt was headed for success. She would be able to introduce him to some of her old schoolfriends: 'This is my fiancé. Matt owns Ballard's.'

He thought she was looking prettier — and more cheerful and welcoming — than she had for a while. He was proud to walk out with her on his arm. With the lorry running he began to make more money, from business attracted by a new set of leaflets which Katy persuaded the local shopkeepers to show. He was able to take out Fleur more often. More and more he was taking over work that would formerly have been done by the Spargos.

Whenever Katy saw Ivor in time she avoided him, but sometimes he ambushed her going to or coming from the shops in Dundas Street. He always taunted her but now his threats that she would be homeless and Ballard's would go broke, were hollow. He knew it and that inflamed him more, but it meant Katy could smile and ignore him. But then came the day when he asked his father, 'When are you going to let me take a lorry out?'

Vera Spargo had gone to see her sister in Blyth and would not return until evening. She had left explicit instructions as to how her husband should deal with the work of the day, and her usual warning that he should not diverge from them. That warning always nettled Arthur Spargo. Did she think he couldn't run the yard? So he told Ivor, 'Aye, you can take one today, but watch what you're doing.'

Ivor was driving through Monkwearmouth and savouring his position, seated above the pedestrians and winking and leering at the girls, when he saw Katy with Louise in her pram. He reached over the side of the cab to squeeze the bulb of the horn and Katy turned at its hooting, at first thinking it might be Matt. She saw the lorry bearing down on her and Ivor grinning malevolently at the wheel. For a horrified instant she thought he meant to run down her and her child and she swerved away from the kerb with the pram. She saw him laugh at her fright and as the lorry roared past her he leaned out of the cab to shout back at her, 'I'll teach you to give lip!' Then he faced forward again.

Too late, he saw the coal cart backing out of a cul-de-sac, its driver at the horse's head. It had appeared while he was shouting back at Katy. He tried to stop, to swerve, but the lorry skidded across the road with a screech of brakes then crashed into the cart. Coal was scattered over the road and the horse reared in panic. Its driver shouted, 'Are you blind or bloody daft?' The front of the lorry was smashed in and a mixture of petrol and water spilled onto the road.

Ivor looked around him wildly. He saw Katy standing on the kerb and shrieked at her, 'You're the cause of this!'

A bystander bawled, 'Get away wi' ye! Ye weren't looking where you were going! I saw ye!'

Ivor did not hear him. Intent on Katy he raged, almost in tears, 'It was you! You've got the evil eye! But I'll get you for this! I swear! I'll see you burn in hell!'

The curious crowd that had gathered now stared at him disbelievingly. A policeman came pushing through them and Ivor shut his mouth but still shook his fist at Katy. She turned away and ran.

Ivor told Vera the next day, 'That Merrick lass has been a curse on us ever since we threw her out for her loose living! That Ballard she works for is taking our trade! We should wreck them, burn them out, before they finish us!'

Vera regarded him with contempt. 'Don't be daft. If you go on like that they'll put you away.' And to Arthur: 'If you'd done as I told you, this wouldn't have happened. Don't let him near a lorry again.'

The incident cast a shadow of fear over Katy. She contrived to hide it from Matt but it was always lurking at the back of her mind. She had known for some time that she had made an enemy in Ivor Spargo, but now she believed he was mad.

14

'We need another lorry,' Katy raised her voice to be heard above the throb of the engine. She had taken to riding with Matt as driver's mate — while Beatrice was at school and Annie Scanlon looked after Louise — on those days when the load could be handled better by two pairs of hands rather than one. At first Matt had agreed only reluctantly, 'What — a woman? It's not a woman's job.'

Katy had replied, 'Why not? If it helps?' And after a while she had her way. Matt found that, though she did not have his strength, she was quick and did her fair share of the work.

Now Matt, seated at the wheel, answered, 'Another lorry? We've got a full order book and could take more. But if we took on a second lorry we'd need a driver for it. We'd have to pay him thirty bob a week and we might not have enough work to keep him and his lorry busy. That's where we could move from profit into loss.'

Katy argued, 'We can afford a lorry under the subsidy scheme.' She knew their balance at the bank to a penny.

Matt shot a startled glance at her, 'You've been looking at that scheme, have you?' Then he conceded, 'All right, we could manage the lorry

189

that way but we can't afford the driver.' Matt braked the Dennis at a level crossing and grinned at her, 'Leaving aside your share as partner, I'm only paying you a few shillings. I wouldn't get a driver for that.'

Katy was silent a moment, then said, 'Teach me to drive.'

'You?' Matt was incredulous.

'There are a lot of women driving nowadays.'

'Rich men's wives playing around in their motor cars, not women driving lorries for a job.' The gates of the crossing opened, Matt let out the clutch and the Dennis rolled forward.

Katy retorted, 'I bet it's no heavier than a day's washing. The actual driving, I mean.'

'Well . . . '

Katy seized on his indecision: 'You've never done a day's washing!'

He laughed, 'I've washed out my clothes in a bucket many a time, but — no, not the way you mean.'

'If I took all the light loads, fitted in their delivery when the girls were with Annie or at school — that would help.' Katy urged him, 'Give me a try! See if I can!'

He glanced aside at her eager face, her eyes fixed on him. As he looked forward again, he laughed, 'I don't know what folks will think, but — all right, next time we have an hour or so to spare, I'll try you out.'

Katy smiled happily as she gazed out at the countryside rolling by. She enjoyed these longer trips — they were headed for Durham with a load that day. Louise was with Annie Scanlon, a ready volunteer to care for the child. Katy reflected that she was very lucky. In the year since they had bought the Dennis they had gained more work, and in particular, more long-distance loads. Their income had increased by leaps and bounds. It was only limited now by the fact that they had only one lorry and its driver. There might be work to keep two lorries busy, or there might not. Katy was convinced there would be and thought, There's only one way to find out.

'Open the throttle part way — like that. Now close the air shutter . . . and switch on.' Two days after returning from Durham they were seated in the Dennis again but this time only in the yard and with Katy behind the wheel. She listened and watched intently as Matt talked her through the starting procedure. As they trundled slowly around the yard with Katy gripping the wheel, Matt said with surprise, 'You got hold of that soon enough.'

Katy admitted, 'I've been watching you.' And so she had, every time she had gone with him in the cab.

At the end of an hour she had progressed from manoeuvring about the yard to driving out of the gates and around the neighbouring streets. That was with many a helping hand from Matt, but as he said, when back in the yard and he was helping her down, 'You didn't hit anything.'

Katy smiled at the praise. She felt exhausted by the nervous strain and concentration of the past hour, but — she had done it!

By the end of a month she was taking turns

with Matt to drive the Dennis out on local work while he sat at her side as driver's mate. Heads turned as she drove past and Matt would grin and wave. 'That's something they've not seen before!'

They bought a spanking, brand new Dennis under the War Office subsidy scheme. Annie Scanlon asked, 'What scheme is that?'

Katy explained, 'The War Office gives us a subsidy of a hundred and ten pounds towards the cost of the lorry, provided we maintain it properly and make sure it's fit for Army use if they have to requisition it. They send an inspector round once a year to check on it.'

Annie peered at her, wary. 'What if they find summat wrong?'

Katy assured her confidently, 'They won't. Matt will be servicing it.'

But Katy drove it. When Matt brought the Dennis into the yard for the first time he walked around it with Katy, both admiring the gleaming paintwork, the shining, slick newness of it. Then he turned to her and grinned, 'Now it's your turn.' He handed Katy up into the cab, though that was a courtesy because for a long time she had swung up into the old Dennis with practised ease. Then with Matt beside her she drove out through the streets and across the bridge into the town. And that was where Ivor saw them.

He reined in his horse as they drove along Fawcett Street, with its clanging electric trams, big shops and crowded pavements, and past the Town Hall. Ivor looked from the immaculate Dennis to Katy at the wheel, then back to the

Dennis as the brightly painted rest of it slid by him. Neither Katy nor Matt saw him as they passed because he was hidden in a long line of traffic on the other side of the road. He watched them go away from him, still not saying a word, let alone shouting an insult after them. But he had got back his tongue by the time he drove his horse and cart into the Spargo yard.

Ivor confronted Arthur Spargo and snarled, 'Ballard and that tart Katy Merrick have got a brand new lorry.' He told his father how they had passed him. 'That makes two lorries they've got now! They're getting bigger all the time and a lot of that is due to her and what she learned here. The bitch has it in for us. I said we had to finish them before they finished us!'

Arthur grumbled, 'Aye, I reckon you're right.' He scowled at Ivor, 'That lass did the dirty on us.' It still rankled with him, how Katy had humiliated Ivor and himself on the day she walked out. He decided now, 'We'll settle her.' He stopped there because he did not know how to set about it.

Ivor did: 'We'll burn them out. Set fire to both their lorries.'

'Aye?' Arthur wasn't sure about that. The immorality of such an attack did not worry him but suppose Vera found out?

Ivor read his thoughts and urged him, 'Ma's away.'

'Aye, she's looking after that poorly sister of hers at Blyth. She won't be back till the end of the week; that's what she said in her letter I got this morning.' Arthur added bitterly, 'That and a

193

string o' bloody orders.' He smarted from Vera's acid-tongued instructions. He would show her.

Ivor said, 'So we'll go tonight. Who will we take with us?'

Arthur scowled, 'Why do we have to take anybody?'

Ivor insisted, 'Somebody has to climb the wall and open the gate for us. I'll do the job after that but I want somebody to watch my back; I'm not going in on my own.'

Arthur still demurred: 'I don't like the idea of taking sombody else in. Suppose he splits on us afterwards?'

Ivor grinned unpleasantly, 'I'll fetch Ernie Thompson. He won't dare to open his mouth.' Ernie was a labourer in the Spargo yard, a skinny underfed little man. He had a wife and five children and they all lived from hand to mouth on his small wage and without it they would starve.

Arthur nodded, 'You're right there: Ernie will be safe enough.'

It was close to midnight when Arthur drove one of his lorries into the street next to Ballard's yard. He put on the brake and switched off the engine. He, Ivor and Ernie Thompson, sitting side by side in the cab, peered out at the silent street with its pools of light from the street lamps. The only sound was the metallic clinking as the engine cooled. Then the clock in the Town Hall across the river chimed twelve times.

Ivor muttered, 'Everybody's abed. Let's get on with it.' He climbed down and a frightened Ernie followed. Arthur came reluctantly, having doubts

194

now. Ivor reached back into the cab and lifted out a gallon tin of petrol. Carrying this, he set off with the others following him. The yard was just around the next corner. Its gates, still painted Docherty & Ballard, were closed. Ivor tested them and whispered, 'They're bolted.' He glanced at the wall on either side of the gates and saw the broken glass on its top glinting in the light from the nearest street lamp. 'You'll have to go over the gate.' He jerked a beckoning thumb at Ernie then he and Arthur gripped the little man's legs and lifted him until he could swing first one leg and then the other over the gate. He hesitated then for a moment, fearful, propped on his stiffened arms holding on to the top of the gate. Then Ivor hissed, 'Get on with it!' And Ernie let himself down inside the yard.

With solid ground under his feet he paused again, his back to the gate and his head turning as his gaze tried to probe the darkness, his eyes blinking nervously. The cobbled yard stretched before him and he could see it was empty. The walls which surrounded it, however, cast deeper, black shadows which hid everything. He could just make out to his left the roofs of a garage or shed and a stable. Ahead of him the office with the flat above stood out in silhouette but cast its own black shadow. The yard was a dark square in a black frame and nothing stirred but the wind which brushed his cheek.

'What're you *doing*?' Ivor hissed. 'Get on with it!'

Ernie obeyed. The bolts and hinges on the gates had been oiled, Matt had seen to that, so there was no noise as the bolts slid and Ernie swung one of the gates open. The breeze tried to blow it shut again but Ernie held it. The others entered cautiously and Ivor muttered, 'You took your time.'

Ernie excused himself: 'I was making sure there was nobody watching.'

'Who'd be watching at this time o' night? Ballard can't afford a watchman.' Ivor brushed past him contemptuously. 'You come with me.' As Ernie released the gate and it started to close at the push of the breeze, Ivor addressed Arthur: 'Hold on to that gate and keep it open. Don't let it slam.'

Arthur whispered, 'You be careful.' His courage was running out now. It had been easy to growl threats back in his own yard but now . . .

'Don't worry,' Ivor told him, 'I know what I'm doing. We're going to settle some scores tonight — with Katy and that bloody Ballard.' He started to cross the yard but then a child wailed faintly in the flat above the office. Ivor and Ernie froze and the wail came again but then faded away into silence. They waited a minute, breathing shallowly, then Ivor muttered, 'All right.'

He set off across the yard again, heading for the garage. Its doors were shut and he went to open one of them, whispering to Ernie, 'Hold this.' He held out the can of petrol and released it, but, fumbling in the darkness, Ernie had not taken it properly. It slipped from his fingers and fell on the hard standing in front of the garage with a tinny clangour. Ivor snatched it up and hissed, 'You bloody clumsy — ' He stopped there, listening, head turned back over his shoulder to peer at the office and flat. But there was still no movement or sound, only the sigh of the wind.

Ivor let out his pent breath and thrust the can into Ernie's hands, but this time making sure he held it. 'You're lucky. Nobody heard that.' Then he pulled open the door of the garage a foot or so. Inside was as black as a pit but he could make out the gleam of metal on the lorries within. He took the petrol can from Ernie again and passed inside.

He had been wrong. Katy had been quick to go to Louise when her daughter awoke, crying in the night. She soothed the child and Louise was soon sleeping soundly again. Katy waited a little while to be sure both little girls had settled and she was about to return to her bed when she heard the *clunk-clank* come faintly from the yard. She tiptoed to the window, drew back the curtain an inch or so and peered out. The yard lay in darkness but over by the garage the deeper shadows moved and she knew someone was there.

Katy's heart thumped as she pulled on her coat over her nightgown, thrust her feet into her shoes and ran silently down the stairs on her toes. She flitted through the office to the counter and reached down to shake Matt but found only the blankets he had cast aside. They were still warm from his body. She gave a little sigh of relief, thinking that it would be Matt in the yard.

197

Still, she wondered, Why?

Katy padded back through the office to its door, opened it and passed through. She paused a moment then, standing in the deep shadow of the building, her gaze fixed on the garage. One of its doors was open and she could just make out a figure standing before it, but surely that was too small to be Matt? She took a hesitant step forward — then an arm wrapped around her, binding her arms, and a big hand slipped over her mouth. She stood still for an instant, frozen in shock by the sudden assault, then a voice breathed in her ear, 'Don't move or make a sound. Do you hear, Katy?' She managed to nod against his hand. He took it away and his arm slipped from around her body. Katy felt herself shaking with reaction from that moment of fear. Now she could see him, that he had pulled on shirt and trousers.

Matt was going on in a whisper, 'I heard a noise and looked out of the office window. There were two of them by the garage. I reckon one of them is inside now. What are you doing here?'

Katy explained, shivering in the night air, and from the tension. She finished, 'I came to ask you what was going on.'

Matt said grimly, 'That's what I'm asking myself.' And then, doubtfully, 'Will you do something for me, Katy?'

She turned her head to face him and breathed, 'Yes.'

He pointed, his finger before her face: 'They've opened one side of the gate — and wedged it, or the wind would have closed it.'

Katy nodded. She saw the grey square opening in the wall that marked the open leaf of the gate. Matt kept two wedges there to hold the gates open when needs be. Katy had used them for that purpose on occasion. Matt said, 'Sneak around in the shadow of the walls so that feller outside the garage won't see you. Then shut that gate. I'm going around the other way to the garage and I'll jump on them when I see you close the gate. Then they won't be able to run for it.' He gave her a gentle push on her way and was gone.

Katy saw his tall silhouette merge into the shadows to be lost. She moved stealthily around the office to the side wall of the yard and then soft-footed along it to the front wall. Her coat was dark grey and covered her from neck to ankles. She was certain she could not be seen by the man outside the garage but hearing was another matter. She felt her way carefully though blindly in the gloom.

Katy knew that Matt, working his way around the square in the opposite direction, had further to go. She would come to the open gate before he reached the garage so he would not have to wait for her. She was edging along the front wall now and the open gate stood square before her, hiding the gateway. She was almost upon it when her toe stubbed lightly against something solid. She crouched to finger it, thinking it might be a brick but she found it was the wedge for the gate. She rose with it in her hand, was conscious of the breeze at her back and flirting with her hair which hung down below her shoulders. She wondered, What is keeping the gate open with the wind trying to close it? Then it came to her, that there was another man on the other side of the open gate.

That shocked Katy again, but only for a few seconds. She told herself that she had to shut the gate — somehow — because Matt was relying on her. At that moment she had confirmation of her suspicion. Someone moved on the other side of the gate, a soft footfall, then a man appeared. He stopped at the edge of the gate, his bulky figure only partly clear of it, his shoulder still propping it open. She could see him in profile and now, so close he was, barely six feet away, she recognised Arthur Spargo.

Katy still held the wedge. She transferred it from one hand to the other as she slipped out of her coat. She knew that the shadows would not hide her now because her white nightgown would give her away. But there was no help for that, and Arthur would see her anyway if he turned his head. She needed the coat because it would buy her a few seconds grace. Holding it by its collar in her right hand, the wedge in her left, she stepped forward.

Matt paused in the shadows just short of the open garage door and only five or six yards from the skinny little man who stood there. Ernie's back was turned to Matt and his head swivelled uneasily as he shifted his gaze from the office on the other side of the yard to the inside of the garage. Matt could hear a faint splashing from in there and wondered what was happening. He could just see past Ernie and the open door to the front wall — and the dark grey square showed the gate was still open. *Where was that girl?* Now he saw another man back out of the garage and pass something to the first. Matt heard a whispered, 'Hold that and don't drop it!' Then the second man turned back to the garage again.

Ivor drew a deep breath compounded of excitement and anticipation. Now for it! He glanced just once towards the gate in the front wall and saw his escape route was open, then he struck the match. It flared for less than a second. He held it, waiting for it to burn steadily, but before that could happen a fist closed over his hand and the match, snuffing it out.

Katy saw the flame flicker by the garage at the instant she lunged at Arthur Spargo. As her slight weight hit the gate it was just enough to send the unprepared Arthur staggering clear of it. Katy swung the coat so it wrapped around his head, muffling and blinding. She released it then and shoved at the gate again. It slammed shut, she shot the bolts across and set her back against it. Arthur fought out of the coat and cast it from him. Katy could see past him to where there was a struggle going on outside the garage and another man running towards the gate. But then Arthur waddled towards her, squeaking, 'Get out o' that!' His voice broke high with panic.

Katy lifted the wedge in both hands, holding it by its thin edge, and skirled, 'Keep back!' He hesitated a second but then came on, fear driving him, and she warned again, 'I will!' But he still kept on and she lashed out.

Arthur lifted an arm and saved his head but yelped with pain as the thick and heavy wedge hit his elbow. He pulled back, clutching it with his other hand. 'You've broken it!' Now the other man came running, only to skid to a halt just short of the gate. Arthur whined, 'Shove her out of it! She's broken me arm!'

The newcomer took a hesitant step forward but Katy remembered him: 'Don't you come near me, Ernie Thompson! You're in enough trouble already!' And: 'I don't know what your wife will say when she hears what you've been up to!' But Katy had a good idea, and so did Ernie. He shifted from one foot to the other, his gaze slid miserably from Katy to the cursing Arthur and back again. He pleaded, 'Give me a chance, Katy, lass.'

She was tempted, suspecting that he had been pressed into this action, but then Matt came striding and shoving Ivor ahead of him. After snuffing out the match he had grabbed the neck of the startled Ivor's jacket and yanked it down. So now the buttoned jacket was gathered about Ivor's lower arms and they were pinioned to his side.

Matt was breathing hard and in a raging temper. He had a kind, approving word for Katy: 'Well done, lass!' She had held Arthur and Ernie at bay, though truth to tell, there was no fight in either of them. Matt had only to deal with Ivor — Ernie had run at the sight of Matt — and took him from behind and by surprise. Ivor was no match for him, anyway. When he turned on the others his voice cracked like a whip: 'You were trying to burn me out! The garage and lorries stink of petrol! Here's the can you used, the box of matches you were going to!' He held both in his free hand. The other was locked on Ivor's shirt collar. Arthur and Ernie shrank from the angry young giant but he snapped, 'Stand still! If one o' you tries to run I'll flatten him!' They froze and he held them for a moment, his gaze shifting from one to the other.

Arthur offered. 'Can't we forget about it? I'll make it worth your while.'

Matt answered, 'Shut up!' His glare did the rest. Arthur closed his mouth, despairing. Matt said, 'Up to the office.' He jerked his head towards it and Arthur and Ernie moved off ahead of him. Ivor followed them, Matt still gripping his shirt collar. Katy had seized the opportunity to pick up her coat and slip into it. She walked alongside Matt and he told her, 'When I've got these beauties inside you can get dressed and fetch a pollis.'

Katy was thinking hard and did not answer that. Ivor gasped, choking, 'The pollis won't do owt. I'll say we came here to offer to buy this place and you turned nasty. It would only be your word against ours. That petrol tin and the matches could ha' been yours and I'll swear they are.'

Matt replied grimly, 'We'll see about that.' He halted them just outside the office. 'This is close enough. We don't want to blister the paint.' When they stared at him, puzzled and uneasy, he explained, 'You're all going to write out what you did here tonight and what you intended. Then you'll swear to it on the Bible.' When Ivor shook his head, Matt went on, 'Or we're going to have an accident.' He lifted the petrol can and shook it so they could hear the sloshing of its contents. Eyeing Ivor, he said softly, 'There's fair drop left. I'll pour it over you and set it alight.'

Ivor swallowed and whispered, 'You wouldn't dare.' Then he gasped as the first of the petrol splashed on his head and ran down his face. He shrieked, '*No! Stop it! I will! I will!*'

Matt lowered the can, 'All right, get inside.' He ranged them against the wall of the office and seated miserably on its floor. Ivor, still shaking and ashen-faced sat nearest the door. Matt lit the gaslight and Ivor jerked as the match spurted. Matt said drily, 'You'll come to no harm there — provided you behave yourself.' Then to Katy, 'Will you fetch the pollis now.'

Instead of answering, Katy tugged at his sleeve and drew him out of earshot of the gang. Matt asked, 'What is it?'

Katy whispered, 'Going to the police would hurt Ernie Thompson badly — he has a wife and children depending on him — and I think they forced him into this.'

Matt protested, 'I'm sorry about that, but I'm not letting them off just for his sake. They tried to put us out of business!' His anger was flaring again. He glanced past Katy at the gang and they took no comfort from his expression.

Katy plucked at his sleeve again. Her voice low and urgent, she pleaded, 'If it goes to court they'll pay lawyers. They won't get off and they know that, but it will drag on for months.'

'So?' Matt insisted, 'I'm not letting them go.' He began to turn away.

Katy put in quickly, 'No, I'm not saying you should, but listen: They have another yard in Yorkshire with a lot of lorries . . . ' She whispered on and Matt listened, at first opposed but finally approving.

When Katy was done, Matt turned back to the gang and stood over them. 'There's paper and pen on the desk.' He pointed, 'You'll take it in turns to write down why you came here tonight and what you did. Then you'll witness each other's signatures. We'll start with you, Ernie.' That was because he judged the little man to be the weakest member. When Ernie had finished his statement, written in a wavering, childish scrawl, Matt read it out. At one point Ernie had written, 'They said they were going to settle you. I didn't want to come with them but they said they would sack me if I didn't.' The Spargos listened, they knew, to what would be Ernie's statement in court. They followed suit.

Matt shuffled the three signed and dated statements together and eyed the Spargos: 'I'll keep these in case of further trouble. They'll be locked in a solicitor's safe first thing tomorrow. But there's one thing more. So long as you were around these parts you'd try to make trouble and I won't have that. So I want you out of it inside of forty-eight hours. This is Thursday morning — just. By Saturday morning you will be gone. You'll shut down your yard here and move to your place in Yorkshire. In the future, if you need to send a man and a lorry up here with

205

a load, that's fine. But neither of you, or Mrs Spargo, comes with it.' Arthur groaned at mention of his wife and Ivor winced. Matt finished flatly, 'If I see any of you in this town again, I'll take these to the police.' He flourished the statements.

Ivor muttered, 'That's against the law.'

Matt replied, 'If you want to stick to the law then we go to the police. D'you want that?'

Arthur shot a frightened glance at his son and ordered, 'Shut up!' He looked at Matt and asked meekly, 'Can we go now?'

Matt stood back to let them pass: 'Get out.' He followed them down to the gate, herded them out of it and bolted it behind them. Then he returned to the office and Katy.

She stood in the middle of the floor, her coat still clutched around her over her nightgown, her hair hanging loosely down her back. For the first time he was conscious of her beauty and his blood was still running hot from the recent confrontation. But then he remembered she was another man's wife, she trusted him and he had virtually promised to protect her when he took her in. Besides, he had a lover and was engaged to be married. There was Fleur who loved and also trusted him. His days as a single man, of easy meetings and partings, were gone.

So he kept his distance, grinned at her and said, 'Well, we won.' He laughed but Katy did not join in, only smiled.

She said, 'I think you did the right thing.'

'So do I,' he agreed confidently, 'but it was your idea. We'll know in a couple of days, but

I'm sure now.' Katy moved towards the stairs and he watched her go, then said, 'You're quiet. Are you worried about something?' Katy hesitated with her foot on the first tread and he urged her, 'Spit it out.'

She met him eye to eye and asked, 'Would you have done it? I mean — set him alight?' Then she waited, fearful, for his answer.

He stared for a moment, disconcerted, then grinned wryly. 'So you thought I might. Well, Ivor thought I would so that was a good thing. It proves there's a bit of an actor in me, because — no, I couldn't do it, not to him or anybody. I once saw a chap caught in a petrol fire — ' He closed his eyes for a second to blot out the memory, then opened them to stare bleakly at Katy and ask, 'Happier now?'

She smiled at him shakily, relieved. 'Sorry. Yes, I'm happier. I couldn't believe you'd do it at first, but you were so — real.'

She started up the stairs again and he called after her, 'Thank you, and good night, Katy.'

'Good night, Matt.' She had the answer she wanted. Otherwise she would have had to admit she had misjudged a man yet again — and would have left this place. Her mind at ease she went to her bed. For a little while she lay listening to the small sounds of movement below as Matt got into his bed under the counter. Then there was silence and despite the excitement of the night, she slept.

When Vera Spargo returned home the following afternoon she found the yard busy but not as she liked it. None of the lorries or steam wagons were out on jobs. Instead they were lined up in the yard. Worried looking men were carrying furniture out of the house and loading it onto the vehicles. Vera could not see Arthur Spargo because he was supervising inside the house but Ivor was out in the yard watching the emptying of the office. As her cab turned in at the gate, Vera shouted at the cabbie, 'Stop!' He reined in and she addressed Ivor through the open window, 'What the hell d'ye think you're doing?'

He eyed her sulkily, but afraid for the wrath to come. He tried to divert it to his father: 'Dad will tell you. He's up at the house.'

'Don't try to squirm out of it, you little worm!' Vera raged at him. '*You* tell me!'

'I can't.' He jerked his head at the men passing back and forth from the office, laden with books and papers they were putting into a van. 'It's private. Family.'

Vera was not one to wash the family's dirty linen in public. She accepted what he said but snapped at him, 'Leave those fellers to get on with whatever they're doing and you come along with me.' Then to the cabbie: 'Drive on!' The jingling cab took her up to the house and Ivor followed reluctantly on foot.

A gaping Vera took in that the lower floor of the house was already stripped. Her buttoned boots echoed on bare boards. The walls were bereft of pictures, the windows of curtains. The furniture, including the mahogany sideboard, the pride of her parlour, had gone. Arthur Spargo was descending the now uncarpeted stairs and as he reached the foot of them, she grabbed him: 'Come in here.' She dragged him into the parlour, pulled Ivor in after him then shut the door behind them. Now they were alone and she demanded, voice cracking with anger, 'Tell me what is going on!'

Arthur shrugged. 'We're giving this place up and moving down to Yorkshire.'

'*What?*' Vera's little boot-button eyes flicked from one to the other as she refused to believe what she had heard. 'Why? What are you talking about? For God's sake! I go to spend a few days with me sister and leave a comfortable home and a business I've built up over the last twenty years. I come home and you tell me I've got to leave it all! *Why?*'

Arthur flinched but stood his ground. He now feared something even worse than Vera and he said stubbornly, 'It's that or prison.' As she stared, for once silenced by him, he began, 'We — that is, Ivor and me — we'd had enough o' Matt Ballard and that Merrick lass so we decided to finish them . . . '

Vera listened to their tale, silent through to Arthur's bitter ending: 'So we have to go or it's prison for the pair of us.' A dreadful calm of acceptance had settle over Vera. Now she looked them over with contempt. 'You pair of stupid, blundering, useless — '

She broke off then, searching for words strong enough to describe them but failing. 'You waited till I was out of the way before you tried this. You knew I wouldn't let you do it because I would ha' known you'd mess it up between you! I've heard of people talking of somebody having a millstone around his neck but I've got two of them around mine!' Her bitterness was increased because she knew she could not let them go to prison. She could do nothing to save the situation. But . . .

Vera strode to the door but paused there to look back at them. 'This dog's dinner wasn't of my making. One of the men can drive me down to the station. I'm going to Yorkshire and I'm staying in a hotel till you get there with all our lorries and furniture and you've found a house — one that suits me!' She walked out, but as her train hissed and clanked away from Sunderland Station she glared back at the town where Matt Ballard and Katy Merrick lived. It was to them she spoke when she whispered, 'I'll see my day with you, damn you!' The threat was repeated by Ivor Spargo as he rode out on the last lorry to leave the yard.

On Saturday morning, Matt and Katy drove round to the Spargo yard in the new Dennis, with Katy at the wheel and the two children sitting on Matt's knees. The gates were closed and a disconsolate group of men were gathered around them. Katy said, 'That's a good half of their men. There's Ernie Thompson.' He slouched among the others, haggard and worried. Another man, better dressed in a neat suit, straw boater and carrying a walking cane, stood reading a notice tacked to one of the gates.

Matt and Katy got down and Matt asked innocently of the group in general, 'Aren't they open today?'

The man with the cane glanced over his shoulder, then stepped aside. He said curtly, 'The blighters have skipped.' He tapped the notice with the head of his cane. Matt read it, Katy peering over his shoulder with Louise on her hip and holding the hand of Beatrice.

Matt turned to her, 'They've gone. It gives the address of their yard in Yorkshire and apologises for any inconvenience.'

'That's no damned use to me!' The cane tapped at the notice again. 'I'm ready to move and Spargos were supposed to have a van at my house first thing this morning — nearly two hours ago. I came round to complain about the delay because I want the job done! I don't want it dragging on until Monday! I have work to do!'

Matt turned to the others and asked, 'What about you?'

One of the men shrugged gloomily. 'Arthur paid us off. He took the drivers 'cause they had to drive the lorries to Yorkshire, but he's only keeping a few of them there. The rest of them are coming back on the train on account of they don't want to work down there.'

Katy whispered to Matt. He stared at her for several seconds, then nodded. Turning to the group, he said, 'I'm Matt Ballard. I've got a little haulage business across the river in Monkwearmouth. I need a man now and I'm taking on Ernie Thompson.' Katy saw Ernie lift his head, his surprise and then the relief flooding into his face. Matt went on, 'I'll take the names and addresses of the rest of you and if I find work for you later on, I'll let you know.' Then he turned on the cane-wielder: 'And if you'll tell me what job you want doing, I'll get on with it.'

'What — now?' He pushed back his straw boater with his cane and stared doubtfully at Matt.

Matt said firmly, 'Now.'

As they drove back to their own yard, Matt said, 'I'm wondering what you've let me in for.'

Katy, her hands on the wheel, her eyes on the road, smiled. 'We'll be getting a lot of extra work now the Spargos have gone.'

Matt agreed, 'I can see that. We'll be able to use Ernie. But all the rest?'

'You won't have to take on all the rest.' Katy hesitated, casting about for tactful phrasing: 'If you like — the decision will be yours, of course — I can suggest who would be best for us.'

'Ah! Now I see.' Matt nodded. 'You know them all.' Katy did: the workers and shirkers, the ones with common sense and the feckless. Matt smiled happily, 'Right. We'll do it that way. We're going to be busy, partner.'

They were both laughing, in boisterous mood, when Katy swung the Dennis into the yard. She got down from the wheel and took the children as Matt passed them across to her. He followed them to take his place in the driver's seat, but then leaned down from the cab to kiss the top of her head. 'I'll see you later.'

He drove off to do the job for the cane-wielder and Katy watched him go, smiling. But she was relieved that he had gone. If he had stayed she might have hugged him and that would have led to trouble. She reminded herself of her vow, never to be taken in by a man again. She was a partner with this one in a business venture, no more than that. She must not let her happiness lead her into another awful mistake. Still, the happiness was there and she sang as she walked back to the office with the children. Ivor was still fresh in her memory but she was sure he would recede with the passing of the days, as Howard Ross had done. He was almost forgotten now, like some long past bad dream.

* * *

Howard Ross had not forgotten her. He was thinking of Katy at that very moment as he walked by the Tyne in Newcastle. A police sergeant with a young constable in tow pointed out the man in the expensive suit with the rings on his fingers: 'See him?'

'The young toff?'

The sergeant nodded. 'That's him. Ralph Norgren. He's a pimp and he's violent. We can't get anything on him because no witness will testify. They're frightened of him. Still, one of these days . . . ' But that was said more in hope than in confidence.

Howard was thinking that one day he would look up that Merrick girl. Her child — that was his — would be two years old soon. He cared nothing for the child but that Katy was a juicy piece. He had sweet memories of her seduction and she would make good money on the streets. Another meeting might be amusing, or profitable, or both. One day . . .

15

'Matthew! Matthew! *Aahh!* Matthew!' Fleur let out a shuddering, rapturous sigh. She lay naked in Matt's arms. She had taken him into her bed some months ago, all part of her plan for binding him to her. At first she feigned being shy and virginal, but soon became adoring and passionate. Fleur pretended innocence but knew exactly what she was doing and how to avoid consequences. An elderly struck off doctor with salacious tastes had schooled her in that when she succumbed to his advances — at a price. The affair was ended by the heart attack which killed him, leaving Fleur to find another bedmate.

Now she lay spent in Matt's arms. On these occasions her mother was dispatched to the theatre. Mrs Ecclestone went reluctantly because of her increasing ill health, but she was too weak to argue with her daughter.

Fleur murmured, 'It isn't long to our wedding day. Then we'll always be together, my darling.' She had named a day in June, had waited this long because she wanted a place in society so her wedding would be handsomely attended and recorded. Fleur knew the places to be seen and the people with whom to be seen. With Matt as her escort and his money to pay their way, they now moved in the town's social circles.

214

Matt had come a long way in a little less than two years. Since the Spargos left, his haulage business had expanded rapidly. Fleur knew he had five lorries — or was it six? She was not sure but always said, 'My fiancé runs a fleet of lorries.' She was sure he was making a lot of money and that she had been clever to select him and cultivate him. It was a bore when he talked about his work, but her best investment by far.

By the time Fleur's mother was due to return they were seated decorously in the sitting-room, as she had left them. Fleur asked of Matt, 'Have you been to the house lately, darling?' She smiled sweetly and stroked his hand because the house had almost caused a rift between them. Fleur had asked for a place in Ashbrooke, one of the best parts of the town, a house much larger and more expensive to rent than Matt was prepared to pay for. He had earlier insisted on buying the freehold of the yard and its buildings and was adamant he could not afford to take on such a big house. Fleur had seen his determination and silently cursed, but settled for another house, still in Ashbrooke but smaller and so at a lower rent.

'No,' Matt replied now, 'I've not been there since the decorators moved in.'

'I wish you would, darling,' cooed Fleur. 'I called in yesterday and the fat man with the big moustache — '

Matt put in: 'The foreman.'

'Yes. He said some of the things we wanted done were extra to the original agreement. He said they would cost more. That's really too bad.

Some of these tradesmen think of nothing but money.'

Matt questioned, 'Which extra things?'

'Oh, I asked for a different wallpaper in two of the rooms and for the bath to be moved. He went on about having to bring in a plumber.' Fleur took Matt's face in her hands and kissed him. 'Shall I come round to the yard in a cab tomorrow afternoon and we can go to the house together? Please?'

Matt smiled fondly, thinking that a young girl like Fleur, with a sheltered upbringing, could not be expected to understand these things. 'Of course.' If the foreman was trying to wangle some pocket money out of the job then Matt would settle his hash.

Fleur refused to think of Matt as a tradesman. She would mention in conversation: 'My fiancé is a haulage contractor.' Then going on to explain: 'He has to earn his living — a younger son, you know.' Thus suggesting that Matt was of landed gentry but without the benefit of inheriting an estate.

Fleur's mother returned, looking tired and ill. Her daughter contrived to be smiling and patient with her until Matt had gone, then she rounded on the old woman: 'For God's sake! You've just been out to enjoy yourself! What's the matter with you *now*!'

⋆　⋆　⋆

Katy was up and about early the next day. When Matt climbed the stairs from the office where he slept she was waiting to set his breakfast before him. Beatrice, seated opposite and ready for school, called, 'Good morning, Uncle Matt.' Louise, alongside her, copied, 'Good mornin', Unca Matt.'

As he ate Matt told Katy, 'I'm going up to the house this afternoon with Fleur; I have to settle an argument with the foreman decorator. But I'll be around the yard the rest of the day because I have a service to do.' Matt serviced all the lorries — there were four more now — himself.

Katy was down in the office, at work at her desk, when the men came into the yard to start the day. There were four drivers, each with a mate to accompany him, and help load and unload, and Ernie Thompson who was a general labourer working around the yard, Katy gave them their orders through the open window and one by one the engines burst into life, roared with acceleration then settled to a steady beat. They were all three-ton Dennis lorries, bought under the War Office Subsidy Scheme. And all were busy every working day except when they were off the road for servicing. Katy kept the servicing records up to date. She watched with pride as they drove out through the gates. She reflected that Matt — and herself — had done miraculously well. In less than a year they had built up the business from one lorry to five. They had taken most of the Spargos' clients and most of their men. Katy told herself she should be happy, but she was not.

There was Fleur. In the two-and-a-half years since Katy came to the yard she had not met

Matt's fiancée face to face. Fleur had occasionally visited the place but had rarely got down from the cab which brought her. She had never seen Katy, who had kept out of the way. Katy had watched Fleur from a distance, read of her in the newspapers when they listed those present at some social function, and heard of her, endlessly, from Matt. He was obviously in love with Fleur, and happy. Katy told herself she was glad, but . . . She knew nothing wrong about this sweet-smiling girl but still distrusted her. She thought that it was no longer down to fear. It had been her constant worry for so long, that when Matt married Fleur they would move into the flat, or Fleur would take Beatrice, that there would be no place for Katy and Louise. But now it cost her no sleep because if need be, she could rent a flat or house for her and Louise — though she still did not relish the thought of losing Beatrice to Fleur. Katy sighed. She just could not take to Matthew's fiancée and did not know why.

Matt clumped into the office, returned from a visit to the bank. He dropped the paying-in book on the desk, took off the jacket of his suit and pulled on overalls. 'I'm off to do that service now. Any chance of a cup of tea later on?'

Katy laughed up at him, 'I'll see what I can do.'

He put his arm around her shoulders and gave her an affectionate, brotherly squeeze. Then he was gone, striding across the yard. Katy watched him until he entered the garage and was lost to sight. She turned back to the day's post. Matt no longer asked if she had heard from her distant sailor husband. Six months earlier she had told him that her husband had written saying that he was finished with her and would not be returning home. Matt had been sympathetic and never mentioned the matter again. That 'husband' was now a part of her past like the other men in her life.

Katy worked quickly, filing, invoicing, posting receipts, logging jobs in the order book, slotting them into the schedules for the days ahead, talking into the telephone which now stood on the desk. Louise had gone to stay with Annie Scanlon for the day while Beatrice was at school. At mid-morning Katy climbed the stairs to the flat, brewed a pot of tea and carried two mugs across to the garage. Matt had his head under the engine cowling but he pulled it out when Katy called, 'Matt! Tea!'

He took one of the mugs and grinned down at her, 'Thanks.'

'How are you getting on?' Katy peered at the engine.

Matt laughed, 'Are you thinking of taking over the servicing now?' Katy had already persuaded him to teach her routine maintenance such as checking oil and water. The men had stared at her, incredulous as she worked on the engine. Katy joined in Matt's laughter now and stayed on, talking as she sipped her tea.

★ ★ ★

219

Fleur stared out of the window of the motor taxi at the passing traffic, day-dreaming contentedly. She thought that life was very good and congratulated herself on her choice of Matt as a husband. She had been unsure of him for a while when the haulage business hit rock bottom after the death of Joe Docherty but Matt had recovered spectacularly. Soon they would be married, though she was in no hurry and enjoying her freedom.

Matt had been sympathetic and generous when she had hinted delicately at her straitened circumstances as the daughter of a widow living on a small annuity. Fleur would not 'lower herself' by taking a job, but explained to Matt: 'I would like to work but I feel it would be selfish to leave mother to manage on her own. She isn't well, as you know.'

Matt felt sorry for her. She could not openly accept money from the man to whom she was engaged because that would make her no better than a kept woman. So instead he secretly supplied her with the cash she wanted for clothes — and the pursuit of leisure. She could afford to travel to Durham to meet Anthony, the black sheep of a good family, with extravagant tastes but no money. Fleur had succeeded in catching his eye when she visited the city to escape from one of those long days of boredom spent with her mother. Anthony would indulge himself and her with Matt's money. Fleur even paid for the hotel room they shared.

She smiled reminiscently. But now was the time to make sure of Matt. Besides, there was no reason why she should give up Anthony — or Denys, in York, whose attentions were becoming pressing. He would not wait much longer. There would be time for both of them. Matt spent long days in that yard of his.

And here it was. The cab puttered in at the open gates and stopped. Fleur got down and ordered the driver, 'Wait here, please.' She could hear Matt's deep laugh coming from the garage and she walked towards it. Then she heard more laughter, light and happy, a girl's laughter. Unthinkingly she quickened her pace and came to the garage. Matt stood with his back to her while the girl was at his side and turned towards him so Fleur saw her in profile. She was dark, slender and young — Fleur judged her to be in her early twenties. She was flushed, pretty and smiling up at Matt. Then she saw Fleur from the corner of her eye and turned to face her, the smile slipping away.

Matt turned, grinning, and said, 'Hello, Fleur, I wasn't expecting you till this afternoon.'

'So I see.' Fleur's tone was icy, but inside she burned with rage and suspicion. She nodded at Katy: 'Who is this — person?'

Matt was surprised, 'This is Katy. You know, Katy Merrick. I've told you about her lots of times.'

So he had. Fleur remembered him talking of a seaman's wife who acted as his clerk. She had pictured someone like the blowsy women coming out of dockside pubs with their men at closing time. Or a drab mouse with steel-rimmed spectacles, her lips moving as she totted up her

221

figures. This girl was not like that.

Matt said cheerfully, 'Well, now you're here I'll wash off this oil, get out of these overalls and we'll be off to the house. Why don't you have a cup of tea while I'm doing that. Katy, will you trot up to the flat and make a cup for Fleur, please?'

Fleur asked, 'She uses the flat?' Not liking the idea.

She liked Matt's answer even less: 'Katy lives in the flat. That's why she came to work here, to put a roof over the heads of her and Louise. I let them have the flat and Katy looks after Beatrice and does the office work.' He saw from her stony face what she was thinking and sought to reassure her: 'It's perfectly respectable. Katy lives in the flat and I live in the office. That's no different to other people living in rooms next door to each other. And Katy is a decent married woman.'

Fleur did not believe him and it was written in her face. Katy saw it. Flushing with embarrassment, she broke in: 'Please, Mr Ballard, if you'll excuse me, I have a lot of work — ' She almost ran past Fleur, out of the garage, across the yard and up to the flat. There she sat down at the kitchen table, her face in her hands.

Matt stared after her as she fled and he was angry when he turned back to Fleur. 'That was a nasty insinuation.'

Fleur denied, 'I didn't insinuate anything.'

'The way you looked — '

'The way I looked,' Fleur cut in, 'was surprised — that you didn't see how this might appear to other people.' She had decided quickly how to present this to him. She would not play the part of the jealous, suspicious wife, but she would put a stop to this affair. '*I* know it's innocent because I love and trust you. But others will see a successful young businessman living, not in a house, but in the office below the young woman he employs. Oh, I know people live quite respectably in rooms side by side, but they aren't occupying your station in life. To put it simply, to them it is commonplace, but you are not one of them. I don't know about this Katy, though I'm sure she is the decent young woman you say she is, but that still does not alter the case.' Fleur laid a hand on his sleeve and pleaded, 'Don't you see, my darling?'

Matt rubbed a fist on his jaw, leaving a smear of black grease. He muttered, troubled, 'I'd never thought of it like that. I won't have people thinking of Katy in that way. I took her in because I couldn't turn her and her little girl away, and I don't know how I'd have managed without her.'

Fleur thought that he would have to. She said, with feigned sadness, 'We've got to do something for her sake, Matt. It's — ' She hesitated, not wanting to dignify the girl with her name, already thinking of her as 'that woman'. But she went on, 'It's Katy's reputation that will suffer. She'll have to go, Matt.'

His head jerked up. 'What? Turn her out of house and home? I can't do that. No, I'll move.'

Fleur did not like that, had wanted to be quit of Katy for good, but she could see Matt's antagonism to that idea and agreed, 'You're right, of course. The simplest and best thing to do now is what you intended in a month or so. Find some lodgings today, and as soon as there's one room fit to live in at our house, then move in. Let's tell that decorator man this afternoon that he must finish one room for you.'

Matt agreed reluctantly, 'I suppose so.' And then: 'I must tell Katy and make sure she doesn't think she's being accused of anything improper. I wouldn't want her hurt.'

Fleur thought that she had cauterised this sore just in time.

They crossed the yard together and Fleur waited in the office while Matt shrugged out of his overalls. She had visited the office once or twice but had hardly got past the door. Now her eyes flicked over the desk with the vase of flowers which Katy had introduced, and sharply noticed the neatly made bed under the counter. It was only a few yards from the foot of the stairs leading up to the flat and her lips tightened.

They climbed the stairs together and Fleur smiled with false sympathy as Matt washed and explained to a quiet Katy, her tears dried, 'I just never thought of — ' he paused to choose his words ' — our arrangement, that way.' Katy thought that Fleur would. He said, 'I won't have old wives talking about you, so I'm moving.' He told her what he intended and Katy listened while Fleur looked on. Matt finished awkwardly, 'This won't make any difference to us. We'll just go on as before.'

Katy saw Fleur's eyes flicker and said, 'I'll

pack your things. They'll be ready when you get back.' Fleur did not like that; Katy saw the flicker again, quicker than a snake's tongue. But Fleur said nothing and Katy knew she was silent because she realised she had won.

Matt left with Fleur then, clattering down the stairs, and he called a farewell. Katy did not go to the window to see them drive off in the cab. After a while she descended to the office and tried to absorb herself in her work because Matt had said, 'We'll go on as before.' She failed miserably. They would not go on as before because Fleur would be watching them now, for any word or action, however innocent, which might be construed as affectionate. Matt might not realise that but Katy did. She thought that she could simply leave as Fleur wanted. Katy had made a lot of money in the past months. She had enough to rent a comfortable house — But then she rebelled. She was a partner there, had helped to make the business successful and would not give it up.

Katy walked to the National School and met Beatrice, then together they called on Annie Scanlon and they all had a cup of tea. Afterwards Katy brought Louise and Beatrice back to the flat above the office, because this was their home and here they would stay.

Matt departed for lodgings that evening, carrying the suitcase Katy had packed for him. In the next few days Katy stripped his bed, washed the bedding and put it away in a cupboard then covered the bed with a dust sheet. Matt asked Katy, 'Can you look after

Beatrice until I'm married?'

Katy answered, 'I'll keep her as long as you'll let me.' She suspected Beatrice would not be happy with Fleur. So Beatrice stayed on in the flat.

Fleur became a frequent visitor at the yard, calling suddenly, unexpectedly, sometimes even on foot and at all hours. Katy greeted her with cool politeness and Fleur would stand with her arm in Matt's or her hand on his shoulder, possessively. Beatrice once asked clearly of Matt when he was with Fleur, 'Who is that woman?'

Old Mrs Ecclestone collapsed a week before the June wedding and died within twenty-four hours. Fleur was distraught — because Matt suggested postponing the nuptials. 'No,' she said bravely, 'we must go on. Mother would have wanted it so.' Fleur certainly did not want a postponement. With the death of her mother she had lost her only official source of income. She had to make sure of Matt now. So she buried her mother with great mourning on Friday and made a gallant recovery in time to walk down the aisle on Saturday.

It was a day of brilliant, burning sunshine. Fleur was ravishing in white silk and Matt handsome in a good suit. Fleur had refused to have a bridesmaid, though Matt had proposed Beatrice. Instead Louise and Beatrice spent most of the day with Annie Scanlon. Katy received an invitation from Fleur — prompted by Matt. Most of the guests were friends and relatives of the bride. Matt's brothers and sisters were scattered far and wide and wrote apologising for

226

not being able to attend. His guests were men he met in the way of business, with their wives. And Katy.

The reception was held at the Palace Hotel and while Fleur had seated several of Matt's guests on or near the top table, Katy found her place at a table furthest from Matt. Afterwards there was dancing and on another occasion Katy would have loved to put Annie's dancing lessons to good use. Instead Katy sought out her hostess. Fleur was on the edge of the dance floor with men clustered around her. She was in animated conversation, eyelashes fluttering and slender fingers gesturing so her rings caught the light.

Katy excused herself, 'I have to go back to the children.' She could not say she was sorry.

Fleur's smile was wide, that of a victor. 'Of course. I can understand how you feel. Goodbye, Mrs Merrick.'

The band struck up then, a waltz, and Matt came to claim his bride because they were to lead off the dancing. He whirled her around the floor, Fleur with her head back and smiling. She knew now that she could relax, was 'home and dry'. She had hooked this man and secured her financial future. She laughed as they passed Katy, who saw the light of triumph in Fleur's eyes.

Katy walked home across the bridge to Monkwearmouth, oblivious to the ships in the river and the clanging electric trams with the Saturday crowds filling the seats and standing in the aisles, swaying to the motion. She collected the children from Annie Scanlon, who chided her, 'Didn't you stay on for the dancing? I'd ha' thought a young lass like you would ha' jumped at the chance.'

Katy forced a smile. 'I think these two little girls will be the better for bed and I can do with an early night. We've been busy at the yard the last week or two.' That was true but it was not that which had wearied her. 'Thanks for looking after them, Annie.'

Katy took the two girls back to the flat. When they were in bed and sleeping sweetly, Katy sat in an armchair staring into the cheerless bleakness of an empty grate; the weather was too warm for a fire. She knew she had made another terrible mistake, instinct told her that. After Howard's seduction of her and his cynical betrayal she had sworn never to trust another man. Now, by her stubborn adherence to that oath, she had let Matt walk out of her life with another woman. She might not have won him but she could — should — have tried. Now it was too late. She would not commit adultery and she was sure Matt would never betray his vows to Fleur. Katy was desolate.

16

It was a fine summer but for Katy it came at the end of a very bad year — and there was worse to come.

Marriage had not changed Fleur and she was always watching, or so it seemed. She appeared at odd times and on odd days, as she had before she married Matt. Katy worked at her desk in the office with one eye always on the gates of the yard. This was not because of any sense of guilt for there was nothing between her and Matt, Katy was painfully aware of that. She watched for Fleur so she could avoid her, because whenever they did chance to meet Fleur would make some comment like: 'You're looking tired, Mrs Merrick. I hope my husband isn't working you too hard.' Katy could not relax even when Matt said ruefully, 'Fleur has gone to Durham for the day to do some shopping.' Because on occasion she returned far sooner than might be expected.

Katy could imagine Fleur shopping. She suspected that a large part of Matt's share in the profits of the partnership were spent by Fleur. That share was not over-generous, either, because they had bought another Dennis lorry with a War Office subsidy, making six in all, and taken on another two men to crew it. Most of the money the firm made was ploughed back in this way. Katy spent some of her share on clothes, crisp white blouses and mid-calf length skirts for her days in the office, a pink silk suit with a skirt which almost hobbled her ankles for day wear and a lilac silk gown which floated lightly. If Matt noticed he did not comment, but Billy Nicholson, who had asked them to move his bricks all that while ago, told him, 'By lad, that lass is a good advertisement for your business!' She also bought some furniture for the flat and decorated it — and finally took a holiday she would bitterly regret.

In the last week but one of that hot July Katy took the two girls to a boarding house in Whitley Bay. They spent their days sitting on the sand, paddling, fishing in rock pools, building sand castles or digging complicated water-courses. It was a happy time and they left for home at the end of it tired but sunburned and happy. Beatrice pleaded, 'Do we have to go home?'

Katy laughed but sympathised. She had found a world of relief in the childhood play, had contrived to forget her latest mistake, or at least had pushed it to the back of her mind. She said ruefully, 'I'm afraid so.' And told herself she was happy.

Howard Ross was not. He sat in a pub on the dockside of Newcastle that was filled with seamen off the ships in the Tyne. Ross stood out from the rest in his expensive checked suit with narrow trousers and ornate waistcoat. Men walked carefully around him; he was known and feared. This was where his girls plied their trade. One of them sat opposite him now. Once a plump and jolly country girl, she was now afraid for her life. Howard demanded of her, 'What the *hell*! She's gone where?'

The girl faltered, 'She said down south. Didn't say exactly but I supposed she meant London. She said she had done a turn or two with this feller and he told her he'd look after her if she went down there.' She shrank back from Howard's glare. She knew he was quite capable of venting his anger on her, violently.

He demanded, 'When did she tell you this?'

'About an hour ago. She was just leaving the house as I came in.' Howard Ross ran a 'boarding house' for his girls. This one went on, 'I saw she was carrying a case and I says, 'Where are you off to? Your holidays?' Joking, y'know. And she says, 'I'm going away down south. I'm finished wi' this place — ' But Howard cut her off then, back-handing her out of his way as he headed for the door. She watched him go with her hand to her bruised face, fear and hatred in her eyes.

He made for Newcastle Central Station and ran at full pelt, shoving aside people who got in his way. He knew the train his girl would be on and when it was due to leave. He arrived only in time to see the tail of it disappearing from sight. He paused for a minute, catching his breath, glaring at the now empty platform and cursing. He had lost a source of income. After a time he shrugged and turned away, thinking that he would just have to find a replacement. It was as he was passing through the station that he saw Katy.

For a moment he could not believe it was her because this girl was not poor and frightened but laughing and well-dressed in a silk suit. Then he could not believe his luck. 'Katy Merrick,' he said softly. 'And done well for herself. She must have married some feller in a good way o' business. And two bairns. One o' them will be mine.' He calculated: 'Must be the little one.' Now he was happy, his fortunes and good temper restored.

When Katy returned to the yard in the early evening she found Matt's Vauxhall, with its fluted bonnet, standing outside the office. He had bought the motor car at Fleur's urging — but he wanted it. She liked him to drive her about the town where she would be seen. To Matt it was a toy. Katy did not begrudge him the car — it was not an extravagance. He could well afford it out of his seventy-five per cent share of the business. Katy was satisfied with her own twenty-five per cent share. That was well-earned, but there would be no business without Matt's mechanical expertise. He kept all the lorries running efficiently.

Some of the men were still working, exchanged cheerful greetings and made much of the children: 'Did you have a nice holiday, Bea?' 'And what about you Louise? Did you go plodging?' Louise nodded vigorously. She had spent most of her time at Whitley Bay paddling in the sea. One of the men explained, 'The boss asked us to stop back to finish a special job, Mrs Merrick, but we're just about done now.'

Matt came out of the office at that moment, shrugging into the jacket of his suit. He hailed Katy: 'It's good to see you all back and looking so well! We've missed you. I tried to keep the office work up to date but it's fallen behind a bit.' He grinned at her. 'But only because we picked up a lot of extra jobs this week. I've been working late every night. We're on top of the world, Katy.' Then he glanced at his watch. 'But Fleur has been complaining at not getting out, so tonight I'm taking her out for supper and a show. I'd better hurry.' He wound up the Vauxhall's starting handle then vaulted into the driving seat. He paused then to call above the tickover of the engine, 'Annie is waiting for you upstairs in the flat. She's wanting to hear all about your week away — and to get her hands on the girls again.' He laughed and drove down the yard and out of the gates.

Katy watched until he was lost to sight, then she turned back into the office. As she entered, Annie Scanlon, ruddy and beaming, came hurrying down the stairs from the flat and calling breathlessly, 'Hello, bonny lass! And two canny bairns! I got your postcard. And you've all had a lovely time?'

The girls told her all about their holiday as she put them to bed. When they were sleeping, Katy and Annie settled down with a cup of tea. It was a half-hour later when Katy heard a knock at the office door. She stood up and peered out of the window. 'I thought all the men had gone.'

The yard was empty and the gates closed but not bolted and she concluded, 'One of them must have forgotten something or want to ask me about a job.' And she told Annie, 'I won't be long.'

Annie assured her, 'I'll listen for the bairns.'

Katy ran down the stairs, calling, 'I'm coming!' She crossed to the office door and swung it open. Howard Ross stood smiling at her.

For a second, shock ruled her. She recoiled and her hands went to her mouth, the blood drained from her face and Howard's Cheshire cat grin danced and wavered before her. Then it steadied as he took a pace towards her to lean on the doorpost. Katy asked huskily, throat dry and tight and heart thumping, 'What are you doing here?'

Howard flapped a hand carelessly, 'Just visiting. I saw you on the station at Newcastle and thought you'd be worth following.' His eyes drifted over her insolently, inspecting, penetrating. Despite herself, Katy felt the blood rush back into her face now and colour her neck. Howard laughed, 'I'll always find you, whenever I want you. And I want you now.'

'I don't want you.' Katy tried to shut the door but his boot was jammed against it.

Howard still smiled: 'It looks like you've done well for your self. Nice clothes and you've somebody in this business — I heard how the men were talking to you, as if you were the boss, or the next best thing. And still using your own name. Are you the boss's bit o' stuff?'

'No!' Outrage wrung that out of Katy. 'No, I am not!'

Howard's brows lifted and he taunted her, 'But you'd like to be.'

'No!' Katy had control of herself again but was furious because he had tricked that reaction from her. 'I work here, that's all.'

Howard shook his head, 'I don't believe you.'

'I don't care. That's the truth.' Katy's fear was now giving way to anger. She grasped the nettle and demanded, 'Why are you here?'

Howard shrugged, 'Just showing a fatherly concern. I heard the men talking to the bairns when you came in here today. I don't know who owns Bea but the little one, that the men were calling Louise, she's mine. You've only got to look at her.'

Katy knew that was true but denied him: 'She's not yours because you deserted her and me. We were nothing to you and you are nothing to us.'

At last Howard's smile disappeared. He said softly, 'You'll be whatever I want you to be, do whatever I want you to do.' His glare burned into her. This had always worked before with the girls who worked for him and he was confident it would again. He leaned towards Katy: 'You can start off with a payment for services rendered. Give me ten pounds and — '

'*Ten pounds!*' Katy cut in, staggered by the request. Ten pounds was a month's wages for a well-paid tradesman. 'You're mad!'

That infuriated him. 'Mad? We'll see who's mad! You pay up or everybody around here will know all about you. I don't know what tale you spun them but we'll see what happens when they hear the truth!'

Katy hesitated for a moment. There was a temptation to give him the money to be rid of him. But then she remembered the kind of man he was and knew he would be back for more. She met his glare and told him coldly, 'You can tell what you like to who you like. I won't give you a penny.' Howard reached out a hand towards her and she shouted, 'Annie!'

'Aye?' came from upstairs. Howard froze, eyes lifted to the ceiling.

Katy called, 'I'll be up in a couple of seconds. Will you pour me another cup, please?'

'Aye! I will! This minute!'

Katy still held the door firmly. Howard's hand hung a few inches before her face but he knew she would scream if he touched her. He was also sure that she would fight. He recognised that instinctively, though it had never happened before with any of the other girls. Then there was this Annie upstairs who would be a witness. He turned away and strode off across the yard. Katy watched him go, turn into the street and out of her sight as the gate swung shut behind him. She ran across the yard and shot the bolts on the gate then leaned back against it, breathing deeply, feeling sick and shaky as reaction gripped her. Then she remembered Annie, walked back to the office and up the stairs to the flat.

Annie pointed to the cup and saucer on the table: 'There it is. I made it fresh but poured it out a few minutes ago. Do you want a hot one?'

'No, this is fine.' Katy managed a smile and held the cup in both hands so that it would not spill with her shaking.

Annie said, 'That took some time. What did that feller want?'

Katy lied, 'He just wanted some details about his job on Monday.'

She contrived to act normally and to talk to Annie until she left for home. Katy let her out of the gate and bolted it again behind her. She locked the office door and also made sure all the windows were fastened. She had never before been afraid to be alone in the flat save for the girls, but now . . . Despite her precautions, she lay awake, twitching as shadows moved on the wall and listening to the sounds of the night, every creaking board and the tiny settling noises of the embers of the fire in the kitchen. She told herself that Howard Ross had gone, but when she closed her eyes she could see his cold smile and burning eyes. She did not sleep for a long time and then only fitfully.

The following days were filled with work and worry. To some extent the former brought welcome relief from the latter, though whenever Katy had a breathing space her fear of Howard would seize her again. But the work kept on, Howard did not return and after a while her memories of his rage and hatred receded. She began to believe that, by standing up to him, she had got rid of him for good. Katy became more and more convinced of this as the days passed.

They were times when she would send Beatrice off to school and take Louise to stay with Annie Scanlon for the day. Louise was in favour of this, as she was spoiled by Annie and was able to play with the other pre-school age children in Annie's street. Beatrice was not sure whether she approved of this, but Katy told her she was lucky to be allowed to go to school while Louise was not. Beatrice accepted this honour being paid to her, but with limited enthusiasm. However, when the schools were on holiday both girls would go to Annie.

This had been the pattern of their days for a year or more. Katy would go back to spend the day in the office, trying to cope with the work and reduce the backlog, but sometimes she had to take one of the lorries out on a job. Still, that was a relief from the 'pen-pushing' and she took pleasure in the work. She and Matt were building a successful business, together, even though they might be miles apart when he was out on the road.

Relief from Fleur's surveillance came at the end of July when Matt acceded to his wife's clamouring and took her away to the South Coast for a fortnight, the two weeks either side of the August Bank Holiday. Matt told Katy wryly, 'This holiday calls for a whole new wardrobe for Fleur. Do you think you can hold the fort while I'm away?'

Katy grinned at him, 'I'll try.' And she did, though it meant long hours of work again.

But it was at the end of July that another worry arose that eclipsed all the rest, the threat of war. Every newspaper carried the warning and the word in huge letters: WAR. In that week leading up to the August Bank Holiday there was talk of little else. On Sunday of that weekend the newsboys ran through the streets with their bundles of the *Sunderland Daily Echo* under their arms, shrieking, 'Special *Echo*! Special *Echo*! General Mobilisation!' Katy heard them, bought a newspaper and read the stark account. Germany was threatening to invade Belgium and the British government had sent an ultimatum to Berlin: Germany must respect Belgian neutrality or Britain would declare war. The ultimatum would expire on Tuesday, 4th of August at eleven p.m.

Army Reservists were being recalled to the colours. She knew that meant Matt. For a time she could not believe that their world was to be turned upside down. She had realised vaguely that he had been a soldier and was still liable to serve if needed but had never thought the occasion would arise. She slept very badly that night and all through Monday there seemed to be an air of hysteria.

On that fateful Tuesday morning Katy delivered Beatrice and Louise to Annie — the schools were on holiday — and kissed them both. 'I'll be back to fetch you later on. Be good for Annie, now.'

Annie assured her, 'They'll be all right. And I'll try to have the little 'un clean when you come for her.' Katy went away, laughing at that because Louise had a reputation for dirtying a clean white pinny in an impossibly short time.

Katy walked back to the yard, worrying about Matt and then saw him with a leap of her heart.

His Vauxhall stood outside the office and he was at his desk. The men were busy about the yard and some were almost ready to go out, only needing their orders for the day. Katy could only say the foolishly obvious, 'You're home early.'

Matt snapped at her, 'I've been told that already. Fleur wanted to stay on for the second week. She seems to think this war will wait until she's ready for it.' He was unshaven, looked tired and went on, 'I had to damn near drag her onto the train. I got the first one I could but it left King's Cross at midnight and it was full of sailors. We only just managed to get seats, let alone a sleeper. It was a hell of a trip for Fleur.'

Katy could imagine how Fleur had reacted, her holiday cancelled and then a sleepless night crammed into the corner of a railway carriage. She said, 'I'm sorry. Look, you can leave me to get the men off to work. Why don't you go home and get some sleep.'

Matt hesitated. 'I want to tidy my affairs before I report to the barracks. I'm nearly done here and I'll take your advice soon, but Harry Rogers hasn't turned in. He's an Army reservist and he's gone back to the Northumberland Fusiliers.' Harry Rogers was one of the drivers. Matt went on to ask, 'Will you take his lorry and his mate and do Harry's jobs? Mine were local and I've postponed them for now, but Harry had a morning's work making deliveries spread out over a few villages and there's no way I can get in touch with them as late as this.'

Katy agreed, 'I'll do it.'

'Good!' He grinned at her, 'I can always

240

depend on you. Now I have to go and pack.'

Katy, bitterness in her soul, said, 'I suppose Fleur is upset at your going.'

Matt nodded gloomily. 'She's taking it very well, no tears. But that reminds me; she was asking about money. If this scare doesn't blow over, if it does come to war, I don't want Fleur to suffer. So I'll make her an allowance out of my share of the profits. I'll look in this afternoon and leave an authority with you so she will be able to draw from the bank. I'll see you then.' He waved and drove away in the Vauxhall.

So Katy climbed up into the cab of the Dennis allotted to Harry Rogers and drove out of the yard to deliver his loads. At that same moment Howard Ross stopped at the end of Annie's street, as he had every day for weeks. He leaned against a lamp-post, apparently reading a newspaper held up before his face but in reality watching the activity in the street. By now he had established the daily routine of Katy's life. He saw Louise playing with some other toddlers only a score of yards away, and Beatrice in another group of older children gathered around a lamppost swing. After a time Annie came to her front door and saw the children were happy in their games, laughing and excited. She watched them, smiling, for a minute, then returned to her kitchen and the meal she was preparing for mid-day. It was all as Howard had learned to expect.

Now he moved, turning his head to nod at the motor taxi-cab waiting behind him. He saw the driver yank at the starting handle then climb into his seat. Howard strolled down the street, apparently just another passer-by, folding the newspaper and stuffing it into his pocket as he went. When he came to the little blonde three-year-old he stooped to smile at her and said, 'Hello, Louise. Your mam sent me to take you back to her at the yard.'

She smiled up at him and took the hand he held out to her. 'Are you one of her workmen, then, Mister?'

'That's right,' he told her, and led her away. 'And your mam sent me and not one o' the others because I'm your uncle. So you call me Uncle Ralph.'

Louise hung back for a moment, asking, 'What about Bea?' She pointed at Beatrice, seated in a loop of rope and swinging around the lamppost, oblivious to anything outside her little circle of friends.

Ross assured Louise, 'She's coming along later. Your mother only wants you at the moment. It's going to be a surprise.' That satisfied Louise. He opened the door of the taxi and lifted her in: 'Whoopsadaisy!' Louise laughed with glee.

Annie came to her front door some ten minutes later and looked in vain for Louise. She acted at once, though concerned rather than afraid, thinking that the child had only wandered off but would be frightened when she found she was lost. She was also surprised because Louise had never done this before. 'Beatrice! Where's Louise?'

Beatrice stopped swinging and peered around

her then said uncertainly, 'She was with them.' She nodded.

Annie sought out the small girls she had last seen playing with Louise and asked worriedly, 'Where's Louise gone?'

Most of them gazed around them blankly, but then one, another grubby little three-year-old, said, 'She went away with the man.' Annie got the rest out of her in disjointed sentences: 'He was a big man with white hair.' And: 'He said her mam sent him.' That was all she knew but it was enough to set Annie's hands shaking.

She ran round to the yard but there was no one there save Ernie Thompson and he told her Katy was not expected back until noon. Annie told her neighbours and the police and the search started.

When Katy drove her Dennis into the yard a few minutes after twelve she was startled to see a policeman standing outside the office. She immediately feared trouble of some sort. Had Matt or one of the men been involved in a crash? But then Annie ran from the office and threw herself against the cab of the Dennis, crying, 'A man's run off with Louise! Katy, I'm sorry, lass, I'm sorry, sorry . . . '

For a second, Annie's face danced before Katy's eyes but then her vision cleared and she clutched at the sobbing old woman. 'It's not your fault! Now, did you see him?'

Annie broke off from her tearful apologies to recount the three-year-old's description: 'A big man with white hair.' Katy's heart lurched within her. She knew who that had to be.

The policeman stood behind Annie and now he said, 'My sergeant's out directing the search but he'll be back any minute, ma'am. Do you recognise anyone from that description?

'Yes, I do.' Katy's voice shook with shock, fear and outrage. All pretence abandoned now and careless of proprieties, she said, 'His name is Howard Ross, he's the father of my child and I know where he comes from.' The police would not have searched for Ross when he abandoned her because he had broken no law, but now he was guilty of abduction.

An hour later Katy was on a train bound for Newcastle. As it pulled into the station she saw the platform was crowded. A police sergeant was waiting for her as she stepped off the train, standing out from the throng in his helmet. He had been warned of her coming and of the circumstances of the case. He put a finger to his helmet in salute and introduced himself: 'Sergeant Leybourne, ma'am. We don't know of any Howard Ross, except where he's gone.' And when she stared, he explained, 'We couldn't trace anybody of that name as living in Newcastle, but when we made inquiries at railway stations and shipping offices we found something. If you'll come with me, please.' His face was serious.

Katy swallowed, suddenly afraid. She whispered, 'What have you found? Is it . . . ?' She couldn't say it.

Leybourne had seen her fear and held out a steadying hand. 'We believe your little girl has come to no harm. We haven't found her but we

244

think we know where she is.' He urged her towards the street, making a way for her through the crowds, and explained their presence: 'All these chaps are Army reservists, called up to join the colours and on their way to their regimental depots.' Katy now saw that the people filling the station were predominantly men of any age from twenty-five to forty. There were tearful women clinging to the arms of some of them. Katy had seen similar scenes at Sunderland before she boarded the train and her thoughts went to Matt, another reservist, as they had then. But now she only cared for . . .

Katy pleaded, 'Where are we going? Where is she?'

'There's a clerk in a shipping office here who says that last Friday he booked passages for a Howard Ross and his niece, Louise, on a German ship bound for Hamburg. We want you to hear what he has to say and ask him any questions you might have.' They were outside the station now and he was handing her into a horse-drawn cab. 'It isn't far.'

Katy stared sightlessly out of the window at streets and shops which had been familiar to her when she had worked and lived in this city. She did not see them now, not even Ashleigh's as they clattered past the gates of the warehouse. Her mind was filled with pictures of a wolfishly grinning Howard and a weeping Louise. The next thing she knew was Sergeant Leybourne saying, 'Here we are.'

They climbed down from the cab outside an office which Katy remembered and was close to the Tyne. The sergeant, helmet under his arm, pushed open the door for Katy to enter. Inside was a counter and beyond it a desk where a clerk, dapper in suit and bow tie, bespectacled, brisk and busy, sat writing. He laid down his pen when he saw them and came to the counter. The sergeant said, 'Them inquiries I was making earlier on — this is the lady. Will you tell her about this feller who booked passages for Hamburg?'

'Aye.' The clerk took off his spectacles and smiled nervously at Katy. 'He came in last Friday afternoon and wanted to book for him and his niece. He gave their names as Howard Ross and Louise Merrick. I thought it was funny, with all the talk about crisis and Germany, him wanting to go there, but that was what he wanted and he paid cash, so that was what he got.'

The sergeant asked, 'And description?'

The clerk lifted his shoulders in a shrug, 'I can only tell you what I told you before: he was six foot or over, strong looking, blond hair, blue eyes, well-dressed — nice suit — a handsome feller.'

Leybourne looked a question at Katy and she confirmed, 'That sounds like Louise's father.' And seeing the curiosity in the clerk's eyes she explained, not caring what anyone thought now, 'Louise is my daughter, born out of wedlock.'

He stared, not saying anything for a moment, storing away this piece of scandal for gossiping purposes later. Then he added, 'Well, that's all I can tell you, except that I gave him the tickets for the *Freya* because she was the only vessel in the

246

river bound for Germany, let alone Hamburg, She didn't complete her cargo till this morning and she sailed just after eleven.' He glanced at the clock on the wall: 'She'll be well out to sea by now.'

He stopped then, seeing the tears running down Katy's face, and looked uncomfortably at Leybourne, appealing for help. The policeman took Katy's arm. 'I don't think we can do any more here, ma'am.'

Katy thought, Nor anywhere else. Louise was out of her reach, gone away with her father and at his mercy for as long as this war might last. And she was suddenly certain that war was inevitable. She could not see either the policeman or the clerk properly because of the tears blinding her, could hardly mouth the words through the grief which was choking her: 'Will you take me to the station, please? I want to go back to Sunderland.' She wanted to hide from the world and went, drooping, with Leybourne.

★   ★   ★

Ivor Spargo made the run from York to Newcastle twice a week. He was in charge of the vehicle inasmuch as he conducted the business but he had a man to drive it for him. Vera, his mother, had bitterly insisted on that. Her anger at having to leave Sunderland had not abated. She daily derided and cursed Arthur and Ivor for the fiasco they had engineered. Ivor was grateful for the trip to Newcastle because it took him out of reach of her whiplash of a tongue for a while, at least.

The business was the collection of miscella-neous goods from warehouses set by the Tyne. It was as he emerged from one of these that Ivor saw Katy being helped into a cab by a police sergeant. Even from across the street, Ivor could see that she was distressed and wiping at her eyes with a scrap of handkerchief. As he stared the cabbie shook the reins and the horse trotted away with the cab swaying behind it. A clerk stood outside an office, watching it go, and Ivor told his driver, 'Wait here a minute.'

The driver protested, 'We can't hang around here all day! Your ma will be expecting us!' He knew Ivor stood in fear of Ma Spargo.

But Ivor was not deterred this time and only snarled back at him, 'You damn well wait!' He ran across the road to catch the clerk before he could re-enter his office, and panted, 'Here! Was that lass getting arrested?' And craftily pretend-ing solicitude rather than vulgar curiosity, 'It must be a mistake, a bonny lass like that.'

The clerk shook his head dolefully. 'No, she's not being pinched. It's a very sad case. I don't know all the ins and outs but it seems she had a bairn by a feller and then he didn't marry her. Now he's taken the little lass and gone off to Germany. That woman you saw is broken-hearted.'

Ivor feigned sorrow, 'Aw! That's terrible! So he's not taking her to the station?'

The clerk chuckled at this. 'Aye, he is, but not the pollis station. She's gone to get the train back to Sunderland.' Then he stared because Ivor was racing across to the lorry and swinging up into the cab. A second later it roared off down the street.

At the railway station, Katy smiled shakily up at Sergeant Leybourne and said, 'Thank you, but I can manage on my own from here.'

He tried, awkwardly, to cheer her: 'Keep your pecker up, lass. They say if this war starts it will be over by Christmas and then you'll get her back. Keep that in mind.' Then he left her with a salute and Katy looked for and found her train. She was oblivious to the crowds of reservists and they were all seeking main line trains. She found a seat easily in the local that would stop at all stations to Sunderland. She stared out of the grimy window, seeing nothing but Louise — and a grinning Howard Ross. There was a slamming of doors, the guard's whistle blew and the train jerked with a preparatory banging of couplings then started to move away. And suddenly Ivor's face took the place of Howard's.

He had run frantically from the lorry to catch this train, had charged through the barrier, brushing past the clutching fingers of an outraged ticket collector, ignoring his bellow of, 'Come back here!' He was gasping for breath but he had caught Katy and that was all that mattered.

He clung with one hand to the door handle as the engine gathered speed, clung long enough to shriek at her, his voice breaking with hate and triumph: 'So that white-headed fancy man o' yours has done you dirt again! Run off wi' the

249

bairn he left ye with! Serve you right, you little bitch!'

He had to let go then, his labouring legs unable to match the acceleration of the train. He fell back and out of Katy's sight but he had been laughing with glee at her pain and she knew he would be laughing still.

★ ★ ★

Matt had packed his kit and carried it down to the hall. He looked in the drawing-room and saw Fleur sitting in an armchair and staring sulkily into space. Matt said. 'I'm going down to the yard for a few minutes to tie up a loose end, then I'll come back here for my kit and catch my train.'

Fleur answered, 'As you wish.' The threat of war had spoiled her holiday and looked as though it would disastrously affect her social arrangements. Matt was running off because of some stupid idea of duty and she could scarcely attend a dance or go out to dinner on her own.

Matt bit off an angry retort. These were the last hours before he went off to war. He did not want them soured by a row. 'Then I'll see you soon.'

'Very well.' She did not turn her head to face him.

He left the house and drove off in the Vauxhall. As the sound of his engine died away, Fleur thought there might be a solution to the problem of the escort.

250

It was some time later that her thoughts turned to Katy Merrick.

* * *

Later Katy remembered little of the nightmare journey back to Monkwearmouth station. She left the train there, rather than cross the bridge into the central station in Sunderland, and walked to the yard. As she entered she saw Matt's Vauxhall standing outside the office. She remembered dully that he had said he would look in that afternoon — something about an authority for Fleur to draw money while he was away — before he left to join the Army. It meant nothing to Katy now. Matt ran out to meet her as she trudged wearily up to the office. He set his hands on her shoulders, peered down into her tear-streaked face and said, 'Annie told me all about it.'

Annie showed behind him. She, too, had been weeping and the corners of her mouth were down. She wailed, 'I had to tell him the truth about Louise's father. Matt thought he was a sailor.'

Katy looked up at Matt and explained, not caring now, 'It was a story I made up because Louise was born out of wedlock.'

Matt said, 'I know. Never mind that now. Did you find Louise?' Katy shook her head dumbly, wordless from the lump in her throat, and he said softly, 'Oh, dear God! I'm sorry, Katy.'

She tried to speak, failed and tried again. It came out chokingly, 'He's taken her to Germany.

251

I can't do anything until the war is over and I don't know how I'll find her then.' Katy's face crumpled and she sagged with it under the weight of emotional exhaustion.

Matt said, 'Oh, Katy!' He opened his arms and she fell into them, they wrapped her round and she lay with her head against his chest and wept. He held her and whispered words of commiseration, stroked her and stooped his head over her to kiss her cheek. 'We'll find her, Katy. As soon as this war is over — they say it will be over by Christmas — we'll find her and bring her back.' Just for a moment Katy, unreasoning because she was not able to reason, felt safe and secure in his arms and hopeful. Then Fleur said harshly, 'And what the hell are you two up to?'

She had come in at the gate unseen and now stood only feet away. The cab that had brought her was turning away outside the gates, the cabbie clicking his tongue at his horse. Fleur glared at Matt and Katy as they turned startled faces towards her, and she went on, voice rising, 'Not as I can't bloody see!' And glaring at Matt she mimicked, ' 'I'm going down to the yard for a few minutes.' That was an hour ago!'

Katy pushed herself away from Matt, her hands on his chest. She tried to dry her tears with a scrap of handkerchief, tried to explain: 'I've lost Louise. Her father took her — '

Fleur broke in, shouting, 'I'll bet that's not all you've lost, by the look of things! Oh, I've had my suspicions about you and him for a long time!'

Matt snapped, 'Don't talk rubbish!'

252

'Rubbish?' Fleur laughed, jeering. 'All those times you were late coming home and said you were working! No wonder you hung around this place so much and so long, with her and her bairn! I wouldn't be surprised if *you* were the father!'

'That's enough!' Matt grabbed her shoulders as he had Katy's but this was no gentle grip. Fleur squeaked as his fingers dug into her but he ignored that and rushed her across to the Vauxhall.

Fleur shouted, 'It's true, isn't it?'

'No! It isn't!' And that came from Annie now standing at the office door. For a second they stared at her and she was able to put in: 'It isn't true because I was waiting here. Katy just got back and she's heartbroken, anybody can see that. Matt was only giving her the comfort any decent man would.' Her angry stare caught Fleur and she told her, 'So don't you go making slanderous remarks or Katy can have the law on you.'

That silenced Fleur and Matt shoved her up into the Vauxhall. As he drove it away he turned his head once to stare back at Katy. Then he swung the motor car out of the gateway and was gone.

Katy, slumping, watched him go. Annie grumbled, 'When he came down here he told her it was to tidy up some odds and ends before he went for a soldier. But when he heard what had happened to Louise and how you were looking for her, he stayed on. She must have wondered why he was so long and come down here for

253

him. But don't you take any notice of what she said; that woman has a poisonous tongue. She ought to be ashamed of herself. But *I* know the sort o' lass you are and it's not the sort she said. She was talking a pack o' lies.'

They entered the office, Annie still chattering, 'I would ha' been out sooner but I was keeping an eye on Beatrice — she's upstairs and ready for bed.'

An open envelope lay on the desk, a letter beside it. Katy glanced at it as Annie commented, 'He said that was for the bank.' It was an authority for Fleur to draw from the firm's account while Matt was away. Katy dropped it on the desk. It would have to wait until the bank opened.

Katy got through the rest of that terrible day and went to bed in the room beside Beatrice but without Louise. She was conscious of the missing child, that Matt had gone, and God only knew when — if — either would come back to her. Her weary mind trudged again and again over the disasters of that awful day as if on a treadmill. She realised Howard Ross had timed the abduction and his escape almost to the minute. The German ship had been dropping down the Tyne on her way to the sea while Katy was still trundling around the countryside doing Harry Rogers' job.

Annie had said Fleur had talked a pack of lies when she accused Katy and Matt of being lovers. But Fleur had been right.

★ ★ ★

Katy had known it and so had Matt when he briefly held her in his arms.

The ultimatum to Germany expired at eleven that night. As Katy had dreaded, it had come to war and her daughter was somewhere on the other side of the battle lines. All communication with Germany now was through neutral countries. She would have tramped barefoot through the length and breadth of Europe to find her child, but while Holland or Switzerland would have passed her through, as soon as she set foot in Germany she would be locked up as an enemy alien, to spend the rest of the war behind bars.

Katy was powerless and she recalled Annie's talk of living trapped inside a bottle. Trying to find Louise was like climbing a glass wall and Katy wept into her pillow night after night. Nevertheless, over the following months she pleaded with her Member of Parliament and wrote frantically to everyone she thought might help, but without result. The war was that wall of glass between herself and Louise.

She was not to know how long she would fret and grieve for her daughter, and her frustration at being unable to act was a recurring torment.

'Louise . . . *Louise!*'

And: '*Matt!*'

17

MONKWEARMOUTH. DECEMBER 1914.

'You be careful when you're out today!' Annie issued the warning as Katy opened the gate to let her into the yard. The older woman had a shawl wrapped around her shoulders over the winter coat she wore. Her breath steamed on the winter air and frost glistened and sparkled on the road behind her and on the yard.

'I will, don't worry.' Katy swung the gates wide and wedged them open, then she and Annie walked up the yard to the office. Katy wore overalls, the legs of them showing under her heavy coat. From the corner of her eye she saw Annie's disapproving glance but was used to it now. She had seen that look numerous times each day since she had first worn the overalls two weeks ago. She had ignored it every time because now she spent all her working days behind the wheel of the Dennis. There was only one now, the first she and Matt had bought when they started the partnership. The others, all purchased under the War Office Subsidy Scheme, had been claimed by the Army. The War Office had paid compensation, of course, but the bank had taken back the money loaned to buy them. Little capital was left and money did not carry any loads. It sat in the bank and earned interest — or was spent. And that was another story.

'Good morning, Ernie!' Katy halted outside the office and called as he came in through the gates. His skinny body was now bulky with an old raincoat and several ragged pullovers. He was blue-nosed with the cold.

'Morning, Mrs Merrick.' Ernie sniffed. 'Shall I start her?'

'Aye, get her warmed up, please.'

Ernie said lugubriously, 'That's what we all want this morning.'

'That's true.' Katy laughed as she watched him cross the yard to the garage. 'I'll be with you in a minute or two.' Ernie Thompson could not drive but he was able to start the Dennis. Katy was grateful for him as he cranked the starting handle and the engine burst into life. She reflected wryly that if the Army had left her the lorries there would have been no one to drive them. Ernie was the only man left to her. All the others had joined one or other of the fighting services. Ernie had volunteered with the rest, despite his brood, but the doctors had turned him down because of his flat feet.

Katy joined Annie in the office. While Katy was driving out on the roads, Annie now looked after the office and answered any enquiries for work. Beatrice was also there, seated at the desk and reading a book. She was ready for school, bundled up warmly with a thick muffler around her neck and would be leaving in a few minutes. She had asked about Louise several times, curious as to where she was and when she would return. Katy had answered brightly that Louise had gone to visit an uncle and would be back when the war was over. She managed to smile while giving this explanation, not wanting to worry the child, but afterwards she was tearful.

Now Katy smiled again: 'All ready, Bea?'

'Um,' answered Beatrice, her nose in the book.

'Off you go, then. Give Annie and me a kiss.' And as Beatrice obeyed, Katy added, 'Be careful how you walk because the streets are very icy this morning. And come straight home at twelve o'clock — '

Beatrice cut in: 'Because Annie will have my dinner ready. Yes, I know.'

Katy smacked her bottom lightly but chuckled, 'Don't be cheeky.' She watched, fondly, as the little girl she regarded as a daughter crossed the yard and turned into the street.

Annie said behind her, equally fondly, 'There's not much wrong with that one.' And then: 'Here's the postman.' He came up the yard with a handful of letters held in fingerless gloves, his nose as blue as Ernie's. Katy took the letters and shuffled through them quickly with the daily surge of hope, but none had come from Germany by way of neutral Switzerland. They were all relating to the business.

Annie asked, 'Nothing about Louise?'

'No.'

Annie started, 'That Howard Ross! I'd like to — ' She stopped her usual diatribe, remembering it hurt Katy. Then she went on gently, 'Nothing from Matt, either?'

Katy turned away so that Annie could not see her face. 'No.'

'He's still on Salisbury Plain, then.'

'I suppose so.' Katy had sent several letters to Matt, businesslike missives detailing how the Army had taken the lorries — and the men. Matt had written only once. A week after he had left, Katy received a picture postcard of Stonehenge. In a few words on the back he had said he was living under canvas on the Plain. He was well but the food was awful. It might have come from any soldier — to anyone. There had been nothing since and Katy knew why.

'We never see anything of *her*.' Annie's tone was sour.

Katy knew Annie always referred to Fleur that way. 'No.' Katy was not going to be drawn. Fleur had never come to the yard since her vitriolic outburst but Katy knew that she had been left a generous allowance by Matt — all his share of the profits from the firm, in fact — and that she was drawing it up to the hilt. Moreover Fleur's name was frequently mentioned when the newspapers reported charity events, balls and suchlike, held to raise funds for comforts for the servicemen. Katy had also seen her out walking in the company of various young officers.

She said briskly, 'It's time we started.' The Dennis was ticking over with Ernie's hand on the throttle. Katy crossed the yard, checked the oil pressure gauge and took off the radiator cap to see that the water was circulating. Satisfied, she climbed up into the driver's seat as Ernie moved over to make room for her. A wave to Annie where she stood at the office door and then she drove out of the gates on the first job of the day. As she steered the Dennis between the gates she wondered bitterly if Fleur ever thought of Matt.

At that moment, Fleur did not, but that was to change. She was woken by the hammering of the big brass knocker on the front door. She stirred sleepily and murmured, 'See who that is, darling.'

The major was a recalled reservist, too old for active service but still energetic and his money also attracted Fleur. Now he was reluctant to move. The fire in the bedroom grate was almost out and he could see the frost on the outside of the window. 'Let your maid do it. I've got a better idea.' He began exploring again.

Fleur giggled, 'No! She doesn't come in for another half-hour and I want you out of here before then. I've got my reputation to think of. Now go and see who it is — and I'll be nice to you before you leave.'

The major would settle for that. He slid out of bed and pulled on shirt and trousers as the knocking came again. He bellowed, 'All right!' Then padded down the stairs in his bare feet and opened the front door.

The boy standing outside wore a pillbox cap and a leather belt and pouch around his waist. His face was pinched with the cold and he held out the buff envelope: 'Telegram for Mrs Ballard.'

The major fumbled in his trousers pocket for coins and tossed a penny to the boy, who snatched it out of the air. 'Thank ye, sir!'

Fleur stretched and smiled as the major returned. Then she saw the envelope: 'A telegram?'

'You can read it later.' His hands fumbled at her but she shoved them aside.

'Give it to me!' Fleur snatched the envelope, ripped it open and scanned the message inside. 'Damn!' She balled the buff flimsy and threw back the bed clothes. At sight of her nakedness the major reached out for her again but she slapped his hands away and brushed past him: 'Get dressed and out of here! My husband's on his way home!' The major fielded the clothes she tossed at him and stood gaping at her with his shirt-tails hanging outside his trousers and his braces dangling. Until Fleur shouted, 'He sent that telegram as he was getting on the train at King's Cross! He might walk in any minute!' That was an exaggeration but Fleur wanted him out of her house and it worked. Thoughts of an angry husband hastened the major in his dressing. They were ready for the street together but left separately, she by the front door and the major by the back.

Fleur would have taken a cab to the station but did not see one and had to use the tram. As it clanked and ground into the town she tried to pull her jumbled thoughts together. The telegram had come as a shock. She had virtually forgotten about Matt, only thought of him occasionally and absently as she pursued her life of pleasure. She had known that he would be given leave at some point but that was in the future and possibly the distant future at that. In truth she did not care when he came home because she was having a good time and his arrival now would spoil it. She did not want him.

261

She was sure that he had been 'carrying on' with Katy Merrick and that had enraged her. When he went back to the Army they had parted in a cold silence. He had written several times but she had not. She needed the money he allowed her but not him. He had been her escort in the days of peace and his success had given her a key to society, but now there were other men to take her to dances and soirées.

So Fleur considered how she should treat this nuisance of a husband and decided to be outwardly sweet and forgiving, to submit to his advances. She was sure there would be advances; he had been away for four months. She felt a little thrill of excited anticipation then, began to look forward to the coming of this big man. She could use his hunger to manipulate him, as she had done with others. Besides, it would only be for a week or so and then she could go on with her life of dalliance.

She stood on the platform as the train puffed into the station with a sigh of steam and rattling of couplings, a grinding of brakes. The men were hanging out of the windows, eager for it to stop. Most were in khaki but there were some in the dark blue of the Navy. As the train halted they spilled out of the carriages into the arms of the waiting women who thronged the platform. Fleur looked for Matt and soon spotted his head above the crowd around him. She waved her handkerchief and smiled tentatively. He smiled in return but it was mechanical. When they met among the embracing couples they did not touch except for the peck Fleur planted on his cheek.

He was unshaven from travelling through the night and his stubble scraped her. She noted the three stripes on his sleeve. She had forgotten he was a sergeant and that it would be awkward. In the circles in which she now moved she had become used to walking on the arms of officers. A sergeant would be out of place. She would just have to stay at home.

Irritated, she said, 'So there you are.'

Matt sensed a coldness and tried to ignore it. 'Aye, the bad penny.'

Fleur smiled politely. 'Will you get us a cab?'

They found a horse-drawn cab outside the station and sat facing each other, Matt's pack on the seat beside him. They conversed politely as the cab took them home and Matt knew then it had all gone to hell but he still tried. During the long nights on the Plain he had told himself he had loved this woman and married her, sworn fidelity and much besides. He would not throw that aside. And when they were in the house Fleur put her arms around him and whispered, 'It's good to have you home.' But then she added, 'I forgive you.'

'Forgive me?' Matt stared down at her. 'What for?'

'When I found you with that woman.'

Matt's face stiffened. 'I explained about that. There was nothing to forgive.'

Fleur's arms slipped away and she stepped back from him. 'It wasn't explained to my satisfaction.'

Matt took a breath, swallowing the first angry retort. He insisted, 'I told you, there was nothing between me and Katy, not all the time we worked together.'

Fleur sniffed, 'I saw how she clung to you.'

'She needed to cling to somebody, *anybody!* The girl had just lost her child, stolen by her father!'

Fleur laughed without humour. 'That's her story. *If* he was the father. You never know with that sort of woman.'

Matt, outraged, snapped, 'I won't have you talking about her like that! She's not 'that sort of woman'!'

Fleur shrugged, pouting, 'If you say so.' And remembering how he had hungered for her, said, 'Now, if you'll excuse me, I think I have a migraine. I'm going to lie down.' She looked for disappointment in his face, thought he might plead, but she was the one to be disappointed when Matt said, 'Of course.'

Fleur turned at the door to have the last word: 'Will you use the spare room? I haven't been sleeping well lately.' Then she left without waiting for an answer.

Matt stared bleakly at the closed door. He did not want her.

He dined with his wife that night and breakfasted with her the next day, then told her, 'I'm going down to the yard.'

Fleur said sulkily, 'To see that woman, I suppose.'

Matt refused to be drawn and only answered curtly, 'To see how the business is running. It pays for your keep, remember.'

He went reluctantly and because he had to,

and not only to see to the business. He drove there in the Vauxhall, making a mental note to sell it. Turkey was in the war now, since Guy Fawkes day, and Matt believed now that the war would be a long one. There was no sense in leaving the car to gather dust in the garage.

Katy was in the driving seat of the Dennis, Ernie at her side, and ready to drive out on the day's work. Then she saw the Vauxhall swing in through the gateway with Matt at the wheel. Her heart leapt instinctively and her first ridiculous thought was that she wished she was not wearing the overalls. She got down from the Dennis and walked towards him as he came to meet her, but they stopped a yard apart by mutual unspoken agreement. They smiled ruefully, lopsidedly at each other because there was an invisible wall between them now. The easy days of comradeship when they had worked together, were over. They both knew it.

He said, 'Hello, Katy.'

'Hello, Matt.'

He asked, anxiety mixed with hope, 'Is there any news of Louise?'

Katy shook her head wordlessly, the fret and fear surfacing as they did every day in some moment when she was not busy.

Matt said, 'I'm sorry.' And in an awkward attempt to get away from a subject which pained her, he asked, 'How are you getting on?'

'We're coping. If you go into the office, Annie will show you the books.'

He stared at that. 'Annie?'

'I took her on to handle the office work. I'm

out on the road most of the time. I told you about the Army taking the men besides the lorries.'

'Aye, you did. I wondered if you would manage.'

'We have — just.'

But while they were talking it was only on the surface and their eyes were exchanging other messages — of hunger and despair.

Katy felt no sense of guilt because Matt had briefly supplanted Louise in her thoughts. She could think of him though her child was a prisoner in a foreign land because she had enough love for both her child and this tall man, and both were tearing her apart. But while thoughts of Louise were always with her, Matt was here now. She could not prolong this and said, 'I'd better get out on the road and try to earn a few shillings.'

Matt agreed heavily, 'Aye. You do that. I'll talk to Annie.'

But when Katy drove the Dennis out of the gates and glanced behind her she saw him still standing where she had left him, outside the office, watching her go from him.

Katy worked mechanically through the morning, her thoughts elsewhere. When she returned to the yard at mid-day she found Matt outside the office again but this time Annie and Beatrice were with him. The little girl was excited: 'Uncle Matt gave me a ride in his motor car. He went *fast*!'

Katy addressed Beatrice but her eyes were on Matt. 'Did you enjoy yourself?'

Beatrice said ecstatically, 'It was *lovely!*'

Matt said, 'It was like old times.'

Katy thought, Old times, past times.

Annie broke in proudly, 'I showed him all the books.'

Matt said, 'You've done very well, both of you.' He glanced across at Ernie who was sweeping out the back of the Dennis, and amended, 'All of you.' His gaze returned to Katy: 'Will you be able to carry on?' And then, without waiting for her answer, 'I think when I go back after this leave I'll be sent over the pond and I don't know when I'll be back.'

Katy had been expecting this but she still flinched inside under the blow. Then Annie laid a hand on Matt's shoulder and said sympathetically, 'And you want something to come home to.'

That could be interpreted two ways and Katy put in quickly, 'We'll cope.'

Matt studied her a moment, then nodded. 'I think you will.'

Annie appealed to Katy, 'I've been trying to get him to stay for a bite of dinner.'

Matt shook his head, 'Thanks, but I think I should get back to Fleur.' He frowned as he thought of the reception he would receive but then strode to the Vauxhall, cranked it into life and swung into the driving seat. He looked back at Katy for long seconds then drove out of the yard. She was left staring at the empty gateway where a faint wisp of exhaust smoke hung a moment in the air then was dispersed on the breeze, leaving no sign of his passing.

The days of his leave slipped by and Katy kept count of them but he did not come to the yard again. She arranged the work schedule so there were no jobs on the day he was to go back to his regiment. She stayed in the office all that day but he did not come. She had not thought that he would, but just in case . . . As the shadows of a winter dusk filled the yard she knew that he would not come, would be on the train racing south by then.

She knew him, that he would keep faith and would be true to Fleur, the woman he had married, and that was why he had stayed away from Katy. She was temptation.

She had not lost him because she had never possessed him in the first place. Now she was sure she never would.

18

MONKWEARMOUTH. JULY 1916.

'They're dying in their hundreds over in Flanders!' Annie Scanlon said it, her face drawn with horror. They were talking in the office, Katy already feeling warm although dressed only in her overalls on top of her underwear. They had suffered two years of war and now the battle of the Somme, the 'Big Push', had begun. Annie were on, her lips quivering, 'That lad Benny Pennington, Hetty Pennington's son, he's home on leave from the Navy and he stopped in London for one night before coming up north. He says the ambulance trains are coming into all the stations day and night, bringing the wounded.'

Katy nodded, 'Aye. I'd heard that.' And inevitably she had wondered if Matt was safe. He had written once, just to say that he was in Palestine, a stilted, formal letter. As it had to be, she understood that.

They were talking in the office and now Katy picked up the job list. 'I'll start the Dennis and get going.' Ernie Thompson had finally persuaded the Army to take him and had gone off to the war. Katy had managed to find a boy to help her with the lifting of cargo on and off the lorry. She could not take on a man because the shipyards on the three rivers of the North-East,

Tyne, Wear and Tees, were working all out to replace the ships lost to the U-boats. The men the Army had not taken were now in the shipyards. The fifteen-year-old Danny was a cheerful, willing worker but she could not ask him to start the Dennis and warm it up as Ernie had done.

As she walked across the yard she reflected that the engine would not take long to warm in this summer weather. And now she thought of Louise as she had earlier thought of Matt. There was not a day she did not think of the man and her daughter. She had nightmare visions of Matt lying dead or terribly wounded. And of a big-eyed, skeletal Louise, because the government claimed the naval blockade had left the people of Germany starving.

Katy shuddered now despite the warmth of the sunlight and the pink-faced Danny, his cap so big it seemed to rest on his ears, stared at her, puzzled. But then Katy saw the postman sauntering in at the gateway and she turned back to take the letters from him. She fanned through the few envelopes, looking for a letter — from Germany or from Matt — but was disappointed. She passed on to Annie all the post except one envelope addressed to herself in a sprawling, ill-educated hand. There was something about it that struck a chord of memory and she ripped it open and glanced first at the signature.

The letter was from her sister, Ursula. Katy thought absently that it was little wonder she had not recognised the writing on sight because she had not seen it since she left home ten years ago.

She scanned it quickly, then read it through more slowly to take in its full import. There was a good deal about how the family should stick together, letting bygones be bygones, forgiving and forgetting, but essentially the message was simple: her father was at death's door.

'Annie, will you write to everybody on the job list and tell them I've been called away on urgent family affairs. I've got to go to Newcastle. Danny, will you sweep out the yard and do any jobs Annie finds for you. I'll see you when I get back.'

It was a strange house in a strange street in Wallsend. Katy saw the neighbours standing at their doors watching her curiously as she passed. She was much better dressed than any of them. The front door was open and she walked along the uncarpeted passage and knocked at the first door she came to. The passage needed sweeping, there was a stale smell of cooking and two near-naked little boys, dressed only in vests, played on the stairs but stopped to stare at her.

Ursula opened the door, blinked at the smartly dressed Katy for a moment but then her expression changed from surprise to relief and she held the door open to admit her sister. 'By lass, I'm glad to see you.' But that was the end of their greetings. They stayed apart and there was no exchange of pecks on the cheek.

There was just the one room, the floor covered with ancient, cracked linoleum. A small fire burned in the grate and an old basket chair stood before it. A table and two straight-backed chairs were set under the window and the bed

271

was in a corner. Barney Merrick lay in the bed. He was sleeping, his breathing laboured, and grey-faced under the stubble of several days. The room had been swept and dusted and the windows cleaned. There was a smell of sweat but the sheets on the bed were clean.

All this Katy took in with one swift glance. Ursula noted it and said defensively, 'I've done what I could. The others don't come near.' And then, pointing to the basket chair, 'Sit down and I'll make you a cup of tea.'

Katy sat down cautiously but the chair held her with only a faint creaking. She was shocked by the appearance of her father, who had been a man of strength and high temper. 'He looks awful. How did he get like this?'

Ursula used an enamelled jug to fill the kettle from a bucket of water by the fireside, then she set the kettle on the coals and a small teapot on the hob to warm. 'He had an accident a year or two back, fell down some steps when he was coming home drunk. It left him crippled and he couldn't get work in the shipyards any more, only odds and ends of jobs. Then his wife died. She left him a few quid but he soon got through it. I think after that he just pawned stuff. I found a lot of pawn tickets when I came here.'

She hesitated, then said with a rush, 'You knew what he was like. I always took his part, thought he was great, but I found out about him at the end. I had money saved for my wedding, I'd put a bit away every week for years. He found it, took every penny and spent it on booze. So when he came round to me a few weeks ago and asked for a loan I told him to go to hell. I thought he wanted it for drink.' Ursula wiped tears from her eyes with the back of her hand then made the tea as the kettle sang. She poured it into two chipped cups and sat down across the fire on one of the straight-backed chairs.

She sniffed, 'I wouldn't have let him starve. One of the neighbours came in when they hadn't seen him for a day or two. They knew where I lived and fetched me because he was in bed and they couldn't get any sense out of him, he just wandered.' They drank tea and Ursula went on, 'I cleaned up the place and him, tried to get his temperature down and some beef tea into him, but he didn't improve, so I got the doctor in.' She lowered her voice: 'He said Dad could go at any time. So I wrote to you.'

Katy said, 'Don't blame yourself. You did all anybody could do.'

They were silent for a moment, then Ursula looked up and asked, 'How are you, then?'

'I'm fine.'

Ursula looked down at the cup on her knee and ventured, 'We heard you had a bairn and were living with a feller.'

Katy eyed her sister and said directly, 'I had a little girl but her father deserted me. I'm not living with any feller.'

Ursula gave an apologetic flap of the hand, primly embarrassed. 'Sorry.' Then she got up quickly, took a slip of paper from the mantelpiece and handed it to Katy. 'That's yours.' And when Katy stared: 'It's Mam's brooch. She always wanted you to have it. Dad

273

must have got it back from that second wife of his, Marina, to pawn it for drink.'

Katy reclaimed it the next day. When she came out of the pawnshop she stopped for a minute under the three brass balls of the sign and looked down at the brooch lying in the palm of her hand. It brought back memories of her mother — and Louise. Katy vowed that one day she would hand on the brooch to her own daughter. It was a promise made with determination and fear. She slipped the brooch into her bag and walked back to the room where her father lay dying.

She and Ursula took it in turns to care for the old man and to sleep in the basket chair under a blanket. They did that for two nights because Barney Merrick, a fighter all his life, fought for it now. It was an animal reaction of the body. The mind was elsewhere. Often he would mumble incoherently when it was impossible to tell whether he was awake or sleeping. When he could be understood his talk was of old times, old places, old fights and old friends, all gone from him now. He never gave any sign of recognising Ursula or Katy, lost in his own world.

The doctor came once when Katy was on duty and Ursula had gone to buy bread and milk. He was an elderly man, too old for war service, and he eyed Katy disapprovingly as he said, 'He should never have been allowed to get into this condition. All he needed was some care.'

Katy could have defended herself against the charge being levelled at her, could have pointed out that she had not known of his destitution and illness while others did, that she had come as soon as she had learned of his condition, that her father had turned her out and disowned her. But she said nothing. She would not argue over his body.

Barney Merrick died in the last cold hour of the night. He did not wake. Katy was on duty, sitting by his bedside, watching him by the light from the fire because that would allow him to rest, rather than using the brighter gas lamp which hung from the ceiling. The flames flickering low in the grate cast shifting shadows on the walls and the old man's face. In sleep it was austere but not hard. Katy hoped he had found some inner peace, wished he had been kinder to her — and she to him. She could feel only pity for him now, his cruelty forgotten. She acknowledged sadly that he would not have thought he had treated her harshly, would have been sure he was acting as much for her good as his.

When he drew his last breath — Katy heard the quick, shallow intake and long sigh — she knew he had gone from her. She had a moment of loneliness then. She had lost Louise, could never have the man she wanted and her family were strangers to her. But then her own fighting spirit buoyed her up. She had a home of her own, a life of her own and one day she would find Louise and bring her back.

She stood up and went to where Ursula sat sleeping in the basket chair and gently shook her awake: 'He's gone.'

Her brothers and sisters came to the funeral and made some attempts at reconciliation but they tried to talk across too big a gap. Barney had left Katy with a reputation and she was a stranger to them, their husbands or wives. Ursula had gone some way towards surmounting this barrier due to the two days she had shared with Katy the duty of caring for their father. But even she was not close, not easy with her sister. If anything the men were kinder than the women but still uncomfortable. Their spouses eyed this scarlet woman with her fine clothes warily. Hadn't she a child born out of wedlock? Didn't her father say she was without a husband and living with another man, not the father of the child? Katy saw their glances and guessed their import. The clothes had all been bought before the war and she reflected grimly that the way business was going she would not be buying any more.

Katy said nothing of the abduction of Louise. They could do nothing to help and she suspected the knowledge might only provoke further speculation about her, doubts as to whether she was wholly or partly to blame, had tailored a story to suit herself. Besides, Louise was hers, to love and worry over, and nothing to do with them.

It was over at last, the interment as they all stood under a soft summer drizzle blown in from the North Sea, the cab ride back to the single room and a sandwich meal eaten with relief. Then the polite talk, the departure and the farewells and half-hearted invitations: 'Come and see us!' Katy set off for home.

She took a cab because she had her suitcase to carry, she was weary from the last two days of nursing and broken nights and wanted to be home. As the cab swayed along behind the trotting horse she thought over the past few days. She decided she would take up the invitations and visit her siblings — but not for some months — or years. They needed time to get used to her. But that was something good come of this visit. And there was the brooch. She looked down at it now, pinned to the lapel of her coat. One day she would pass it on to Louise. She had been gone for two years and would be six years old in December. Katy closed her eyes, out of weariness and to try to picture her daughter now. Then she woke with a jerk, looked out of the window — and saw Louise.

It was a mere glimpse. One moment the child was seen in a busy street and the next she was lost in the hurrying crowds. Katy shrieked, '*Stop!*' She jumped out of the cab before it came to a halt, the startled cabbie on his box staring down at her. She ran back the way they had come, threading her way between the people on the pavement.

Katy heard the cabbie, afraid he was about to lose his fare, shout, 'Here! You come back here!' She ran on, but slowing. It had been her, she was sure. Katy stopped, peering about her, eyes frantically scanning the crowd. *There!* She started forward then stopped because the little girl she saw now was not Louise, though about her size. *Now!* But again this was another small girl but not her daughter. Her shoulders slumped as she faced reality. She had been half-asleep and had been thinking about Louise, had awakened to see a small girl and thought it was her daughter. It was no more than wishful thinking. Louise was hundreds of miles away across the cold North Sea.

Katy walked slowly back to where the cab stood at rest, the driver down on the road beside it, both cabbie and horse looking back at her. She was close to tears as she apologised, 'I'm sorry. I thought I saw someone I knew but I was imagining it.'

He grinned sheepishly, 'You had me worried for a minute.' And then, concerned as he peered into her face, 'Are you all right, lass?'

Katy smiled wanly, 'I will be.' She went to climb into the cab.

'Here y'are. Ups-a-daisy!' He took her arm and almost lifted her into her seat. Then he dug into the pocket of the ancient coat he wore and brought out a flat bottle, unscrewed the cap and offered it to Katy: 'Have a drop o' rum. That'll cheer you up.'

'No.' Katy shook her head. 'But thank you. You're very kind.'

He took a swig himself, then climbed up onto his box and the cab rolled forward. Katy sat back in the corner of the cab and wept.

19

MONKWEARMOUTH. FEBRUARY 1917.

'*No!* I simply can't manage on this — this *pittance!* I want another pound a week at least.' Fleur posed in the middle of the office floor, head thrown back and looking down her nose at Katy where she sat at her desk. When Fleur had stormed into the office, Katy had offered her a chair but that offer had been ignored. Fleur raged on, 'The price of everything has gone up, *if* you can get it — because most of the time the shops are sold out! You ask them for something and they look at you and say, 'Shortages.' It's *ridiculous!*'

Katy could sympathise there to a certain extent. There were shortages in this third year of the war. Nobody knew it better than she because petrol was now restricted. That had reduced the firm's income even more because some days the lorry stood idle for want of fuel. Katy did not complain because she knew that the petrol brought into the country came at the cost of men's lives as the U-boats were sinking the ships. It seemed Fleur did not care.

She fumed, 'And it's degrading that I should have to come to you to beg for money that is mine by *right*, and at this unearthly hour! When I called yesterday that old woman said you were out. Was that true?'

Katy, stung by this reference to Annie, snapped back, 'Of course it was! Annie wouldn't lie to you.'

Fleur insisted, scowling, 'I'm not so sure. She was offhand to the point of rudeness. God knows why you employ her. It seems to me like a waste of the firm's money.'

Katy tried to keep her temper. This was Matt's wife and he would want her treated with respect. 'Annie earns her keep and more. Most people wanting jobs done come to the office. If they don't find anyone here they take their custom elsewhere.'

Fleur sniffed, 'Well, anyway, I want more money, an increased allowance.'

Katy looked out of the window and across the yard. Danny was sitting in the driving seat of the Dennis and its engine was ticking over. He had learned quickly over the past months and now started the Dennis every morning. He had become a useful assistant and Katy had paid him a rise because of that, but now he was talking of joining the Navy. Katy sighed, 'I have to start work soon.' She tried to explain as calmly as she could: 'Matthew authorised the allowance and only he can increase it. Have you asked him?'

Fleur bridled, 'No, I haven't. As his wife I'm entitled to the money.'

Katy tried another tack: 'I know prices have gone up but we're all in the same boat.'

'No, we're not,' Fleur cut in furiously. '*You* aren't in *my* position! All the money passes through your hands before it gets to the bank so you'll never be short! I think *that* needs looking into!'

Katy was stunned by the allegation for a moment. Then she jerked to her feet and pointed at the door, '*Get out!*'

Fleur fell back before her anger but paused in the doorway to hurl a final threat: 'I'll get a solicitor onto this and he'll see I get what is mine. *And* I'll write to Matthew this very day to tell him just how you're mismanaging his business and keeping me short of funds!' Then she was gone, flouncing across the yard to the motor taxi-cab which waited for her with its engine running.

Katy sat down with a bump. She felt sick. Fleur was greedy and in the wrong because there was no way that a solicitor could obtain more money for her. Her allowance already took up all of Matt's share of the profits of the firm. The firm still made a profit but only because Katy worked six long days every week. She was not worried by the charges levelled at her, could account for every penny earned and spent by the firm. But if the solicitor took the case to court? Or wrote to Matt? And Fleur was going to do just that. Katy could not let that happen to him.

She changed from her overalls into a dress, pulled on her coat and told Danny, 'Annie said she was going to queue at the butcher's for some meat and then come to work. Will you wait and help with any jobs she can find you? I'll be back in a couple of hours.'

She had to wait at the bank because she did not have an appointment but the manager saw her after some twenty minutes. Her business completed, or rather, the easiest part of it, Katy went on to deal with the worst. She had never been to Matt's house in Ashbrooke and was not looking forward to this visit. It was one of a terrace, with a long garden and steps leading up to the front door. She rang the doorbell and a maid, a girl of seventeen or so in black dress, white apron and cap, opened to her.

Katy asked, 'May I see Mrs Ballard, please?'

Before the girl could answer, a male voice called, 'Who is it?'

The maid replied, 'A lady wants to see madam.'

'A lady?' There was a pause and then the owner of the voice appeared at the maid's elbow. Katy noted that the girl not so much stood aside as shrank from him. The newcomer was tall and slender, with oiled hair parted in the middle and brushed flat, like patent leather. He stroked this as he ran his eyes over Katy. Then he eased the maid aside and opened the door wide. 'Come right in! Fleur's at her dressmaker's but she should be back real soon.' And to the maid: 'OK, kid, I'll see to this.'

Katy recognised the accent as North American because she had once heard such spoken by some seamen whose ship had berthed in Sunderland. She hesitated a moment, but she had to see Fleur, so she passed him to enter the house and he followed her. 'I'm Harry Dawkins,' he drawled, 'originally from New Orleans but lately I've played in London and a few other spots.' They stood in a hallway with a wooden floor polished until it shone. Katy guessed that the maid had done the polishing down on her knees. Harry Dawkins guided her with a hand in the small of her back. 'In here and sit right down.' It was a drawing-room crowded with chairs and small tables. A huge mirror on one wall reflected an image of the room. The seat Dawkins indicated was a couch. Katy perched stiffly at one end of it and he sat next to her. 'So what did you want to see Fleur about?'

Katy answered, 'A personal matter.'

'Well, any friend of Fleur is a friend of mine.' He sat smiling at her and she could feel his eyes probing her body. 'And nothing's lost that's given to a friend, that's what I say.' Now his smile was suggestive. Katy stared straight in front of her and she saw a clarinet lying in its open case on an occasional table.

To distract him, she asked, 'Do you play?' She nodded at the instrument.

He got up from his seat. 'Sure.' He picked up the clarinet and blew a ripple of notes, then bragged, 'I'm one of the best jazz players around. That's how I met Fleur; she came to a dance where my outfit was playing. I guess she hadn't heard anybody play like me before and that goes for a lot of other folks around here.'

He started back towards Katy and that was when the front door was opened. They heard the turning of the key in the lock and then the tapping of high heels on the polished floor. Fleur called, 'Mary Ann! Take a brush and sweep the front path and steps. You shouldn't need to be told.' And then, 'Hulloo, darling! I'm home!'

Dawkins slid into an armchair several feet from Katy just before Fleur entered the room. Then he stood up in leisurely fashion as she did so.

Fleur was smiling but her face changed as if a curtain was pulled across when she saw Katy. 'What are you doing here? That girl had no right to let you in.'

Dawkins said nothing but stood close behind Fleur. Katy got to her feet and now she could see in the mirror that he was fondling Fleur's haunches. She said, 'This — gentleman — invited me in.'

Dawkins said quickly, 'She said she was a friend of yours, Fleur.'

Katy denied him: 'No, I didn't. You assumed that.' Her gaze switched to Fleur: 'I told him I wanted to see you on a personal matter.'

Fleur snapped, 'Then tell me what you want and get out. I don't want you here.' Katy glanced at Dawkins but Fleur waved a hand impatiently. 'I don't mind him hearing and I'm not going to be left alone with you. The way you looked at me this morning — murderous!' She shuddered. 'So?'

Katy said, forcing out the words, anger and revulsion choking her. 'I talked to the bank manager and they are going to increase your allowance as you asked.'

'Aha!' Fleur threw back her head triumphantly. 'So you've seen sense and given in! That shows you told me a pack of lies this morning!' Katy walked past her and made for the door. Fleur shouted after her, 'Yes, get out! Harry! See her off the premises!' Then she laughed. Dawkins got to the front door just before Katy reached it. He swung it open but only wide enough for her to sidle through. As she did so he slid an arm around her waist and whispered, 'I'll come and visit some time.' His face was close to her and Katy seized his nose and twisted it. He yelped with pain and she shoved him aside. He fell back holding his nose, tears in his eyes and bleating, 'You Goddam bitch!'

Katy left them, sickened. As she walked down the path she came on the maid, industriously sweeping. The girl stood aside but she was grinning. 'I saw that, miss. Good for you. I wish I had your nerve.'

Katy paused and asked, 'You're not happy here?'

The girl's grin slipped away. 'I'll be off out of this before long. I'm working my notice now. I have to do that to get my money. The way they carry on! I take up the tea in the mornings and they're in bed together. But there's others *he* doesn't know about, nor anybody else around here. They're in and out by the back way. They think I don't know but I've seen these fellers going out of a morning. And what he does to me . . . He's all hands, but *she* doesn't know about that.' The girl was watching the house all the time and now she resumed her sweeping: 'She's looking out o' the window.'

Katy went on her way. She reflected bitterly that Fleur had won, got all she wanted, but there was nothing Katy could do. How could she tell Matt, thousands of miles away, about his wife's demands — and about Dawkins and the rest?

She could not torment him like that. So she had authorised payment of Fleur's increased allowance out of the firm's account, which was the same as out of Katy's money because Fleur had already had all of Matt's share. But — Fleur had described Katy as murderous. She was close to that now.

★   ★   ★

The winter passed, summer came and went. Perversely and as if to torture her, where once Katy had seen Fleur scarcely at all, now she saw her every few weeks. As Katy drove the Dennis about her business she caught glimpses of Fleur: sauntering along the High Street, strolling in Mowbray Park in a summer dress and a wide picture hat, going to a dance. Once, returning from a long trip after midnight, Katy even saw her coming out of the Palace Hotel after attending some ball. Katy had stopped the Dennis because of people crossing the road. The door of the Palace opened, sending a shaft of light which cut through the blackout imposed because of air raids and lit a party which spilled out onto the pavement. Katy saw Fleur was one of them and Dawkins was holding her, his arm around her waist. She was in a low-cut silken gown that clung to her as she clung to him and he was peering down into the valley of her breasts. Katy drove on, raging inside. Dawkins was with Fleur more often than not but she was never alone. There was always a man fawning on her, usually a young officer.

It was in October that Katy set out to drive to a mining village in West Durham. She went without Danny because he had gained his heart's desire and joined the Royal Navy just a week before. Katy and Annie had gone with his mother to see him off at the central station and they all wept together afterwards. So Katy drove alone on that foul morning of fog and driving rain. She had much to occupy her mind as she strained her eyes to make out the road which wound about and up and down. She needed a man or a strong boy to replace Danny and help her lift the heavy loads. It would not be easy to find one because the shipyards took those the Army left behind. The yards were so desperate for labour now that they were employing women. That had been unheard of before the war. The yards had always been a male preserve. Katy could manage on her own for a short time but it meant turning down heavy work — and most of the work was heavy. If she found a man she would have to pay him a man's wages and that would not be easy. There were too many days when she could not get the petrol to work. She still grieved over Louise, yearned for her. She had not heard from Matt . . .

The Dennis was climbing around the outside of a hill. Katy knew the road and that the view out over the countryside was lovely despite the pitheads which scarred the landscape. This day the view was hidden by drizzle and fog. It was a road on which there was little traffic as a rule but Katy was on her own side of it anyway. It was the lorry on the other side and coming down the hill which skidded on the turn and slid across the road. Katy twisted the steering wheel frantically to avoid a head-on collision and succeeded, but only at the cost of sliding off the road. She glimpsed the white, frightened face of the driver of the other lorry then the Dennis bucked as it lurched over the rocks marking the roadside and slewed across the turf beyond them. Katy saw the almost sheer drop ahead of her, let go of the wheel and jumped.

She landed on moss and long, tufted grass that was sodden from the rain but at least broke her fall. As she lay there gasping for breath and shaking she watched the Dennis roll over and over, sometimes falling twenty or thirty feet at a time to land with a shuddering crash before rolling on. It finally came to rest some two hundred feet below, was still for a second or two, then burst into flames. Katy stood up, feet sinking into the grass, feeling it soak through her overalls up to her knees. She watched the Dennis burn for a time then turned to look for the other lorry. It was nowhere to be seen. The road was empty.

Katy climbed up to the road, stood on its edge and looked left and right. She could see some two or three hundred yards through the mist and rain and there was no lorry. She could not believe that the driver had not seen the Dennis; they had passed within feet of each other and she remembered his face, eyes staring into hers. His obvious fear gave her the answer. He had seen her go over the edge, recognised he was to blame and fled from the scene. Katy shook her head in rage and started to walk back to the nearest village. A half-hour later she reported the accident to the village policeman and an hour after that she was on a bus meandering back to Sunderland.

Two weeks later, no one else had admitted being involved in the crash and the police could find no evidence to point to anyone. Katy sat at the kitchen table in the evening when Beatrice was in bed and asleep, and faced the facts. She had tried desperately hard to keep her promise to Matt and the business in being, but the loss of all the men and all but one of the lorries, petrol shortages and cost of maintenance — Matt was not there to service and repair the Dennis — all had whittled away the firm's money. And then there was Fleur's allowance.

The Dennis had been purchased six years before and was second-hand then. The insurance for it would not buy another lorry worth running, even if she could find one in wartime. Without the Dennis there was no business. But for Matt's insistence on buying the freehold of the yard, flat and office, there would be nothing left to show for seven years of work and the one hundred and fifty pounds she had originally invested in the firm. A small amount of capital would remain after all outstanding bills had been paid, about fifty pounds, but she would not touch that. She and Matt would share that; he had to have something to come back to.

It was not the first time she had sat and pondered thus but she was reluctant to make the final decision. Matt had asked, 'Will you be able to carry on?' And Katy had answered, 'We'll cope.' Now she felt she had failed him, though God knew she had tried.

She heard the first tap at the door of the office below but did not run to open it, wondering who it might be at that time of night. The second knock was firmer and now she rose from her chair, ran down the stairs and looked out of the office window. She could see the man only by the diffused light from the room upstairs and just in profile but she knew him and opened the door.

Charles Ashleigh said, 'Hello, Katy.'

20

Charles Ashleigh was older, of course, still tall and lean but heavier in the shoulders. He raised a hand to his cap in salute and there were the three gold rings of a commander on his cuff and a block of medal ribbons on his broad chest made a subdued splash of colour against the navy blue of his jacket. He said, 'Hello, Katy.'

'Hello.' It came out shakily, incredulous, and she held on to the doorpost for support. After all these years — *Charles Ashleigh*! Katy realised she was staring at him, a hand to her open mouth. 'I'm sorry. Will you come in?'

Upstairs in the kitchen she sat him in the other armchair, the one she always thought of as Matt's chair. Now, in the gaslight, she could see that Charles was bronzed, burned by the sun, and there were streaks of silver in his butter-coloured hair. She knew he was only thirty-one or two but also that the war aged men — and women for that matter. But, for all that, he was a handsome — she corrected herself — *very* handsome man.

He looked at her across the fire and asked, 'Am I welcome?'

Katy wondered why he asked. 'Of course you are.' And explained, 'I know it was your father's idea to have you sent to China and I'm sure your

291

mother drove him to it.' And when he stared she told him the whole story, how she had seen the letter from his father's friend in the Admiralty, how she had left Ashleigh's and eventually Newcastle.

Charles sighed, 'I concluded something like that had happened, but not for a very long time. I wrote from China, again and again, but you never replied.'

'I had no letter, ever.' Katy thought a moment, then asked, 'You wrote to the address where I was living when you left, I suppose?' And when he nodded she said, 'And as I've told you, I moved — and I think my landlady would not forward your letters. I expect she burned them.' She did not say that Mrs Connelly regarded her as a harlot because of her affair with Charles.

He said, 'I guessed as much. When I came home from China I had three months' leave before joining my next ship in the Med. I spent the time looking for you. I even put an advertisement in the personal columns of the papers but there was no reply. Then mother persuaded father to rent a house in London for the Season and you know what goes on there.'

Katy contradicted him: 'No, I don't.'

He blinked at that but then said slowly, 'No, of course, you wouldn't — I'm sorry. Well, it's a marriage market. Mothers give balls for their daughters in the hope they will make a good marriage. By that they mean to a man with plenty of money and hopefully a title as well. I met my wife there.' He was meeting Katy's gaze directly. 'I hadn't seen or heard from you for six or seven years. I hadn't forgotten you, still loved you, but — Eleanor was there. She was good to me, good *for* me. I think I was good to her, and love came. Can you understand that?'

That the prolonged absence of one lover could make room for another? Katy could, only too well. 'Yes, I can understand.'

Charles said, 'She gave me two sons. She died just over a year ago.'

Katy said softly, 'Oh, Charles, I'm sorry.'

He fell silent for a minute then glanced up at the clock on the mantelpiece and rose to his feet. 'It's late. I only came because I got off the train just a half-hour ago. I should have waited, I suppose, but I couldn't. I wanted to see you now, just to be sure you were really here. I have a lot to say but not tonight. I'm staying at the Palace. Will you have dinner with me tomorrow night? I understand they have a band for dancing.' He waited, unsure.

Dinner and dancing! Katy felt like Cinderella. She wondered if she should, but then thought that she had worked and worried too long, was worrying still. 'For old times' sake? Yes, I will.'

His face broke into a smile, teeth showing white against his tan. 'I'll call for you in a cab.'

Katy was sorry to see him go, briefly to lose this excitement which had come into her life, but at least she had gained a breathing space, time to think. She thought for a long time that night because sleep was slow to come, and all through the following day. She arranged with Annie to care for Beatrice that night and worked on her wardrobe. She dressed with care in the lilac silk

293

evening gown she had bought in the long ago days of peace. When she was ready, Beatrice stared open-mouthed and said, 'Ooh! You're beautiful!'

Annie agreed, 'She's right. And you enjoy yourself with this old friend of yours. You've earned it.'

Katy found herself blushing and turned away.

Charles arrived on time and handed her into the horse-drawn cab — there were few motor taxis now because of the petrol restrictions. He escorted her into the restaurant of the Palace and across the dance floor to one of the best tables and Katy could see heads turning as she passed, the eyes of the men on her.

Charles said as they were seated, 'You've caused something of a sensation.'

Katy laughed, 'More likely because of you, the grand naval officer. You have gone up in the world.'

He shrugged, 'I'm expecting my captaincy soon, assured of it, in fact. The war makes for rapid promotion and I've been very lucky. But when it's over I'll leave the Navy. Both my parents are dead. Tomlinson — you'll remember him?' Katy did remember the young manager very clearly, and nodded. Charles went on, 'I'm sorry to say he was killed early in the war.'

Katy whispered, 'Oh! What a shame! He had a young wife and children.'

'Yes,' Charles agreed. 'He was a good man in every way. We're paying them a pension, of course, but it can't make up for his loss.'

They were both silent for a moment, their

thoughts in the past, then Charles stirred and continued, 'Now Ashleigh's is being run by an older man. He's a very good manager making a great deal of money for us, but he's coming up to retirement. I feel I should take over, now my father has gone.'

Katy agreed. 'I think you would do it very well.' She meant it, was sure Charles would run the business competently, but she said it absently. Louise was never far from her thoughts, though she tried not to worry at a situation she could not affect, and now she wondered if she should tell Charles about the kidnapping of her daughter. The temptation was there, to pour out her tale of grief and misery, but then she decided it was not his problem, it would not be fair to him.

And now Charles said, 'I think I'm being too serious.' He cocked his head on one side, listening. Then he smiled at Katy, 'This is a foxtrot, isn't it? Would you like to dance it?'

Katy would, and stepped up and into is arms. He danced well though stiffly at first, but after a minute he shifted his hold on her and drew her close. Katy found that Annie's verdict when teaching her had been correct; she was a natural dancer. As they circled the floor, Katy saw Dawkins, with his patent leather hair, sitting in the band and playing his clarinet. He recognised her, took the instrument out of his mouth and gaped at her. Katy stared back and after a moment his eyes fell. She told herself to forget him and Fleur and found it easy.

Back at their table again, Katy asked one of

the questions which had come out of her thinking: 'How *did* you find me?'

Charles grinned, more at ease now. 'I employed a detective agency. They found your father. I didn't know anything about him, of course.'

'And he told them where I was?' Katy said drily, 'He wasn't so helpful as a rule.'

Charles looked embarrassed. 'I understand they paid for the information.'

'That sounds like him.' Katy hoped the money had done her father some good but doubted it. Also that Ursula had never mentioned this, so Barney Merrick had pocketed the money and told no one.

They dined and danced, talked and laughed. It was late in the evening when Charles became serious and said, 'I should never have let them part us but I just didn't know what was going on. I should have told them to keep out of my life, left the Navy and made a life for us elsewhere, maybe in Africa.'

Katy touched his hand, 'It wasn't your fault any more than it was mine. Don't blame yourself. You were young.'

'So were you. All through the years I kept thinking how young you were and how I'd failed you.'

'You didn't fail me. We both suffered from the way of the world.' Katy stood up: 'Now, shall we dance this one?' And this time she held him close, trying to console him in his sorrow and for the lost years of his grieving. He held tight to her and she knew he could feel her body against his through the thinness of her dress.

They drifted through the rest of the evening on a tide of remembered love. At one point Katy saw Fleur seated at a table with a party of young officers. She stared at Katy and Charles with a mixture of rage and disbelief; they were far and away the most handsome couple in the room. Katy looked through her and forgot her, only noticed some time later that she had gone. Fleur had stormed home, jealous.

Charles escorted Katy back to the flat, handing her into the cab. In its sheltering darkness, as the horse clip-clopped along, the good man at her side put his arm around her and she rested against him. But when he lowered his head to kiss her she whispered, 'No, Charles, please.' Because she knew what was coming next and there would be an awful temptation. She would be able to live in the Ashleighs' big house, with his money to buy her whatever she wanted, and servants at her beck and call. He would do everything he could to make her happy and it would be a marvellous life.

The cab wheeled into the yard and halted outside the flat. Charles handed her down and walked her to her door. He stopped there with a hand on her arm and looked down into her face. He said, 'I know you're not married. The detective agency told me that. If you had been married then I wouldn't have come here. But there is someone else, isn't there?'

'No.' Because she thought there wasn't. She would be wishing for the moon if she hoped . . .

Charles nodded slowly. 'I didn't know what I

had all those years ago. And I haven't got you now. There's someone else.'

With him looking into her eyes Katy faced it and admitted it to herself. She said, 'Yes, there is.' She had known that long ago, when Fleur had come upon her and Matt laughing in the garage in those days before the war, three years ago. In all that time she had told no one, never put it into words, kept that secret locked in her breast. Until now. 'I'm sorry, Charles.'

He said heavily, 'And this is goodbye, then.'

'Yes.' She would not lead him on to no purpose.

'I'll never forget you, Katy.'

He started to turn away but now she reached up to take his head in her hands, pull it down and kiss him on the lips. 'I won't forget you, Charles.'

He climbed into the cab then and Katy watched him driven out of the yard and out of her life. She mounted the stairs to the flat and found a sleepy Annie sitting by the fire. Katy asked, 'Will you take on Beatrice, Annie, please? I have to go away.'

21

The drivers were told when a hospital train loaded with wounded was due to come in from Flanders. This was the fourth such train Katy had attended with her ambulance on this tour, which had started in the evening. Now it was close to morning and she had been on duty for nearly ten hours. She was both hungry and thirsty, but when the shattered men arrived they had to be cared for. She was a member of the Women's Legion and attached to the London Ambulance Column.

Katy drove the Ford up from the Embankment, through the tunnel, and emerged into Charing Cross Station. There she braked behind another ambulance, a queue of them stretching ahead of her onto the platform. They were seen as silhouettes in the half-dark of the blackout now enforced because of the air raids on the city. A pall of smoke smelling of soot hung around her, and mixed with that the sickly sweet, acrid stench of poison gas and gangrene; the hospital train had arrived. She could see it now, as the line of vehicles edged forward, the panting locomotive at its head breathing steam, a red cross painted on the side of each carriage. Katy got down from the cab for a moment to stretch her legs as the queue was briefly halted. She

299

wore her Army pattern greatcoat over her neat brown jacket and skirt, the soft brown felt hat tipped slightly rakishly on one side. She breathed in the tainted air and shuddered in anticipation, bracing herself. This was her life now.

Katy had walked to the Labour Exchange and joined the Women's Legion the day after she parted from Charles Ashleigh. She yearned for Louise but could not go to Germany to search for her until peace came, and that seemed far distant in 1917. She had signed on for a year or the duration of the war. Annie had agreed, needed no persuasion, to care for Beatrice but Katy had found it hard to part from them when the time came. She had written to Matt, telling him how the business had finished — and why. She had wished him well and told him she was going where women were needed to drive, but she did not know where. She sent it to the only address she had, the one he had sent her when he went abroad early in 1915. She could not ask Fleur for his more recent address, knew she would receive a poisonous tirade of accusations — and no address. Katy did not know how long the letter would take to reach Matt. She had never heard from him. She did write to Fleur, a short note in businesslike terms, advising her that Ballard's had ceased trading but there was money in the firm's account to pay her allowance up to the end of February, when it would finish.

The line of ambulances was moving again and Katy jumped up into the cab of the Ford to keep her place in it. She drove out onto the platform and halted. A crocodile of men bearing stretchers was heading towards her with a nurse in the lead. Katy saw it was Sybil Northcote, a Fany — First Aid Nursing Yeomanry. She trotted up to Katy, a small, slight girl, her fluffy blonde hair escaping from her cap, her grey eyes wide with nervousness. Sybil had travelled with Katy several times before, and once already this day. She said, 'I say, Katy, I've got one serious chap and I have to come with you, but I have two other ambulances to watch out for.'

Katy got down from the Ford: 'So we'll bring up the rear.' That was standard procedure when one nurse had to tend the inmates of more than one ambulance: she would ride in the last with the most seriously injured. If any of the other wounded needed her assistance their ambulance stopped and waited until she came up.

Sybil said, 'Oh, thanks.' Then with a quick, relieved smile, 'I like being with you.' She was barely nineteen, a veteran with a year's service, but glad of the company of the older Katy.

'Here y'are, miss.' That came from the first stretcher bearers with their burden. There were four bunks in each ambulance and the stretchers slid into them on rollers. The bunks were filled with rapid efficiency. As the bearers did their work, Sybil had a moment to spare to whisper, 'They're all from field hospitals. We're going to be busy.' The field hospitals were always emptied before an attack. When the attack went in, the cases on the ambulance trains were not only from field or base hospitals. Many of the wounded came straight from the battlefield, still in their muddied and blood-soaked clothing. Katy had that hollow feeling inside again. At times like these she pictured Matt on a stretcher like these men. Or worse.

The bunks were full and so were the other two ambulances in their party. Sybil said, 'The Commandant said this was the last train. We're stood down after this run.' And then: 'I'm starving. And there won't be anything at my hostel at this time of night.' Nor would there be at Katy's. Worse still, because of food shortages at this stage of the war, they would not find a café able to serve them anything but a slice of toast. Sybil climbed into the back of Katy's Ford and perched on the little seat behind the driver, but by the head of the seriously injured soldier and looking out of the rear. The backs of the ambulances were all open, draughty and chill. Katy checked that the stretchers were lashed in so that they could not slide out, then she cranked the Ford and drove out of the station, following the other two. And now, prompted by her fear for Matt, she feared for Louise. Was her daughter starving in Germany?

As the Ford wound through the streets of London she thought about them, and Annie and Beatrice. Katy had shut up the flat and the office and put the key in its hiding place between door and step. She had padlocked the gates of the yard and given the key to Annie to keep. Beatrice had cried when Katy had left, Annie had sniffed and wiped her eyes and Katy herself had done her weeping in the train carrying her south. She wrote once a week at least and sent money for

Beatrice's keep. Katy still had some money in the bank, what was left of her share of the profits when the firm ceased trading. Matt's share — and some of Katy's — had gone to Fleur. But that little sum of money, now in a bank in London, was sometimes increased by a few shillings, but never drawn. That was Katy's last, fragile bulwark against penury. The money sent to Beatrice came out of Katy's pay of forty-five shillings a week.

Katy braked the Ford at the doors of the hospital in Hampstead just before dawn. She was aware of her hunger again. Was Louise going hungry at this moment? The stretcher bearers were waiting for them and came hurrying out. Katy went round to the rear of the Ford and found Sybil still inside, holding the hand of the seriously wounded man. She held on to it awkwardly as his stretcher was eased out of the ambulance by the bearers, biting her lip. Katy saw him in the first grey light, his face drawn and ashen, eyes closed. She could just make out the label tied to him: 'MGW' — Multiple Gunshot Wounds. She knew now that was probably due to a machinegun. Another nurse came hurrying down the hospital steps to take charge of him from Sybil. She gripped his hand instead and Sybil leaned back against the side of the Ford, tears on her cheeks. Katy wrapped her arms around the girl, comforting.

The last of the stretchers had been carried into the hospital. Katy and Sybil climbed into the front of the Ford and Katy drove them back into London as the day grew. She stopped outside a building that had once been a theatre — there were billboards with faded posters each side of the entrance — but now a sign above the door said it was a canteen.

Sybil, dozing in her seat, woke and asked blearily, 'What have we stopped for?'

'Breakfast, I hope,' Katy told her. 'I found this place a few nights ago. Come on.'

They got down and entered the building. The stage was lit and the canteen was set up there like a café. The floor between door and canteen, where once there had been rows of seats, lay in darkness and was covered by sleeping soldiers. Katy and Sybil picked their way through them and were served with poached egg on toast and strong tea by a girl no older than Sybil. As they ate, seated at a trestle table, the sleeping men were behind them and out of sight. But with the little meal over they rose and turned to leave. The soldiers still lay in their ragged rows, unmoving, and Sybil shivered and whispered, 'They look like corpses.'

Katy nodded agreement, and now the awful thought came: Did Matt lie thus, dead on some distant field? She tried to banish the picture from her mind but failed. She crawled into her narrow bed in the hostel but lay awake for a long time despite her weariness. When she finally slept it was to dream of Matt lying dead, Louise crying for bread and her father, Howard Ross, laughing madly.

* * *

Ivor Spargo sidled into the public house on Newcastle's dockside. He paused just inside the door, eyes flicking over the crowd of drinkers. When he saw no police, military or civil, he moved in further, bought a pint of beer and sat down at a small round table with a marble top. The old suit he wore, with a scarf knotted around his neck, was in tune with the workmen and seamen around him. He had not shaved for over a month but he had trimmed the resultant beard. The former thin moustache was now a ragged, drooping walrus.

He sat at the table for a half-hour before the man he waited for came in. He looked more prosperous than the others, with a collar and tie, and smiled about him. Ivor waited until the newcomer had bought a drink and settled at a table, then crossed the room to join him. Ivor said, 'Any luck, Mac?'

The other man was a steward on a merchant ship, with a profitable sideline in smuggling contraband — or people. He shrugged, then said in a thick Glaswegian accent, 'It depends. I've found a berth for you.'

Ivor said eagerly, 'Well done!'

'He wants fifty quid.' Mac sipped at his beer.

'Fifty — ' Ivor gaped at him. 'I can't pay *that*! I can't pay *half* that! I've already given you five quid!'

Mac pointed out, 'That was for me finding you a berth. I've done that.'

'You — !' Ivor stifled the imprecation; he dared not antagonise Mac because the Scot could be his salvation. With Mac's cold eye on him he pleaded, 'Where am I going to get fifty quid?'

Mac shrugged, 'That's none of my business. But if you want a passage, unofficial-like, on a ship to Holland, that's what it will cost ye.'

Ivor stared ahead of him, fuming inside — and frightened too. He was no stranger to fear now. He had run from home to avoid conscription into the Army and now knew he would be hunted as a deserter. He believed his only hope was to escape to neutral Holland and hide himself there. He could not go home for money because he would not find any there. He knew who to blame for that . . .

He saw the man walk in off the street, thought he was familiar — and then remembered. This man was tall, blond and well-dressed in a good suit. He carried a Homburg hat and kid gloves in one hand, leaned on the bar and called for a whisky. Ivor stood up and Mac asked, 'What about it, then?'

Ivor glanced at him and asked, 'Who's that just come in?' Mac warned, 'You keep clear of him if you don't want to be cut up.' He went on to answer Ivor's questions.

At the end Ivor grinned at him, 'I know where to get the money. How long have I got?'

'How the hell should I know?' Mac told him curtly. 'This isn't bloody P and O. There are convoys running across to Holland all the time but you never know whether some feller will slip you aboard on the quiet. You just get the money and I'll fix the rest.'

Ivor made for the door. The blond man still

leaned on the bar and sipped at his whisky. Ivor whispered to himself, 'And I'll pay you off as well.'

When Annie Scanlon answered the knock on her door an hour or two later she did not recognise Ivor Spargo. She had heard about him from Katy but never met him. She eyed the bearded, moustachioed stranger in his shabby, old clothes and asked, 'Aye?'

Ivor smiled, 'I saw the notice on the gate of the yard. It said Mrs Scanlon had the keys and gave this address.'

Annie repeated cautiously, 'Aye? What do you want with them?'

Ivor shook his head, 'I don't. I was looking for Katy Merrick. I'm a friend of hers, of the family, like — Freddie Tait. My ship has docked here and I thought it would be a chance to see her again after all these years.'

'Freddie Tait?' Annie frowned. 'She never mentioned that name to me.'

Ivor shrugged carelessly, 'That's not surprising. I've not seen her in years. I only got the address of the yard from her father before the war — Barney, that is. Though he wasn't good to her as I remember.'

That was a name Annie recognised, and now she recalled the North Country demands of hospitality and opened the door wide. 'You'd better come in and have a cup o' tea.' She sat Ivor down in an armchair by the fire and put the kettle on the glowing coals to boil. 'Won't be long.' Then she warned Ivor, 'I can't give you her address without asking her, but I'll write to her and tell her how she can get in touch with you. How about that?'

Ivor said enthusiastically, 'That'll be fine, Missus. Very kind o' you.' And thought, Bloody suspicious old cow!

Annie beamed at him, 'Right y'are, then. I'll make us both a cup o' tea in a minute. I've just got to see to the dinner.' And as she went out to the scullery, where she prepared her vegetables: 'I've got a bairn coming in to be fed in half-an-hour . . . ' She disappeared from his sight but chattered on. Ivor did not listen. He had spotted the sheaf of envelopes behind the clock on the mantelpiece. With one eye on the door to the scullery he stood up and plucked out the letters. He did not recognise the hand but did not need to, nor did he need to look into the envelopes. Katy had written her name, and the address of the hostel where she was living, on the back of each envelope, as was common at the time. He read it, then stuffed the letters back in their place and was in his seat when Annie returned.

She made the tea and as they drank it Ivor gave her a fictional address for Katy to write to, and an equally fictitious account of his doings since the start of the war. But he left as soon as he could, refusing Annie's offer of: 'I can give you a bite o' dinner.'

'No, thanks. I've got a train to catch. But give Katy my best and tell her I'd love to hear from her after all these years.' He made his escape and got a bus out to the Great North Road. He dared not take a train because there were

Military Police on all the main line railway stations. However, he was lucky and just north of Durham he was picked up by a lorry travelling south. That was the first of a succession of lifts. He spent some time sitting at the roadside and that night he stayed in the house of an old woman who did bed and breakfast. He arrived in London close to midnight of the following day.

And at that same time Annie answered another heavy knock at her front door and Matt Ballard said, 'Hello, Annie. I'm looking for Katy.'

22

Matt was very brown, thinner in the face and harder. His khaki uniform was worn but fitted him as if he had been poured into it, the knack of the veteran soldier. Annie exclaimed, 'There's a surprise! You're home on leave?'

He said grimly, 'Aye. I've got just one week before I go to France. It's my first home leave since December 1914, but it seems they are short of Service Corps non-coms out there.' But then he seemed to dismiss that as of no importance. Annie could sense the pent up anger when he said, 'What the hell is going on? I sent a telegram to Fleur, telling her I was coming home. She didn't meet me at the station and when I got to the house the maid there told me 'Madam' was out at some dance and she didn't know where. I came to the yard and it's locked and there's a notice saying the key is with you. Where's Katy?'

'In London. She wrote to you.' Then Annie remembered there was a blackout and she was standing with the door wide open, casting light into the street. 'But come in, come in!' And when she had sat him in the chair used by Ivor she asked, 'Didn't you get her letter? She wrote to you, telling you all that had happened.'

310

Matt shook his head. 'I got no letter.' He thought a moment, then: 'I think the only address she had was the one I sent when I first went abroad. I've moved about a lot since then: Egypt, then Gallipoli, East Africa, Mesopotamia, back to Egypt. That letter could be anywhere.' But in fact it lay on the seabed in the Mediterranean, inside the ship which had carried it, torpedoed by a U-boat.

Annie handed him a cup of tea. 'Can I get you something to eat? A sandwich, or I could fry — '

Matt waved away the offer. 'No, but thanks for the tea. I'm not hungry.' He looked at her and asked, 'So what happened, Annie? I went away thinking that if anyone could keep that business going it was Katy.'

'And you were right!' Annie insisted. She sat down opposite him. 'Now, I don't know all the ins and outs, mind, but . . . ' And she told him how the petrol restrictions had cut down the time the single lorry could work, how Katy could only get a boy to help her and he had gone into the Navy, and then the crash.

When she had finished, Matt sat in silence for a while, but then said reluctantly, 'I would have thought there would have been some capital left to tide the business over.'

Annie stiffened in her chair. 'Katy wasn't dipping her fingers in the till, I'll swear to that.'

Matt shook his head. 'That's not what I was thinking, but there's something that doesn't add up.'

Annie said, 'Well, I told you I didn't know everything. But the final accounts and the books

311

are still in the office. Do you want the key to the gate?'

'Yes. I'll go there tomorrow. Do you have an address for Katy?' Matt stood up.

Annie gave him Katy's address and the key to the yard then saw him to the door. Just before she let him out she said, 'I had another friend of hers come here today looking for her: Freddie Tait.'

Matt said absently, his thoughts elsewhere, 'I don't recall the name.' He was facing up to the knowledge that the business built up by Katy and himself was no more.

Annie explained, 'He knew her — and her father — in Wallsend. I've got his address and I'm sending it to her.' Then she added, 'Not that he stands much chance with her. He didn't look Katy's type at all.' Then reprovingly, 'Pity you married that Fleur. I always thought — '

Matt broke in on her: 'But I did. Good night, Annie.'

Annie's lips tightened at the snub but she remembered where he had come from and what he was going back to: the killing ground of Flanders. So she said, 'Good night, bonny lad. Come and see me again.'

Matt went back to his house and told the sleepy maid to go to bed. He sat up, waiting for his wife to return. Fleur came back in the early hours of the morning. She was alone in the motor taxi which set her down outside the house, and modestly attired in a high-collared, dull grey dress. Matt opened the door to her and she greeted him brightly, 'Hello, darling! Sorry I

312

couldn't come to meet you but this dance was arranged absolutely weeks ago and you can't disappoint people, can you? And really I was working — it was for a war charity, you know — that's why I wore this dreary old thing.' She flapped the skirt of the grey dress. 'I'm saving my best clothes because I don't know when I'll get any more, the price of things these days.' In fact she had changed in Dawkins' room at the Palace Hotel before she came home.

Matt answered, 'You disappointed me.'

Fleur's smile vanished and she pouted as she pulled off her silk gloves then turned for him to catch her coat as she slipped it from her shoulders. 'I hope you aren't going to sulk. It won't make this war any better for you if I stay home all miserable. I can only go out on these charity dos because I don't need an escort; there are a lot of women like myself whose husbands are away and we stick together.' Then she added darkly, 'Mind, there are some . . . '

She left it there, suggestively, and went on, 'I'm not that sort but I need to have a *little* pleasure. It's very scarce these days. Like money. I hate to talk about it but I must. That Merrick woman simply refused at first to increase my allowance. I soon showed her the error of her ways!'

Matt demanded, incredulous, 'She increased it?'

'Of course she did!' Fleur tossed her head. 'But then she had the insolence to write to me — I got the letter from her months ago — saying it would *stop* in March! I wrote back, of course, and told her I would see a lawyer if she interfered like that.' Fleur smirked with triumph for a moment. 'And my allowance has been paid without any bother.' Now she pouted again. 'But I went to see the manager at the bank and he said the business *had* shut down and my allowance *would* finish at the end of the month. I wrote to you, of course, because that's absolute *nonsense* and I suppose that's why you're here. You must do something about it, darling, transfer some cash into the account or something.' Fleur gave him a quick smile, gone as soon as it appeared, and got no reply. This was not the old adoring Matt. He watched her coldly, his face set. She chattered on uneasily, 'I can't understand why you left the handling of the money to her. It's so *humiliating* for me to have to go to her for every penny. If you'd left the firm's money in my hands I could have given her what she actually needed and kept a tighter hand on the purse strings. I know you think she's marvellous.' That was accompanied by a sneer. She went on, 'But I believe she's not to be trusted.'

Matt had listened with bewilderment and rising anger. Now he broke in: 'I didn't get your letter about the allowance because I've been in a transit camp or on a troopship for the past six weeks. They didn't fetch me home to sort out your financial affairs but because they want me in France at the double. And you've been talking bloody rubbish!'

Fleur stared at him open-mouthed. '*Oh!* How can you speak to me like that!'

'I'll go down to the office tomorrow and find out what's been going on.' Then, as Fleur gaped at him, he went on, 'Katy Merrick couldn't increase your allowance without my permission and you didn't ask for it. You didn't write to me about anything.' Matt threw her coat onto the hallstand. 'The capital left in the firm's account was for the firm. Katy was supposed to use it for the firm. You say she gave you more money?'

'Of course she did! I had to have it! But she made me practically *beg* for it!' She flounced past him and began to climb the stairs. Her boldness was an act. She was frightened, knew Matt was in a towering rage and his silence now only made it worse. She wanted to sleep alone and tried to summon up the courage to say so. It was not needed.

Matt said, 'I'll sleep in the spare room.'

Fleur tossed her head, 'Suit yourself.'

It did suit him. His desire for her was dead.

The next day he opened the gates of the yard with the key given to him by Annie. There was one letter in the post-box and he recognised Fleur's writing. It was her letter to Katy, threatening legal action if her allowance from the firm was not continued. He read it and winced at the abuse it contained, then crumpled it into a ball.

He found the office key hidden in the crack between doorstep and door and let himself in: The air was stuffy so he opened the window, then dusted off the chair with his handkerchief and sat down at the desk. The books, accounts and bank statements were in a drawer and he set them out on the desk and began to read.

As the morning wore on the picture steadily fell into shape like the pieces of a jigsaw puzzle. He saw how Katy had worked to keep the business going and how it had failed. He also saw where the money had gone. He sat with his head in his hands. Loyalty and duty had always been the keystones of his life. He had married Fleur out of love but now the love was gone. The duty remained but that was all.

He looked up and remembered Katy sitting at this desk, or out there, crossing the yard, slender and graceful and laughing. He sighed and wrote her a formal little note asking if he could see her when passing through London on his way back to his regiment. He posted it on the way back to his house.

Arrived there, he sought Fleur and the maid answered him, 'Madam is still in bed, sir.'

Matt asked, 'How much does — madam — pay you?'

'Seven shillings a week, sir.'

'Pack your belongings and go home. There's a week's notice and a bit besides.' He gave her ten shillings.

'Ooh! Thank you, sir.' This was not the girl Katy had seen, and there had been others filling the post of maid since then. But this one, like her predecessors, had had enough of Fleur and Dawkins and was working her notice. A friend of hers worked in a factory for a pound a week and had told her there was a job for her if she wanted it.

Five minutes later, Matt walked into Fleur's

room without knocking. She started up in bed, her nightdress slipping off one shoulder, and asked querulously, 'What d'you mean by barging in here — '

'I'm your husband and we need to talk.' Matt stood over her. 'There are going to be some changes. For a start, I've just paid off the maid and the cook.'

'*What!*' Fleur hitched at the strap of the nightdress and threw off the covers to get out of bed. 'What the *hell* do you think you're doing?'

'I went down to the yard this morning.' Something in his tone made Fleur shut her mouth and as he took a pace towards her she retreated. He continued, 'I read through the accounts of the business, the books and bank statements. They can't lie and they tell a different story from the one you told me last night. You've milked that business, *my* business, dry. I left you an adequate allowance on top of the allowance from my Army pay and you've frittered it all away and demanded more. God knows what you spent it on but I can guess and anyway, it's gone. There'll be no more money from the yard.'

Fleur gaped at him, 'What do you mean — gone? The yard is still there. Isn't it?'

Matt snapped impatiently, 'Of course it is! But you wouldn't know because you only went there when it suited you. The business closed down nearly six months ago. It hasn't made a penny since then.'

Fleur attempted to shift the blame. 'That little bitch, Katy! She's had the money!'

Matt shook his head contemptuously. 'No, she hasn't. It's clear where the money went. Katy authorised the bank to increase your allowance out of *her* share of the firm, so long as it lasted. She used the firm's capital to pay your damned allowance! Now it's finished. You'll manage on what I send you from my Army pay, and if you want more you'll have to find work.'

Fleur tried to salvage the situation. She smiled up at him tremulously and gave a twitch of the shoulders so that the strap slipped again and showed one breast. She stepped close to him and stroked his face. 'You poor darling. No wonder you're upset.' Her mind was racing frantically, trying to find a way to escape this threat to the life she lived, and she remembered: 'But you still have the yard. You bought the freehold of that just before we married. Weren't you wise! That must be worth a lot of money.'

'I'm not selling.' Matt was definite. 'For one thing, it's all I have left to come home to if I survive this war. For another, I can't. Katy Merrick put up some of the money for that purchase. She is part owner and I can't sell without her agreement.' Now he brushed her hand away. 'You're my wife and I'll honour that obligation. While you are faithful to me, I will keep my share of the bargain. I won't let you starve, but that's all.' He pushed her aside so she fell across the bed and he strode out of the room. Her wailing followed him down the stairs. It was partly contrived, a last effort to weaken his resolve, but also had an edge of real sorrow. She had married to secure her financial future and now that was lost.

The next days dragged for both of them. Fleur sat about the house, sulking and silent. As she failed to cook, Matt made meals for himself. He spent most of each day walking, examining his life. His present existence he regarded as like being in prison. It seemed the rest of his life would be spent in that prison.

Katy found the letters waiting for her on the table in the hall of the hostel, spartan and uncarpeted, when she came in from a day spent driving her ambulance. The first was from Annie and told her of the visits of Freddie Tait and Matt. Katy did not recall anyone by the name of Freddie Tait from her childhood in Wallsend. She set that one aside, deciding to do nothing about it for the time being. She thought she might write to her sister, Ursula, to ask if she knew this Freddie Tait.

The second letter was from Matt. Her heart thumped when she recognised the writing on the envelope. She took it to her little hutch of a room and sat on the bed to read. Matt asked in a formal, brief note, if she could meet him. Katy wondered if she should think hard about this because the man she loved was already married, but her instinct would not let her. She wrote back to him: 'I am glad you are safe and well. I would like to meet you as you pass through London but my hours of duty are irregular. I am driving most days but also often through the night. If you come here, there is a room where we can talk, or where you could wait for me to come off duty, if this would be convenient.'

Matt opened the letter on the fourth morning of his leave. He read it, put it carefully away in his breast pocket with his Army pay book then packed his kit. Fleur was still in bed when he walked into her room. He told her, 'I'm going to London then back to the regiment. Remember what I told you.' When she did not answer but lay with her head turned away, he snapped, 'Did you hear me?'

Fleur muttered an answering, 'Yes', hating him but fearing him too. She need not have done because he would never have struck her.

That was all their parting and he turned on his heel and left her.

Fleur listened to the tramping of his boots on the stairs, then the slam of the front door. She threw back the covers and swung her legs out of bed. She had wasted enough time.

She found Harry Dawkins at the Palace Hotel and just about to start a rehearsal. He was in his shirtsleeves and had not shaved but his patent leather hair was smooth and glossy with oil. He was not in the best of tempers and greeted Fleur moodily: 'What the hell are you doing out of bed this early? I'm only here 'cause I'm working.'

Fleur said breathlessly, 'I came to tell you he's gone back. You can move in again.'

Dawkins scrubbed at his stubble with one hand. 'Well, great, only I've had enough of this country. The blackout, the grub — what there is of it — I can't take any more. So I'm going home. My old man owns a restaurant. I'll stay with him and maybe start my own band. One thing's for sure, I'm getting the hell out of this place. This guy — ' and he jerked his head to indicate the bandleader up on the stage' — he doesn't like the way I behave. So I'm off to Liverpool tomorrow to book a passage.'

The bandleader called impatiently, 'Come on, Harry, we have to make a start!'

'OK, OK! I'm coming!' Dawkins turned back to Fleur for a moment, 'Stick around and we'll have a drink later — or something.' He winked and made for the stage. Fleur stared after him, wondering . . .

The train pounding south towards London was crowded with sailors and soldiers, going on leave or returning from it. Matt stood in the corridor as far as York but a lot of the men got out there to change trains and he squeezed into a seat in the corner of a compartment. But all the time he was thinking of Katy and Fleur.

Katy's thoughts were of another man.

23

In the darkness the bare branches of the trees
waved above Katy's head like the arms of giants.
The night sky was overcast and dark, with only
an occasional star glimpsed in a rift between
racing clouds. The trees were black with rain and
stood like soldiers on either side of the street
where the hostel lay. Katy had written to Matt
only the day before. Now she was returning to
the hostel after a long day spent at the wheel of
her ambulance. The collar of her greatcoat was
turned up against the wind and rain and she felt
her feet cold and wet in her shoes as she
splashed through puddles she could not see. She
had a torch in her pocket but because of the
blackout that could only be used in emergencies.
The hostel loomed ahead of her, a large old
house requisitioned for the duration of the war, a
huge silhouetted block without a light, also
because of the blackout. She was close to the
entrance when a shadow moved under one of the
trees and a man said in a hoarse whisper, 'Hullo,
Katy! Remember me?'

She shrank away, immediately wary, not
recognising the voice. 'Who is it?'

There was the scrape of a match and as it
spurted flame she glimpsed a bearded face and
eyes gleaming in dark sockets. He said, 'Don't

say you've forgotten me, Ivor Spargo.'

She recognised him now and demanded, 'How did you find me here?' But her voice shook.

Ivor heard it and grinned. 'I went to see your friend, Annie.'

Katy denied him: 'That's a lie! Annie wouldn't tell anybody!'

Ivor agreed, 'No more she would, but I spun her a tale I was an old friend of yours. She let me in, then when her back was turned I got your address from a letter of yours that was stuck up on the mantelpiece. It was as easy as that.'

Katy thought bitterly, Freddie Tait. She said with contempt, 'So you tricked an old woman. You won't trick me into anything so you've wasted your time coming here.' But she was having difficulty keeping the tremor out of her voice. She was alone with him in the darkness.

Ivor laughed harshly. 'I've come to pay my debts, Katy.'

She answered him, 'I'm not frightened of you.' But she fumbled for the torch to use as a weapon. 'And what debts are you talking about?'

The flame of the match had faded and died. Now she could see him only as another shadow but she could sense his hatred as he spat out, 'I owe you a hell of a lot. You got us turned out of our yard so we had to go down to Yorkshire. Ma used to curse you every day and in the end she had a stroke and that was the end of her.' Katy winced, but reminded herself that Ma Spargo had been a woman full of hatred; now it had killed her. Ivor snarled on, 'Pa went on the booze and then the war came along and the business went kaput. I was left without a bloody penny! Then they brought in conscription and put me in the Army. I wasn't starving but when they wanted to send me to Flanders I run off. Oh, I owe you, Katy Merrick!'

'Don't be damned silly,' said Katy, trying to sound braver than she felt. She had the torch in her hand and tried to edge away.

Ivor saw this and jeered, 'It's no use you running. I've got you on a string and I can haul you back when I want.' Katy heard this with unease but still edged along the wet pavement. She was on the point of making a run for the hostel when Ivor said softly, 'I can tell you something about your fancy man and your bairn.'

That stopped Katy dead, but only for a moment. She knew Ivor for a liar among other things but also knew now that he was not lying about this. He was too sure of himself. She moved back towards him as if drawn on a string as he had said. 'What do you know about Louise?

Ivor taunted her, 'That's got you toeing the line, hasn't it?'

Katy reached out and grabbed his coat, wet under her hands, and shook him: 'What is it? What do you know?'

He retreated further under the trees, dragging her with him. He was laughing softly now. 'Changed your tune, haven't you? And you want me to tell you where to find your babby? Because I can.'

'Find her?' His arm was around her but she

did not care, had to know. 'Where is she?'

'She's not in Germany — never was. She's in England.'

'I don't believe you.' But she did. 'Where in England?'

'Aha! I've given you a taste, now I'm going to have one.' He pressed his lips on hers, bruising.

Katy tore away: 'There's someone coming.' She was lying, had heard no one, but then there came the sound of hurrying footsteps. Katy said, 'I think it's the policeman on his beat.'

Ivor swore, then hissed, 'You be in Barker's Lane tomorrow night. It's down in the East End. Bring sixty quid and you'll find out where your little bairn is now. Tell anybody else and you'll never know. She'll end up working the streets.' He shoved her away, out onto the pavement, then he was gone, disappearing into the deeper darkness under the trees. Katy stood with the rain running down her face. Ivor had knocked off her felt hat and her hair hung loose.

The hurrying footsteps came up to her. She recognised another girl returning to the hostel and was greeted by her: 'Hello, Katy. Lord, you're getting soaked! Where's your hat?'

Katy answered mechanically, 'It blew off.' The other girl helped her find it by the light of the shaded torch and they walked on together. They talked about the events of the day but all the time the words drummed in Katy's head, 'She's in England. *In England!*' And: 'She'll end up working the streets.'

In the hostel she went up to her little hutch of a room, sat down on her bed and tried to think.

Some conclusions were easy. Firstly, she meant to learn what Ivor Spargo knew, cost what it may. If there was any chance of finding Louise then Katy would take the gamble. She could draw the money from the bank the next day. That was essential because Ivor would not talk without it. But suppose he was lying? She did not believe he was, but how could she make sure he did not take her money and walk out of her life?

Katy saw her commandant next day and asked for leave of absence, which was granted. She drew the money she needed from the bank and in the early evening was ready to go. She had a little time to spare before the hour she had decided to leave and sat on her bed, the tension mounting inside her. She started when someone rapped on her door, but then Dorothy, one of the girls on her floor, called, 'Katy? Are you there?'

'Yes.' And Katy opened the door.

Dorothy was plump and giggly and she giggled now: 'There's a man asking to see you, a sergeant-major in the Army Service Corps. *Nice!*'

Matt! Katy swallowed and got out, 'I'll come down.'

She picked up her coat and her bag with the money in it and ran down the stairs. A room by the front door was set aside for male visitors. Inside were a half-dozen small tables with chairs and Matt sat at one of these. He rose to his feet as Katy entered, his cap in his hand. 'Hello, Katy.'

'Hello, Matt.'

They stood for some seconds, looking at each other, seeking changes. She thought his face was thinner but he seemed bigger than she remembered as he looked down at her. He knew he had never seen anyone so lovely. It hurt.

Katy said shakily, 'We'd better sit down.' She sat opposite him, both on straight-backed chairs with the width of the table between them. Katy began the polite exchange: 'How are you?'

'Fine, fine. And you?'

'Yes. I quite like this job. I feel I'm doing something useful.'

Matt asked, 'Have you heard anything of Louise?'

She could not tell him, would not involve him in this extortion by Ivor. She shook her head.

He said, 'I'm sorry, Katy.'

She shifted away from the subject: 'How was your leave? I thought you had a few more days.'

That was the end of the well-worn, stilted phrases. Matt answered jerkily, speaking his mind: 'I have three more days. I thought I'd spend them down here. I thought we could go out together.'

Katy said gently, 'No, Matt, I don't think that would be a good idea. Nor do you. You're married and you're not the sort to play games. Neither am I.'

'No,' he agreed. 'I came to see you but not intending . . . That just — slipped out. And the leave was bloody awful, that's why I'm here.' He looked about him absently and Katy guessed he was working out what to say next. She waited for him. There were three other couples in the room, seated round tables like Matt and Katy, each with its little private world of murmured conversation.

Matt's gaze came back to Katy and he said, 'When I left the business to you I didn't know how bad things were going to be. I've seen the books and accounts so I know you've had a hell of a time. A lot of that, I think, was down to Fleur. You stripped the business for her, took money from *your* share to pay her the allowance she wanted. You must have known that was your future you were giving away. God knows how we'll start up again with the little capital we have left.' He scowled down at his hands, folded on the table before him. They were big, calloused and scarred from years of working on engines. Katy's own slender hands lay only a foot away and she could have reached out to touch him but did not. She knew that would be dangerous.

She looked up at the clock on the wall, a sideways glance that he could not see, and saw that she had to leave soon. She knew temptation but resisted it again: she would not tell Matt about Louise. He could not help and he had enough trouble of his own.

Now Matt looked up from his hands and asked, 'Why did you do it, Katy? Why give her *your* money? I wouldn't have let her have it. I'd have told her to cut her expenses down. Why did you do it?'

For love of him, of course. Katy admitted, 'I thought if I didn't let her have the money she would write to you.'

Matt said wryly, 'I think you're right there. I'm damned sure she'd have written to me for the money. That's probably the only time she would write.'

'I'm sorry, Matt.' Katy hesitated, then added, 'I couldn't do that, couldn't have you tormented that way, when you were thousands of miles from home.'

Matt sighed, 'I guessed that would be it.' He was silent for a time, staring past Katy absently, recalling the experience. His eyes returned to her and he said, 'I talked to Fleur. I told her all I'd found out and that from now on she had to live on the allowance I send her from my Army pay. I'll support her because she is my wife, so long as she is faithful to me.' He stopped there because he had caught a flicker of change in Katy's expression, gone as quickly as seen, but he seized on it: 'What is it? You know something, Katy.' His hand reached out and gripped hers. His voice rose, demanding, '*Tell me!*' It cut through the hum of conversation in the room, stilled the other voices and the girls and men turned their heads to stare.

Katy begged, 'Matt! Please! Don't make a scene here!'

He followed her glance and saw the others watching. They looked away from his glare but when he went on he lowered his voice. He was still insistent, still clamped Katy's slim fingers in his own. 'Well?'

She confessed, 'There's a man.' She was sure there had been more than one but would not say. One was bad enough. 'He was living in the house. I saw him, talked with him. The maid told me he and Fleur were living together.'

Matt said softly, 'Dear God! And I loved her. Her extravagance and moods and the way she used to try to manipulate me, I learnt about all these after we were wed but I made excuses for her, told myself she would change back to the girl I'd fallen for. But that girl never really existed. She was just a pretence. What's that saying? 'All things to all men.' That was Fleur.'

He released Katy's hands and now she reached out to hold his. 'I'm sorry, Matt.' She could have wept for him.

Matt was not going to weep. He stood up and said grimly, 'It's time to put a finish to this. Now.' He looked up at the clock. 'I can just catch the next train out of King's Cross.' He looked down at Katy, now on her feet. 'I'm sorry, Katy. This has been a rough ride for you. Thank you for all you did.'

He started for the door, long striding, and Katy pursued him. She caught up with him outside on the pavement. 'Matt! Wait! Don't go off like this!' A motor car with hooded headlights because of the blackout, a Vauxhall like that used by Matt before the war, pulled into the kerb and Matt shouted, 'Cab?'

The driver, swathed in a khaki greatcoat, responded, 'No, this is a private car.'

Katy clutched Matt's sleeve and pleaded, 'Don't get yourself into more trouble! She's done enough damage to you!'

'She won't do any more.' Matt brushed off her hand as he turned from the car and set off

330

along the pavement.

The driver of the Vauxhall was out on the pavement now and asking, 'Miss Merrick?'

'Yes.' Katy was still staring helplessly after Matt.

'This is the car you asked for, miss.'

Matt had disappeared into the darkness under the trees. Katy turned, climbed into the rear of the car and it pulled away. She was afraid for Matt but this other matter came first. She wiped the tears from her eyes and braced herself. Ivor Spargo would be waiting.

Katy left the car several streets away from Barker's Lane. This was a familiar environment for her, an area of close-built terraces of little houses down by the docks of London's river. She wound her way through the darkened streets, seeing few people, until she came to Barker's Lane. Here there were a half-dozen pubs crammed into one short, narrow thoroughfare and two little music halls besides small cafés. The pavements were thronged with people and Katy saw why Ivor had chosen this place. He could watch for her from some dark doorway to confirm she was alone, and disappear in the crowd if he needed to run.

She began to pace up and down the street, her eyes searching for Ivor in the crowd flowing past. There were no trees here and the blackout was not complete so she could make out faces at some distance. Outside one pub, halfway along the street, stood a little group of four men, arguing. They stood on the steps leading up to the door and so could see her as she passed but they did not look her way. Katy walked for a half-hour and at some point she noticed that the group had now moved to the steps of a music hall opposite the pub where they had been before. And then she saw Ivor.

He showed briefly on a corner of an alley some ten yards away, standing in the light leaked from a café as its door opened and closed. In that blink of an eye he beckoned and she turned towards him. For a moment he was seen as just a shadow as the door of the café was shut and the gloom closed in again, then he was gone. Katy followed him into the alley and hurried after his receding back. They traversed a network of streets. Every now and again she would see the pale blur of his face as he turned to confirm she was still there — and that they were not being followed. She trailed him, but cautiously and not too fast, stopping at each turning. She knew he would wait for her and she was in no hurry to walk into his trap. He would wait because he wanted the money. Katy wanted Louise.

At last Ivor turned into a dark and silent house. Katy paused at the door. The passage inside was a place of impenetrable shadows. She delayed again, calling, 'There's no light! I can't see my way!'

Ivor was impatient now: 'Aw, come on!'

Katy insisted, 'I want to see where I'm putting my feet.'

She heard the tread of his boots on the stairs, then the scrape of a match and a lamp glowed. Ivor grumbled, 'Come on up.'

Katy climbed the uncarpeted stairs. There was

a stale smell of cooking and of damp. Mouldering paper hung on the walls. Ivor held open the door at the head of the stairs and ushered her in with a mocking flourish. The oil lamp he had lit stood on the table. There was one straight-backed chair and a dishevelled bed. As Katy passed him to enter, Ivor shut the door behind her and turned the key in the lock. Katy swallowed.

Ivor demanded, 'Have you brought the money?' He held out his hand.

Katy reached into her bag and took out a wad of banknotes. Ivor snatched them and began to count. Katy said, 'There's thirty. I'll give you the other thirty when you tell me where to find Louise.'

Ivor glared at her. 'If you haven't got it I'll tell you nothing.'

Katy confirmed, 'I've got it.' Then added quickly, 'If you try to take it I'll scream the place down.'

Ivor grinned then: 'All right. A bargain's a bargain. Louise, is it? I'm told she takes after her father, white-headed. I saw him in Newcastle just a few days ago, knew him right off. The feller I was with, he told me about him — and his little blonde lass. He never went to Germany. He played some trick on you. Him and Louise have been living up there all along.'

Newcastle! Katy's face was frozen in disbelief. But then she remembered the day she had thought she had seen Louise on Tyneside but then concluded she had been mistaken. She had been right all along. Howard had booked the passages to Germany for Louise and himself, but only as a red herring. *He had not taken them up!* All this time Louise had been only ten miles away, but securely hidden as one small child in a big, sprawling city.

As these thoughts tumbled through her dazed mind she was still listening to Ivor as he spouted the poison he knew would hurt her: 'They don't call him Howard Ross, either. His name there is Ralph Norgren. He's been getting rich for years and has a big house where he keeps these girls. He lives off them but they don't ply their trade there; he sends them down to the riverside to do that so he's in the clear. Folks let him alone because he uses a knife and those lasses of his are terrified of him. The feller I talked to told me to steer clear of Norgren, said the police wanted him but could never get anyone to give evidence.'

Ivor stuffed the banknotes into a pocket and instead took out a scrap of newspaper. He held it up and Katy could see it was torn from the *Newcastle Daily Journal*. Ivor waved it. 'I wrote his address on here. That's where you'll find him — and her.' Katy could see the pencilled writing on the margin of the scrap of paper and stepped forward, reaching for it, but he snatched it back. 'Money first!'

Katy got out the second wad of notes but clutched it to her breast. 'Give me the address.'

Ivor held it out but as Katy went to take it he let it go. As it fell she stooped to snatch it out of the air, and Ivor seized the chance to whip one arm around her, the other over her mouth. His voice in her ear said, gloating, 'You'll do no screaming now.' Katy panicked for a moment because it had all gone wrong. But then rage took charge of her, outrage at the way this man had pursued her, tried to extort money from her, was keeping her from her daughter. She kicked out, caught the table and sent the oil lamp flying to fall with a splintering crash. Ivor cursed. 'You stupid bitch!' His grip on her mouth slackened slightly in that instant of blackness and Katy sank her teeth into a finger. He yelled with the pain of it and tore his hand away as the first flames licked up from the spilled oil of the broken lamp. Katy pulled one of her arms loose from his grip and her scrabbling fingers found the whistle in her bag. She put it to her lips and blew a long blast.

They both heard the boots drumming along the passage below and then on the stairs. Ivor shouted, 'You've cheated me!' He threw her aside, ran to the window and drew the curtain.

A voice outside bawled, 'There he is!'

Ivor turned back into the room and then the door burst inwards and men shouldered through it. Ivor went down under them but there was no fight in him, no chance for him. Hand torches suddenly blazed, lighting up the room. Katy saw Ivor lifted up and handcuffs snapped on his wrist. She recognised the two big men, police in plain clothes. They had been part of the group who had stood outside the pub in Barker's Lane, and later by the music hall. One of them took her arm, steadying. 'You did very well. If you hadn't delayed at every corner, then when you got to this place, we might have lost him. As it is, they'll put him away for a long time, that's certain.'

Katy was not listening, was smoothing out the scrap of newspaper carefully and reading the address pencilled on it. She took back her money when the police found it, then let them escort her downstairs and through the little crowd of curious spectators who had already gathered. She noticed that the driver of the Vauxhall standing at the kerb was the same who had met her at the hostel. But all that was seen in a daze.

The big policeman put his head into the car to say, 'My thanks for this night's work. Is there anything we can do for you?'

Katy had Louise's address tucked away in her bag and burned into her memory. 'I want to go back to the hostel to pack and then to King's Cross to catch a train. Will your driver take me?'

Seconds later she had started on her journey, in search of those she loved.

24

SUNDERLAND AND NEWCASTLE.
FEBRUARY 1918.

Katy was torn two ways, but as the night train pounded north she progressed from instinctive mother love to cold logic. She reasoned that she had waited nearly four years to reclaim Louise; she could wait another few hours. She had to set her mind at rest about Matt. She reached the bleak decision as the carriage swayed and she rocked gently between a sailor and a burly private in the Durham Light Infantry, his boots and gaiters still caked with the mud of Flanders. The men in that crowded train slept soundly, except for the private, who jerked and muttered in his sleep and sometimes shouted out and briefly wakened them all. Katy also dozed from exhaustion, but when the train ran into the station at Durham, the castle and cathedral looming in the grey dawn, she was wide awake. She had a ticket through to Newcastle but got off the express. A few minutes later she was on the slow stopping train to Sunderland.

Katy walked up to Matt's house from Sunderland Station, partly to clear her head after the night in the train, partly because she was uneasy as to what she was walking into. Sight of the house did not reassure her. No smoke rose from the chimney and the place had an abandoned look; she realised there were no curtains at the windows. Katy used the brass knocker, unpolished and green with verdigris, to bang on the front door. She heard a heavy, echoing tread in the hall and then Matt opened to her. He was in his shirtsleeves, freshly washed and shaved, still drying himself on a towel. He stopped when he saw her, the towel held up to his face, and said, 'Katy? What are you doing here?'

'I — came to see how you were.' Katy smiled weakly after she had said it. As if it was a casual call, 300 miles by train!

Matt lowered the towel and she saw he was red-eyed and his face was drawn. 'I'm fine.' That was patently a lie. He said sardonically, 'Or I will be when I get out of here.' Then he set the door wide and invited, 'Come in and I'll tell you all about it. I'd ask you to make yourself comfortable but you'd find that difficult.'

Katy entered and found the hall inside was bare. There was no hallstand, pictures or carpet. That explained Matt's echoing footsteps. She could see into the sitting-room where she had sat with Harry Dawkins and that was also stripped bare. Matt sat down on the stairs and patted the space on the tread beside him: 'Come and sit here. There's nothing else left. I slept last night on the floor under my greatcoat. There's a stale loaf and some coffee in the kitchen but that's all.' He fumbled in the breast pocket of his tunic and brought out a folded sheet of paper. 'That explains it all.'

Katy sat down beside him, smoothed out the

paper and read Fleur's cramped and ornate script. There were two pages, for the most part of abuse, but the gist of it was that she had gone to America with Harry Dawkins. His father owned a restaurant and Harry was going to have his own band.

Katy folded the letter and handed it back to Matt. 'I'm sorry, Matt. She's hurt you a lot.'

He shrugged. 'She'd have hurt me a lot more if she'd stayed with me longer. To hell with her.' He tucked the letter back in his pocket: 'That's evidence.'

Katy questioned, 'Evidence?'

'For a divorce. I don't know a damned thing about the law but I think I have grounds.' Now he looked at Katy. 'It's a certainty Fleur wouldn't have come all this way on my account. Why did you?'

Katy confessed, 'I was coming anyway. I know where Louise is.' She told him about Ivor, and Louise being in Newcastle. 'I'm on my way there but I wanted to be sure you were all right.'

Matt grinned, 'You thought I might have been charged with assault and battery on this Dawkins?'

Katy answered, pink-cheeked, 'Something like that.' But mainly she had come in case he needed comfort.

Matt said drily, 'I would have been, if he'd been here.' He stood up. 'I'll fetch my kit and we'll get started.'

Katy asked, 'We? Where?'

Matt answered, 'Newcastle. It sounds as though you have as much trouble as I did. If you're going after Louise then I'm going with you.'

Katy argued, 'Matt, you can't! You'll have overstayed your leave if you don't report back tonight. They'll treat you as a deserter!' She recalled what the policeman had said about Ivor: 'They'll put him away for a long time.'

He shrugged, 'That can't be helped.' Then grinning, 'What about you? Are you a deserter?'

'No. I told the Commandant and she gave me a week's leave. So, please, Matt, go back.'

But Matt was adamant. 'I'm coming with you.'

They drank a cup of bitter coffee and caught the train to Newcastle.

At the police station Katy talked to a Sergeant Bullock, tall, lean and greying. He sat at his desk and listened patiently to her story until she mentioned: 'Howard Ross is known here as Ralph Norgren.' At that, Bullock interrupted, 'Norgren? Just wait a minute.' He left, but a few minutes later returned to usher them into an office: 'This is Inspector Formby.'

Formby was trim in his dark blue uniform, stocky alongside Bullock but upright. A scar from a knife wound, received when he had broken up a fight in a pub, ran from his ear to his chin and gave him a sinister look that was totally misleading. He listened to Katy in his turn, then said, 'We'll need a warrant.'

An hour later he had his warrant and they were on their way. Katy and Matt shared one car with Formby, Bullock and the driver, while another car followed behind with a Sergeant

Garrett, stout and red-faced, and four constables. The cars halted short of a corner and then Formby said, 'That's our street, just around the corner. Norgren's house is halfway down. It's a long terrace so there are no side doors, just front and back. I want two men round the back. Send them off now. We'll give them a few minutes start then drive down.'

Bullock passed on the order and two constables set off. Then Formby's driver said, 'Begging your pardon, sir, but I was down here only yesterday and they've got all the road up.'

'Damn!' Formby got down and walked to the corner. It was a crisply clear day with a bright, blue sky which promised a frost come nightfall. He squinted against the glare of the low winter sun and saw the hole in the road, cutting it almost completely. A massive steam lorry was being loaded with rubble by two shovel wielding navvies. The lorry cut off what road was left so there was no way that the cars could get through. Formby cursed, turned back to the car and ordered, 'Come on, all of you! We'll have to go from here on foot.' So he and his men, followed by Katy and Matt, turned the corner and started down the street towards the house in the middle.

The street comprised two long terraces, as Formby had said, of tall, old houses that had once been lived in by professionals, doctors and solicitors and the like. They had moved out to the suburbs and now the houses were tenements for the most part. Housewives stood gossiping at their doors with their shawls wrapped around them, making the most of the winter sunshine,

341

despite the cold breeze from the sea that came with it. Children, the boys in ragged jerseys and shorts, the girls in white pinnies, swarmed back and forth across the road, playing games, or gathered about the hole in the road and the workmen, watching them curiously. Another little group stood around a barrel organ man as he wound the handle and played his *tinkle-tankle* tune: 'You Made Me Love You.' Katy's heart thumped when she saw the urchins, the little girls among them. And she gasped when she saw one little blonde-haired lass, then turned it into a sigh when she saw it was not Louise. She had an awful fear that even at this late stage something could go wrong and she would not find Louise.

In the house, Howard Ross shrugged into his expensive overcoat and stepped into the living-room. The child playing with her dolls by the fire looked up and asked, 'Can I go out to play, Daddy?'

'No, because there won't be anybody here to watch out for you.' He turned on the woman and snapped, 'I'm going to see how the other girls are getting on. I don't want you hanging around here, Meggie. You've been lying in bed all morning. Get down the road and earn your keep.'

Meggie was dressed in tawdry finery, a dress that had been ripped more than once and poorly mended, and which showed off her bosom and scrawny neck. She was a woman old before her time. She whined, 'I was just boiling an egg for my breakfast.' The pan stood on the glowing coals. 'As soon as I've eaten that I'll be away.'

'Mind you are.' And Ross grumbled, 'Why the hell didn't you do it in the kitchen?'

'It's cosier in here beside the fire.'

'Slut!' Ross started towards the door but called to the little girl, 'You behave yourself while we're out or it'll be the belt for you.'

The child cringed. 'Yes, Daddy.'

Ross went on to the front door, opened it and paused to glance up and down the street, as always, before stepping out. When looking to his right he had to squint against the bright sunlight, but on turning his head the other way he could see without trouble — and did not like what he saw. The group were marching steadily down the street towards him and children were leaving their games to follow in the wake of the police. Ross knew Formby, and the sergeant, Bullock. The soldier he could not place for a moment, then he remembered the tall man in the yard when he had trailed Katy. Her he recognised at once. He muttered an obscenity and shut the door.

Formby and his party, with the sun in their eyes, had not seen Ross. As they approached the house Formby said, 'Blast! We could have sent those two men through there to get to the back.' Because now they could see that, before Ross's house, there was a gap in the terrace. A lane about six or seven feet wide ran back between his house and the next. But now they were at the front door. Sergeant Bullock hammered on it and demanded, 'Open up! Police!' The call brought more children running in droves and drew the attention of the gossiping women, but the door did not open. The sergeant tried again, still without result, and looked to Formby. He nodded and Bullock bellowed, 'Open up or I'll break this door down!' One of the policemen stepped forward carrying a sledge hammer. And then the door opened.

A slatternly looking young woman stood in the opening. She asked sullenly, 'What d'ye want?' But she was nervous, Katy could see the twitching of the hand which hung by her side, clutching a fold of her skirt, and her eyes jumped from one member of the group to another.

Formby said, 'Now then, Meggie lass, I've got a warrant to search these premises so get out of the way.' And to Sergeant Garrett and his men, 'In you go!' They passed him at a run, big boots thundering in the hall, then they split up to go through the house. Matt went with them, heading straight for the stairs. Formby shouted, 'Here! Not you!' But Matt did not or would not hear and Formby swore, a mild oath but he apologised to Katy, 'Sorry, madam.' But then he warned, 'Don't you go rushing off. You stay with me.' He turned on Meggie: 'Now we'll have a chat inside.'

When Matt reached the head of the stairs he briefly halted. One passage lay ahead of him, another to the right. Which way to go? But he saw a constable preceding him along the passage ahead so he took that to the right. For an instant he thought a soldier faced him, but then saw it was his own reflection in a huge mirror at the end of the passage. There was a door on one side of it. He threw this open, fists clenched ready for

344

whatever or whoever he might find, but found himself in a bedroom at the front of the house. It was empty, but the suits in the big wardrobe marked it as that of the master of the house. This was the lair of the beast who had plagued Katy and made her life miserable. The mirror outside was where he admired himself. Matt kicked aside a chair, stormed out and went on with the search.

In the sitting-room, Formby leaned back against a round table set at its centre and eyed Meggie where she sat by the fire. Sergeant Bullock stood stolidly by the door. The pan on the coals spat like a cat as it boiled over and Meggie slid it onto the hob where it bubbled steadily. Formby said, 'What's that?'

Meggie answered, 'I'm going to boil an egg for my breakfast.'

Formby said, 'D'you want to eat it here or down at the station?'

Meggie complained, 'What do I have to go down there for? I haven't done anything.'

'Just to have a talk.' Formby showed his teeth. 'But we could get it over with here. Where's the little lass?'

'I don't know.' Meggie stared at the fire.

Formby asked, 'What do you know about her?'

'Louise?' Meggie shrugged. 'She's his daughter, that's all. He brought her back just as the war was starting. I suppose she'd been living with her mother.'

Katy broke in fiercely, 'She had. I'm her mother.' Formby gave her a disapproving look at this interruption but she kept on, 'Where is she?'

345

Meggie was staring at her, looking her over from head to foot. 'You were married to him?'

'I was going to be. When he found I was pregnant he disappeared.'

Meggie shook her head, 'A lass like you?' But then she sighed, 'Well, he can make himself out to be a proper gentleman when he wants. He got us all that way. That's how I started. You can thank God he didn't marry you.'

Katy pressed her, 'Where's Louise?'

Meggie's gaze flickered and fell. 'With him.'

Katy felt cold inside. 'Where is he?'

Sergeant Garrett, from the second car, appeared in the doorway. He had been leading the search of the house and now Formby snapped at him, 'Well?'

'He's not in the house, sir.' Garrett looked uncomfortable under Formby's glare, his red face even redder. Now Matt loomed behind him, caught Katy's eye and shook his head with frustration.

Formby swung back to glower at Meggie, 'So where is he? And the little lass?'

Meggie still stared into the fire. 'He was just going out the front when he saw you lot coming. He went out the back way.'

Formby turned to Garrett, standing in the doorway and asked, 'What about those men at the back?'

Garrett answered glumly, 'I found the back door open, sir. The constables were just arriving. They'd had a long run to get round the end of the street to the back lane. They hadn't seen anybody.'

Formby smacked his fist into his palm, 'Damn! We've missed him. But we'll soon pick him up. We know him well and the little lass will give him away. Don't you worry.' That last was addressed to Katy. She stood pale-faced, knowing now that something had gone terribly wrong. Should she have kept Matt and the police out of it, come here on her own? Howard Ross would not have run from her. But nor would he have let her walk away, with or without Louise, she was sure of that. And Louise was with him still. But he could not have gone far . . .

Formby seemed to act on that thought: 'The quicker we start the better. Come on!' He led the way out of the room and his men followed.

Matt took Katy's arm and tried to reassure her: 'Formby's right, they'll soon pick up Ross.' He led her from the room and Katy went obediently, but turned her head to catch one last glimpse of Meggie where she sat by the fire. The woman looked up furtively then quickly away.

Katy asked, 'Is she all right?'

But Meggie only shrugged.

Katy let Matt lead her to the front door but there she stopped. 'I'm going back to talk to her.'

Matt said, 'We ought to get after Louise.'

'The police will do that better than I could.' Katy turned back, 'She's the only one who can tell me about Louise.'

Matt also turned. 'I'll come with you.'

'No, Matt, please. She might talk to me alone but not with you or the police there.'

Matt hesitated, then saw the point, nodded and stepped back. Katy closed the front door on

347

him and returned to the sitting-room.

Meggie looked up from the fire, startled. 'Hey! What are you doing here? I thought you lot had gone.' She craned to peer behind Katy.

'They have,' replied Katy. 'I'm on my own.' She walked to the fireside. A cracket stood there, a little four-legged stool, and she sat on that, her face turned up to Meggie.

'What d'you want, then?' Meggie demanded suspiciously. 'I can't tell you any more about him.' Her voice rose, frightened, 'I can't, I tell you!'

'I don't want to hear about him!' That came bitterly from Katy. 'I never thought I could hate somebody, really hate them, but him . . . ' She paused a moment, her face in her hands, then lifted it and wiped away the tears. She said simply, pleading, 'I just want to know about Louise, my little girl he stole from me.' And Katy told her the whole story, from her seduction to Louise's kidnapping.

Meggie listened, at first wary but then increasingly sympathetic. At the end she whispered, 'That's awful! I'm sorry about you and the bairn.'

Katy asked, 'Is she well looked after? Is she happy?' She looked up anxiously into Meggie's face.

Meggie hesitated, pity fighting fear, then pity won a small battle and she said, 'She always has enough to eat, decent clothes.'

Katy pressed her, 'But is she happy?'

But Meggie would not answer that: 'How should I know?'

Katy reached out to grip her hand, asked the question though afraid of what the answer might be: 'Is he cruel to her?'

'He gives her a clip now and then — '

'He beats her?' Katy's hand tightened on Meggie's.

Meggie winced at the pain of it. 'Aye, but he only once put her in the cupboard, that I know — ' She broke off there, her free hand to her mouth, fearful.

'In the cupboard?' Katy felt faint but her grip tightened further. 'What do you mean? *Tell me!*'

'If I told you anything he'd kill me!' Meggie tried to prise Katy's fingers from her wrist but failed.

Katy insisted, 'The police will protect you! It you give evidence they won't do anything to you and neither will he! He'll go to prison for a very long time! Would you like *your* daughter to be with him — or in this cupboard?'

Now Meggie was weeping. 'He has a room. If any of us lasses crosses him, doesn't do as he says, he locks us in there all day and night. You're just sitting on the floor in the dark and not knowing what he's going to do when he opens the door. It's next to his room. He likes to hear us crying in there. It's behind a big mirror — that's the door. He's in there!' She bent over, sobbing.

Katy realised Ross had played the same trick he had used on her four years ago. He had led her to believe he had gone to Germany when he was still in Newcastle. Now he had laid a trail that had sent the police off on a wild goose chase while he lay hidden in the house.

'*I told you to keep your bloody mouth shut, Meggie!*' Howard Ross stood in the doorway, stripping off an expensive overcoat and tossing it aside.

Meggie whimpered and put her hands to her face as Katy's grip on her loosened, shrank back in the chair and wailed, 'I did like you told me!' Then seeking frantically for any excuse, 'She won't tell anybody, will you, lass?' That last was addressed, pleadingly, to Katy. But Katy was on her feet now, staring wide-eyed at Ross.

He threatened Meggie contemptuously, 'I'll settle with you in a minute.' Then he glared at Katy and reached back into the hall behind him: 'Is this what you're looking for?' He dragged Louise into the room to stand by his side. Katy started forward but Ross snapped, 'Stay where you are!' She saw he held a knife in his right hand, a wicked instrument with a wide, shining blade. She froze. Surely he would not use that — But Katy was not sure. Ross was going on, 'That's right. You keep quiet and do just what I tell you, or else.' That was said softly but with menace. He paused, his cold, mad stare boring into Katy and he saw the fear transfixing her, as it always did when he used that stare on his victims. And as always he thought, She's like a frightened rabbit.

'Stand still.' He left Louise by the door and moved towards Katy, holding her with his eyes. 'You're going to get me out of here. You, me and Louise, we're going out together.' He approached her with certainty and Katy's gaze

350

flicked wildly from him to Louise and back again. Her legs felt loose under her and she was aware of the knife, casually held by his side but a potent threat. What would her life be worth if she went with him? Or the life of Louise? She glimpsed her daughter's frightened face for just an instant longer, saw the fear and pleading in her eyes, then Ross moved between them and blocked her view.

That broke the spell. Katy began to think again, and to fight. She reached down to the fire, scooped up the pan and hurled its contents into Ross's face. He shrieked, scalded and blinded, if only for precious seconds. He clutched at his face that streamed water and Katy saw her chance. She ran past him and snatched up Louise, whisked her out into the hall then slammed the door shut behind them. She heard Matt shout, 'Katy? *Katy!*' She struggled with the catch on the front door then started back as it swung in towards her under the impact of Matt's charging shoulder. Katy glanced behind her and saw Ross burst out of the room she had just left. For a second they all froze, Katy holding Louise, Matt with his arm around her, Ross with his mad glare and his face raw and discoloured. Then he turned and ran.

Matt followed, but first had to round Katy and Louise. Then he and Ross were both leaping up the stairs, though Ross led by several strides. Katy cried out, 'Matt!' She was afraid for him because Ross still had the knife. She thrust Louise into Bullock's arms as the sergeant appeared at the front door, then ran after Matt.

The two men raced upwards through the house. Matt was fitter and faster but Ross threw obstacles in his path — chairs, a small table — that briefly checked him. Because of this Katy was able to keep in touch, though half of a flight of stairs behind Matt.

So they came to the top of the house, where there was a landing. Several small rooms opened off this, rooms in which the servants used to live. Ross dashed into one of these and slammed the door shut behind him. Matt tried to open it but failed. Katy appeared at his side and he panted, 'I think he's shoved a chair up against it.'

Katy said breathlessly, 'Leave it, Matt! He has a knife! Let the police — '

He cut her off: 'I reckon he has a way out of here, or why should he climb to the top o' the house?' He set his shoulder to the door and it tore off its hinges then fell inside. Now they could see Ross, crouching on top of an old chest of drawers in the open dormer window, with one leg out on the roof. As Matt lunged across the room, Ross swung out onto the slates and pushed the window down, closing it in Matt's face. Katy grabbed at Matt's arm but he shook her off and told her, 'I want him for what he did to you!' He grabbed the broken chair from the floor and rammed it through the window, sending the glass spraying across the roof. Ross had disappeared, but when Matt stood on the chest of drawers and cautiously lifted his head out of the window frame he saw Ross walking along on the wide ridge tiles which ran along the apex of the roof. He was now some yards away.

Ross laughed at him and Matt climbed out onto the ridge of the dormer window. Balancing precariously with his feet on that, he could lie flat on the black slates and reach up to the ridge tiles. He began to haul himself up over the slippery slates, as Ross had done. But now Ross turned back, ran nimble as a cat along the ridge and struck at Matt's hands with the knife. Matt saw the attack coming and took one hand off the ridge. He whipped off his cap and dashed it in Ross's face, blinding him, then seized the hand which held the knife. He twisted it savagely and the blade fell from Ross's fingers. It skittered down over the roof to fall in the yard thirty feet below. But now Ross used his free hand to prise the other out of Matt's grasp, then he stamped on Matt's fingers which were hooked on the ridge so that they opened nervelessly and Matt had to let go. It was then that he lost his footing on the dormer window and he slid down the roof after the knife.

Katy, standing in the dormer, saw it all. She leaned dangerously far out, lying on the roof, to grab the skirt of Matt's tunic as he slid past. The jerk seemed almost to tear her arm from its socket, but she checked his fall and dragged him over to the window. As Matt clamped a hand on its frame, Ross shouted from above, 'Try again and you'll get the same!'

Matt said nothing but started to climb onto the roof of the dormer again. Katy pleaded, 'No, Matt!' But she saw he was unheeding in his anger, and she remembered that anger was because of the way Ross had treated her. She called up to him now, 'You might as well give yourself up! You can't stay up here for ever!'

'No, I won't!' Ross shouted in reply. 'And I'll be back to deal with you and that pretty face of yours!' He turned then and ran along the wide ridge tiles.

Matt said, 'He's going to jump across to the next house. He's hoping to get away through there before the police twig what he's doing.'

Katy said, 'He'll never do it!' And then she shouted a warning, forgetting the harm this evil man had done to her, instinctively trying to save him: *Don't! You can't!*

The cry came as Ross was about to leap. It distracted him for a split second but that was too much and his foot slipped as he jumped. He almost cleared the gap but fell short by inches. As his torso thumped against the gable end of the next house his hands scrabbled desperately at the end of its roof. They found a hold on the ridge tile there but it was loose and came away. It fell into the alley between the two houses and he plummeted with it. His shriek came echoing up to them and then was cut short by a sickening thud. There was a terrible silence.

25

Katy turned away, shaking. Matt helped her back into the house and put his arm around her. Policemen came crowding into the little bedroom, panting from their race up the stairs. Matt told them what had happened in a few words, then he and Katy descended through the house together. They found Formby in the hall with Meggie. Her tears had dried but she still twisted a pleat of her skirt in nervous fingers.

Formby addressed Matt severely, 'We were halfway up the road before we noticed you two were missing. You were supposed to be following us. You've no business taking the law into your own hands.'

Katy answered him, pallid and weak but she would not allow Matt to be blamed: 'We didn't. All we did was find out where he was, and that was by accident. I went back to talk to Meggie because I thought she could tell me about Louise. I didn't know he was upstairs all the time, hidden in a room behind a big mirror.'

Matt exclaimed, 'So that was where he was!' He turned on Formby: 'You can't blame your men for not finding that place. I saw the mirror and never guessed.'

Formby grumbled, 'Aye, but that doesn't

355

excuse what you did. That was against regulations. Anyway, now I want statements from all of you. So come along — and walk in front of me this time where I can keep an eye on you.'

Katy and Matt left the house with Meggie and Formby following behind. Outside they found Sergeant Bullock waiting with Louise holding his hand. Katy took her from the sergeant, putting her arm around Louise instead. She could hardly believe she had won back her daughter, kept wanting to touch Louise, wrap her arms around her, but she restrained herself.

Katy said, 'I'm your mother, Louise. I suppose you don't remember me. You were little when your father stole you away.' Louise stared, bewildered, and Katy went on, 'Never mind. I'll explain it all to you later. The important thing is that you're safe now and he won't hurt you again — ever.'

Louise was still uncertain, nervous and frightened, cheeks smudged where the tears had run. Katy could have broken down again at sight of this pale waif of a daughter of hers but thought it better to smile and found it easier. It extracted a tremulous twitch of the lips from Louise and that wrung Katy's heart. Louise would need a long time to get over this trauma.

Formby said with satisfaction, 'Well, there'll be no trial, just an inquest.' He jerked his head at the alley as they passed its mouth, where a policeman stood on guard. Involuntarily, Katy glanced that way, and saw in the shadow between the two houses, a still shape lying on the cobblestones. Someone had found a blanket and covered the body but there was no mistaking what it was. Katy looked away quickly and put a hand up so that Louise would not see.

Matt said grimly, 'That could have been me, if you hadn't grabbed me.' Katy did not want to think about that and tried to close her mind against the pictures it conjured up. Now, by a macabre coincidence, the barrel organ was playing 'Broken Doll.' The jerky *tinkle-tankle* followed them up the street.

They drove back to the police station and made statements, gave details. It was late in the evening when Katy, Matt and Louise finally got down from a cab at Newcastle Central Station. Matt was leaving on the express bound for King's Cross. Katy, holding Louise by the hand — she had refused to be parted from her since being reunited — went with him onto the platform to see him off. She asked anxiously, 'What will they do to you?'

Matt grinned, 'Put me on a charge, that's a certainty. I'll have been absent without leave for eight or ten hours, because when I get to London I'll still have to go on to my regiment on Salisbury Plain. But don't worry. I'll get my knuckles rapped, might lose my rank, but that's all. They won't shoot me.'

Porters were slamming doors — most of them were women at that stage of the war, with so many men on active service — and the guard was standing ready with his flag, whistle in his mouth. Matt set his hands on Katy's shoulders and smiled wryly down at her. 'I've been a bloody fool for a long time, couldn't see what

357

was right under my nose. I love you, Katy. I can say it now.'

Katy slid an arm around his neck while still keeping her grip on Louise. She stood on tiptoe to kiss him, then pushed him up into the carriage and stepped back as the whistle shrilled and the train started to move. She waved until it rounded a bend in the track and Matt was hidden from her; but before that happened the tears had misted her sight of him — but she was smiling.

Katy took Louise home on the local stopping train. They got off at Monkwearmouth and walked down Barclay Street, passed St Peter's Church and so came to Annie Scanlon's little house. Annie answered Katy's knock, with Beatrice in her nightdress peering around Annie's skirts. Katy said simply, 'I've found Louise.'

'Come in! Come in!' Annie was overjoyed, reached out to take Louise but saw Katy's warning shake of the head and planted a kiss on the child's cheek instead. 'Come and sit down by the fire with your mammy.' So Katy was able to relax in the warmth and a comfortable old chair, with Louise in the crook of one arm, Beatrice in the other, while Annie made a pot of tea. She was eager to hear how Louise had been found, but when Katy avoided the subject, tactfully waited until the children had been put to bed. Then Katy told her the full story.

Annie shook her head, appalled, 'You poor lass! You've had an awful time. Now, I hate to ask, but how long have you got?'

'I've got a week.'

Annie nodded, 'A week at home with me and the bairns will do you good, them as well.' Then she asked, 'And how long before you get out altogether?'

Katy hesitated, then ventured, 'I suppose now I've found Louise I could make a good compassionate case for being demobilised now. But I want to keep on with my job down there. I think the Commandant will let me come home fairly often, and I feel I'm doing some good. The wounded men need us.' And there was always the possibility that a train would draw in one day and Matt would be aboard, needing her.

Annie said, 'And you want to know if I can look after Louise as well? Course I can!' She beamed at Katy, 'I'm looking forward to it!'

So that was settled. Katy spent a week that was alternately joyous and heartrending, a week of loving her daughter and seeing her come back to life and loving again. Beatrice welcomed Louise as a playmate in the house but inevitably was somewhat shy. At first Louise was shy with everyone and flinched at every sudden noise or movement, lifting a hand in pathetic defence. By the end of that week, however, she was a different child, chattering with Beatrice and Annie, putting her arms around Katy to say, 'I love you.'

It was a wrench for Katy to leave, but as she set out for the station she looked back and saw Annie with her arms around Louise and Beatrice and both of them waving. Katy went on her way with her mind at rest. She knew she had a long way to go to completely heal Louise's wounds and bring the child fully back to her, but she looked forward to that.

In London again, Katy wrote to Louise at least once a week. She spent a great deal of her spare time writing. Her Commandant offered to find her a post nearer home but a letter from Matt had told her that he had gone to Flanders the day after returning to his regiment. Suppose he came back on one of the hospital trains? So Katy politely refused the Commandant's offer.

Matt had also written: 'The colonel chewed me up but that was just for the look of things, to show that anyone late back from leave was in trouble. But he had a letter of commendation from that Inspector Formby in front of him — I'd had to tell Formby my Army Unit but he wrote of his own accord — so I kept my rank.' For the rest, he poured out his heart. He wrote often, almost every day, sometimes a page or two, sometimes just a few lines scribbled in blunt pencil on an oil-stained sheet torn from a signal message pad. Katy kept the letters carefully and replied to each one as it came.

'I understand I am now a free man.' That letter came in July. Fleur had written to Matt that she had obtained a divorce in America and married Dawkins. They were going to St Louis where they would live with his parents. Besides that information Fleur had written two pages of abuse and sneers. Matt had commented, 'But you won't want to read all that. I don't mind. I don't hate her. I'm just sorry about the time I wasted on her.'

Katy agreed; hate was poisoning.

At that moment Fleur was listening to her father-in-law. Harry's father ran a small restaurant staffed entirely by the family, all of whom worked hard at the business. Now he was demanding of Harry, 'Where the hell were you two when we opened a half-hour ago? You didn't wake up, you tell me? That's a reason? Listen: you never helped around here, didn't do a damn thing except blow on that clarinet all day long. When I threw you out you said you'd had enough of this place and you were going to England. Now you come back and you say the money was lousy and so was the food, you're flat broke and you've got a fancy wife and you want to move back in! OK. Your ma wants it so you come home. But you work. You're a waiter. You get here a half-hour *before* we open and see everything is ready on the tables. She helps your ma in the kitchen. But you both work. Everybody here works.'

Fleur listened miserably and went on washing the greasy dishes which her mother-in-law inspected with an eagle eye.

In October Katy had news of another of the men in her life. It came in a letter from a Newcastle solicitor. He said that Charles Ashleigh had been killed in action just a month before. Katy broke down at that. When she took up the letter again she read:

The bulk of the estate is inherited by his two sons, but he telephoned me before leaving on his last voyage to make an appointment to see me with a view to adding a codicil to his will.

He mentioned your name and that you worked for the Ambulance Column and so I was able to find your address. While he was not specific I nevertheless talked with the executors who agreed that it was obviously his intention to make some bequest. The cheque enclosed comes with their best wishes.

It was for two hundred pounds.

Katy whispered, 'Those poor boys, to lose their father.' She could have wept again for them.

She also thought that the lawyer and the executors probably thought she had been Charles's mistress. Well, let them. They were wrong but she didn't care. She would not write to correct them because that would be like denying Charles. He deserved far better than that.

The Armistice was signed in November and the guns fell silent. Katy celebrated with the rest of the country, but could not rid herself of the memories of the wounded, the dying and those who had died as she held their hands. Her feeling was not so much of joy as relief that the war was over. She was discharged from the Women's Legion and the Ambulance Column early in December but she stayed on in the hostel for a few days while she conducted her business. The hostel was much cheaper than a hotel and she was intent on saving every penny she could. At the end of a week she had become the owner of a lorry, a three-ton Dennis Subsidy model sold off by the Army as surplus to requirements. A whole load of spares came with it. She drove it up the Great North Road, starting very early in the morning, stopped and slept in the cab for an hour in the early evening, then drove on. She finally braked it outside Annie Scanlon's house just before midnight.

Katy climbed down wearily. The house, like all the others in the street, was dark and silent in the moonlight, the people abed. She did not want to wake Annie or the children but neither did she wish to leave the cargo of spares in the street only protected by a tarpaulin. So she used the key Annie had given her, opened the front door and tiptoed inside. The key to the yard was on the mantelpiece as usual and she picked it up and crept out as she had come in.

She drove the Dennis round to the yard, unlocked the gates and put the Dennis in the shed. The top half of the stable door was open and she went to shut it. In the moonlight she could see the collar and harness of the old horse, Sergeant O'Malley, hanging from a nail. That brought back bittersweet memories and a reminder that this was home. She paused a moment then. The yard lay before her with the square silhouette of the office and flat opposite. The sky was clear and that might have meant a frost later in the night but she was not cold. Still . . . Katy had intended to sleep in the cab again, wrapped in her greatcoat. But now the office beckoned and she walked over to it, carrying her small suitcase she had carried in the cab of the Dennis. She fumbled for the key in the crack between doorstep and door, and again, fingers scrabbling backwards and forwards. Then she stopped. The key was not there.

Someone had taken it, that was obvious. The wall around the yard, and the gate, were only meant to keep out the curious. A determined thief could easily climb into the yard, could be in the office now, watching her. Katy's eyes flicked to the window but that was blank, only reflecting her own image in the bright moonlight. She was about to take a pace backward, then turn and retreat, when she thought of another possibility. Who else knew where to find the key? On the instant she was certain of the answer, opened the door of the office and stepped inside. She saw his pack standing on the counter, could just make out the length of him below it, that he was sleeping under the counter as he used to do.

Katy shut the door behind her but it creaked and rattled as it closed. Matt awoke and propped himself on one elbow. His bare shoulders gleamed as he growled, demanding, 'Who's there?'

'It's me, Katy.' She answered low-voiced, though there was no one to wake. 'How long have you been here?'

Matt said, 'They've given me leave — two weeks to see me over Christmas and into the New Year. It was late when I got here and I didn't want to wake Annie, so I threw my coat over the broken glass on top of the wall, shinned over and bedded down in here. What about you?' He watched her, listening to the rustling.

Katy breathed, 'The Women's Legion released me. Matt, I've bought a lorry, a three-ton Dennis with a load of spares. It's old but it runs well. I drove it up here.'

He said, 'It'll do for us to get started. You can run it till I come home for good in a month or so.'

Katy saw he was lying in a big sleeping bag. The rustling had stopped now and she stood before him silver-naked in the moonlight. She shivered in the night air then slid into the arms of her man.

THE END

Other titles in the
Charnwood Library Series:

FALLING SLOWLY

Anita Brookner

Beatrice and Miriam are sisters, loving but not entirely uncritical; each secretly deplores the other's aspirations. Their lives fall short of what they would have wished for themselves: love, intimacy, exclusivity, acknowledgement in the eyes of the world, even a measure of respect. Each discovers to her cost that love can be a self-seeking business and that lovers have their own exclusive desires. In search of reciprocity, the sisters are forced back into each other's company, and rediscover their original closeness.

THE LADY ON MY LEFT

Catherine Cookson

Alison Read, orphaned when she was two years old, had for some years lived and worked with Paul Aylmer, her appointed guardian. Paul, an experienced antique dealer whose business thrived in the south-coast town of Sealock, had come to rely on Alison, who had quickly learned the trade. But when he had asked her to value the contents of Beacon Ride, a chain of events was set off that led to the exposure of a secret he had for years managed to conceal. As a result, Alison's relationship with Paul came under threat and she knew that only by confronting the situation head-on would her ambitions be realised.

FLIGHT OF EAGLES

Jack Higgins

In 1997 a wealthy novelist, his wife and their pilot are forced to ditch in the English Channel. Saved by a lifeboat crew, they are returned to land at Cold Harbour. But it is the rediscovery of a fighter pilot's lucky mascot — unseen for half a century — that excites the greatest interest at the disused airbase. The mascot's owners, twin brothers Max and Harry Kelso, were separated as boys and found themselves fighting on opposite sides when the Second World War broke out. They were to meet again under amazing circumstances — and upon their actions hung the fate of the war itself . . .

ON BEULAH HEIGHT

Reginald Hill

They needed a new reservoir so they'd moved everyone out of Dendale that long hot summer fifteen years ago. They even dug up the dead and moved them too. But four inhabitants of the dale they couldn't move, for nobody knew where they were — three little girls, and the prime suspect in their disappearance, Benny Lightfoot. This was Andy Dalziel's worst case and now fifteen years on he looks set to re-live it. It's another long hot summer. A child goes missing, and as the Dendale reservoir waters shrink and the old village re-emerges, old fears and suspicions arise too . . .

Dismantling
TRUTH

Dismantling TRUTH

REALITY IN THE POST-MODERN WORLD

Edited by

Hilary Lawson and Lisa Appignanesi

Based on a series of papers presented at a conference at the ICA and related materials

St. Martin's Press
New York

First published in the United States of America in 1989

Printed in Great Britain

ISBN 0-312-03261-7

Library of Congress Cataloging-in-Publication Data

Dismantling truth: reality in the post-modern world: based on a series of papers presented at a conference at the ICA and related materials/edited by Hilary Lawson and Lisa Appignanesi.
    p.   cm.
    Bibliography: p.
    Includes index.
    ISBN 0-312-03261-7: $29.95 (est.)
    1. Truth—Congresses.   2. Reality—Congresses.   3. Postmodernism—Congresses.   4. Science—Philosophy—Congresses.   5. Representation (Philosophy)—Congresses.   I. Lawson, Hilary.   II. Appignanesi, Lisa.   III. Institute of Contemporary Arts (London, England)
BD171.D57   1989
001—dc20   89-32214
                                                        CIP

Contents

n-realist
realist
n-realist
realist

v

Prefatory Note

This book began its life as a conference, 'Dismantling Truth: Objectivity and Science', held at the Institute of Contemporary Arts in London in the spring of 1986. It may seem curious that an arts institute should turn its programming gaze on science and the philosophy of science, areas which conventionally might be thought to be outside its domain. However, at the ICA we have never been party to the 'two cultures' notion.

Moreover, we had spent some time within our programme discussing and analysing the post-modern predicament and those theories and practices now generally labelled 'post-modernist'. It seemed a logical progression to focus on the status of 'reality' in science and the debates which science's particular relationship to truth were now generating.

The conference, which Hilary Lawson chaired, provoked interest and controversy. It brought together disparate voices – scientists, philosophers, social scientists. To give the conference a longer, more permanent life in book form seemed desirable. We were well aware, however, of the differences between live discussion and written text and, for the purposes of this volume, we commissioned additional contributions – from Bruno Latour, John Forrester, Hugh Tomlinson – which enlarged the book's philosophical scope.

We hope the book will prove accessible to as wide a variety of people as those who participated in 'Dismantling Truth' at the ICA.

Lisa Appignanesi

List of Contributors

Richard Rorty is a leading American philosopher and author of *Philosophy and the Mirror of Nature* and *The Consequences of Pragmatism*. He is Kenan Professor of Humanities at the University of Virginia.

W.H.Newton-Smith is Fairfax Fellow of Philosophy at Balliol College, Oxford and Director of the Inter-University Centre at Dubrovnik. His books include *The Rationality of Science, The Structure of Time* and *Logic: An Introductory Course*.

Hugh Tomlinson is a philosopher and practising barrister. He is the translator into English of Gilles Deleuze, one of France's leading theorists, and is also the author of *Civil Action Against the Police*.

David Ruben is Senior Lecturer in Philosophy at the LSE and author of *Marxism and Materialism* and *The Metaphysics of the Social World*.

Harry Collins is the Director of the Science Study Centre and Reader in Science Studies at the University of Bath. His books include *Changing Order: Replication and Induction in Scientific Practice* and *Frames of Meaning; The Social Construction of Extraordinary Science*.

Richard Gregory, CBE, is emeritus professor of neuropsychology and Director of the Brain and perception Laboratory at the University of Bristol. His many books include *Eye and Brain, The Intelligent Eye, Mind in Science* and *Odd Perceptions*.

Bruno Latour teaches at the Centre de Sociologie de L'Innovation at the Ecole Nationale Superieure des Mines in Paris. His books include *Laboratory Life* and *Science in Action*.

Steve Woolgar is Lecturer in the Department of Human Sciences at Brunel University and is co-author of *Laboratory Life* amongst other publications.

List of Contributors

John Forrester is Lecturer in History and Philosophy of Science at Cambridge University and the author of *Language and the Origins of Psychoanalysis* and the forthcoming *The Seductions of Psychoanalysis*.

STORIES ABOUT STORIES

Hilary Lawson

I DISMANTLING TRUTH

IF WE ARE certain of anything, it is that we are certain of nothing. If we have knowledge, it is that there can be none. Ours is a world awash with relativism. It has seeped into our culture, it threatens to become our faith. The tide may have begun with the end of belief in a universal morality and religious code, but it has swelled with a recognition of the limited and particular perspective of our culture, our time and our society. Its full force is now being felt in the name of post-structuralism and post-modernity.

Caught in a whirl of intellectual fashion the term 'post-modern' is in danger of becoming a vacuous epithet conveying no more than approbation or criticism depending on the prejudices of the writer. But at its philosophical core post-modernism is an attack on truth. It is an attack that originates not so much in an awareness of alternative perspectives as in a critique of the very possibility of objectivity. From a post-modern perspective the central characteristic of modernism, in a philosophical sense, is not that truth is assumed to have been attained, but that objective truth is assumed to be in principle attainable.

In contemporary writing one can discern two strains of attack on truth: one can be loosely labelled as relativism and the other as post-modernism. Inevitably there will be those whom we may place in one or other category who would themselves reject the label; the classification is intended as a broad-brush guide rather than a definitive description.

The relativist tradition can be seen to stem predominantly from the social sciences, from anthropology, sociology and the history and philosophy of science. In the decades before the Second World War, writers such as Mannheim, Fraser and Malinowski[1] highlighted the cultural and historical character of our outlook and opinions. Against this background of an awareness of the social particularity of our perspective, writers such as Winch, Kuhn and Feyerabend[2] were, in the decades after the war, able to carry relativist arguments through to our understanding of reality itself. By contrast, the post-modern tradition has less emphasis on the social sciences and is more closely associated with concerns about language and the relationships between language, text, meaning and reality. Retrospectively, post-modernism can be seen to have originated with Nietzsche. Retrospectively, because at the time Nietzsche was alive his writings were interpreted very differently. In more recent times, post-modernism is characterized by Lyotard, Foucault and, perhaps above all, by Derrida (although neither Foucault nor Derrida use the term 'post-modernism' themselves).

If relativism initiated an unsettling of truth and objectivity postmodernism is an attempt to engage in the complete dismantling of the edifice. To this extent post-modernism is a radical version of relativism. While relativism can be described as the view that truth is paradigm-dependent, post-modernism might be described as the view that meaning is undecidable and therefore truth unattainable. It would be a mistake however to assume that these two traditions were easily separable. Although, at first sight relativism can appear to be a concern of English-speaking philosophers, and post-modernism a concern of continental (primarily French) philosophers, such an easy distinction is of limited value. Relativism combined with its self-reflexive consequences yields an outlook with many points of contact with continental postmodernism. As a consequence a major figure like Wittgenstein is probably better understood with a post-modern label rather than a relativist one.

From whatever source, these arguments about truth are not limited to arcane philosophical seminars. On the one hand, there are those who argue that the dismantling of truth undermines rationalism, and so calls into question the basis of Western culture.[3] Without facts the great enterprise of knowledge is little more than an Enlightenment error. Moreover, without some notion of objectivity there is no progress, theoretical or social. As a result of what they see as the potential consequences of dismantling truth there are many who insist that truth cannot be abandoned; they fear that without objectivity an untamed irrationalism will sweep all our civilized values from under us. We will be loose in a world without constraint, a world without guiding principles, a world in which anything goes for those with the power to exercise it.

aren't? we now.

On the other hand, adherents of post-modernism deny that dismantling truth will have these consequences. Instead they paint a picture of freedom from the faith of rationality. Truth is a misleading goal that distracts us from the task in hand. Without a metaphysical attachment to grasping reality we can get on with the business of doing as good a job as we can. The real danger is not of irrationalism but of the belief in truth. For it is under the guise of the rhetoric of truth that the most terrible acts can be justified.

The combatants in this argument have therefore no doubt about the seriousness of the battle and the extent of the territory at stake. But if the status of truth is the most central question of our time, it is science that finds itself at the cutting edge of this question. In the past the basis of truth has been sought in God, in phenomenological experience, in the laws of history, but it is above all empirical observation that has provided the most successful and most persuasive basis for truth. And it is in science that empiricism and rationalism have been wedded to produce a system that yields the truth in a manner that other disciplines have sought to copy. Science is not simply an institution that calls on truth to support its claims and give them a special insistence, it is the institution which provides an archetype on which are based almost all other contemporary attempts at truth. There is no discipline that has not been infected, at least to some extent, by this scientism. Literary criticism, aesthetics, even theology have spawned theorists who have wished to give the discipline a 'firmer' scientific footing. Unlike science these disciplines have never achieved widespread acceptance that their conclusions were objective. The claims of the social sciences – anthropology, sociology, history – to objectivity have been undermined by relativistic attacks on their 'truth'. Science alone, of all human endeavour, has been able consistently to have its claims accepted as being true.

The special status of science confers on practitioners an authority akin to that enjoyed by the theologians of the middle ages. Like theologians, scientists are figures who have the knowledge of key texts and the relevant expertise to decide on matters of truth. Traditionally, the most plausible explanation for the special status of science has been found in its empirical base and its method, which have been seen to insulate it from the subjectivism that has beset other disciplines. Science, it appears, is based on fact and observation, not on value and opinion. From Descartes and Locke through Kant to Russell and the Vienna circle, many philosophers have aimed to provide a secure space for science to operate without fear of attack.

In the seventeenth century providing science with a sphere in which to operate meant demonstrating that empirical knowledge was not tainted and could be trusted. If our senses were misleading us, then any observations we might make were of little value. This was one of the central arguments that the Church used against Galileo. It was not so much that his observations were wrong, but that if they led to his conclusions they must be wrong. In the wake of Descartes and Locke in conjunction with the theories of Newton, the veracity of observation was established. There remained epistemological problems relating to whether reality could be inferred from sensation, but aside from students of philosophy the argument was essentially won. For everyone else, whether the table really existed when it was seen and touched was more likely to be a caricature of philosophical argument rather than a serious question in its own right.

Once the veracity of observation was accepted, the task was to ensure that value-laden, non-empirical elements did not creep into the scientific enterprise and thereby sully it. The method and practice of science was supposedly designed to ensure that all subjective concerns were weeded out, leaving only repeatable, objective results. The inevitable and intentional effect of insulating science from the mere opinion of other disciplines was to enhance the standing and authority of science. It is hardly surprising that as a consequence other disciplines either attempted to emulate science or chose to regard themselves as engaged in a wholly different kind of enterprise. The dominance of science was assured from within and without. Those with a scientific training saw scientific method as the only means to providing objective knowledge, while those in the arts and humanities implicitly accepted the scientific model, even if they personally regarded science as being dull and irrelevant to their concerns.

One indication of the profound dominance of science in contemporary society is the extent to which those in the arts and humanities often regard science as being beyond and outside a realm over which they feel they have any jurisdiction or critical capacity. Quite commonly, historians or literary critics adhere to the view that there is no objective truth. Although this view is applied in their own sphere, it is not generally applied to science. Scientific laws, and the scientific explanation of the universe with its planets and atoms, light waves and forces, is somehow immune. Yes, of course, the laws might change in the light of future discoveries, but in principle scientific claims retain their special status. Gravity and electrons exist; they are not regarded as cultural phenomena, the product of one particular theory. No literary or historical theory could hope for such treatment, although in the heyday of structuralism some may have dreamed of it.

Science's claim to truth is now under serious attack. It is not for the first time. But it is more widespread. It has stemmed from those who, as a consequence of their overall philosophical outlook, have come to deny the special claim of science to be capable of providing an objective description of reality as well as those examining the history and the current practice of science. Science is therefore at the cutting edge of the question of the status of truth in two ways: first, a general dismantling of truth leads to a questioning of the implications for science; and secondly, descriptions of the history and method of science which deny its claims to neutral observation and objectivity lead to a more general philosophical questioning of the nature of truth.

There are essays in this collection which start from each of these perspectives. In general, those essays in the first section, 'Stories about Truth', are usually attempting to apply general philosophical accounts of truth to the specific practice of science, while in the second section, 'Stories about Science', the thrust of the argument tends to run in the reverse direction: an analysis of the practice and history of science has implications for the nature of truth in general. The third section, 'Stories about Representation', approaches the issue from the general question of how we represent the world, and examines the possibility of new forms of representation, and new ways of understanding the relationship between our theories and 'reality'.

2 SCIENCE AND THE SUBJECT; SCIENCE AND LANGUAGE

If science and truth have had a special relationship, what has resulted in the current unsettling of such a powerful combination? The answer can be found in our understanding of the relationship between theory or language and the world.

Scientific claims operate at very different levels: some are observational, others theoretical. Since theoretical claims are supposedly based on observational claims, if we cannot determine the truth of the latter the former will fall by default. Traditionally, to question the truth of an observation was to question the reality or existence of the matter in hand. If in the test tube I see a red residue, to doubt the truth of this observation is either to doubt my ability to see or to doubt the epistemological link between my sensation and the reality of the residue. The questioning of my ability to see on this occasion is a philosophically trivial matter. But, if I have good eyesight and normal colour vision and I see a red residue, to doubt the truth of this claim is to question the inference of existence from my sensation. The questioning of this link between my subjective experience and the objective reality has been a central concern of philosophy. Indeed, between the seventeenth and nineteenth centuries the relationship between the subject and the object was perhaps the guiding concern of philosophy.

The problem of subject and object is simple enough: we have immediate knowledge of our sensations; we do not have immediate knowledge of reality. I can be certain of a sensation in a way that eludes me when it comes to reality. If I see red, no amount of doubt can convince me that I see another colour. To have the experience is to know that it is for certain. It is quite another matter when it comes to reality. I may think I see a chair, but it could be a painting, it could be a reflection in a mirror.

A consequence of the apparent primacy of experience over reality has been that philosophers have tended to start from the certainty of sensation and have then attempted to build a bridge to reality. The problem is inevitable – the bridge can never be completed. There have been few, like Berkeley, who have drawn the conclusion that reality does not exist other than in our minds; instead, most have tried to square the common-sense feeling that reality does exist with the philosophical failure to prove it.

Scientists have, quite sensibly, for the most part ignored these

Consider the assumed existence here of a "reality" is this not the Platonic ideal once again?

philosophical problems concerning the existence of reality. There is, however, an associated problem with our understanding of truth. The common-sense notion of truth is simply that a claim correctly describes reality, but if reality is always beyond our reach, if we are trapped within subjective experience, we are never in a position to know whether a statement describes reality or not, and consequently we are unable to know that a statement is true or false. In order to overcome the problem that reality is beyond our reach, we can try to define truth without reliance on direct knowledge of reality. These definitions might be in terms of our sensations, or in terms of the satisfaction of a certain procedure of justification, or in terms of some ideal rational process. What all of these accounts have in common is that truth is not defined in terms of correspondence with reality. As a consequence, all of these accounts are likely to seem unsatisfactory to the common-sense realist for whom truth is simply a matter of whether reality is or is not like the statement in question.

*

Very few philosophers would endorse the claim that there is no truth. Many would regard the claim as being meaningless since it is reflexively paradoxical, for if there is no truth it cannot be true that there is no truth.[4] In addition, few would wish to deny that we must distinguish between true and false statements, and if there are only false statements such a distinction is not possible. So when we have referred to 'dismantling truth' this should not be understood as denying that there is a meaning to the term, or that the category can be applied to certain propositions. If, however, truth is understood to mean 'something I like' it no longer carries the weight associated with our common-sense notion. 'Dismantling truth' is therefore shorthand for 'dismantling realist truth', truth understood as a correspondence to reality.

Since the scientist, as a human subject, is not able to see or touch reality in itself, issues arise as to what can be inferred about the external world from subjective experience. In the past these issues have been the centre of debate: Can we be certain about the nature of reality? Can scientists verify a claim or can they only falsify it? Can general laws ever be deduced from individual instances? These are important questions but they are not at the heart of the current unsettling of science's special claim to truth.

The present concern is not so much with the subjective character of the scientist's observation, as with the linguistic, theoretical and symbolic frame within which the observation takes place. For if, between the seventeenth and nineteenth centuries the central question of philosophy was the relationship between subject and object, the central question in the twentieth century has been the relationship between language and the world. And it is the role of language rather than the role of the subject that threatens to dismantle the edifice of objective truth.

For empiricists like Locke and Hume language was a transparent medium that enabled us to communicate. Individual words stood for ideas or concepts, which in turn were derived from sensation. Concepts were therefore derivative on sensation, and words on those concepts. Such a view remains the common-sense opinion. The word 'chair' is understood to stand for the idea which refers to the object. The idea and the word are thus derived from the object or the sensation. In this respect they are neutral. Although we could of course have a different word to stand for the same idea, neither the word nor the idea impinge on the object. The object exists independently of our concepts and our language.

In 1781, in his *Critique of Pure Reason*, Kant made a radical shift from this position. Instead of concepts being simply derived from sensation, they were an essential part of experience. No longer were concepts to be understood in a passive role; instead they were to provide the structure within which experience could take place. While the empiricists had seen sensation as providing the raw data of experience, and therefore the task of philosophy was to demonstrate how this raw data could be combined to yield experience and knowledge, Kant denied the possibility of immediate access to sensation, and the task of philosophy was to explain how knowledge was possible.

Kant set out to provide an account of how it was possible for us to have knowledge of the external world, but, in the process, instigated a strain of idealist philosophy which at its high point regarded the world as the outcome of the mind. Kant had been impressed by Hume's empiricist arguments that there was nothing in sensation that could lead us to knowledge of cause and effect or to the identity of the self. Since he was not prepared to endorse such a sceptical view, he abandoned the assumption that experience was derived from sensation alone. He argued that certain concepts were essential for experience to take place at all. These key concepts, or categories as Kant called them, provided the formal framework necessary for experience. It was Kant's argument that certain concepts were necessary that enabled him to avoid Hume's scepticism. Since concepts were necessary, we could not doubt them, for without them we would have no experience at all. By the use of this so-called transcendental argument Kant claimed that we could have knowledge of the external world, of the identity of the self, and of cause and effect. But at a cost. Experience and reality had as a consequence become inherently conceptual.

Through linking concepts and sensation Kant was able to overcome the epistemological problem of how knowledge was possible. Kant had bridged the gap between subject and object by denying the possibility of experience that was either purely subjective or purely objective. Realist critics would argue that, far from providing us with objective knowledge, Kant made the world irretrievably subjective. Kant's reply, although he would have used different terminology, would be to say that the world was indeed irretrievably subjective but it was also irretrievably objective. Knowledge and experience require both concepts and sensation: the two can never be separated.

Kant was still writing at a time when the opposition of subject and object, rather than language and the world, dominated philosophy. Kant was therefore unconcerned with the relationship between language and what he referred to as concepts. For us, concepts are immediately linguistic, but for Kant they were ideas in the mind. However, in the late nineteenth century and for all of the current century, Kant's arguments have been replayed in linguistic terms. In place of concepts and sensation, we have concepts and reality, language and the world. If Kant argued that experience necessarily involved a subjective element in the sense that experience was partly dependent on concepts, so it is now argued that experience and reality are necessarily linguistic.

Although Kant made a good attempt, the issue of subjectivity was never settled. The gap between subjective experience and knowledge of reality remained a problem, and to some extent has continued in much the same form. But it was no real threat to anything. Scepticism about the external world based on the subjectivity of experience may have been a useful tool in engendering philosophical debate and entertaining students but it was never likely to have any impact on the general public or the practice of science. The argument that experience and reality are dependent on concepts in the sense of dependent on language has, however, widespread implications. For, unlike subjectivity, language appears to be in our control.

We considered earlier the observation of a red residue in a test tube. Leaving aside control of the objective conditions such as lighting and so forth, a recognition of the subjectivity of this statement might lead us to check the eyesight of the individual concerned, but it is unlikely to have further ramifications. But what if the concepts partly determine the observation? For example, the word 'residue' implies that this matter is left over from something else. The observation therefore carries with it a theoretical implication. Those who argue for the irreducibly linguistic character of experience will insist that this theoretical element can never be eradicated. There can never be a neutral observation language. Just as Kant argued that we can never experience pure sensation, sensation must be always combined with understanding. As a consequence there can never be a neutral observation either. It is this conclusion that threatens the dominance of science and its claim to truth.

For those in the arts and humanities, attacks on truth are often interpreted at the most general level, as if truth is used with a capital T to mean an all-embracing account which is universally true. As a consequence there are few who wish to insist on truth, in the sense that there is one true account of an historical period or one true analysis of a poem. Of course there are many. The attack on truth in this manner is thus of little consequence. It is the attack on truth with a small t that is more unsettling. If each observation is dependent on language which carries with it a point of view, a theoretical content, what is the relationship between our statements about the world and reality? It is, one suspects, because of the difference between truth at a general theoretical level and truth at the observational level that many non-scientists are able to endorse with some equanimity the view that there is no truth, while there are few scientists who would do likewise. For scientists truth is immediately understood to refer to individual observations. To deny truth is to deny that statements such as 'the residue in the test tube is red' or the 'apple fell to the ground' can have a single truth value independent of context or circumstance. And to undermine these observations is also to undermine theories based on them.

The most threatening attacks on science and truth therefore operate not at the most general level of theory but at the most mundane level of individual observations and facts. If it is possible to have data we already have more than enough. There are, of course, many subsequent queries and question-marks. There are limits perhaps to our knowledge. We may not be able to hallow our theories with the same certainty as our data. But nevertheless we have truth. We have eternal nuggets of certainty that can provide a solid foundation, an anchor, to our theories and opinions about the world. This truth may not satisfy the desires of some to have knowledge of a grand metaphysical plan. It looks pale perhaps in comparison to the tales of religion. But despite this limitation we have truth. We may not be able to know everything, but the world is a knowable place.

There are those who have been unimpressed with this observation level of truth. Somehow all that was interesting and valuable in the world seemed to be left out in an account which generated mere data. As a consequence the assertion of truth for these data has appeared to some as a claim of little consequence. But this is deeply misguided. So long as there are nuggets of truth we not only have the basis on which to build theories that may also be deemed to be true, but we have an archetype that other claims can aspire to; we have a method and a procedure which can guide all of our activities. Above all, we have a core of solidity in an otherwise uncertain world. Science and factually based disciplines can advance the frontiers of knowledge. There is a direction to their endeavour. They are part of the real world, while so-called creative pursuits such as art and literature are seen as little more than high-class entertainment for the educated. Without this mundane level of truth there is no finality in any observation, there are no facts on which our theories can be built, there is no core of certainty that can provide the basis for knowledge. And without this still centre there is nothing against which all our other claims, including those of progress and advancement, can be judged.

So truth with a small t is not a matter about which we can be indifferent, as if we could leave it to logicians to sort out for us. It is a matter which affects every discipline and every sphere of activity. Once every text had to take account of the theologians and the authorities, so today every text is written against the back-drop of science and the authority of truth with a small t. This is as true of poetry as it is of social science. And without this truth the distinctions between science and art, between literature and philosophy, between stories and truths, begin to look precarious. The question that runs throughout this collection and provides its focus is whether we can do without this truth. If truth cannot be abandoned what are we to understand by it, and if it is to be abandoned how is it possible to proceed?

3 ANTI-REALISM AND REFLEXIVITY

Attacks on the conventional, correspondence view of truth can be found in both English language and European philosophy. For English-speaking philosophers it is the pragmatists Dewey and James and the later Wittgenstein who perhaps are most clearly associated with an attack on a realist notion of truth. Richard Rorty has to a great extent been responsible for the renewed interest in the pragmatist tradition, and in his essay 'Science as Solidarity' outlines a pragmatist notion of science and truth.

The pragmatists denied that truth had anything to do with reality. Truth is defined in terms of utility. Those views which it is useful to believe are true. There is no metaphysical meaning to truth over and above this. At first sight this might appear an absurd view. After all, there are all sorts of claims one might make which could be considered useful – by the criminal a claim of innocence, by the scientist the confirmation of his or her theory by experiment (but which might well be false). The pragmatist will however define utility in a more general sense. Although on any individual occasion it might be useful to the criminal to claim that he or she was innocent or to the scientist that the experiment was successful it would not be useful for either of them to endorse the general view that others should make similar claims in an equivalent position. Thus truth defined in terms of utility comes to mean what a rational person or group of persons would endorse in the relevant circumstances. A rational person could not advocate assertions of innocence when guilt was known because this would conflict with many other beliefs and threaten notions of consistency and law and order.

A common criticism made of pragmatism by realists is that

pragmatism makes no allowance for falsehood, a criticism that David Ruben elaborates in his essay 'Realism in the Social Sciences'. The realist wishes to argue that a statement is true or false independent of reasons for asserting it. A statement which we currently believe to be true may in fact turn out to be false. Truth is not simply a matter of our wishing to assert it, or even of our rationally deciding that it can be ascribed; it depends crucially on correspondence with reality. The pragmatist can, however, introduce a notion of falsehood by appealing to ideal circumstances. A claim can be false because, although it is useful now, if we only had all the information and were making a purely rational choice we would decide that it was not true. There is a variety of similar responses that the pragmatist can make when challenged to show the possibility of error. What remains less clear is whether the pragmatist has not reintroduced truth by the back door. Although the notion of an objective reality may have been abandoned, as little more than a metaphysical hang-up, the charge can be made that a similarly unreachable absolute has replaced it in the form of an idealized rational decision. This is an argument developed by W. H. Newton-Smith in his critique of Rorty's position.

The writings of the later Wittgenstein have much in common with pragmatism although they originate from very different preoccupations. Wittgenstein started out from the reverse perspective. In the *Tractatus*, his major early work, he can be regarded as proposing an ultra-realist position. Propositions are laid against the world in order to determine their truth value. They either picture facts, in which case they are true, or they do not, in which case they are false. The world is fully described by the totality of true propositions. As a consequence the limits of language are the limits of the world.

The *Tractatus* is a masterful attempt to describe the relationship between language and the world. It is, however, caught in a self-reflexive paradox. The theory it proposes is denied in the very theory itself. For the theory is a theory about the relationship between language and the world, and yet the theory claims that we cannot step outside language, that the limits of language are the limits of the world. Any theory which describes the relationship between language and the world must be standing outside language. We cannot from inside language picture what it is like

from the outside. Indeed we cannot picture what language is picturing, other than within language. It is for this reflexive reason
that Wittgenstein says at the end of the book that having climbed
the ladder we must throw it away.

Perhaps as a response to this reflexive paradox, in his later work
Wittgenstein denies any attempt to provide an overall metaphysical
picture at all. We find ourselves caught in a language game, a
game that provides us with what we understand as the world.
But it is not a game that we can describe because we are lost
to it. The overall metaphysical picture of the relationship between
language and reality lies outside our grasp, for it lies outside language. As a consequence Wittgenstein abandoned any notion of
truth as correspondence with or picturing of reality, and instead
understood meaning and truth as an internal function of language.
The meaning of a word or sentence was not to be found in some
external reality but simply in terms of its use within language.
Wittgenstein is referring to use not in the pragmatist sense of
useful, but in the descriptive sense of the way a word is in practice
used. So what is truth? It is no more and no less than the way
we use the term. It does not describe some transcendent relationship between sentences and reality, nor does it describe a method
of justification. It is, like every other word, a term in our language,
a term that we make use of in a multitude of ways, for a variety
of purposes.

For the later Wittgenstein therefore not only is there no objective
reality, but there is no single meaning. Any sentence or proposition
has as many meanings as there are contexts. Furthermore, anyone
who desires to provide a final account is to be treated as if suffering
from a philosophical disease. There are no answers in any ultimate
sense, there are only responses within language.

If Wittgenstein's early work is threatened by reflexivity, so is
his later position. Although he studiously avoided providing any
overall account of what he was up to, we need an implicit understanding of his position in order to make any sense of his writing
at all. Once we are able to say to ourselves 'Wittgenstein is wandering around in the language game sorting out the odd conundrum'
we can understand the exercise. But as soon as we have provided
this account, we have an ultimate truth after all. We know what
is going on, namely that we are trapped in a language game. But
to know this is to know the ultimate metaphysical picture, as

if we could stand outside ourselves and language and look down and say 'they are trapped in language'. But if we are trapped we certainly can't know that we are, for to do so would mean that we were not trapped after all.

The addition of this reflexive concern to Wittgenstein provides a link with the continental tradition. Like Wittgenstein, Derrida starts from critique of a realist account of language. Unlike the later Wittgenstein it is not a critique of his early work but of Husserl. The outcome of Derrida's critique is the denial of singular meaning. Meaning is radically unstable in that it is a function of the play of other meanings. Not only does language not refer to reality, but there is no presence for language to refer to. Derrida argues that it is the assumption of presence that has dominated philosophy and thought. In denying presence Derrida is denying that there is a present, both in a spatial and in a temporal sense.

Derrida's denial of the present is immediately linked to his denial of a stable meaning. The traditional realist view has a fixed meaning which refers to a fixed reality. The corollary of there being no single meaning is that there is no single reality. There is no present. We have the illusion that there is a something which is my experience now, which we call the present. But that thing is the outcome of a complex web of meanings that can never be held still. The illusion of a present, in the sense of a thing that is here and now, is the result of fixed meanings. Derrida's writing is usually rather abstract and theoretical. But similar arguments can be applied to the most elementary observations.

If we look around us we have a sensation of objects, of things in relation to each other. I see a mug on a desk in a room. But each of these terms carries with them the weight of the rest of language. They have their meanings only in relation to the meanings of other words. Do I also see, for example, a cup on a table in a space? Or a drink on a working surface? Each of these descriptions shifts the experience slightly. It is not simply a question of which is the correct term to describe the experience. If I was in a fight I might see the mug and the desk as weapons and defences. If I was a child I might see the cup and table as a hat and a house. The realist in us may want to say, 'But in the end it is such and such, it is a mug on a desk.' But according to these arguments there is no final resting place of meaning. There is no simple observational language that can neutrally describe what I see. And as a consequence there is no single present that is seen. The idea of a present is something that is imposed on flux, through the assumption of fixed meaning.

But if there is no fixity of meaning, we cannot know there is no fixity of meaning. For that would be to have captured presence, albeit in a negative way. As if we could say, 'So, it is not a cup on a desk.' This reflexive cycle is, as I have argued elsewhere,[5] central to post-modernism. Derrida does not avoid the reflexivity of his position. If there are no stable meanings, Derrida's own terms must be unstable. If there is no presence there can be no presence for Derrida to describe. There can be no ultimate account including his. As a result Derrida abandons his initial terminology; he abandons his account of presence. The metaphysics of presence is just one strategy of story telling among others. He plays and jests with his readers, teasing them with different accounts and different tales. The meanings of Derrida's texts evaporate in your hands, but then they are meant to. As Wittgenstein avoided providing any overall account, so Derrida provides many but they all disintegrate, and no one version is to predominate over the others.

4 THE POST-MODERN WORLD

Where do these overall accounts of truth, that are at once not overall and not accounts of truth, leave our everyday practice? The irony is that while at times relativist or post-modern attacks on truth are challenged for threatening to undermine all existing institutions, they are at other times criticized for being essentially conservative.[6] There is some justification in this charge. The two apparently contradictory tendencies towards anarchy and towards conservatism are found in both relativism and post-modernism. They threaten anarchy by removing the stability of reality and truth, but they endorse conservatism by appealing to the only thing that is left, namely, what we already have. The pragmatists, Wittgenstein and Derrida have all been charged with a concealed conservatism. Although these outlooks destroy all authority and propose a permanent revolution from within, they are thereby denied authority themselves and it is precisely for this reason that they risk having nowhere to lead us. And without goals, without direction, is it not easiest to stay where we are?

The developments in philosophy that have posed a challenge to traditional notions of truth, meaning and reality have been mirrored by work in the history and philosophy of science. The history of science, which in the heyday of realism was seen as a gradual series of discoveries that uncovered the true nature of the universe, has been extensively reinterpreted. If objectivity is a mirage, experiments cannot in a self-evident manner demonstrate the truth, as H. M. Collins argues in his paper, 'The Meaning of Experiment'. So there is now an alternative to the realist history of science. In this new story the great heroes of science – Galileo, Newton, Einstein – are not neutral painstaking observers but active rhetoricians. Scientists do not draw inevitable conclusions from unavoidable evidence but impose their meanings and construct their worlds.

Perhaps the central question for those historians and sociologists of science who wish to dismantle truth is to account for the success of science. If science is true it is not in any way surprising that it works. But if science is our fairy story where does it derive its force? Are we to look to the success of science in its institutional and organizational procedures? Or is it to do with some special character that its theories embrace? As yet, to a large extent these questions remain unanswered. Non-realist accounts of the history of science have so far been predominantly concerned with providing an alternative to realism. But in the debate between a conventional realist perspective and non-realist outlook the realists from being in the ascendancy are now on the defensive. If, however, the battle over truth is nearing its completion, it is far from clear where the victors are heading. Rorty, who wishes unequivocally to abandon our conventional notions of reality and truth, also regards science as a model of rational behaviour, while another anti-realist, Feyerabend, regards the current practice of science as being authoritarian and anti-democratic.

The intention of this collection is not only to be concerned with the debate between those who advocate a realist truth and those who wish to dismantle such a truth, but to attempt to move on from this debate to the question of how we operate in a post-modern world, a world without truth in the conventional sense. How we should proceed is, as we have seen, deeply unclear, for a denial of truth is at one and the same time an assertion of another truth. The radical consequences of this reflexivity are explored in the papers by Hugh Tomlinson and Steve Woolgar. Should we as a consequence adopt a conservative stance, on the ground that our current beliefs and patterns of behaviour are the only safe basis on which to proceed, or should we advocate a theoretical anarchy on the ground that hidden vistas are waiting to be discovered? Some will argue that the position is simply untenable and the only alternative is a retreat to realism. The practice and method of science, as the archetype of truth with special access to objectivity, is central to our attempt to answer these questions and determine a way forward.

There are those who would apocalyptically argue that we are at the end of a two-thousand-year-old tradition. We are at the end of rationalism. The ancient Platonic vision of an ideal to strive for, a good to endorse and a truth to uncover, a vision that has provided the framework for both Christianity and socialism as well as science, is finally losing its hold. The tradition is undoubtedly under threat, but it is less clear whether this heralds a revolution, or whether a post-modern world is indistinguishable from the modern world. For in the post-modern world we may abandon our idols of truth and reality only to choose to reinstate them in the name of usefulness, or effectiveness, or simply because they are already with us. We may laugh at the metaphysicians of the past, but can we do without them? If we abandon everything, is not everything the same?

The dismantling of truth is both a strength and a weakness. It is a strength because it is a challenge to all that is past. It is a weakness because it prescribes nothing. The dismantling of truth provides the character and the vacuity of our time. The character because it is becoming our predominant belief, the vacuity because we are left with a question-mark. It would, as a consequence, be absurd to imagine that this collection might come to definitive conclusions. It is too much to hope for and too much to ask that these stories and fables of our time provide the truths and certainties of all time. All our truths are, in a sense, fictions – they are the stories we choose to believe. To that end, this collection does not present its papers as truths but as possible rhetorical moves within a category of stories, in the belief that it may become more apparent what sort of options are open to us, and what sort of stories we are able to tell.

STORIES ABOUT
TRUTH

Hilary Lawson

INTRODUCTION

WHEN A contemporary philosopher asks the question 'What is truth?' the intention is to engage in the apparently mundane task of asking what the term 'truth' means, what is it for something to be true, rather than demanding an exploration of the essential character of the world. That the question is construed in this way is not merely a consequence of 'language' philosophy in the narrow linguistic sense which in the 1950s and 1960s risked appearing to reduce all philosophical issues to a matter of definition, but is a function of the central role that language has played in philosophy throughout this century.

Language has dominated twentieth-century philosophy because it has ceased to be regarded as the transparent medium between thought and the world. As a consequence the relation between thought and language, and language and the world has been called into question. Traditionally it has been widely held that for a claim to be true the claim must correspond with reality – the world must actually be as the statement claims that it is. However, as soon as the relation between language and the world is questioned it becomes a complex matter to describe what correspondence with reality entails. To ask for the meaning of truth is not therefore the mundane question that it might appear, for at once it raises the central question of contemporary thought, namely the nature of the relationship between language and the world.

If we have direct access, independent of language, to the world, the truth of a claim can in many cases be straightforwardly ascertained. 'Snow is white' if when we go and look at the world snow actually is white. But if our access to the world is through language we are never in a position to compare the world to the statement in order to ascertain whether it is true. It then begins to look as if 'snow is white' is true because we have chosen our categories in that way. If someone told us that snow was green we would be less likely to tell them to go and look again, and more likely to question whether they were using the word 'snow' and 'green' in the everyday sense.

For the realist, statements always have clear truth value: they are either true or false. 'Snow is white' is true, because the world is like that. For a non-realist the truth of a claim can be dependent on time and circumstance. For example, 'Snow is green' might be true for an environmentalist arguing about Antarctica. The realist may respond that such examples use language in a metaphorical way. The non-realist can reply that there is no such thing as the core, non-metaphorical meaning. Meanings are constantly shifting against one another, and so as a consequence is the world as we see it through language.

In its broadest terms, the problem facing a realist account of truth is to explain how language is hooked on to the world, something essentially independent of language, while the problem facing the non-realist is to explain falsehood in a world dependent on language. However, to see the task as an attempt to solve these problems is in part already to have adopted a realist position, as if there was a correct answer to the question of truth which will emerge once we have found a coherent position. From a non-realist perspective what matters are the consequences of these accounts, these stories about truth. All of the papers in this section, although ostensibly about truth, are at the same time trying to persuade us of the force and value of their position and the consequences.

Richard Rorty and Hugh Tomlinson fall roughly into the non-realist camp, and W. H. Newton-Smith and David Ruben into the realist camp. Richard Rorty has been the central figure behind a renewed interest in the American pragmatist tradition. In his paper, 'Science as Solidarity', he is concerned to defend the practice of science while retaining a non-realist account of truth.

W. H. Newton-Smith wishes to convince us that the consequences of this position are unattractive and that it should therefore be abandoned. Hugh Tomlinson hopes to convey the creative possibilities of non-realism, and David Ruben argues that a realist position does not make social science impossible. All of these stories, if we choose to adopt them, have consequences for our understanding of reality and how we should pursue knowledge and truth.

On a final disquieting reflexive note: if we knew how to choose between these stories, we would already have chosen. For we are presumably trying to choose the 'true' story among them, and these stories are attempting to tell us of what such a story would consist.

Richard Rorty

SCIENCE AS SOLIDARITY

IN OUR culture, the notions of 'science', 'rationality', 'objectivity' and 'truth' are bound up with one other. Science is thought of as offering 'hard', 'objective' truth – truth as correspondence to reality, the only sort of truth worthy of the name. Humanists – philosophers, theologians, historians, literary critics – have to worry about whether they are being 'scientific' – whether they are entitled to think of their conclusions, no matter how carefully argued, as worthy of the term 'true'. We tend to identify seeking 'objective truth' with 'using reason', and so we think of the natural sciences as paradigms of rationality. We also think of rationality as a matter of following procedures laid down in advance, of being 'methodical'. So we tend to use 'methodical', 'rational', 'scientific' and 'objective' as synonyms.

Worries about 'cognitive status' and 'objectivity' are characteristic of a secularized culture in which the scientist replaces the priest. The scientist is now seen as the person who keeps humanity in touch with something beyond itself. As the universe was depersonalized, beauty (and, in time, even moral goodness) came to be thought of as 'subjective'. So truth is now thought of as the only point at which human beings are responsible to something non-human. A commitment to 'rationality' and to 'method' is thought to be a recognition of this responsibility. The scientist becomes a moral exemplar, one who selflessly exposes himself again and again to the hardness of fact.

One result of this way of thinking is that any academic discipline which wants a place at the trough, but is unable to offer the predictions and the technology provided by the natural sciences, must either pretend to imitate science or find some way of obtaining 'cognitive status' without the necessity of discovering facts. Practitioners of these disciplines must either affiliate themselves with this quasi-priestly order by using terms like 'behavioural sciences' or else find something other than 'fact' to be concerned with. People in the humanities typically choose the latter strategy. They describe themselves either as concerned with 'values' as opposed to facts, or as developing and inculcating habits of 'critical reflection'.

Neither sort of rhetoric is very satisfactory. No matter how much humanists talk about 'objective values', the phrase always sounds vaguely confused. It gives with one hand what it takes back with the other. The distinction between the objective and the subjective was designed to parallel that between fact and value, so an objective value sounds as vaguely mythological as a winged horse. Talk about the humanists' special skill at critical reflection fares no better. Nobody really believes that philosophers or literary critics are better at critical thinking, or at taking big broad views of things, than theoretical physicists or microbiologists. So society tends to ignore both these kinds of rhetoric. It treats humanities as on a par with the arts, and thinks of both as providing pleasure rather than truth. Both are, to be sure, thought of as providing 'high' rather than 'low' pleasures. But an elevated and spiritual sort of pleasure is still a long way from the grasp of a truth.

These distinctions between hard facts and soft values, truth and pleasure, and objectivity and subjectivity are awkward and clumsy instruments. They are not suited to divide up culture; they create more difficulties than they resolve. It would be best to find another vocabulary, to start afresh. But in order to do so we first have to find a new way of describing the natural sciences. It is not a question of debunking or downgrading the natural scientist, but simply of ceasing to see him on the model of the priest. We need to stop thinking of science as the place where the human mind confronts the world, and of the scientist as exhibiting proper humility in the face of superhuman forces. We need a way of explaining why scientists are, and deserve to be, moral exemplars which does not depend on a distinction between objective fact and something softer, squishier and more dubious.

To get to such a way of thinking we can start by distinguishing two senses of the term 'rationality'. In one sense, the one I have already discussed, to be rational is to be methodical: that is, to have criteria for success laid down in advance. We think of poets and painters as using some other faculty than 'reason' in their work because, by their own confession, they are not sure of what they want to do before they have done it. They make up new standards of achievement as they go along. By contrast, we think of judges as knowing in advance what criteria a brief will have to satisfy in order to invoke a favourable decision, and of business-men as setting well-defined goals and being judged by their success in achieving them. Law and business are good examples of ration-ality, but the scientist, knowing in advance what would count as disconfirming his hypothesis and prepared to abandon that hypothesis as a result of the unfavourable outcome of a single experiment, seems a truly heroic example. Further, we seem to have a clear criterion of the success of a scientific theory – namely, its ability to predict, and thereby to enable us to control some portion of the world. If to be rational means to be able to lay down criteria in advance, then it is plausible to take natural science as the paradigm of rationality.

The trouble is that in this sense of 'rational' the humanities are never going to qualify as rational activities. If the humanities are concerned with ends rather than means, then there is no way to evaluate their success in terms of antecedently specified criteria. If we already knew what criteria we wanted to satisfy, we would not worry about whether we were pursuing the right ends. If we thought we knew the goals of culture and society in advance, we would have no use for the humanities – as totalitarian societies in fact do not. It is characteristic of democratic and pluralist soci-eties to redefine their goals continually. But if to be rational means to satisfy criteria, then this process of redefinition will be bound to be non-rational. So if the humanities are to be viewed as rational activities, rationality will have to be thought of as something other than the satisfaction of criteria which are stable in advance.

Another meaning for 'rational' is, in fact, available. In this sense, the word means something like 'sane' or 'reasonable' rather than 'methodical'. It names a set of moral virtues: tolerance, respect for the opinions of those around one, willingness to listen, reliance on persuasion rather than force. These are the virtues which members of a civilized society must possess if the society is to endure. In this sense of 'rational', the word means something more like 'civilized' than like 'methodical'. When so construed, the distinction between the rational and the irrational has nothing in particular to do with the difference between the arts and the sciences. On this construction, to be rational is simply to discuss any topic – religious, literary, or scientific – in a way which eschews dogmatism, defensiveness and righteous indignation.

There is no problem about whether, in this latter, weaker sense the humanities are 'rational disciplines'. Usually humanists display the moral virtues in question. Sometimes they do not, but then sometimes scientists don't either. Yet these moral virtues are felt to be not enough. Both humanists and the public hanker after rationality in the first, stronger sense of the term: a sense which is associated with objective truth, correspondence to reality, method and criteria.

We should not try to satisfy this hankering, but rather try to eradicate it. No matter what one's opinion of the secularization of culture, it was a mistake to try to make the natural scientist into a new sort of priest, a link between the human and the non-human. So was the idea that some sorts of truths are 'objective' whereas others are merely 'subjective' or 'relative' – the attempt to divide up the set of true sentences into 'genuine knowledge' and 'mere opinion', or into the 'factual' and the 'judgemental'. So was the idea that the scientist has a special method which, if only the humanists would apply it to ultimate values, would give us the same kind of self-confidence about moral ends as we now have about technological means. I think that we should content ourselves with the second, 'weaker' conception of rationality, and avoid the first, 'stronger' conception. We should avoid the idea that there is some special virtue in knowing in advance what criteria you are going to satisfy, in having standards by which to measure progress.

One can make these issues somewhat more concrete by taking up the current controversy among philosophers about the 'rationality of science'. For some twenty years, ever since the publication of Thomas Kuhn's book, *The Structure of Scientific Revolutions* philosophers have been debating the question of 'whether science

9

is rational'. Attacks on Kuhn for being 'irrationalist' are now as frequent and as urgent as, in the 1930s and 1940s, were attacks on the logical positivists for saying that moral judgements were 'meaningless'. We are constantly being warned of the danger of 'relativism' which will beset us if we give up our attachment to objectivity and to the idea of rationality as obedience to criteria.

Whereas Kuhn's enemies routinely accuse him of reducing science to 'mob psychology', and pride themselves on having (by a new theory of meaning, or reference, or verisimilitude) vindicated the 'rationality of science', his pragmatist friends (such as myself) routinely congratulate him on having softened the distinction between science and non-science. It is fairly easy for Kuhn to show that the enemies are attacking a straw man. But it is harder for him to save himself from his friends. For he has said that 'there is no theory-independent way to reconstruct phrases like "really there"'.[1] He has asked whether it really helps 'to imagine that there is some one full, objective, true account of nature and that the proper measure of scientific achievement is the extent to which it brings us closer to that ultimate goal'.[2] We pragmatists quote these passages incessantly in the course of our effort to enlist Kuhn in our campaign to drop the objective–subjective distinction altogether.

What I am calling 'pragmatism' might also be called 'left-wing Kuhnianism'. It has also been rather endearingly called (by one of its critics, Clark Glymour) 'the new fuzziness', because it is an attempt to blur just those distinctions between the objective and the subjective and between fact and value which the criterial conception of rationality has developed. We fuzzies would like to substitute the idea of 'unforced agreement' for that of 'objectivity'. We should like to put all culture on an epistemological level – or, to put it another way, we would like to get rid of the idea of 'epistemological level' or 'cognitive status'. We would like to disabuse social scientists and humanists of the idea that there is something called 'scientific status' which is a desirable goal. On our view, 'truth' is a univocal term. It applies equally to the judgements of lawyers, anthropologists, physicists, philologists and literary critics. There is point in assigning degrees of 'objectivity' or 'hardness' to such disciplines. For the presence of unforced agreement in all of them gives us everything in the way of 'objective truth' which one could possibly want: namely, intersubjective agreement.

As soon as one says that all there is to objectivity is intersubjectivity, one is likely to be accused of being a relativist. That is the epithet traditionally applied to pragmatists. But this epithet is ambiguous. It can name any of the three different views. The first is the silly and self-refuting view that every belief is as good as every other. The second is the wrong-headed view that 'true' is an equivocal term, having as many meanings as there are contexts of justification. The third is the ethnocentric view that there is nothing to be said about either truth or rationality apart from descriptions of the familiar procedures of justification which a given society – *ours* – uses in one or another area of enquiry. The pragmatist does hold this third, ethnocentric view. But he does not hold the first or the second.

But 'relativism' is not an appropriate term to describe this sort of ethnocentrism. For we pragmatists are not holding a positive theory which says that something is relative to something else. Instead, we are making the purely *negative* point that we would be better off without the traditional distinctions between knowledge and opinion, construed as the distinction between truth as correspondence to reality and truth as a commendatory term for well-justified belief. Our opponents call this negative claim 'relativistic' because they cannot imagine that anybody would seriously deny that truth has an intrinsic nature. So when we say that there is nothing to be said about truth save that each of us will commend as true those beliefs which he or she finds good to believe, the realist is inclined to interpret this as one more positive theory about the nature of truth: a theory according to which truth is simply the contemporary opinion of a chosen individual or group. Such a theory would, of course, be self-refuting. But we pragmatists do not have a theory of truth, much less a relativistic one. As partisans of solidarity, our account of the value of co-operative human enquiry has only an ethical base, not an epistemological or metaphysical one.

To say that we must be ethnocentric may sound suspicious, but this will only happen if we identify ethnocentrism with pigheaded refusal to talk to representatives of other communities. In my sense of enthnocentrism, to be ethnocentric is simply to work by our own lights. The defence of ethnocentrism is simply that there are no other lights to work by. Beliefs suggested by

another individual or another culture must be tested by trying
to weave them together with beliefs which we already have. We
can so test them, because everything which we can identify as
a human being or as a culture will be something which shares
an enormous number of beliefs with us. (If it did not, we would
simply not be able to recognize that it was speaking a language,
and thus that it had any beliefs at all.)

This way of thinking runs counter to the attempt, familiar since
the eighteenth century, to think of political liberalism as based
on a conception of the nature of man. To most thinkers of the
Enlightenment, it seemed clear that the access to Nature which
physical science had provided should now be followed by the
establishment of social, political and economic institutions which
were 'in accordance with Nature'. Ever since, liberal social thought
has centred around social reform as made possible by objective
knowledge of what human beings are like – not knowledge of
what Greeks or Frenchmen or Chinese are like, but of humanity
as such. This tradition dreams of a universal human community
which will exhibit a non-parochial solidarity because it is the
expression of an ahistorical human nature.

Philosophers who belong to this tradition, who wish to ground
solidarity in objectivity, have to construe truth as correspondence
to reality. So they must construct an epistemology which has room
for a kind of justification which is not merely social but natural,
springing from human nature itself, and made possible by a link
between that part of nature and the rest of nature. By contrast,
we pragmatists, who wish to reduce objectivity to solidarity, do
not require either a metaphysics or an epistemology. We do not
need an account of a relation between beliefs and objects called
'correspondence', nor an account of human cognitive abilities
which ensures that our species is capable of entering into that
relation. We see the gap between truth and justification not as
something to be bridged by isolating a natural and trans-cultural
sort of rationality which can be used to criticize certain cultures
and praise others, but simply as the gap between the actual good
and the possible better. From a pragmatist point of view, to say
that what is rational for us now to believe may not be *true*, is
simply to say that somebody may come up with a better idea.

On this pragmatist view of rationality as civility, enquiry is

a matter of continually reweaving a web of beliefs rather than the application of criteria to cases. Criteria change in just the way other beliefs change, and there is no touchstone which can preserve any criterion for possible revision. That is why the pragmatist is not frightened by the spectre of 'cultural relativism'. Our interchange with other communities and cultures is not to be thought of as a clash between irreconcilable systems of thought, deductively inferred from incompatible first premises. Alternative cultures should not be thought of on the model of alternative geometries – as irreconcilable because they have axiomatic structures and contradictory axioms. Such geometries are *designed* to be irreconcilable. Individual and cultural webs of belief are not so designed, and do not have axiomatic structures.

Cultures can, indeed, protect themselves by institutionalizing knowledge-claims, and making people suffer who do not hold certain beliefs. But such institutional backups take the form of bureaucrats and policemen, not of 'rules of language' or 'criteria of rationality'. The criterial conception of rationality has suggested that every distinct culture comes equipped with certain unchallengeable axioms, 'necessary truths', and that these form barriers to communication between cultures. So it has seemed as if there could be no conversation between cultures but only subjugation by force. On the pragmatic conception of rationality there are no such barriers. The distinction between different cultures differs only in degree from the distinction between theories held by members of a single culture. The Tasmanian aborigines and the British colonists, for example, had trouble in communicating, but this trouble was different only in extent from the difficulties in communication experienced by Gladstone and Disraeli. The trouble in all such cases is just the difficulty of explaining why other people disagree with us, and of reweaving our beliefs so as to fit the fact of disagreement together with the other beliefs we hold. The same pragmatist (and, more specifically, Quinean) arguments which dispose of the positivists' distinction between analytic and synthetic truths dispose of the anthropologists' distinction between the inter-cultural and the intra-cultural.

Another reason for describing us as 'relativistic' is that we pragmatists drop the idea that enquiry is destined to converge to a single point – that Truth is 'out there' waiting for human beings to arrive at it. This idea seems to us an unfortunate attempt to carry a religious conception over into a secular culture. All that is worth preserving of the claim that rational enquiry will converge to a single point is the claim that we must be able to explain why past false views were held in the past, and thus explain how we go about re-educating our benighted ancestors. To say that we think we're heading in the right direction is just to say, with Kuhn, that we can, by hindsight, tell the story of the past as a story of progress.

But the fact that we can trace such a direction and tell such a story does not mean that we have come closer to a goal which is out there waiting for us. We cannot, I think, imagine a moment at which the human race could settle back and say, 'Well, now that we've finally arrived at the Truth we can relax.' Paul Feyerabend is right in suggesting that we should discard the metaphor of enquiry, and human activity generally, as converging rather than proliferating, becoming more unified rather than more diverse. On the contrary, we should relish that thought that the sciences as well as the arts will *always* provide a spectacle of fierce competition between alternative theories, movements and schools. The end of human activity is not rest, but rather richer and better human activity. We should think of human progress as making it possible for human beings to do more interesting things and be more interesting people, not as heading toward a place which has somehow been prepared for us in advance. To drop the criterial conception of rationality in favour of the pragmatist conception would be to give up the idea of Truth as something to which we were responsible. Instead we should think of 'true' as a word which applies to those beliefs upon which we are able to agree, as roughly synonymous with 'justified'. To say that beliefs can be agreed upon without being true is, once again, merely to say that somebody might come up with a better idea.

Another way of characterizing this line of thought is to say that pragmatists would like to drop the idea that human beings are responsible to a non-human power. We hope for a culture in which questions about 'the objectivity of value' or 'the rationality of science' would seem equally unintelligible. Pragmatists would like to replace the desire for objectivity – the desire to be in touch with a reality which is more than some community with which we identify ourselves – with the desire for solidarity with that community. They think that the habits of relying on persuasion rather than force, of respect for the opinions of colleagues, of curiosity and eagerness for new data and ideas, are the *only* virtues which scientists have. They do not think that there is an intellectual virtue called 'rationality' over and above these moral virtues.

On this view, there is no reason to praise scientists for being more 'objective' or 'logical' or 'methodical' or 'devoted to truth' than other people. But there is plenty of reason to praise the institutions they have developed and within which they work, and to use these as models for the rest of culture. For these institutions give concreteness and detail to the idea of 'unforced agreement'. Reference to such institutions fleshes out the idea of 'a free and open encounter' – the sort of encounter in which truth cannot fail to win. On this view, to say that truth will win in such an encounter is not to make a metaphysical claim about the connection between human reason and the nature of things. It is merely to say that the best way to find out what to believe is to listen to as many suggestions and arguments as you can.

My rejection of traditional notions of rationality can be summed up by saying that the only sense in which science is exemplary is that it is a model of human solidarity. We should think of the institutions and practices which make up various scientific communities as providing suggestions about the way in which the rest of culture might organize itself. When we say that our legislatures are 'unrepresentative' or 'dominated by special interests', or that the art world is dominated by 'fashion', we are contrasting these areas of culture with areas which seem in better order. The natural sciences strike us as being such areas. But, on this view, we shall not explain this better order by thinking of the scientists as having a 'method' which the rest of us would do well to imitate, nor as benefiting from the desirable hardness of their subjects compared with the undesirable softness of other subjects. If we say that sociology or literary criticism 'is not a science', we shall mean merely that the amount of agreement among sociologists or literary critics on what counts as significant work, work which needs following up, is less than among, say, microbiologists.

Pragmatists will not attempt to explain this latter phenomenon by saying that societies or literary texts are squishier than molecules, or that the human sciences cannot be as 'value-free' as the natural sciences, or that the sociologists and critics have not yet found their paradigms. Nor will they assume that 'a science' is necessarily something which we want sociology to be. One consequence of their view is the suggestion that perhaps 'the human sciences' *should* look quite different from the natural sciences. This suggestion is not based on epistemological or metaphysical considerations which show that enquiry into societies must be different from enquiry into things. Instead, it is based on the observation that natural scientists are interested primarily in predicting and controlling the behaviour of things and that prediction and control may not be what we want from our sociologists and our literary critics.

Despite the encouragement he has given it, however, Kuhn draws back from this pragmatist position. He does so when he asks for an explanation of 'why science works'. The request for such an explanation binds him together with his opponents and separates him from his left-wing friends. Anti-Kuhnians tend to unite in support of the claim that 'merely psychological or socio-logical reasons' will not explain why natural science is so good at predicting. Kuhn joins them when he says that he shares 'Hume's itch' – the desire for 'an explanation of the viability of the whole language game that involves "induction" and underpins the form of life we live'.[3]

Pragmatists think that one will suffer from Hume's itch only if one has been scratching oneself with what has sometimes been called 'Hume's fork' – the distinction between 'relations of ideas' and 'matters of fact'. This distinction survives in contemporary philosophy as the distinction between 'questions of language' and 'questions of fact'. We pragmatists think that philososphers of language such as Wittgenstein, Quine, Goodman, Davidson and others have shown us how to get along without these distinctions. Once one has lived without them for a while one learns to live without distinctions between knowledge and opinion, or between subjective and objective, as well. The purposes served by the latter distinctions come to be served by the unproblematic sociological distinction between areas in which unforced agreement is relatively infrequent and areas in which it is relatively frequent. So we do not itch for an explanation of the success of recent Western science any more than for the success of recent Western politics. That is why we fuzzies applaud Kuhn when he says that 'One does not know what a person who denies the rationality of learning from experience is trying to say', but are aghast when he goes on to ask *why* 'we have no rational alternatives to learning from experience'.[4]

On a pragmatist view, the contrast between 'relations of ideas' and 'matters of fact' is a special case of the bad seventeenth-century contrasts between being 'in us' and being 'out there', between subject and object, between our beliefs and what those beliefs (moral, scientific, theological, etc.) are trying to get right. Pragmatists avoid this latter contrast by instead contrasting our beliefs with proposed alternative beliefs. They recommend that we worry only about the choice between two hypotheses, rather than about whether there is something which 'makes' either true. To take this stance would rid us of questions about the objectivity of value, the rationality of science, and the causes of the viability of our language games. All such theoretical questions would be replaced with practical questions about whether we ought to keep our present values, theories and practices or try to replace them with others. Given such a replacement, there would be nothing to be responsible to except ourselves.

This may sound like solipsistic fantasy, but the pragmatist regards it as an alternative account of the nature of intellectual and moral responsibility. He is suggesting that instead of invoking anything like the idea–fact, or language–fact, or mind–world, or subject–object distinctions to explicate our intuition that there is something out there to be responsible to, we just drop that intuition. We should drop it in favour of the thought that we might be better than we presently are – in the sense of being better scientific theorists, or citizens, or friends. The backup for this intuition would be the actual or imagined existence of other human beings who were already better (utopian fantasies, or actual experience of superior individuals or societies). On this account, to be responsible is a matter of what Peirce called 'contrite fallibilism' rather than of respect for something beyond. The desire for 'objectivity' boils down to a desire to acquire beliefs which will eventually receive unforced agreement in the course of a free and open encounter with people holding other beliefs.

Pragmatists interpret the goal of enquiry (in any sphere of culture) as the attainment of an appropriate mixture of unforced agreement with tolerant disagreement (where what counts as appropriate is determined, within that sphere, by trial and error). Such a reinterpretation of our sense of responsibility would, if carried through, gradually make unintelligible the subject–object model of enquiry, the child–parent model of moral obligation, and the correspondence theory of truth. A world in which those models, and that theory, no longer had any intuitive appeal would be a pragmatist's paradise.

When Dewey urged that we try to create such a paradise he was said to be irresponsible. For, it was said, he left us bereft of weapons to use against our enemies; he gave us nothing with which to 'answer the Nazis'. When we new fuzzies try to revive Dewey's repudiation of criteriology we are said to be 'relativistic'. We must, people say, believe that every coherent view is as good as every other, since we have no 'outside' touchstone for choice among such views. We are said to leave the general public defence-less against the witch doctor, the defender of creationism, or anyone else who is clever and patient enough to deduce a consistent and wide-ranging set of theorems from his 'alternative first principles'.

Nobody is convinced when we fuzzies say that we can be just as morally indignant as the next philosopher. We are suspected of being contritely fallibilist when righteous fury is called for. Even when we actually display appropriate emotions we get nowhere, for we are told that we have no *right* to these emotions. When we suggest that one of the few things we know (or need to know) about truth is that it is what wins in a free and open encounter, we are told that we have defined 'true' as 'satisfies the standards of our community'. But we pragmatists do not hold this relativist view. We do not infer from 'There is no way to step outside communities to a neutral standpoint' to 'There is no rational way to justify liberal communities over totalitarian communities'. For that inference involves just the notion of 'rationality' as a set of ahistorical principles which pragmatists abjure. What we in fact infer is that there is no way to beat totalitarians in argument by appealing to shared common premises, and no point in pretending that a common human nature makes the totalitarians unconsciously hold such premises.

The claim that we fuzzies have no right to be furious at moral evil, no right to commend our views as true unless we simul-taneously refute ourselves by claiming that there are objects out there which *make* those views true, begs all the theoretical questions. But it gets to the practical and moral heart of the matter. This is the question of whether notions like 'unforced agreement' and 'free and open encounter' – descriptions of social situations

18

– can take the place in our moral lives of notions like 'the world', 'the will of God', 'the moral law', 'what our beliefs are trying to represent accurately' and 'what makes our beliefs true'. All the philosophical presuppositions which make Hume's fork seem inevitable are ways of suggesting that human communities must justify their existence by striving to attain a non-human goal. To suggest that we can forget about Hume's fork, forget about being responsible to what is 'out there', is to suggest that human communities can justify their existence only by comparisons with other actual and possible human communities.

I can make this contrast a bit more concrete by asking whether free and open encounters, and the kind of community which permits and encourages such encounters, are for the sake of truth and goodness, or whether 'the quest for truth and goodness' is simply the quest for that kind of community. Is the sort of community which is exemplifed by groups of scientific enquirers and by democratic political institutions a means to an end, or is the formation of such communities the only goal we need? Dewey thought that it was the only goal we needed, and I think he was right. But whether he was or not, this question is the one to which the debates about Kuhn's 'irrationalism' and the new fuzzies' 'relativism' will eventually boil down.

Dewey was accused of blowing up the optimism and flexibility of a parochial and jejune way of life (the American) into a philosophical system. So he did, but his reply was that *any* philosophical system is going to be an attempt to express the ideals of *some* community's way of life. He was quite ready to admit that the virtue of his philosophy was, indeed, nothing more than the virtue of the way of life which it commended. On his view, philosophy does not justify affiliation with a community in the light of something ahistorical called 'reason' or 'trans-cultural principles'. It simply expatiates on the special advantages of that community over other communities. Dewey's best argument for doing philosophy this way is also the best argument we partisans of solidarity have against partisans of objectivity: it is Nietzsche's argument that the traditional Western metaphysico-epistemological way of firming up our habits is not working any more.

What would it be like to be less fuzzy and parochial than this? I suggest that it would be to become less genial, tolerant, open-minded and fallibilist than we are now. In the non-trivial,

pejorative sense of 'ethnocentric', the sense in which we congratulate ourselves on being less ethnocentric now than our ancestors
were three hundred years ago, the way to avoid ethnocentrism
is precisely to abandon the sort of thing we fuzzies are blamed
for abandoning. It is to have only the most tenuous and cursory
formulations of criteria for changing our beliefs, only the loosest
and most flexible standards. Suppose that for the last three hundred
years we had been using an explicit algorithm for determining
how just a society was, and how good a physical theory was.
Would we have developed either parliamentary democracy or relativity physics? Suppose that we had the sort of 'weapons' against
the fascists of which Dewey was said to deprive us – firm, unrevis-
able, moral principles which were not merely 'ours' but 'universal'
and 'objective'. How could we avoid having these weapons turn
in our hands and bash all the genial tolerance out of our own
heads?

Imagine, to use another example, that a few years from now
you open your copy of the *New York Times* and read that the
philosophers, in convention assembled, have unanimously agreed
that values are objective, science rational, truth a matter of correspondence to reality, etc. Recent breakthroughs in semantics and
meta-ethics, the report goes on, have caused the last remaining
non-cognitivists in ethics to recant. Similar breakthroughs in the
philosophy of science have led Kuhn formally to abjure his claim
that there is no theory-independent way to reconstruct statements
about what is 'really there'. All the new fuzzies have repudiated
all their former views. By way of making amends for the intellectual confusion which the philosophical profession has recently
caused, the philosophers have adopted a short, crisp set of standards of rationality and morality. Next year the convention is
expected to adopt the report of the committee charged with formu-
lating a standard of aesthetic taste.

Surely the public reaction to this would not be 'Saved!' but
rather 'Who on earth do these philosophers think they *are*?' It
is one of the best things about the form of intellectual life we
Western liberals lead that this *would* be our reaction. No matter
how much we moan about the disorder and confusion of the current philosophical scene, about the treason of the clerks, we do
not really want things any other way. What prevents us from
relaxing and enjoying the new fuzziness is perhaps no more than

cultural lag, the fact that the rhetoric of the Enlightenment praised the emerging natural sciences in a vocabulary which was left over from a less liberal and tolerant era. This rhetoric enshrined all the old philosophical oppositions between mind and world, appearance and reality, subject and object, truth and pleasure. Dewey thought that it was the continued prevalence of such oppositions which prevented us from seeing that modern science was a new and promising invention, a way of life which had not existed before and which ought to be encouraged and imitated, something which required a new rhetoric rather than justification by an old one.

Suppose that Dewey were right about this, and that eventually we learn to find the fuzziness which results from breaking down such oppositions spiritually comforting rather than morally offensive. What would the rhetoric of the culture, and in particular of the humanities, sound like? Presumably it would be more Kuhnian, in the sense that it would mention particular concrete achievements – paradigms – more, and 'method' less. There would be less talk about rigour and more about originality. The image of the great scientist would not be of somebody who got it right but of somebody who made it new. The new rhetoric would draw more on the vocabulary of Romantic poetry and socialist politics, and less on that of Greek metaphysics, religious morality or Enlightenment scientism. A scientist would rely on a sense of solidarity with the rest of her profession, rather than a picture of herself as battling through the veils of illusion, guided by the light of reason.

If all this happened, the term 'science', and thus the oppositions between the humanities, the arts and the sciences might gradually fade away. Once 'science' was deprived of an honorific sense, we might not need it for taxonomy. We might feel no more need for a term which groups together paleontology, physics, anthropology and psychology than we do for one which groups together engineering, law, social work and medicine. The people now called 'scientists' would no longer think of themselves as members of a quasi-priestly order, nor would the public think of themselves as in the care of such an order.

In this situation, the 'humanities' would no longer think of themselves as such, nor would they share a common rhetoric. Each of the disciplines which now fall under that rubric would worry as little about its method, cognitive status or 'philosophical foundations' as do mathematics, civil engineering or sculpture. For terms which denoted disciplines would not be thought to divide 'subject-matters', chunks of the world which had 'interfaces' with each other. Rather, they would be thought to denote communities whose boundaries were as fluid as the interests of their members. In this heyday of the fuzzy, there would be as little reason to be self-conscious about the nature and status of one's discipline as, in the ideal democratic community, about the nature and status of one's race or sex. For one's ultimate loyalty would be to the larger community which permitted and encouraged this kind of freedom and insouciance. This community would serve no higher end than its own preservation and self-improvement, the preservation and enhancement of civilization. It would identify rationality with that effort, rather than with the desire for objectivity. So it would feel no need for a foundation more solid than reciprocal loyalty.

W. H. Newton-Smith

RATIONALITY, TRUTH AND THE NEW FUZZIES

SCIENCE IS under attack: an attack marked by, if not actually launched with, the publication some twenty-five years ago of T. S. Kuhn's *The Structure of Scientific Revolutions*.[1] Not surprisingly the onslaught on science by various historians, philosophers and sociologists of science has left the institution of science little affected. If anything the intervening period has seen a further increase in the proportion of society's resources placed at its disposal. Some critics, notably Feyerabend, intended to redeploy resources away from science, and no doubt a serious discussion of our priorities in this regard was, and remains, overdue. In most cases, however, the attack only appeared to be directed against science. In the case of Kuhn himself the object of criticism was not science itself but only a certain image of science. That image has it that science is jointly constituted by the pursuit of the worthy goal of truth and by the possession of the Scientific Method, a device uniquely designed to bring progress towards the goal. The institutional embodiment of science is a group of men (for the most part) who dispassionately and disinterestedly apply the method in the successful pursuit of the goal.

The time had come to dissolve that image. That this is so would be agreed by virtually all parties to the debates of the last quarter-century save for Karl Popper. The question of the viability of the image is no longer of interest. What is of interest are the questions of the best perspective from which to advance a critique and the best image to put in its place. For Richard Rorty the perspective is the pragmatism of Dewey and James. From that perspective, for Rorty at least, the critique goes much deeper. For the image rests on traditional philosophy, which is itself to be dissolved. Rorty tells us that philosophy as invented by Plato and as practised in the continuing Anglo-Saxon tradition is burdened with an untenable theory of truth, the correspondence Theory of truth, which generates a series of false dichotomies: mind–world, appearance–reality, subject–object, truth–pleasure. As befits a pragmatist Rorty argues that this framework has simply not worked and needs to be set aside. The framework consists of a vocabulary that has not proved useful. Once we think our way out of the morass of this tradition our new image of science should be one of solidarity. What makes science, science and what makes it special is the solidarity of the members of the scientific community one with the other. The specialness has nothing to do with the goal of truth or the Scientific Method. The details of this new image are to be fleshed out with the help of the vocabulary of Romantic philosophy and socialist politics.

What is on offer from the latterday pragmatists is much more than a new image of science. Going the pragmatic way, we are told (Rorty, p. 17), will end the division between disciplines, end the quasi-priestly status of scientists, end concern with foundational and methodological issues. It will focus attention on communities instead of disciplines, and incline these communities to identify with the preservation and enhancement of civilization. One might well question, as indeed I will, whether all these consequences are to be desired. In any event it is heartening to think that a philosophical movement might have consequences of this magnitude. Given the strength of the claims, one wants to know both whether Rorty's pragmatism is a viable alternative to what he regards as the traditional philosophical perspective and how one gets from the new perspective to the supposed consequences. In the first part of this paper, Rorty's 'first philosophy', his pragmatism, will be considered. The position and the objections to be offered may be familiar but reminding ourselves of them will assist in seeing why Rorty thinks that pragmatism has something powerful and exciting to offer. That being done the alleged consequences, particularly in regard to science and the relation between science and the humanities, will be examined in the second part of the paper.

According to Rorty the central error of our philosophical tradition is the correspondence theory of truth. That theory assumes that there is a way in which the world is mostly independent of ourselves. Our beliefs are true just in case they correspond to how the world is. Not without justice Rorty claims that the nature of this correspondence has never been properly explained. And the very project of trying to make it out is held to involve the concealed assumption of something like a God's-eye perspective from which the realm of human beliefs is held up against the world itself. Much needs to be said if the traditional view is to survive in any recognizable form, and much can be said. That I forbear to do, preferring in the context of this paper to examine Rorty's alternative, difficulties in which may well inspire us to try again the traditional way.

Rorty proposes that we set this framework aside on the grounds that no one has ever cashed out the metaphor of correspondence and, more generally, that it simply has not worked. Our concern should not be with beliefs we confusedly hope correspond to the world but with what we are warranted in saying; with what it is reasonable for us to say. We determine this and that should be the focus of our concern. Truth is to be understood by reference to the notion of what it is reasonable to say. Many styles of argumentation that might be deployed against this suggestion are held by Rorty to beg the question by assuming the standpoint of traditional philosophy. For instance, any argument that proceeds by reference to the meaning of 'true' or the correct analysis of the concept of truth is countered by Rorty's rejection of the traditional categories of meaning and analysis. One cannot fight on all fronts at once – at least not if one wants to do more than make a heroic gesture. And so I propose to use only strategies that a pragmatist is bound to respect. These are at least three. First, one can enquire whether pragmatism does in fact avoid what it finds unattractive in the traditional perspective. Secondly, one can consider the relative explanatory powers of the perspectives, for this is a consideration which Rorty remarks that a pragmatist must respect. Thirdly, a pragmatist must respect arguments that look to the benefits or otherwise of conversion to a particular perspective.

The common ground one can find with the pragmatist for the

sake of discussing one's differences includes a respect for science. That is what makes it possible to appeal to the notions of problem-solving and explanation. In this regard it is to be stressed that Rorty is no Feyerabend. Science itself is not to be dissolved. There is something special about science for Rorty and our new framework must do justice to that fact. Indeed, it is hard to see how any follower of Dewey and James could be an enemy of science. Dewey and James (as construed by Rorty) and Rorty himself are enemies of philosophy. That makes them opponents not of science but of the associated traditional image of science. As will be seen this creates something of a tension in Rorty's new perspective.

It is agreed on all sides that there is some distinction to be drawn between something's being reasonable to believe now and its actually being true. Rorty says that something which it is reasonable to believe now is false just in case someone may come up with a better idea. Two questions arise. Who is this someone? In virtue of what would his or her idea be better? Presumably the someone is not any actual person. If a currently reasonable belief of mine is only false if some actual person comes up with something better in regard to that belief, a nuclear holocaust which decimated the human race would guarantee the truth of all my reasonable beliefs. And even if the human race is destined to continue indefinitely, genetic engineering might lead to an accidental erosion of the IQ of all future members of the race to the point where no one had any better ideas than I do now. And that eventuality does not seem a way of making my reasonable beliefs true. Or, again, the triumph of a permanent fascistic regime might ensure that no one formed more reasonable beliefs than I do without thereby making it the case that my beliefs are true. Thus it is not surprising that pragmatists have tended to talk not of some actual person who might have better ideas than we do but of hypothetical persons or communities of persons. For instance, according to Peirce, if I reasonably believe that P but P is false, that amounts to the fact that if human enquiry were continued indefinitely and properly the community would converge in a stable way on the belief that P is false. Thus in order to avoid the unpalatable consequences outlined above, we have to say that what makes my currently reasonable beliefs true or false is what some hypothetical, or as Rorty says 'imagined', believer or community of believers would believe.

This hypothetical community must not only continue its labours indefinitely, it must also have unlimited access to the evidence without restriction to time and place. To illustrate the need for this, consider the very real possibility that some primitive man or woman had an entirely reasonable but false belief about the numbers of some long-extinct species living in his or her vicinity. We can well imagine that no one since has had any decent ideas whatsoever about this matter. The hypothetical community can only come to have better ideas than the primitive if they have access in some mysterious way to the evidence available at the long-past time but no longer. One recent pragmatist has even gone so far as to suppose the community to be capable of time-travel![2]

Our hypothetical community must continue its enquiries indefinitely (otherwise there is no possibility that their reasonable beliefs at a particular time may be false) and it must have unlimited access to the relevant evidence. And what is more, they presumably have enhanced perceptual faculties. For it is easy to imagine that we have false but reasonable beliefs due to the limitations of our sensory equipment. Finally, given the history of the way in which we have improved our methods of dealing with such evidence as is available, and given that we have good reason to think that further improvement is possible, we need to imagine the members of this community as capable of dealing with the evidence in ways quite unfamiliar to us.

Rorty, in saying that someone might come up with a better idea, is discretely quantifying over these ideal beings. It is instructive to ask whether we would recognize one of these creatures if it were to come among us. After the best possible investigation that we can actually conduct we have concluded that P is so. We believe reasonably that P is true. This creature believes that P is false and *ex hypothesi* it, the creature, is correct. But to us the creature's view seems just bizarre. It is as if someone told us confidently that the earth is flat. To recognize the creature as superior we would have to recognize that he or she was right and that is just what we could not do. For by our lights the reasonable thing to believe is that P is true and this the creature denies. I suppose the creature might perform 'miracles'. He or she might exploit his or her superior knowledge to produce spin-off technology that so impressed us that we would take them on authority.

But we would not recognize them through seeing that they were right. We would have to take them, Christ-like, on faith.

Rorty is fond of deploying theological imagery in decrying the traditionalist. Pragmatism is described as furthering the prospect of doing without God.[3] Presumably this is because the traditional realist needs God to do what is impossible for us: to step outside our skins and compare ourselves with something absolute.[4] And certainly the restriction to reasonable or warranted belief appeared to give us something more available than the world of facts apprehended only by God. But in order to avoid making ourselves gods by making our reasonable beliefs true just because they are our reasonable beliefs, we have had to invoke beings so ideal that we would not recognize one in our midst. These beings, imagined to be in human form, are still gods. In Rorty's theological imagery one is tempted to say that his position has all the attractions of the New Testament over the Old Testament. This fantasy does have a point. It is a form of *tu quoque*. Rorty objects that, for the traditionalist, truth is something which may transcend our capacity to recognize it. But truth is equally transcendent for Rorty. The fact that the God who recognizes the truth for Rorty has taken human form does not mean that it is recognizable by us here and now.

Rorty no doubt regards what I have offered as an attempted definition or theory of truth. And he professes not to be interested in such things. That is all very well. If one does not want to have theories or definitions that is one's choice. However, if Rorty wants to be able to explain how it is that a reasonable belief can be false he is going to have to tell some story along the lines given. He may prefer not to describe the story as a definition or a theory, but, however labelled, he is stuck with the story.

There is more to be said by the traditionalist and by the pragmatist in defence of their respective conceptions of truth. But enough has been said to show that the pragmatist does not obviously avoid what he feels to be problematic about the traditionalist's approach. Even if there is a stalemate at this level, it may be possible to make progress by considering the explanatory potential of the rival approaches. The traditionalist in the context of the philosophy of science is the realist. The realist has attempted to make a great deal of the apparent explanatory force of his theory. He asks what it is about, say, relativistic mechanics that enables it to generate more correct predictions than, say, Newtonian mechanics. His answer is that it is the improvement in their truth content. The world is more like the way the relativistic theory describes it than the way the Newtonian theory describes it. For the realist, it would be a total mystery that the relativistic theory should deliver the goods if it were not for the fact that that theory encapsulates more truth about the world at the theoretical level. This argument, a version of which I have spelled out elsewhere,[5] is fraught with difficulties. But it has an undeniable appeal. And the onus is on the pragmatist to say something using only his soft and fuzzy notion of truth in answer to the question what it is that makes contemporary physical theories better than their predecessors.

What is the pragmatist's line? Rorty suggests, citing Kuhn and Dewey, that 'we give up the notion of science travelling towards an end called "correspondence with reality" and instead say merely that one vocabulary works better than another for a given purpose'.[6] No doubt Einstein's vocabulary is better than Newton's for one who wants to make correct predictions. But what is it about that vocabulary which makes it better? Is it just, as Rorty puts it, that Einstein 'lucked out'? Maybe, but it would be respectable scientific practice to assume that there is more to it than this. Scientists are not inclined to answer questions about the demise of the dinosaur by saying that their luck ran out. At least initially one expects something better; similarly in this case. A scientist is going to expect a decent answer to the question why Einstein is better. Rorty certainly cannot evade the analogy by reference to the fact that while the demise of the dinosaurs belongs to science, the demise of Newton does not. For given his Quinean framework, his opposition to traditional philosophy and his fuzziness about disciplines, there is no demarcation in kind between science and philosophy. It may be that at the end of the day Newton and the dinosaurs just had bad luck. But that is what we say at the end of a bad day. The realist, unlike the pragmatist, does have something to say in explanation. And he has further puzzles to draw to the attention of the pragmatist. If it is just a matter of vocabulary, why do we not find a plurality of equally viable vocabularies for dealing with the world? If there were two alternative vocabularies (genuinely different vocabularies) for particle mechanics, geology, genetics and so on, the realist perspective would be in trouble. It is for this reason that realists have always been nervous of under–determination. But we do not find these alternatives. What explanation is there of this lack of plurality? Lack of imagination or ability on our part? That is puzzling. We have had a history of genii who have produced extraordinarily successful theories, or, as Rorty would say, extraordinarily successful vocabularies. Why, given all that talent, has it never manifested itself in alternatives? Vocabulary is up to us. Why have we not been able to come up with a plurality? The answer is obvious: the vocabulary we have is tending to cut the world at its joints. That is why there is no plurality. On the very explanatory grounds that the pragmatist is bound to respect, there are good reasons for preferring realism.

The pragmatist has not supplied a satisfactory vocabulary to replace the traditionalist's talk of truth. Nor has a framework been created which represents an explanatory advance. However, if the pragmatist were able to provide a new and satisfactory model of science and a new and beneficial way of thinking about rationality, one might be attracted to join forces in tackling the problems of the programme in the light of the admitted difficulties in the traditionalist's approach. Rorty does purport to have delivered these goods – goods which are examined below.

In our culture, according to Richard Rorty, the notions of 'truth', 'rationality', 'science' and 'objectivity' have become bound up together. Objective truth, truth as correspondence, is what we arrive at using rationality, of which science provides the paradigm. And we think of scientific rationality as 'a matter of following procedures laid down in advance' (p. 6). Taking rationality in this way gives science a special position. For the arts and the humanities cannot offer such procedures, or so Rorty says. Vain attempts to do so only produce the sort of grotesque distortions involved in converting the study of human action into a 'behavioural science'. Rorty wants those other than scientists to have a chance at being rational. And so he proposes another sort of rationality. To be rational in his way is to be sane, reasonable, civilized and various other good things, including eschewing dogmatism, defensiveness and righteous indignation.

Rorty does not see himself as making a trivial linguistic proposal for the use of the word 'rational'. He sees two models of rationality at work in our culture and proposes that we give up valuing rationality in the sense of the scientific model as he, Rorty, construes that model. This sort of rationality will be called *criterial rationality*. Rorty's style of rationality will be called *fuzzy rationality*. Each of these models is taken to embody claims about what we ought to value; about the procedures we ought to follow; about how we ought to organize ourselves and our lives. Rorty is quite clear where he stands. There is, he says, no special virtue in 'knowing in advance what criteria you are going to satisfy, in having standards by which to measure progress'. We should stop caring about criterial rationality and care only about fuzzy rationality.

The thought that there are no standards laid down in advance is a little puzzling. At the very least, are not the rules of deductive logic and the axioms of the probability calculus laid down in advance as necessary conditions of rationality? And are there not better and worse ways of choosing between rival scientific hypotheses? Even if we agree that we may change our minds about the rules of deductive logic or the best methodology for science, it looks as though there are principles guiding us at each moment. In view of the *prima facie* implausibility of thinking that there are no standards laid down in advance, it is instructive to ask what it is about pragmatism that leads to this conclusion. In Rorty I do not find any satisfactory general argument to this conclusion. At times pragmatism is simply defined as the doctrine that there are 'no constraints derived from the nature of the objects, or of the mind, or of language, but only those retail constraints provided by the remarks of our fellow inquirers'.[7] On this definition one gets easily from pragmatism to the rejection of criterial rationality. But the route is boring. What one wants to know is how the rejection of the correspondence theory of truth in favour of the pragmatist's 'non-theory' of truth supports the rejection of criterial rationality. An argument suggested to me by Rorty's remark about absence of constraints derived from the nature of the objects, and by other remarks to the effect that truth is not something to which we are responsive, is given below.

The traditionalist thinks that there is a world, a world largely independent of us and in virtue of which our beliefs are true or false as the case may be. If there are these facts and these truths about them, there will be better and worse ways of finding out these truths. Facts about these facts, these truths and ourselves (our biological nature) mean that some ways of finding out are good, some bad and some indifferent. The good ways are good quite independently of decisions or beliefs on our part. Of course we can change our conversational styles and our vocabularies but the viability of those changes will answer to something outside our control. In one very good sense the traditional approach does support criterial rationality. There are standards laid down in advance whether we have or even can recognize them as such. Facts about polar bears, the North Pole and our perceptual apparatus mean that going to the North Pole is a better way of finding out about such bears as may be there than going to the source of the Amazon. The traditionalist has to admit to the existence of criteria about which we have no choice. If, on the other hand, truth is just what our methods of enquiry produce, so to speak, and if those methods are up to us, there is a sense in which there are no criteria laid down in advance. Or so it would seem.

But this is mere appearance, appearance created by Rorty's claims not to have a theory of truth. As we have seen, he has committed himself to something rather like a theory of truth. For, to permit reasonable beliefs being false, Rorty has to hold that truth is what idealized methods of enquiry would produce if correctly used by certain hypothetical communities of enquirers. But in that case what is true and what is false is so in virtue not of ourselves and our enquiries but of these ideal beings and their enquiries. In which case there will be better or worse ways of proceeding in our enquiries. What is true will make some ways good, some ways bad and some ways indifferent. The pragmatist is committed to criterial rationality just as much as the traditionalist. There are criteria just as much laid down in advance if truth is correspondence to the world or if truth is the results found by a community of enquirers among whom we cannot number ourselves.

In so far as one finds an argument in Rorty it is of a rather different style. In his paper he suggests that his position can be made more concrete by considering the issue in the context of a recent debate in the philosophy of science. By attacking a criterial conception of rationality in the context of the philosophy of science he hopes to render the non-criterial approach plausible there. The intention is to transfer that conception to the humanities having rendered it respectable. As such the project is reminiscent of the positivists' desire to transfer the methods of science to the humanities. We need to consider whether there is any sense in which arguments from the philosophy of science support a fuzzy conception over a criterial one. And we need to ask if Rorty can derive the results he hopes for (the dissolution of subject boundaries, etc.) from this fuzzy conception.

In the literature of the philosophy of science there is most definitely a criterial conception, a conception of the scientific method as consisting in a system of binding, exceptionless, timeless rules for choosing between rival hypotheses in the face of a given body of evidence. That conception has been subjected to lively attack, particularly by Kuhn and Feyerabend,[8] both of whom Rorty enlists on his side. There is here an easy target. However, the fact that such an extreme conception is to be ridiculed does not show that there is something wrong with criterial rationality in science. *Prima facie* the idea that there are no criteria laid down in advance in science is bizarre. For example, the community of mathematicians is pretty solid on the matter of Peano's axioms of arithmetic. If someone shows or appears to establish a result incompatible with those axioms such as that $1 = 0$ (there are notorious 'proofs' of this result generated by covert division by zero), it is assumed without any serious examination of the proof that there is a mistake here. Such a criterion as this was not given *a priori* by the gods. It as a history, it is open to re-evaluation. But at any moment in time it is quite natural to describe mathematicians as operating with criteria fixed in advance. Rorty cites businessmen and judges as operating with criteria of success laid down in advance. But if that is acceptable there, why not in other areas as well? On reflection it may be that Rorty is counting the activities of the legal and business communities as evidence against criterial rationality.

Just what Rorty has in mind by criterial and fuzzy rationality is a bit fuzzy. And I propose to try and get clearer by using the procedure he recommends – contrasting Popper and Kuhn. For Rorty, Popper is the 'bad guy', Kuhn the 'good guy'. Before proceeding, there is a fundamental confusion in Rorty's thinking that needs to be noted. I do not think that anyone (anyone party to the Popper–Kuhn debate) thinks that whatever it is that is laid down in advance or is taken to be laid down in advance gives the meaning or content of rationality. Rationality in matters of belief is a matter of being reasonable. And as such it is a topic-neutral notion. Being reasonable in a scientific or mathematical context may amount to following criteria laid down in advance.

33

In defending criterial rationality against Rorty I want to make it clear that what is being defended might better be called scientific methodology; that is, it is a defence of the particular procedures to follow if one wants to be reasonable in a scientific context. That being said I will continue to use the misleading terminology of Rorty.

Popper certainly believes in criterial rationality. Indeed, for him the criteria are laid down in advance in a very strong sense. For his falsification criterion, which is offered as a great intellectual advance, is purported to be established by *a priori* philosophical argument. Popper then proceeds to show that it fits the great scientists, namely, Newton and Einstein. Somehow the cunning of reason revealed itself to Newton though this was not made explicit until Popper. Newton would have loved this. For he thought that Moses knew the Newtonian laws. Newton saw his own genius to lie in merely making public what the ancients had known! The criterion Popper initially articulated was simple, indeed simplistic. A rational scientist was one who produced theories with predictive power and who rejected his theory when once an observation was made which was incompatible with a prediction of the theory. And this is clearly what Rorty has in mind by his attacks. For he refers (p. 8) to the scientist who abandons a hypothesis as a result of the unfavourable outcome of a single experiment as seeming truly heroic. On the Popperian conception it was not rational to be a Marxist or a Freudian because such theories had issued in false predictions or in no predictions at all. There is no doubt that this was intended as a criterion laid down in advance. For, as noted above, it was supposed to have been established by *a priori* philosophical argumentation.

But as Kuhn, Feyerabend and others pointed out, no scientist ever abandons a theory just because someone somewhere has made an observation incompatible with the theory. If that was the procedure, the only rational response to the results of undergraduate physics experiments would be to reject all scientific theories. Obviously in the face of an apparent falsification, one has to exercise judgement about the instruments used in the experiment, about the reliability of the experimenter and so on. As Kuhn has remarked, at times the experiment tests the experimenter not the theory.

Popper cannot allow that one simply exercises one's judgement whether to reject the theory or to blame something else in the case of an apparent falsification. For in that case the very activities he wished to condemn as non-scientific, as non-rational, could avoid censure. In order to castigate Freud and Marx he elaborated the criterion in ways that play into the hands of Rorty. For Popper required that the rational scientist specify in advance the circumstances under which the theory would be regarded as falsified. One no longer had to give up the theory because of the results of a clumsy physics undergraduate, but one had to say (to oneself at least) when articulating the theory just which adverse results in which sort of circumstances would lead to rejection. This might involve experiments done by sober Nobel prize winners in one's own presence, for example. This has such an air of fantasy about it that one briefly has some sympathy with Rorty's polemic. It is certainly a criterion on which Popper's favourite rational scientists would lose status. The idea, for example, of asking this of Einstein is quite ridiculous. Einstein notoriously was not interested in the result of Eddington's observation of the eclipse. And even when asked what his response would have been if the observation had been incompatible with general relativity, Einstein answered: 'I would pity the dear Lord.' And Newton, knowing his laws to have been revealed to him by the Lord as the Lord's truth, would have found the very idea of entertaining the possibility of falsification an impiety. At the very least we have an ironic result. Popper, not content with an *a priori* justification, has sought to display his methodology functioning in the work of Newton and Einstein. But on his methodology Newton and Einstein do not come out any better than Freud and Marx, who Popper imagines would be unwilling to specify in advance the circumstances under which they would abandon their theories.

If what Rorty has in mind by criterial rationality is a Popperian methodology, such a form of rationality is neither a part of actual scientific practice nor a part of some ideal form of scientific practice. As Lakatos and Kuhn have pointed out, what it is right to do when theory seems at odds with experiment is something that cannot be settled in advance. The best response depends in part on what alternatives are available at the time. If there is no rival theory, for instance, then it may be reasonable to cling to the existing theory, blaming the tools or the experimenter.

Rorty seeks to enlist Kuhn on his side, calling his own position 'left-wing Kuhnianism' (although, as noted below, it is more accurately described as 'right-wing Kuhnianism'). But this is somewhat problematic. For in spite of Kuhn's remarks about the variation of standards across paradigm change, he has always insisted that there are certain beneficial features of theories, what he calls the 'scientific values', which are common to all scientific communities. These 'values', which include simplicity, fertility, consistency and accuracy, are paradigm-neutral. There may be different interpretations of them and there may be different assessments of their relative importance but they define the parameters of debate for all members of all scientific communities.

If Kuhn is correct, and I think he is, there certainly are criteria of theory-choice laid down in advance. And furthermore the standards of achievement are determined in advance of the production of scientific theories. Some have argued that these standards are based on prediction and control. According to Kuhn the standards are based on problem-solving capacity, a major ingredient of which is predictive power. In explicating fuzzy rationality Rorty cites poets and painters as examples of those who proceed by making up 'new standards of achievement as they go on'. But science is not like this and it could not be. A traditionalist would say that, if some institution did not care about this, prediction would by definition not be a scientific one. But given Rorty's horror of talk about meaning and definition we have to say things like 'prediction is what it's all about', 'prediction is the name of the game'. But the substantial point remains, a point made by Kuhn himself: science is based on agreed criteria of success.

Pragmatists including Rorty respect science. After all, it works. This involves according respect to the means whereby it achieves its successes. And if that involves criterial rationality, criterial rationality is vindicated at least in the scientific context. The community believes that certain features of theories (including Kuhn's scientific values) are good signs of future success. These criteria are applied. They are not 'up for grabs' on each occasion. But they are not fixed for all time. As we learn more, we learn more not only about the world but also about the best methods for getting at the world. We do change our minds about the criteria to be used but at any given moment there are criteria about which we might change our mind.

Rorty could be making the point that there are no algorithmic criteria in science. Contrary to what Popper and Carnap thought, such criteria as are laid down in advance do not give a definite, mechanically generated decision-procedure. There is always the need to exercise judgement. But if that is what Rorty is saying, it is hard to see who constitutes the opposition. The project of having such an algorithm has a venerable history running from Leibniz through Mill to Carnap and Popper. But that project has already been abandoned. And abandoning that project is not the same as using the poet and the painter as our new model of rationality. What we might call Kuhnian rationality in science is far from the model of the poet and the painter.

Is there any special connection between Kuhnian rationality and Rorty's pragmatism? It does not seem so. A traditionalist may happily and indeed enthusiastically embrace Kuhnian rationality. The traditionalist in the philosophy of science holds that the aim of science is to discover explanatory theories that are ever more approximately true. He thinks that the increasing observational success of science is a reason for thinking that we are in fact achieving this. And he thinks that that fact provides grounds for thinking that our current criteria for theory-choice have something in them. He can accept that they function as Kuhn takes them to function, as guiding principles. He can accept with Kuhn that as working criteria we change our minds about what are the most efficacious criteria to use in achieving the goal of science. The traditionalist does differ from Kuhn in seeing the criteria of theory–choice as criteria for determining which theory is more likely to take us towards the goal of increasing the truth content of our theory. For Kuhn the criteria indicate only the likely problem-solving capacity of theories. But there need be no disagreement on the criteria and their functioning.

One cannot consistently combine respect for science, acceptance of Kuhn's account of science and a rejection of criterial rationality unless the rejection is limited to algorithmic criterial rationality. And if the target is in fact algorithmic criterial rationality, hitting it is about as impressive as hitting one's target with a thrown stone where the target is the earth's surface. Charity might incline one to think Rorty must have something more in mind than merely castigating algorithmic rationality. Perhaps what he is telling us is this. Such Kuhnian rationality is not all that important in characterizing the nature of science. Perhaps what makes science special is not the possession of some kind of criterion for rational theory-choice but something else.

For Rorty science is special; it is exemplary. But what makes it special is not the possession of a method, it is rather that it is 'a model of human solidarity':

> We should think of the institutions and practices which make up various scientific communities as providing suggestions about the way in which the rest of culture might organize itself. When we say that our legislatures are 'unrepresentative' or 'dominated by special interests', or that the art world is dominated by 'fashion', we are contrasting these areas of culture with areas which seem to be in better order. The natural sciences strike us as being such areas. But, on this view, we shall not explain this better order by thinking of the scientists as having a 'method' which the rest of us would do well to imitate, nor as benefiting from the desirable hardness of their subjects compared with the undesirable softness of other subjects.

This will not do. Science is in order, in good order relative to its goals. So too are painting, music and poetry. To suggest that art ought to emulate the solidarity of science is to go well beyond the already extreme scientism of the positivists. The solidarity of science is a solidarity about results and, as Kuhn has argued, about criteria. If you do not accept certain results, if you insist the earth is flat or that Newton was the final word, you are excluded from the community or kept on as a mere curiosity. If you cannot accept that, all things being equal, predictive power counts in favour of a theory, you will be excluded from the community. In contrast, the charm and importance for us of music, poetry and painting is just this absence of solidarity. It would be emasculating and dehumanizing to promote artistic endeavours based on the model of scientific solidarity. But there is no accounting for taste and perhaps Rorty really would like an art world which was solid on the matter of styles in painting, music and poetry. Perhaps diversity is not for him the spice of art. And if solidarity was the fundamental characteristic of science, various religious and political groups must turn out to be the very model of good science: you cannot get more solidarity than you find in the Church of Latter Day Saints or the Communist Party of Albania.

Whatever the pros and cons of the proposed emulation of science, we must face the prior question: Has Rorty correctly characterized what is special about science? Is solidarity the fundamental characteristic? There is no doubt that the scientific community displays solidarity. But this solidarity itself needs explanation. And that explanation requires reference to things agreed in advance. First, we identify science as an activity which seeks prediction and control over nature (possibly among other things). Either we think with the instrumentalist that this is the end of science itself or we think with the realist that this is the best way of achieving the true goal of explanation. Secondly, given that at any moment we do not know which of two rival theories will better achieve that goal, we agree on which features determine the theory with the greatest promise: the one which best exemplifies Kuhn's 'scientific values'. The criteria play a role in generating the solidarity. And the solidarity once generated reinforces agreement on the generating values. The lack of solidarity on results in the case of painting must in part be explained by the absence of anything agreed in advance. It is not as if science in some mysterious way generates solidarity. Science is constituted by a certain project and in the pursuit of that project it is found by trial and error that certain procedures, certain values and certain beliefs are more effective than others as means to the end. There is no possibility of explaining what is special about science by reference to solidarity alone: that solidarity arises from and reinforces the Kuhnian rationality, the criterial rationality, that Rorty rejects. Fuzzy rationality could never explain this. Indeed, it is incompatible with solidarity. If scientists did not have standards of success and standards of theory-choice laid down in advance they would exhibit the sort of diversity that prevails in the artistic community. Fuzziness would transform science into non-science, a sort of Feyerabendian heaven.

Rorty could be wrong about the role of criterial rationality in science; he could be wrong about the specialness of science and yet still have a case for adopting a different model of rationality outside the sciences: fuzzy rationality. But just what is being proposed is not clear. At times, fuzzy rationality is equated with being reasonable. In which case we are all fuzzies. Fuzzy rationality will not be in opposition to criterial rationality in science. For criterial rationality is just part of what being reasonable in science comes to. On this understanding of fuzziness he is not offering anything controversial, nor is he providing anything fundamentally different to guide us outside the area of science. At other times Rorty adds to reasonableness a list of liberal virtues – sanity, civility, tolerance. No doubt these are virtues we should seek to acquire and use in all contexts. Again, if that is the message of the fuzzy it is hard to see from where the opposition will come. It will certainly not come from the traditionalist, who will have just as much reason to value these virtues as the pragmatist. And at yet other times Rorty builds into fuzziness a rejection of standards of achievement laid down in advance. We have already seen that no one who respects science and certainly no one who accepts a Kuhnian account of science can accept fuzziness in this sense as a virtue in science. And it is doubtful that it is much of a virtue outside science. Within the confines of this paper this question cannot be discussed. Space permitting one would want to consider the following sort of questions. Is it really the case that Michaelangelo had no idea of what he wanted to achieve before he worked on the block of marble which was to become his David? Are not historians agreed before they begin their narratives that accounts of historical actors must be compatible with our beliefs about the basic features of human motivation?

Whatever the fuzziness of Rorty's proposed fuzziness it is supposed to offer us a new and different world, a world in which culture would be described in the vocabulary of the romantic poet and the socialist politician. In so far as the inspiration of this vision is supposed to come from a Kuhnian account of science, the reference to the vocabulary of socialist politics is particularly puzzling. For if there is anywhere that the rhetoric of the right is appropriate, it is in science. After all, Rorty himself speaks of the sciences as providing the spectacle of fierce competition. Science might well be likened to a free market where theories and scientists fight it out, with the weak going to the wall. It is hard to see how such rhetoric as 'From each according to his ability, to each according to his need' could have application to science.

The world that will arrive in the 'heyday of the fuzzy' would have the following attributes according to Rorty:

1. The division between disciplines would disappear.

2. Scientists would lose their status as members of a quasi-priestly order, both in their own eyes and in the eyes of others.
3. 'Disciplines' would no longer be concerned with foundational or methodological questions.
4. The focus of interest would be particular communities rather than particular disciplines.
5. Members of these communities would identify with the larger community, the goal of which would be the preservation and enhancement of civilization.

Let us imagine that we have made Rorty's leap and have embraced fuzzy rationality. Is there any reason to think that this would deliver the goods listed above and if so should that count in favour of the proposal? In the case of the division between disciplines, it is not clear that the border between science and non-science would erode, given that successful scientific procedures do involve criteria laid down in advance. And if the border is blurred, it can only be because Rorty is mistaken about the humanities. For he has characterized them as typically not having criteria in advance. In any event, why should it be assumed that it is a good thing to break down the divisions between the disciplines? The sciences have divisions among them, and there are divisions between the sciences and the humanities, and both the sciences and the humanities are flourishing. That provides a pragmatic argument in favour of divisions.

With regard to the second claim, that scientists would lose status, there is no need to go over to fuzziness to achieve this. We need simply to remind ourselves that what science aims at is not all there is to achieve and that the techniques of the scientist are particularly adapted for pursuing the goal of science. They are not to be emulated in other areas of endeavour. And so long as scientists continue to deliver the goods, one can well imagine them retaining their prestige for that reason alone. In fact going over to fuzziness might well enhance the priestly qualities. If they achieve all they do without having criteria, they look like shamans, like magicians.

On the third point, there is no good reason to think that, having dropped criterial rationality, we would not be interested in foundational and methodological questions. It is as if Rorty thinks that these arise for the humanities only because they have nervously sought to bring themselves into line with science. There are bound to be questions about fundamental assumptions and about what criteria to make up as we go along. In so far as dropping criterial rationality would mean dropping concern with foundational and methodoligical questions, there is no reason to think that this counts in its favour.

Rorty's fourth claim is innocuous. There are good reasons to focus on the communities of practitioners of a discipline. But that is not excluded from the concern of the traditionalist who sticks by criterial rationality. As for the last claim, not a shred of evidence has been provided for thinking that a pragmatist, a fuzzy, is going to be more concerned with the enhancement of civilization than a traditionalist. There is no reason to think that some pragmatists will not come to believe that some horrible doctrines will 'work'. And in so far as a concern with whether things work is civilizing, it can and ought to be equally the concern of the traditionalist. For the traditional realist, whether things work is relevant to determining what is true.

Rorty's fuzzy, liberal vision of how things might be, may have merits, but it has no merits that warrant abandoning the traditional approach. The liberal values it embodies are available to the traditionalist. In the end no pragmatic considerations have been provided which favour pragmatism over traditionalism.

Hugh Tomlinson

AFTER TRUTH: POST-MODERNISM AND THE RHETORIC OF SCIENCE

INTRODUCTION

IT IS GENERALLY imagined that science has an intimate relationship with truth. The highest purpose and justification of scientific activity is said to be the attainment of 'true theories' about the world. It is claimed that the accounts of the world given by scientists are superior to those of mystics or witchdoctors because of their (potentially) unique adequacy to objective reality. In short, science aims for truth and truth justifies science. But, despite the intimacy of their relationship, 'truth' is not itself a 'scientific' notion. It is of no practical assistance to scientists and does no work within scientific theories. 'Truth' has its function in the work of those who defend and justify science.

'Truth' is the basis of a powerful and persuasive apologetics – the rhetoric of science. Over the past two centuries this has swept away all rivals. It is a key part of the 'modern' perspective on the world, an unspoken assumption at the heart of our thinking. Rationality and truth have become so interwoven that any attempt to question the notion of truth seems irrational and incoherent.

'Who', asks Paul Feyerabend, 'has the fortitude, or even the insight to declare that "truth" might be unimportant, and perhaps even undesirable?'[1] This insight is a starting point of what can be called 'post-modernism'. For present purposes, this is not a

43

cultural theory but rather an (anti-)philosophical view flowing from a 'suspension' of the notion of truth. The post-modernist does not 'suspend' truth for 'romantic' or 'irrationalist' reasons – such attitudes are simply the other side of the coin of truth. Rather, the post-modernist 'takes truth seriously' and tries to make sense of it. He carries out an 'internal critique' of 'truth' itself. It is not that 'truth' *ought* to be rejected in favour of something like beauty or intuition but that the disciple of truth, the rationalist, cannot give a coherent account of it in his own terms. Thus in one sense the post-modernist is a super rationalist: if we take rationalism seriously it cannot measure up to its own standards. As Nietzsche says, it is truthfulness which destroys our belief in truth – 'truth kills, kills itself'. This is the 'negative' side of post-modernism.

The 'positive' side of post-modernism involves the development of new rhetorics of science, new stories of knowledge 'after truth'. 'Truth' is central to the self-understanding of modern culture. Its suspension involves radical cultural change. In particular, the distinction between 'truth-seeking' science and 'story-telling' myth can no longer be maintained. The boundaries between science and non-science become quantitative rather than qualitative. The story of the power and utility of science cannot be avoided but it must be told in a whole variety of new ways, none of which can be definitive.

The aim of the account that follows is to provide a sketch of the post-modernist attack on the rhetoric of truth. This account moves from the internal difficulties of common-sense realism, through the failures of sophisticated realism to the delusions of pragmatism. Many of the particular arguments deployed by the post-modernist are the familiar currency of contemporary epistemology and philosophy of science and they are not developed here. The strategy is, rather, to sketch out the grounds on which science might get its divorce from truth and to suggest that life unsupported might not be as dangerous as the rationalist would have us believe.

COMMON–SENSE REALISM

The modern notion of truth draws much of its plausibility from a set of metaphysical views which form an 'externalist' perspective on the world, what Putnam has called a 'God's Eye point of view'.[2] This perspective is now deeply embedded in our 'common-sense' attitude to the world. The 'common-sense realist' sees the world as being objectively ordered independently of all human activity. Science seeks to provide theories which 'mirror' this objective ordering, theories which are, in a word, 'true'.

The basic 'given' of common-sense realism is unobjectionable: the world is relatively independent of our dealings with it. But this is elevated into an ontological thesis that there is a single, objectively structured reality independent of human thoughts and actions. According to the realist:

> the world consists of some fixed totality of mind–independent objects. There is exactly one true and complete description of 'the way the world is'. Truth involves some sort of correspondence between words or thought-signs and external things and sets of things.[3]

It follows that the key feature of language is 'reference': bits of language are used to 'refer' to bits of the world. A statement is true if it successfully refers to the world. Whatever our subjective perceptions, the world is objectively 'out there' and the aim of our theorizing is to provide a theory which 'copies' or 'corresponds' to it.

This correspondence view of truth provides an apparently straightforward and easily applicable picture of the relation between words and world. It is a picture which fits with the way which we use simple sentences about ordinary material objects. We look to the world, to the 'thing referred to', in order to decide whether such sentences are appropriate or not: to decide whether 'there is food in the fridge', I can look in the fridge.

The common-sense realist wants to expand this picture into a general account of the relation between words and world, a general theory of truth. There are immediate difficulties with this move. What seems obvious in relation to ordinary physical objects such as cars or houses is difficult to apply in relation to the objects of the physicist or the astronomer. There is no straightforward and clear sense in which talk about quarks or quasars 'corresponds' to the world. The acceptability or utility of such talk depends

45

on complex procedures of observation and calculation which are entirely unknown to most of us.

These problems multiply when we move outside the 'natural' sciences. The language of 'social science' often lacks clear 'objective reference': statements about the mind, social classes or historical changes have no obvious 'objects' to correspond to. The difficulties are even more formidable in areas such as religion, aesthetics or ethics. There is no uncontested way in which we can even decide on what might count as the 'objects' of such theories. On the common-sense realist view, 'true' theories about God, beauty or the good life seem impossible.

The common-sense realist has a number of moves to deal with these worries. 'Objects' are constructed to correspond to the complex theoretical constructions of physical theory and the subject matter of social theory. The problem of truth in religion, aesthetics and ethics is solved by removing them from the cognitive realm altogether. The logical positivists (although, strictly, not realists) were being perfectly consistent in relegating such disciplines to the realm of the 'emotive'.

Difficulties of this kind are central to philosophical debates within realism but they are not decisive. Common-sense realism cannot be challenged by means of direct counter-examples. Once the 'realist picture' is accepted they *must be* resolvable. The question is: can the basic picture be made coherent? Can the realist give a coherent account of the correspondence view of truth?

According to the realist picture 'truth' is given by a particular relationship between words and world: a sentence is true when it corresponds to the world. This involves two aspects: the items to be related and the relationship itself. From his own perspective, the realist must be in a position to give a coherent account of both.

The items to be related seem obvious and straightforward: words and objects. The common-sense realist thinks of the world as consisting, paradigmatically, of unproblematically identifiable physical objects with simple properties. From a 'God's Eye point of view' the world 'really is' divided up into objects, independently of human description and ordering.

This view of objects runs counter to the whole thrust of modern philosophy since Kant. It is ultimately dependent on the idea of the world as 'God's project', divided up according to divine categories. It was Kant's fundamental insight that 'we are giving the orders', that both concepts and experience are necessary components of knowledge. We can only have experience of a world which is already structured by our concepts; it is 'our world'. What counts as a particular object depends on the classificatory concepts which we use. We cannot 'leap outside' these concepts and directly compare them with 'unconceptualized objects'. If we accept Kant's argument the two sets of items which 'correspond' have lost their independence. The 'bits of world' which are to be related to 'bits of language' seem to be only their shadows. The common-sense realist must abandon the view that scientific theories can be directly compared with unconceptualized bits of world to see whether or not they correspond.

The realist has sought to protect his basic picture in a number of ways. Most promisingly, it has been suggested that 'objective ordering' is preserved because there is a set of 'basic concepts' which are necessarily used in descriptions of the world. 'True statements' expressed in terms of these would be the 'raw material' for explanation by scientific theories. For example, some philosophers of science argued that 'observational terms' were basic and 'theory-neutral'. The difficulty with such a view is that 'observation' and 'theory' can never be fully separated out. All the proposed 'observational terms' have been found to contain irreducible 'theoretical components' – 'theory' goes all the way down.[4]

It seems that all that words can ever be related to are objects which depend on the words used. Truth is, then, not 'objective' and unique, but 'subjective' in the sense that it depends on the particular language used. There are as many truths as there are languages and the notion of truth can no longer provide a final and objective justification for science.

Analogous difficulties arise when the common-sense realist tries to explicate the *relationship* between words and world, the 'correspondence' which constitutes the truth of theories. In order to support the notion of 'truth' this must be a simple 'one-to-one' relationship between bits of language and bits of world.

The realist's first move is to explain the relationship in terms of 'similarity' or 'picturing'. But 'correspondence as similarity' is untenable for, as Putnam points out, there is no unique similarity to produce the one-to-one correspondence that the theory requires, because 'everything is similar to everything else in infinitely many respects'. The realist wants theories to be like 'maps' of reality but there are an unlimited number of equally 'accurate' maps of the same piece of land, depending on the mapping conventions employed. This will not do for the realist. He wants there to be 'one true map', the one drawn by God. But there is no simple self-justifying relationship which will give him this because words can be mapped on to the world in a whole range of ways. No unique truth relation is given.[5]

In summary, the correspondence view of truth depends for its power on a simplistic view of the relationship between words and world. It derives a general model from everyday talk about ordinary physical objects, assuming a world already divided up into facts and a single vocabulary to deal with it. Neither of these assumptions are tenable. In order to 'single out a correspondence between two domains one needs some independent access to both'.[6] The 'world as it is in itself' does not dictate a single vocabulary in which it must be described nor does it prescribe a unique 'mapping convention' by which words are to be related to world. The world is 'always already' conceptualized and the simple correspondence view cannot be made coherent.

SOPHISTICATED REALISM

In recent philosophy of science, the defenders of realism have retreated from simple 'common-sense realism' to a more sophisticated view. They accept many of the points made against their common-sense predecessors. The emphasis is switched from the establishment of a direct correspondence between words and world to consideration of the 'method' which guarantees the 'correspondence' of whole scientific theories. This involves an abandonment of most of the metaphysical intuitions of common sense.

The sophisticated realist acknowledges that theories cannot be simply 'compared' to the world as revealed to empirical observation because all observations are 'theory-laden'. He accepts that the world is always already conceptualized and that, in consequence, scientific theories must face the world 'as a whole', not 'sentence by sentence'. He shifts attention from the relationship of correspondence to the 'method' of science which is seen as 'setting tests' which theories must pass in order to establish their credentials as 'truth candidates'. These tests are not definitive and theories are always open to revision. Truth is the property of an ideal theory which passes all possible tests. Such an ideal theory will correspond to the world and mirror its objective structure. The methodologies of 'critical rationalism' are attempts to provide a mechanism for determining which theories more closely correspond to reality in terms of 'increasing verisimilitude'.[7]

There are two types of difficulty with this approach. The first is a 'practical' one. All the 'methodologies' which the sophisticated realist proposes are, in practice, incapable of dividing what is commonly thought of as 'science' (for example, astronomy and chemistry) from what is generally regarded as 'non-science' (for example, astrology and alchemy). The methodologies proposed are either so weak that they perform no proper exclusionary function at all or so strong that they exclude much of 'science'. They are, in Feyerabend's words, 'either useless or debilitating'.[8]

The second difficulty is more fundamental. This is the problem of 'incommensurability'. The scientific method will allow us to judge between competing theories only if they are in fact comparable. But, if we look at theories as 'wholes', the meaning of individual terms must be linked to the 'principles of construction' of the whole theory. Thus there is no 'theory-independent' way of comparing the contents of theories.[9] This means that competing theories are not directly comparable and that the choice between them cannot be governed by the 'rational principles' of the scientific method. As Feyerabend has consistently argued, theory choice is ultimately governed by 'irrational factors' such as 'prejudice, passion, conceit, errors, [and] sheer pig-headedness'.[10]

The scientific method of the sophisticated realist cannot provide the hoped-for positive content to the notion of truth. There is no set of tests to be applied to theories which will guarantee that the ones which pass are in ever closer correspondence with the nature of reality itself. Method cannot generate truth.

THE INDISPENSABILITY OF TRUTH

The realist believes that truth is indispensable to thought. Whatever the difficulties with positive attempts to define it, he relies on a series of negative arguments in its defence. The initial set of

moves involve the claim that truth performs an *explanatory* function, that it is less of a theory and more of an explanatory hypothesis. 'Truth' is advanced in an attempt to do justice to our
'metaphysical intuitions' and to make sense of the power and utility
of our theories.

First, it is claimed, the correspondence view explains the 'objectivity of truth'. We regard truth as being, in some sense, independent of our activities and beliefs. According to the 'realist' a
statement could turn out to be objectively false however strongly
we believe it and however well it fits our 'tests for truth'. He
therefore appeals to the notion of truth to make sense of the 'intuition' that truth is independent of belief – that a theory could be
rationally acceptable, useful, powerful and so on and yet still be
false.

But this does not advance matters much further. The 'objectivity
of truth' is the very thing that the post-modernist denies. He finds
unintelligible the supposition that a theory which meets all possible
tests for truth 'might *really* be false'.[11] The realist is seeking to
justify his own picture by appealing to the intuitions deriving
from it.

Secondly, the notion of truth is said to explain why science
in fact works – because it corresponds to reality as it objectively
is.[12] The notion of truth is called on to explain the success of our
theories and, in particular, the success of natural science. But it
is difficult to see where this gets us. Unless an independent account
of truth can be provided, there is no difference between saying
'science succeeds because it succeeds' and 'science succeeds because
it is true'.

It is not that 'science succeeds' is the last word; for the post-
modernist there is never a last word. It is rather that 'because
it is true' cannot be the last word about science. Many different
accounts can be given of the success of science, none of them
is definitive, none takes ultimate priority.

The second type of realist defensive move is a general argument
from the nature of assertoric language. According to the realist
all assertions by their nature make 'truth claims'. The attack is
then turned on the post-modernist for asserting that 'there is no
truth' – which implicitly makes a truth claim. Thus the post-
modernist is 'helping himself' to the very notion he pretends to
reject. The assertion 'there is no truth' cannot stand because it

is implicitly affirming truth while explicitly denying its truth. In the very act of being stated such a view refutes itself.

The post-modernist stands charged with pragmatic self-refutation. He admires this argument, it is a version of the ploy he has been using against the realist, but it does not hit home. It depends on two points – neither of which the post-modernist accepts. First, post-modernism does not involve making any general metaphysical assertions like 'there is no truth'. Rather, it involves turning the realist's assumptions against himself. From the point of view of the realist, this means that there is no truth. From the point of view of the post-modernist there are many different stories to be told. Secondly, the argument depends on the acceptance of the view that all assertoric discourse sets out to be 'truth-stating' – which is just what the post-modernist rejects. Like the post-modernist's own 'anti-realist' arguments, it only has force against someone playing the realist game. The post-modernist does not accept that there is any general notion of 'truth' implied by all assertion. He uses the language but refuses the metaphysics. We can discuss the contents of the fridge and accept that looking in will be decisive of some of these discussions without committing ourselves to a 'realist ontology' or a 'correspondence theory of truth'.

The realist's final move is fundamental. Truth, he says, is the regulative principle which saves us from theoretical (and ultimately moral) chaos. Without its constraints 'anything goes', and theory collapses into gibberish. But, once again, this is precisely what the post-modernist denies. Where the realist sees chaos and disorder the post-modernist sees plural possibility. There is no 'neutral' way of deciding between these two intuitions. The post-modernist has no 'positive arguments' for his views, he simply 'assembles reminders' to try and shake the realist out of his obsessions.

RELATIVISM AND POST-MODERNISM

This account of realism can be summarized by saying that, on close examination, it collapses into relativism. This collapse has two phases. First, the insight that the world is 'our world', that what counts as a fact depends on our theories, means that there is no 'reality' for theories to correspond to. As Kuhn puts it, there is 'no theory-independent way to reconstruct phrases like "really there"; the notion of a match between the ontology of a theory and its "real" counterpart in nature ... seems to me illusive in principle'.[13]

Secondly, if there are a number of incommensurable theories there are as many worlds as there are theories. In Feyerabend's words, 'we ... cannot assume that two incommensurable theories deal with one and the same objective state of affairs ... Hence, unless we want to assume that they deal with nothing at all we must admit that they deal with different worlds.'[14] This view is commonly called relativism.

Relativism is often misunderstood. It is not another theory about the nature of truth. We cannot accept it as an 'alternative' to realist absolutism – as a 'theory of truth' it is clearly incoherent. The statement 'all truth is relative' is inconsistent because, at the same time as denying the possibility of absolute truth, it appears to be claiming absolute truth for itself.[15] As Nietzsche says, 'There are many kinds of eyes ... and consequently there are many kinds of "truths" and consequently there is no truth.'[16]

The post-modernist is not advancing a 'theory of incommensurability' or a 'relativist theory of truth'. Rather, he is drawing out a consequence of the realist's own position. Relativism *is* incoherent but this incoherence belongs to realism not to its opponents.

The post-modernist story is a simple one: realism, in any of its forms, cannot be made coherent in its own terms. We have, as Putnam says, reached 'the demise of a theory that lasted for over two thousand years. That it persisted so long and in so many forms in spite of the internal contradictions and obscurities which were present from the beginning testifies to the naturalness and strength of the desire for a God's Eye View.'[17] The question is: where do we go from here?

PRAGMATISM AND TRUTH

The 'pragmatist view of truth' in the work of Richard Rorty sets out to provide a version of life after truth. Rorty develops many of the anti-realist arguments sketched out above. He rejects the notion that truth is 'the sort of thing one should expect to have a philosophically interesting theory about'.[18] Instead, he urges us to give up the worship of 'scientific truth' or our own 'poetic nature' and to accept the 'contingency' of our position in the universe.[19]

With characteristic provocativeness, Rorty describes his view as 'post-modern bourgeois liberalism'. It has been said that the last two words are more appropriate than the first two, but our challenge is not directly political. The question is: has Rorty in fact broken with the realism and the rhetoric of truth? On examination it seems that, despite the apparently radical nature of his pronouncements, Rorty is still wedded to the 'God's Eye point of view'. The pragmatist remains a closet realist.

According to Rorty we cannot go beyond the procedures of justification of our society. He adopts the 'ethnocentric view that there is nothing to be said about either truth or rationality apart from descriptions of the familiar procedures of justification which a given society, ours, uses in one or another areas of inquiries'.[20] But, in telling us this, Rorty is standing 'beyond' society, giving an overview of the way it 'really is'. In a powerful series of analyses, he has given detailed accounts of matters such as the domination of philosophy by the notion of the mind as 'the mirror of nature',[21] and the oppositions between 'Platonism' and 'pragmatism',[22] 'objectivity' and 'solidarity'.[23] But these accounts continue to rely on realist notions of representation. Rather than acknowledging their own 'mythical' nature and the availability of a variety of potentially useful alternative accounts, they implicitly claim superiority over all rivals. They set out to describe 'things as they are', to give a 'uniquely adequate' account of recent cultural history. Despite his elegant exposition and fast footwork, the rhetoric of Rorty's account is the rhetoric of truth.

Rorty would reply that the 'truth' of these accounts is not the metaphysical 'Truth' of the realist but the anti-essentialist 'truth' of the pragmatist.[24] Not 'correspondence to reality' but 'what is good in the way of belief'. Thus 'truth' becomes 'truth for us', for our 'ethnos'. This is what can be called an 'absolute relativist' account. It involves acceptance of the claim 'that there is no standpoint outside our own particular historically conditioned and temporary vocabulary by which to judge this vocabulary in respect of rationality or morality'.[25] Truth is relative to our tradition but, given that we can only operate from within this tradition, there can be no 'alternative truths'. Truth, *for us*, is as absolute as can be. There can be no incommensurability because *either* alternative traditions can be understood in our terms *or* they cannot be understood. In the former case they are commensurable, in the latter it does not even make sense to call them traditions at all. They are strictly nonsense.[26] Rorty's 'absolute relativist' position is completed by a familiar appeal to the 'numerous platitudes' which all societies have in common. Our ethnos turns out to differ little from apparently alternative accounts of the world. The absolutist rhetoric of science can then be supported without metaphysics. Science is defended 'not as an ahistorical teleology – e.g., an evolutionary drive towards correspondence with reality, or the nature of language – but as a particularly good example of the social virtues of the European bourgeoisie'.[27]

But this is not sustainable. First, our society offers not one, but a whole multitude of 'rationalities', of the 'forms of justification'. To claim to be ethnocentric is to beg the question of which version of the ethnos is being appealed to. The 'absolute relativist' position threatens to collapse into the privileging of a single idiolect. Rorty, in effect, attempts to deal with this problem in the classical pragmatist manner: the version of the ethnos appealed to is that which would find favour with an idealized community of enquirers. This idea is itself relativized to the present as he appeals to 'the best elements of our present selves'. But this again begs the question of what these 'best elements' are.

> The pragmatist thinks, in effect, that 'we' ought to consider ourselves as forming part of the spectacle of human progress which will progressively include the whole human race, and he is ready to accept that the vocabulary that 'we' use – we, western social democratic intellectuals of the twentieth century – is the best vocabulary that the race has been able to find.[28]

But, although Rortyan social democrats may be able to accept that this vocabulary is the best, there are many other groups within our ethnos that cannot. The pragmatist's self-justification depends on a particular version of that 'ethnos' already having been accepted. It attempts to justify its own prejudgements by what amounts to an arbitrary ruling that the alternatives are incomprehensible.

Secondly, and more importantly, the same 'reflexive' arguments used against the realist can be used against 'absolute relativists' of all forms. Rorty is trying to have it both ways. If it is not possible to make sense of the idea of alternative traditions then neither is it possible to make sense of the idea that we operate within a tradition. 'Our tradition' can only be viewed as a whole if there is some external 'God's Eye point of view' from which to do the viewing. If there is 'no standpoint outside' our 'historically conditioned and temporary vocabulary' it does not make sense for us to regard it as 'historically conditioned' or 'temporary'. 'Absolute relativism' in the style of Rorty (or Quine or Strawson) either turns out to be an extreme version of ordinary relativism or an absolutism in disguise. In either case it is susceptible to the self-referential collapse drawn out by post-modernism.

POST-MODERNISM AND TRUTH

Nevertheless, the post-modernist approach has many features in common with that of the pragmatist. It does not seek to provide a 'new theory of truth' or a single new 'rhetoric of science'. It has no 'alternative theory of science' which can be 'made coherent'. When challenged to provide such a 'theory' the wise post-modernist steps over the gauntlet and goes off about his business. The absolutist notion of 'theoretical coherence' is one for the realist. The post-modernist knows that coherence is only one factor in the complex and fluid process of theory choice and theory use. What is more he knows that theories are only one factor in the complex and fluid process of living. 'Knock-down' arguments are employed against the realist only because he appears to have a strange penchant for that kind of thing.

The post-modern question is not 'Is it true?' but 'What does it do?' This question must be asked of the whole rhetoric of science which is based on truth. What it does is close off options. It seeks to lay down a definitive and 'guaranteed' stopping point for enquiry: 'the world prevents this being discussed further'. The post-modernist, in contrast, says that enquiry stops where enquiry stops. We simply get to the point where it is uninteresting to discuss a topic any further. 'As if giving grounds did not come to an end sometime. But the end is not an ungrounded presupposition: it is an ungrounded way of acting.'[29]

The difference between post-modernism and pragmatism is that the post-modernist recognizes that the questions raised by realism can never be definitively 'flattened out' and ignored. Rorty's is a 'passive pragmatism' which has 'no more to offer than common sense ... about knowledge and truth'.[30] In contrast, the post-modernist practises a constructive pragmatism. The aim is not the urbane continuation of cultural conversation, but the exhilarating and dangerous task of post-modernity, the telling of new stories, the invention of new worlds, 'the manufacture of materials to harness forces, to think the unthinkable'.[31]

Post-modernism recognizes that science will always require new rhetorics. It can no longer be justified by its 'truth' or its 'methodological rigour'. But its power and utility are not simply self-justifying. The new rhetorics of theory recognize that science tells a powerful story, a story which interacts with the world in a wondrous way. But this story is not in a separate compartment from all others. It has points in common with them as well as points of difference. The distinction between science and non-science is a quantitative and not a qualitative one. Post-modern rhetorics of theory look at the force of different stories, their excitement, their fit – in short, what they do.

Post-modernism does involve radical cultural change. Certain kinds of stories can no longer be told in the same way. Certain moves to cut short discussion are no longer available. One side of the metaphysical pair of truth and fiction has disintegrated. But 'falsity' does not become the new 'principle'. Our metaphysical notions of 'truth' and 'falsity' are interdependent. 'Truth' is not 'abolished' but rather 'suspended'. To use Derrida's metaphor, the opposition between 'truth' and 'fiction' is deconstructed – there turns out to be fiction at the heart of truth. This does not mean that 'everything is *really* fiction'. The notion of what things *really* are belongs to the rhetoric of truth. The 'suspension' of truth involves, in Derrida's terms, a 'reversal of values', an 'undoing of the opposition'. This is done for strategic reasons – hoping you'll catch on, hoping I'll catch on. Post-modern is the discourse which sloughs off the pretended guarantees of 'fact' and 'reality' – which is thrown into the arena and perhaps works, perhaps doesn't ...

EPILOGUE

This has been a story about suspending truth but it is a story which must itself suspend truth. It can make no 'truth claims', pretend to no unique status. It could have been told in an unspecifiable number of other ways. Some might work better, some worse. The post-modern world is without guarantees, without 'method'. After truth there is no 'dialectic', no high road to powerful and useful theories. All we can do is invent. We must construct and exemplify the rhetorics of the future. Post-modernism is paradoxical, against the common opinion, and, in the terms of its ever present realist opponent, it is absurd. Nevertheless, the greatest paradox remains that of truth itself: truth, the enemy of rhetoric, is at the centre of the most powerful rhetoric there is – although rhetoric has the best arguments, dialectic has the greatest force. This is the paradox of post-modernism, the paradox which it seeks to conjure away through its endless stories. Like this one.

David Ruben

REALISM IN
THE SOCIAL SCIENCES

THERE IS AN old Russian proverb, quoted in the autobiography of Vladimir Medem, the former leader of the Jewish Bund, that says: 'An individual in Russia was composed of three parts: a body, a soul, and a passport.' The proverb speaks of three kinds of entities: material, mental and social. I shall, in what follows, often speak of three realms or even worlds, but I mean nothing more dramatic by this than what can be cashed out in terms of either three kinds of entities or three kinds of properties. There may be other kinds of entities or properties in addition to these three kinds, for example, mathematical or moral ones. But these three are the only ones which shall concern me here.

Some philosophers believe that the mental is reducible to the material; others believe that the material is reducible to the mental. Analogous possibilities are on hand for the relation between the social and each of the other two. For the purposes of this paper, I wish to remain neutral on these issues. My choice of a triple terminology is made out of convenience, and not as the result of a prior philosophical decision.

I once defined 'realism' as the view that something existed which was essentially independent of mind, thought or human agency.[1] My idea was to capture the notion that, to whatever extent human beings managed to impress their imprint on the natural world, that world *could* have existed even if that imprint had not been impressed. The agency–world connection, even if ubiquitous, was not essential, at least not essential in the direction of world on agency. The connections between human agency, in which I would include scientific theorizing, and the material world were always contingent relations, not necessary or essential ones. It could hardly be denied that the natural world affected our agency, and that our actions and practice affected the natural world. But such affectings as there were had always a non-essential character as far as the world is concerned; it could always have been otherwise and the world could still have been just as it is.

This may be an acceptable way in which to characterize realism as a view about the material or physical world (I use these terms interchangeably in what follows), although even here there are difficulties about how to draw the essential–inessential distinction in some way which is not just language-relative. There are some ways in which to describe the natural world such that, described in that way, it is essentially dependent on the human. If it only be required that there be at least one description of the natural world such that, relative to that description, it is independent of the human, surely the social world will pass that test of human-independence as well. But even if some acceptable way is found to set out the idea of the essential independence of the natural world from human agency, it still cannot serve as a way of charac-terizing realism about the social or mental worlds. Couldn't one be a realist about the mind? On my previous characterization, one could not be, since it is trivially true that nothing mental could exist essentially independent from itself. As for the social world, one can think of it as the realm in which mind and matter, or the mental and the physical, meet. To that extent, it is Janus-faced. What, for example, is a credit card? A credit card is a piece of material, a piece of plastic, which is produced with a certain intent, that is, to be used in a particular way. It is something which has a function that we impose on it. It has, as it were, both material and mental (or intentional) elements. Thus my previous definition of realism encounters the same difficulty here as it did with the mental. It is utterly impossible for a credit card to exist if there were no minds or consciousness to invest the material world with function or intentionality. Nothing social could exist essentially independently of mind or human agency. There could not possibly be credit cards, or prisons, or nations, or wills, unless there were human beings engaging in certain sorts of activities, with certain specific intentions and purposes. So, on my previous characterization of realism, it would be impossible to be a realist about the social world, for the same reason that it would be impossible to be a realist about the mind. This result tells us rather less about realism regarding the social or the mental than it does about the arbitrariness of my initial characterization of realism.

A new characterization of realism is necessary, which will allow us to pose the question of realism and the social world in a non-trivial way. I think that a good way to do so is this. What realism proposes is a dualism, not between mind in general and nature (for that involves us in the difficulty of how to characterize realism about the social world), but a specific dualism between our theories or beliefs about something and that thing itself, whether the thing under discussion is material, mental or social. For a realist, the reality a theory is about is always an independent 'other', relative to that theory, and as such serves as a means by which we can check or measure the theory. Reality is what we can test our beliefs and theories against (this might mean either verifying our theories or falsifying our theories). The essential point for realism, recharacterized in this way, is that it is always possible that our theories are wrong. Error and mistake are always possible. Where there is this distinction between theory and theorized reality, our theory, or our beliefs about that reality more generally, may have *failed* to grasp adequately or comprehend what they are about.

There are two 'essential independence' claims that need to be distinguished. The first, which is the only one that concerns me here, says that the reality a theory is about is always essentially independent of the theory; the second says that a theory is always essentially independent of the reality it is about. The first claim is a realist claim sans qualification. Reality could logically have been just as it is, even if there had been no theory about it. Notice that this characterization of realism must inherit any difficulties about 'essential independence' that our former characterization had. We cannot just say that there is always a factual or a causal independence of reality from theory, because it is well known that, in some cases, theories or beliefs will bring about the facts that make them true, so that those facts would not have been unless there had been just those beliefs about them. I am thinking here of self-verifying predictions and related phenomena, and these will be especially pertinent in the case of the social sciences. What we have to argue is that, whatever factual ties may bind reality to theory, these ties are always strictly inessential, in the sense that it is always logically possible for the state of affairs or whatever to have been but not the theory or belief about that state of affairs.

The second claim was the essential independence of theory from reality. This, too, is often taken to be a realist claim, but if it is to be taken as such, it can be only with qualification. Matters are controversial here, but many realists accept that there are some singular beliefs, of the form, 'Concerning y, x believes that y is P', and that these beliefs, if intelligible (and not just if true), presuppose that the objects of the beliefs exist. For example, concerning Oscar, if I believe that he is a spy, then if that belief is an intelligible singular belief, it follows that Oscar exists. For some realists, then, there is one kind of belief, singular existential beliefs, which are not essentially independent of the reality they are about. If I believe that Oscar exists, and if my belief is an intelligible singular belief, then my belief must be true, and therefore the reality the belief is about must exist.[2] But if we exclude this case, the case of existential singular beliefs, then we can say that all other beliefs, general beliefs and non-existential singular beliefs, are essentially independent from the reality they are about. The beliefs could have been, even if reality had not been as they assert. I shall not discuss this second independence claim any further in what follows; only the first interests me.

An anti-realist denies just this first essential independence claim, the essential independence of reality from theory or belief about it. Weaker but common characterizations of anti-realism will not do. Sometimes anti-realism is described as the view that reality cannot be accessed independently of the theory, that our knowledge of reality is theory-dependent. This characterization is a mistake. A realist can accept the theory-dependence view of all descriptions of the world, and many have accepted the view (Popper is an example of this). Suppose we must use some theory T, in order to describe reality. All of our descriptions of the world will be T-dependent. However, it does not follow from this that if theory T had not been thought up, created or whatever, the world could not have been just the way it is. All that follows is that if the theory had not been thought up, we would not be able to describe the way the world is. Even if descriptions of reality are linguistically dependent on theory, this would not by itself commit us to the view that reality is itself metaphysically dependent on theory or belief. So I stick to my characterization of realism and anti-realism.

So we are realists in so far as we believe that what our theory is about is essentially independent of the theory itself, and can thereby serve as an external criterion for assessing the truth or falsity of the beliefs or theories. Realism is a view about the thought–world connection. The possibility of error is the mark of a realist understanding of the connection between thought and the reality which the thought is about. Where there is a bifurcation between theory and theorized reality, one can expect to find the possibility of mistakes.

Much less has been written by philosophers about error and ignorance generally than has been written by them about knowledge. Perhaps this is not surprising, when one recalls the extent to which philosophers write in conscious opposition to scepticism and sceptical attacks on the possibility of knowledge. What very often happens is that they then produce views which have the converse difficulty: they show knowledge to be so possible that they then find it hard to account for the possibility of error or ignorance. An example of this is Descartes, who showed that we must know such things as that there is a physical world, since a wholly good God would not allow us to be deceived in our beliefs. But since we are, as a matter of fact, sometimes so deceived, Descartes then had to develop an explanation of how error is possible.

Anti-realism arose historically as one type of rejoinder to scepticism. Anti-realism solves the epistemological problem of how we can know about reality by eliminating the gulf between thought and reality. Anti-realism assures our epistemic access to the world by telling us that we are, as it were, already there, that we have no distance to go. Hegel is an example of this. Reality is, for him, simply thought in its moment of otherness. The fully self-conscious mind is one which has come to understand that there is nothing alien to it, since everything is only, in the end, its own product and creation. If mind makes the world, it is not easy to see how mind could either make any mistake about the world or fail to know some truth about it. So knowledge is thereby assured. But with this assurance of knowledge comes the *prima facie* impossibility of error. Hegel couples with this anti-realist metaphysics an attack on the correspondence theory of truth. Since the mind makes the world, the world cannot serve as an external check on the truth of beliefs or theories. But of course there is no need for such a check anyway, since it will be difficult for an anti-realist to explain how there could be any mistaken beliefs to account for. A similar difficulty arises for Wittgenstein, at least on one common anti-realist interpretation of his writings. Many of the problems in accounting for error in social theory, that arise for Wittgenstein and for Peter Winch, have been discussed at length by Ernest Gellner, and I shall only mention these issues here.[3] What Gellner argues is that on this anti-realist reading, Wittgenstein confers infallibility on a form of life. Gellner then claims that this 'infallibility thesis' is false, for it cannot account for a wide range of phenomena, which includes the way in which a form of life can change its own attitude about something, see its own prior position or belief as erroneous, misguided or whatever. The anti-realist has only internal coherence of a form of life as a test of 'truth'. The realist has both internal coherence and independent fact, which together yield both a genuine possibility of fallibility and of correctability, whether for an individual or a group or a society at large.

One might put the dilemma in this way. Realism is fallibilist; we can be ignorant of and make mistakes about reality. But then the difficulty for realism is that we become too fallibilist; given the gulf between thought and reality, it is not clear how we can really know anything. Anti-realism shows how we can know things, by eliminating the gulf. But then it tends towards infallibilism; it is not clear how we can really fail to know anything.

My recharacterization of realism brings out the special affinity between realism and a full-blown concept of truth. I spoke above of internal coherence being a test of 'truth', rather than of truth, for internal coherence alone could not really be a test of truth in the full sense. It is difficult in this regard to see how to improve upon Aristotle: a belief is true when it says of what is that it is and when it says of what is not that it is not; otherwise a belief is false. There are pale imitations of truth that non-realists may use as surrogates for the full-blown notion – one might think, in this regard, of coherence and pragmatic conceptions of truth, and the replacement for a notion of truth by the idea of assertability conditions. But these are weaker and hence different ideas, for they will fail some strong condition that realist truth passes. For example, on the coherence view, there is no obvious reason why two contradictory beliefs cannot both be true, if each one coheres with some different system of beliefs.

In an important paper entitled 'Philosophical Materialism', Colin McGinn gives four semantic features of classificatory terms which indicate that they are to be understood realistically rather than anti-realistically (or, as he puts it, as natural-kind terms rather than nominal terms).[4] These four features are indicative of our conception of a world essentially independent of our thought about it. First, the way in which we group or classify things into sorts or kinds is susceptible to revision or change, in the light of scientific discovery. If the physical world were not fixed independently of what we think about it, there would be no obvious rationale for changing our classificatory scheme to better comprehend the reality we are attempting to describe. There are many examples of this reclassification: air is not a kind of gas but a mixture of kinds; fools' gold is not gold; a tomato is a fruit, not a vegetable.

Second, there is a tendency to eliminate ordinary language terms, in favour of a technical jargon that introduces distinctions and terms unavailable to ordinary language. Whatever can be said in favour of ordinary language, it is ultimately inadequate for fully understanding the physical or material world realistically conceived.

Third, classificatory terms in natural science exhibit a high degree of division of linguistic labour. I understand the meaning of 'californium', in spite of the fact that I know almost nothing about it, could not identify it if it were shown to me, and couldn't teach the meaning of the term to another person. My grasp of the meaning of the term, and my undoubted ability to construct and use meaningful sentences in which it appears as a constituent, depend on the existence of a specialized scientific community which is able to do those things that I cannot do, that is, identify californium, teach the meaning of the term to others, and so on.

Fourth, McGinn says that we can construct twin earth cases for terms which describe realistically. What he means is this. Suppose that there is some distant planet, twin earth, which is just like earth, except that on twin earth people apply the term 'water' to a substance which, although it looks, tastes, feels and smells just like H_2O, is in fact a chemically distinct substance XYZ. This is sufficient to lead us to say that the term 'water' is ambiguous between the two communities. On earth, 'water' means H_2O, and on twin earth, 'water' means XYZ. Notice that what is 'in the speakers' heads', namely the phenomenological criteria of taste, smell, feel and look, upon which the classification of something as water is made, are insufficient for determining the meaning of 'water', since the criteria are the same on earth and twin earth, but the meanings are different. In this sense, the meanings of terms which have realistic reference are not wholly 'in the speakers' heads'. The real world itself plays an indispensable part in fixing meaning, for what the difference is between earth and twin earth, which accounts for the ambiguity of 'water', is a difference in their chemical composition, and this difference, far from being in the speakers' heads, may be something completely unknown to them.

McGinn mentions other differences between terms realistically and non-realistically employed, but these four are sufficient for my discussion here.

McGinn's four criteria connect with our earlier discussion of realism and anti-realism and the issues of ignorance and error. First, the fact that we revise a classification makes sense only if we think that we have got that classification wrong on the first attempt. And that makes sense only on the supposition that the world is different from the way we thought about it at that first attempt. Second, the elimination of ordinary language in favour of technical jargon is appropriate only if the former vocabulary was either erroneous or neglected some feature of reality that the second vocabulary does not neglect, so the world cannot have been just the way in which it was conceived to be by that first vocabulary. Third, the division of labour must mean that at least some of us remain in ignorance about some matters, even if not all of us do. Reality must be much richer and more complex than the majority of us think it is. Fourth, and finally, the twin-earth example shows us that knowledge of what a natural-kind term means is at least partly outside the head, knowable only *a posteriori*, and that therefore we can be mistaken about what these words mean, ignorant of the fact that two communities might be using the same word ambiguously, because speaking about two different chemical realities.

None of this proves or demonstrates the truth of realism with regard to the natural or physical world. That we construe the terms we use in our description of the natural world in this way might, for all that we have said, be based on an enormous illusion on our part. In this way, the foregoing remarks are not able, and not intended to be able, to rebut anti-realism. Rather, what the argument shows is that we use such terms as if these four types of error or ignorance were possible, and hence as if realism about the external world were true. Our actual scientific and linguistic practice reflects our conviction that realism about the external physical world is true, but of course such practice cannot show that these convictions really are true. I have elsewhere argued, and see no need to retract my claim, that there are no deductively sound arguments for the truth of physical-world realism, whose premises do not beg the very question at issue. Analogously, there are no good inductive or non-deductive arguments for external-world realism which do not rely on principles of non-deductive inference at least as contentious as external-world realism itself.[5] However, I believe that realism concerning the external or physical world is true, in spite of our unfortunate inability to show the sceptic and anti-realist why such a belief is justified. I believe that physical-world realism is a coherent belief, and has no more, and perhaps quite a few less, intellectual difficulties and challenges to meet than does physical-world anti-realism. However, it is not my intention to say anything more about physical-world realism here.

What McGinn then argues is that none of these telltale signs of a belief in realism are reflected in the way in which we think about descriptions of our mental life. McGinn concludes that mental talk is discourse we are not prepared to treat realistically, not prepared to treat as discourse about an essentially independent reality, in the way in which we do treat realistically our discourse about the physical world. McGinn argues that, although we are physical-world realists, we are mental-world anti-realists (*qua* the mental. He also subscribes to a token–token identity theory for the mental and the physical, but this aspect of McGinn's paper will not concern me). Let me repeat just two of the ways in which this is so. If we return to the twin-earth case, let us imagine that the only difference between earth and twin earth is that, although in both communities the term 'pain' is applied to states of consciousness which cause acute discomfort of the sort we on earth experience when we apply the word 'pain', in fact on earth persons in pain are in brain state ABC, whereas on twin earth persons said to be in pain are in brain state XYZ. McGinn concludes, in my view rightly, that it would be wrong to infer that 'pain' was thereby ambiguous, meaning brain state ABC on earth, and meaning something different, brain state XYZ, on twin earth. 'Pain' would be unambiguous, but it would be 'realized in' two very different types of brain states. Second, reclassification of some mental item as belonging to one kind rather than another seems out of the question. Suppose you were disposed to think that some experience you were having was a pain, and then some psychological expert tried to convince you that what you were experiencing was not a pain at all, but really a thought, or a belief. This seems utterly inconceivable. In short, mental terms are not construed realistically. Classification is not about something essentially independent of our knowledge and belief. Nor can we speak about a mental reality (again, *qua* mental) independent of our discourse about the mind, which can be grasped scientifically in a manner that would grossly unsettle our naive and ordinary classificatory scheme. McGinn's arguments about the impossibility of certain kinds of error about the mental connect up with older discussions about the incorrigibility of beliefs about the contents of one's mind, but add greater precision and clarity to that earlier debate.

For my purposes, I want to take all of this as read. One can be a realist about one of the three realms (the physical, the mental and the social) and not be a realist about another. One isn't necessarily a realist *tout court*, but rather a realist about this realm or that. So let's assume we are realists about the physical world, non-realists about the mental. The question that interests me is how things stand with the social sciences. Are we to construe our talk about society realistically, in the way in which we construe our talk about the physical world? Or are we to construe it non-realistically, in the way in which we construe talk about our mental life? As I said before, one way in which to think of society is the location where mind and matter meet. Credit cards, pound notes, banks, prisons, and so on are, *inter alia*, physical things, and as such one would expect them to be like physical things. But, on the other hand, they are things which are designed for specific purposes. Indeed, they are just the embodiments of our intentions, purposes and designs, and as such one would expect them to be like mental things. One might, then, ask: which are they most like?

It is not only social objects that constitute a realm in which mind and matter meet. The realm of human artifacts is just the same sort of realm, for artifacts too constitute the physical embodiments of human designs and purposes. One could never account for thermometers, or compasses, or staplers, without importing some idea of the *function* that they serve or could serve. But these artifacts are not necessarily social objects in the way in which credit cards, pound notes, banks or prisons are, for it is logically impossible for a social object to exist in a one-person universe, but not logically impossible for artifacts to do so.

How do artifacts stand with regard to McGinn's criteria for taking discourse realistically or non-realistically? Concerning artifacts, McGinn says that a general artifact term, like 'thermometer', is defined non-realistically, in terms of a function things of that kind have, and that things of that functionally defined kind can have any one of indefinitely many different physical embodiments or realizations. The last point suggests that we cannot construct, for thermometers or artifact kinds, twin-earth examples. If thermometers on earth and twin earth are phenomenologically indistinguishable, but on earth they are made of glass and filled with mercury and on twin earth made of the phenomenologically indistinguishable but chemically distinct substance, crass, and filled with the phenomenologically indistinguishable but chemically distinct substance, percury, this argues to no ambiguity in the meaning of 'thermometer'. Since thermometers on earth and twin earth have the same function, in spite of their physical differences, sameness of function across the two communities suffices to ensure sameness in the meaning of 'thermometer' across the communities. The term would be unambiguous.

If we wish to define an artifact term non-realistically, in terms of function, shall we construe 'function' in the sense of 'function that an object successfully has', or in the sense of 'function that an object is meant or intended to have'? Surely the latter. There are thermometers that fail to measure temperature, and clocks that fail to keep time. Nor does it seem impossible that we find out that some of our thermometers or clocks are actually doing something other than what they were intended to do. If things are only thermometers or clocks when they succeed in measuring temperature or telling time, then our original, naive classification would be open to revision. Consider ouija boards. The dictionary says that a ouija board is a device consisting of a planchette and a board bearing various symbols which is supposed to convey and record messages from the spirits. But since nothing can successfully have such a function, we cannot define 'ouija board' in terms of the function it actually has, if our artifact classification is to be immune from scientific challenge in the way McGinn claims. What we cannot have got wrong is what purposes we thought or supposed our artifacts to have, or wanted them to have, not the purposes they actually do have. So, if artifacts, like mental states but unlike physical objects, are to fail McGinn's tests for realistic construal (and I'm not sure, at the end of the day, that they do), this must depend in part on the non-achievement sense of function that we are using in their definition.

Let's return, now, to the question of the social world. For the purposes of our discussion, I think we should consider the social world as composed of certain acts and objects. Any social theory will at least have to include items in these two categories, although I do not say that items in these categories exhaust social ontology. So what we are contemplating is a world in which there are social acts and social objects. Social objects might include: prisons, pound notes and insurance policies. Social acts (and events) might include: purchases, inaugurations and paying taxes.[6] This too is a world in which mind and matter have met, in so far as physical things and physical movements or behaviour are impressed with the imprint of intentionality, purposiveness and so on.

With the social world, as with the mind and the physical world, there have been many earlier debates about the possibility of error and ignorance in our knowledge of society. I referred earlier to Gellner's discussion of Wittgenstein and Winch. MacIntyre has also contributed to this debate,[7] but in addition there have been many discussions around such topics as false consciousness, ideology and reification, and self-deception. What I want to do, though, is to restrict my discussion to the four types of error that McGinn has identified for us, and to see how matters stand regarding them in social theory. The thought is that, in so far as we can detect the possibility of these errors in social theory, to that extent we have evidence that we regard our social theorizing realistically, about a social reality essentially independent of that theorizing. If we cannot detect the possibility of these types of errors, to that extent we have evidence for anti-realism about the social world.

As with artifacts, twin-earth cases seem quite impossible to construct for many cases of social objects and social events and acts. A pound or a dollar can have, indeed do have, different physical realizations: there are dollar bills and silver dollars; there are both pound notes and pound coins. Nor does there seem to be any definite limit to the physical realizations there might be for a dollar or a pound. A pound can be any sort of physical entity, as long as it plays a specific economic role and has a certain and identifiable economic function. This, I take it, is the point of Marx's distinction between use value and exchange value. Money is or can be any commodity that *serves as* universal equivalent. Any sort of physical activity may constitute a purchase, if it functions to transfer ownership of something from seller to buyer. In general, social objects and social actions are defined functionally, not physically.

But is the functionality or purposiveness of social objects to be understood in terms of the function they actually have, or in terms of the function they are thought or meant to have? The category of unintended consequences in social life has been much discussed in the literature. I sometimes act, and my act has consequences which I never intended and which I may never even become aware of. Indeed, everyone in a society may act in a certain way, and those actions may have a consequence, singly or collectively, which none of the actors intended or may be aware of. I wish to introduce a category which is the converse of unintended consequences: intended non-consequences. In this case, I (and perhaps every person in the society) act in a certain way, intending to bring about something. But I (or we) am unable or fail to bring about the result I want or which I intended to bring about. The failure may be something I (or we) am unaware of. For example, I pass an item which I take to be a pound note, hoping thereby to purchase something, but am unable to do so, because the pound note, let us say, is counterfeit. So far, from this example, it would seem that at least some social objects and acts are defined in terms of the purpose or function they actually have, not the function or purpose they are thought to have. Money that can't actually be used in exchange isn't money at all; a purchase which doesn't succeed in transferring ownership isn't a purchase at all; a prison which is incapable of holding prisoners (for example, the rooms are too small for even a single person to fit in) isn't a prison. I agree that there is a fine line between what is a poor example of a certain kind and what isn't an example of that kind at all. A prison from which prisoners escape easily and frequently is a prison, just a bad one. But it can at least hold prisoners for brief periods.

It is open to us to find that these social objects and acts are wholly incapable of fulfilling the purpose for which they were constructed, and if we do find this out, we conclude that they are not things or acts of that kind at all. We can be in error in classifying something as of a specific social kind, on the ground that that item does not actually have a certain function which it was intended to have. Thus far, it seems that we have a contrast between mental items (and artifacts, if they indeed are like mental items) and social objects and acts. Many, if not all, social objects and acts are defined functionally in terms of what they succeed in doing, not just in terms of what their function was intended to be. Even if we cannot be wrong about what function something was supposed to have, we can certainly be wrong about what function something actually can have.

The upshot of the discussion so far seems to be this. As in the natural sciences, and in contrast with mental items like pains or beliefs and in contrast with artifacts (although I am not really certain that artifacts should be grouped with the mind for these purposes), the social sciences rely on a system of classification which is open to correction. Our original naive classification of social objects and acts can be wrong. I may falsely believe that some object is a piece of money when it isn't, and may falsely believe that some act is a purchase when it isn't. We may put it this way. In natural and social sciences, our beliefs that something is of a natural or social kind are fallible, whereas with mental items, beliefs that something is of a specific mental kind are non-fallible. I refer to these sorts of beliefs as classificatory beliefs. So, in the natural and social sciences, but not with beliefs about mental items, our classificatory beliefs can be wrong.

The discussion thus far overlooks two important distinctions. So far, we have only considered singular classificatory beliefs, of the form, 'Some specific item i is of social kind s.' First, we need to distinguish between a singular classificatory belief on the part of one person or a few persons, and singular classificatory beliefs on the part of everyone in a society. Second, we need also to think of general classificatory beliefs, of the form, 'There are things of social kind s', both as held by one or a few persons and as held by everyone in a society. So far, I have argued that, in social science, we find singular classificatory beliefs about which a person, or indeed everyone, might be wrong. If I can falsely believe that this is a dollar bill, everyone in the society can falsely believe this same thing. Whether or not something is a dollar bill depends on its not being counterfeit, on where it was made and under what circumstances, and this is something that we may all get wrong. The dollar bill can be counterfeit, even though forever undetected as such. Similarly, the belief that this act is an act of purchase is something that everyone may get wrong. For a necessary condition for my purchasing something from you is that you have title to it, and it may later transpire that, unbeknownst to anyone at the time, you did not after all have the title you then thought you had. Let's call this fallibilism concerning singular classificatory beliefs, which we find in both natural and social science, limited fallibilism. Notice that even this limited fallibilism is untrue with regard to the mind.

How does the matter stand with regard to general classificatory beliefs? Surely I can believe that there are things of some social kinds, when in fact there are none. For example, I may believe that there are, today, British shillings, Confederate money and a Russian stock exchange, when there are none of these things. But where I think we have difficulty in finding the possibility of unlimited error is in the idea that everyone in a society might be wrong in some general classificatory belief that they hold. Here the intuition is that we reach a point at which generalized thinking really does make things so, that there is no distinction at this point to be drawn between a general illusion about the social world and the reality of such a world. And this is surely, if anything is, a feature of anti-realism.

Let's take some examples. Suppose, in society s, everyone believes that there is money, some medium of exchange. What might these people be wrong about? They can be wrong concerning some particular item that it is a *bona fide* example of money. But what would it be like for them all to entertain a false general belief that there is money? They act just as if there is. They transfer title by handing over physical tokens of some sort. They regard those tokens in this way, just as if they were money. What more would have to be the case for there to be money? The plausible answer is: nothing more.

What can be said about a social object, like money, can also be said about a social act or event like a purchase, or a payment of taxes. A person might falsely believe, on some particular occasion, that he had paid his taxes by doing something (maybe the person to whom he handed the money wasn't really an official after all). Indeed, concerning this singular classificatory belief, everyone might be wrong, since everyone could be deceived about the so-called official, including the impostor himself. But could the general classificatory belief that we all have, that there is an institution of tax payment and that sometimes we do pay taxes, be wrong? We do act as if we pay our taxes, in the sense that the tax authorities believe that we do, and that both we and they believe, and act on the belief, that they are richer and we poorer after tax payment than before tax payment. Again, what more would have to be the case for there really to be tax payment? The plausible answer is: nothing more.

I confess that I find this result surprising. If everyone can be wrong, concerning each specific item i, whether or not it is of kind κ, one might think that everyone ought to be able to be wrong about whether anything whatever was of kind κ. Since I am a realist about the physical world, I do think that everyone *can* be wrong about whether there is anything at all of some physical kind κ, or indeed about whether there is anything physical at all. But in the social realm, this sort of generalized error concerning a general classificatory belief does not seem possible in the same way.

This gives us, then, a contrast between the natural and social sciences. We can see that McGinn's original concept of classificatory fallibilism was too simple for our purposes. In the natural sciences there is full fallibilism. Everyone can be wrong in the general belief that there are things of natural kind κ (e.g. unicorns, mermaids, philosophers' stones), as well as in the particular belief that some item is of a natural kind. On McGinn's view, there can be neither full nor limited fallibilism regarding the mental, since no one can be wrong either about whether some particular

73

state of consciousness is of mental kind κ or about whether there are things generally of mental kind κ. The social sciences present an intermediary case. We grant limited fallibilism, but not full fallibilism. There are limits to the possibility of human error, for we reach a point in the social world at which a kind of traditional anti-realism is true. Consistent and widespread error or illusion regarding general classificatory beliefs about society is indistinguishable from reality.

We should not, I think, overstate the anti-realist implications of this. My argument has been, in effect, that if everyone believes that there are social objects of kind s, then there must be some things of kind s. That is to say, to put the matter succinctly, widespread general classificatory belief that there are things of social kind s is *sufficient* for there being things of social kind s. But I have not said that a necessary condition for there being things of social kind s is that there be such widespread general classificatory beliefs. There can be social things which no one has any beliefs about or recognizes in any way. Exploitation, alienation and many other social phenomena can exist undetected, consistently with my argument. The realist belief in the essential independence of social reality from belief or theory about it might mean either of these two things. If so, in one sense realism about the social world is vindicated; in the other sense, it is disproved.

Let me conclude by drawing out an implication of the above argument for something else I have argued elsewhere. Several recent writers have connected realism with explanation.[8] In a recent book, I did something similar.[9] I argued, in opposition to methodological individualism, that we do not explain social facts by reference to psychology (e.g. agents' beliefs about those facts), but rather that we explain rationally held true beliefs about social facts by reference to those social facts themselves. I now need to qualify that earlier argument. In the case of singular classificatory beliefs, or even in the case of a general classificatory belief held by one or a small number of persons, explanation runs in the direction I earlier proposed. But in the case of at least some widely held general classificatory beliefs about society, explanation seems to run in the opposite way and contrary to the direction for which I earlier argued. We can explain why there is money in terms of beliefs about money; we do not explain why people believe there is money by reference to the fact that there is money.

Explanatory priority at this very general level is awarded to the belief rather than to the social reality that the belief is about. I agree, then, in a perverse sort of way, with the realist writers who wish to connect the issues of realism and explanation. I am an anti-realist at this level of general classificatory beliefs about society, widely held, and so, consistently with this, I hold that what such beliefs are about is incapable of playing an explanatory role, at least incapable vis-à-vis the beliefs themselves.

STORIES ABOUT
SCIENCE

Hilary Lawson

INTRODUCTION

SCIENCE MAY not be universally admired – environmental concern and nuclear weaponry have damaged its image – but its effectiveness and power cannot be questioned. Science and technology have not only provided the motor for progress but, until recently, ensured Western supremacy. And, if that supremacy is now in doubt, it is threatened not by an alternative non-scientific, non-technological culture, but by a more technological culture than ourselves. Seen in this light science has been more persuasive than any political creed, and more successful than any religious belief. The story that is science has conquered the world.

For many the success of science is straightforward. The theories of science work because they are correct descriptions of the world – descriptions which lay bare the hidden workings and laws that govern nature. As a consequence the stories about science with which we are familiar are stories of triumph and heroism: figures such as Galileo and Copernicus, Kepler and Newton, who pursued truth over adversity and who, sometimes at risk and cost to themselves, insisted on drawing inevitable conclusions from simple observations. Contemporary accounts of new breakthroughs and new understanding are perhaps less heroic but they are equally triumphant: theories which open up areas of knowledge previously hidden.

The implicit belief behind these stories is that science has painstakingly built up an accurate description of the world based on neutral experimentation and analysis. Every scientist can stand on the shoulders of his or her predecessors and attempt to add a further piece to the vast edifice of knowledge that has accumulated. Unlike practitioners of other disciplines, scientists make observable progress based on proven results and tested theories.

Over the last twenty years this realist picture of science has been challenged by an alternative account in which the history of science is more ambiguously triumphant. One of the first steps away from simple realism is to argue that scientists operate not in a vacuum but within the context of a particular set of theories and beliefs. In general, the scientist will attempt to assimilate results within the current framework of belief rather than propose an entirely different model. Kuhn has been the most influential figure with such an account of science, arguing that 'normal' science operates within certain paradigms that govern the manner in which results are interpreted and understood.

A Kuhnian model of science does not, however, have to abandon realism. A distinction can be made between observation and theoretical interpretation. The interpretation of an observed result may take place within the context of a theoretical paradigm, but the observation itself can remain neutral. Moreover, even though scientists operate within paradigms, advance is possible through the overturning of the paradigm. Science can thus still be regarded as progressing towards a true description of the world based on true observations. The paradigmatic model of science may muddy a simple realism but it does not fundamentally threaten it.

The next and more significant step away from realism is to question the neutrality of observation. According to the traditional view, what Galileo saw through his telescope is unambiguous even if the interpretation can be questioned. Paul Feyerabend provides us with a different history. Galileo's evidence was not the irrefutable data of legend. It was ambiguous and questionable. The point of Feyerabend's history is not to cast doubt on Galileo but to cast doubt on all scientific observation. There is no such thing as data, there is only data within the context of a theory and to that extent data is always value-laden.

The central question that faces any non-realist account of science is to account for how science works. For the realist it was easy: science uncovers the truth and therefore we should adopt the methodology of science in all areas of endeavour. For the non-realist not only is there the question of how science achieves its power, but there is the subsequent question of whether it should be endorsed. Feyerabend is fervently opposed to what he regards as the monolithic power of contemporary scientific institutions. But to be a non-realist does not necessarily imply that one is anti-science. As we saw in the first section, Richard Rorty is a non-realist who not only wishes to endorse science but regards it as a model of rationality.

All of the papers in this section attempt to describe the practice of science and thereby to explain how it is successful. Of the three contributors Richard Gregory is the closest to being a realist. He does not think that theories can simply be laid against the world to determine their truth but he does wish to defend the claims of science to verify and falsify theories. Experiments are games that scientists play against nature and these games produce unequivocal results.

Harry Collins and Bruno Latour are more clearly in the non-realist camp. Collins argues that experiments are not self-evident arbiters of truth. It is only retrospectively in the light of a social agreement between the protagonists that the experiment is seen to be replicable. The result of an experiment is therefore a matter of how we choose to interpret it. As a consequence science is an outcome of social judgements in much the same way as art, literature or politics.

Bruno Latour wishes us to abandon the view that rationality and truth are the reasons for the success of the scientific enterprise, but he does not wish to endorse social relativism. To believe that our theories can be explained by the claim that they are true is to hide the extent to which a wide range of resources must be mobilized in order for the theory to exist. Bruno Latour argues, therefore, that it is in the practice and organization of science that we must look to find its power and its truth.

The importance of an understanding of the practice of science and scientific institutions goes beyond the discipline of science itself. It may give us a clue to the nature of truth. For if science is not powerful because it is true, but is true because it is powerful, the key to its power will also be the key to truth.

H. M. Collins

THE MEANING OF EXPERIMENT: REPLICATION AND REASONABLENESS

INTRODUCTION

EXPERIMENT IS an essential feature of the physical sciences. All reasonable people would 'agree in advance' that, given a choice between two opposed and mutually exclusive claims in science, the claim supported by experimental results is to be preferred to the other. Without this there could not be an experimental science. Since it is widely accepted that individuals are not perfect, we can go one step further and agree in advance that an experimental result that can be replicated is to be preferred to one that cannot. This is because we cannot imagine what it would be like if real things didn't have some degree of constancy and steadiness, and constancy should be expressible in the reproducibility of the corresponding experiments. Let us call this the 'rule of replicability'. Reasonable people are bound to prefer to base their science (as opposed to, say, their magic) on that which is constant and reproducible by anyone, rather than on personal or idiosyncratic reports of capricious or singular events.[1] We can find this view forcefully expressed in Popper's book *The Logic of Scientific Discovery*:

> Only when certain events recur in accordance with rules or regularities, as in the case of repeatable experiments, can our

82

observations be tested – in principle – by anyone. We do not take even our own observations quite seriously, or accept them as scientific observations, until we have repeated them and tested them. Only by such repetitions can we convince ourselves that we are not dealing with a mere isolated 'coincidence', but with events which, on account of their regularity and reproducibility, are in principle inter-subjectively testable.[2]

Any empirical scientific statement can be presented (by describing experimental arrangements, etc.) in such a way that anyone who has learned the relevant technique can test it.[3]

These very reasonable demands are as universally necessary for an experimental science as certain aspects of rational thought are necessary for the existence of thought at all. For example, we cannot imagine any society in which both 'p' and 'not-p' were treated as true at the same time. We might call this 'the law of contradiction'. The question I address in this paper is the significance of these reasonable and necessary advance agreements. I will argue that, while they may satisfy some philosophers and historians, their practical significance is slight. I will argue that such generalizations are unambiguously applicable only *retrospectively* – after debate has been closed off – whereas 'real-time', open instances of scientific dispute are characterized by disagreement about how to apply general rules of method just as much as by disagreement about particulars of the physical world. I will concentrate on experimental replication, but I will start with a brief look at 'p and not-p' to set the style of the analysis and to show how it applies to the most general case.

CONTRADICTION

Consider the law of contradiction. What advantages does knowledge of this universal law of logic confer on, say, anthropologists? What do anthropologists know about cultures yet unstudied by virtue of the law of contradiction? What things cannot happen in a society because of the law of contradiction which might have happened if the law of contradiction did not hold? When logically aware anthropologists visit new unfamiliar cultures, what work can they avoid while their less aware colleagues press on in ignorance?

Imagine a Martian anthropologist who wants to know about earthly rain. He or she (or it) arrives in London on a dull day with a heavy, drizzly mist and requests of a native: 'Is it raining?' 'It is and it isn't,' the native replies. The Martian has heard an utterance which, on the face of it, is equivalent to 'p and not-p'. There are two possibilities: either the native is mad or there is an interpretation of this utterance that is compatible with the law of contradiction. But the law of contradiction itself cannot help the Martian to work out which of the two possibilities is correct. Neither did the law of contradiction help the native to formulate the response. This is a paradigmatic instance of the difficulties involved in applying such a general law. It has become more and more evident in psychiatry and social psychology, as well as in anthropology, that there is nothing that an earthling can say or do that could not be compatible with the law of contradiction. In psychiatry we have been shown how the schizophrenic's world can be seen to make sense.[4] In social psychology, the theory of cognitive dissonance, which is about the way people cope with internalized contradictions, has foundered on the difficulty of determining what people experience as contradictory. (Thus, if it is reported that man will one day visit Mars, and that man will never leave the Earth's atmosphere, is this belief in p and not-p? Not if the subject also believes that Mars will one day enter the Earth's atmosphere, or that Earth's atmosphere already stretches to Mars, or that a bit of Earth's atmosphere travels with man wherever he goes or ... or ... or!)[5] Whenever one tries to use the law of contradiction its practical import slips through one's fingers. It does not seem much use to anthropologists, psychiatrists, social psychologists or anyone.

I will argue that the idea of experimental proof in science and its handmaiden, replicability, stand in the same relationship to scientific practice as the law of contradiction stands to life. Though one can see how to apply reasonable generalizations about experiment after the facts have been settled, they confer no *a priori* benefit on the sociologist or historian of science – or even on the scientist. In themselves ideas about experiment and replication rule out nothing in the way of new scientific activity or belief. In every scientific dispute the meaning of experiment and of replication has to be settled anew for the particular phenomenon in question. 'Replicate results' is a valuable imperative, but its value lies in the way it makes scientists attend to contentious issues, not in the way it demarcates the true from the false. To see how this can be it is necessary to understand experiment.[6]

EXPERIMENT

Experiments are very hard to do. In most philosophical approaches to science experiment has been treated as an unproblematic source of data, the only difficulty being the articulation between fact and theory. The odd thing about this state of affairs is that the contrary is so obvious. Almost all of us have done experiments of at least a very elementary kind – we did them at school – and most of the time they did not work, but an extraordinary yet ubiquitous confidence trick leads us to think that they did. Our attention is never allowed to focus on the one big fact that we might discover in our school science, the fact that experiments are hard, and succeed only rarely. Instead this self-same experience is made to tell us precisely the opposite – that the experimental method is the ultimate touchstone of scientific truth. Here indeed is a nice reflexive example of the radically different ways in which experience can be interpreted. When we did our scientific experiments at school, we were also doing a much larger experiment on the nature of scientific method. The outcome of that experiment is never brought to the forefront of consciousness even though what happens in the classroom is a microcosm of science proper.

When our experiments fail in class we are told that it is *our* lack of expertise that is the problem. We are told that it is the particular conditions pertaining *here and now* and the deficiencies in the apparatus that *we* use that accounts for our failures. This state of affairs is contrasted with an idealized model of proper science. Our attention is directed to the few experiments that work in spite of the adverse conditions of the classroom. These few successes are said to represent and reveal the normal course of events in real scientific research.

But real science is actually like classroom science in a number of respects. All science is full of failed experiments, preliminary runs and breakdowns. 'Normal' science runs by attending to experiments selectively in just the same way as the schoolteacher and the class, so that failures become insignificant or invisible – just part of the learning process.[7] Only in contentious or 'extra-ordinary' science do failures achieve salience. But even here the schoolroom provides yet a further lesson. The way the school-teacher and the pupils achieve evident reproducibility of results from a mixed bag of failures and inadequacies is, in microcosm, very like the way that consensus is achieved over a longer period in grown-up science. Again the key is selective attention to results – though in real science the opposition is much fiercer and more tenacious than would be countenanced in the classroom.[8]

SKILL AND THE EXPERIMENTERS' REGRESS

The conventional view of experimental practice holds that all results should be impartially reported so that there is no place for selection 'prejudice', conscious or unconscious. This idea rests on the notion that, given some ingenious but essentially neutral technical help, what is true will, in a sense, *reveal itself* in exper-iment without more active human intervention. Residual preju-dices can be finally eliminated by repetition of the experiments by others. But this ideal neglects the simple fact that experiments are hard to do.

Experiments are so hard to do because they involve skilful mani-pulation. Like other skills, learning to do an experiment needs trial and error. No amount of book-learning, or careful inspection of an inventory of broken-down categories of ability, can make it certain that a skill has been mastered before the trial-and-error period commences. One may learn to pedal, sit on a saddle, ring the bell and press the brakes, but one cannot *know* if one can ride a bike without the actual experience of failure or success. Thus, just as failure is an inevitable feature of learning to ride a bike, so it is an inevitable feature of doing experiments, and just as uncertainty about one's ability prior to 'trial' (trial and *error* is the method!) is an inevitable feature of learning skills, so uncertainty about ability is an inevi-table feature of experiment. This turns out to be of very great significance.[9] In particular, as I now go on to explain, it leads to the 'Experimenters' Regress'.

One might say that the reason it is not possible to test for experimental ability in a direct way – for example, by investigating the contents of the head as in other academic 'exams' – is that the knowledge needed to achieve the desired outcome is 'tacit knowledge', knowledge that cannot be articulated, and therefore it is knowledge that cannot be displayed.[10] We must use an indirect test for experimental ability. The indirect way that we actually test ourselves is to look at the results of our experiments to see if they agree reasonably with our expectations; this is what we do in the classroom, and this is what happens in regular science. For example, a study of scientists trying to build a new kind of laser showed that experimenters could not be sure that they knew how to build a successful device until they tested their completed models. Often they believed they had built a successful laser and discovered its flaws only when they tested it. However good their sources of information, however much they knew about lasers and related aspects of science and technology, however experienced they were, these scientists could still not be certain that they would succeed first time. Some of the scientists persevered for years without success, and eventually abandoned their efforts. In one unusually revealing case a scientist built a laser almost identical to another that he had made himself and then used for several years. Even in this instance, the second laser would not work for reasons that could not be foreseen. The problem was not solved without many agonizing and speculative explorations of blind experimental alleys.

In the case of the laser most scientists who tried to build the device succeeded in the end in spite of these difficulties because they knew it could be done. They knew what the correct outcome of their experimental manipulations ought to be, and so they pressed on until they achieved the right outcome. When their efforts failed it did not cause them to doubt the existence of the laser; its existence was already part of the scientific consensus. All the laser-building scientists knew when they had done their work properly, and they knew when they had not – they had only to inspect the result.

The Experimenters' Regress arises when an experiment is done without knowing what the right result should be. That is, the Regress applies in those important cases where an experiment, or a series of experiments, is done in order to *establish* certainty. It occurs when there is dispute at the outset. In such cases it is not possible to inspect the outcome to know whether or not the experiment has been done properly for the experiment is meant to establish what the outcome is.

Precisely this situation applies in a number of areas of science which have been the subject of detailed case studies. For example, in the early 1970s Professor Joseph Weber's claim to have detected high fluxes of gravitational radiation was disputed. A number of scientists set out to repeat Weber's experiment in order to test the claim. It was not clear at the outset whether a properly designed experiment should detect gravity waves or should not detect gravity waves because their detectability was the very subject of the dispute. To settle this question, experimenters needed to know whether or not gravity waves existed, and to find this out they needed to do some well-performed experiments. But to know whether their experiments were well performed they needed to see if their experiments produced the 'correct' results, and to determine this they needed to know whether gravity waves existed – and so on. This is the Experimenters' Regress.

The Regress prevents scientists knowing whether an experiment is a satisfactory copy of another before they know what result it should produce. It prevents them from using the rule of replicability to demarcate genuine results from spurious claims unless they already know the answer by other means. Of course, it does not prevent them from knowing which set of experiments comprised a set of successful replications *after* they know what the experiments should have found! It is after we know the answers that the idea of replicability acquires its logical force.

I have provided empirical illustrations and exemplifications for my arguments, but it should not be thought that they rest on the choice of example. On the one hand the Experimenters' Regress could be said to be the practical counterpart of the very general 'Duhem–Quine' thesis.[11] This holds that an experiment cannot uniquely test a theoretical prediction. The significance of a test depends not only on the theory being tested but on the validity of the various theories that support the experiment itself, therefore no experiment can be decisive unless the indefinitely ramifying network of theories that support it are taken for granted.

On the other hand the Experimenters' Regress stands on its own very general feet so long as experiments need skill and the only criterion of skilfulness is virtuosity. In a more automated world than the one we have, things might be different. It is no surprise that most of the worlds described by rationalist philosophers of science are inhabited by automata.[12]

The implication of the Regress is that in new and disputed areas of science scientists are *forced to be selective* in their choice of experimental runs. They must select which runs are to count as producing 'signal' and which are to count as producing 'noise' if they are to reach a conclusion. They cannot simply report every experimental run for, assembled one way, a set of experimental data can look like a multiply replicated confirmation of an hypothesis, while, assembled another way, the very same entries in laboratory notebooks, the very same instrument readings, the very same 'traces of nature', can look like a disconfirmation. More experimental results will not help because just as there are no neutral criteria for assessing a first set of experiments there are no neutral criteria for assessing subsequent sets. In the end decisions have to be made according to criteria which stand outside experiment itself.

What happens in such cases is that the focus of dispute changes from the existence of the phenomena to the performance of the experiments. And since there is no direct way of checking how well the experiments were done, critics will and must resort to a proxy – any proxy – such as the competence of the experimenters themselves, theoretical descriptions of the experiment, calibration of the apparatus, history and institutional affiliations of the experimenters, personal acquaintanceship, trust, more general scientific theories concerning the possibility of the existence of the phenomenon, and so on. Thus, the Regress shows, first, how it is that disputes in science go on so long in spite of the normal application of scientific method and, secondly, why it is that scientific disputes so readily take on a character that seems to have little to do with rationalist models of scientific method. As one critic of Joseph Weber's work remarked to me: 'You see, all this has very little to do with science. In the end we're going to get down to his experiment and you'll find that I can't pick it apart as carefully as I'd like'.[13]

The Regress shows why scientific disputes are so like disputes in other areas of cultural endeavour. It shows how science is part of the history of the cultural world rather than standing outside it. There is nothing disreputable about this. There is nothing to be censured, and nothing about which we must be specially vigilant. Argumentative resources which are not drawn from the canonical version of scientific method are an inescapable part of creative science, however exemplary.[14] The only consequence is that we must abandon any too formalistic ideas of the role of experiment and begin to treat experimenters in the same way as we treat other wise and skilful persons. The scientist is still the expert, but an expert like any other craftsman – a person who knows how to do things.

REASONABLENESS AND REPLICABILITY

Now, to return to the question of the universal replicability of genuine phenomena: it is inconceivable that we should not think of genuine physical phenomena as *in principle* replicable; what is more, without replicability as the demarcation criterion between the valid and the spurious, we would not know how to act. The experimenter in a field of 'normal' science – such as laser-building – knows that the existence of the laser is coextensive with its, in principle, replicability. The experimenter therefore knows how to select the results of experiments, discarding those that do not result in 'lasing' while pressing on until lasing is achieved. Precisely the same applies in the classroom. If valid phenomena were thought of as essentially capricious, their validity would carry no clues about how to carry on in the laboratory. The experimenter would have no idea how long to continue experimenting or how to assess the significance of experiments. Could it ever be the case that the general distinguishing feature of competently performed experiments was failure to produce consistent results? Of course not. The notion is so counter to common sense as to be unimaginable. We must agree that, in principle, genuine results and only genuine results are replicable. This is a vital tenet of science, but what does it mean for the study of science?

There is now wide agreement that studies of the way scientific knowledge is made should avoid the essentially retrospective circularity that goes with explaining the outcome of a passage of scientific knowledge by reference to the truth. That is to say, it is recognized that to argue, for example, that oxygen replaced phlogiston because oxygen exists whereas phlogiston does not is as much use as explaining the soporific effects of opium by its dormative qualities. There are at least four reasons for avoiding this kind of explanation, it is circular, it is boring, it is open to continual revision as we discover that what we once thought was true of nature is no longer true, and it fails to capture the world of science.

This last reason is perhaps the most important. The scientist works in a state of uncertainty. Certainty is the outcome of what scientists do – it is their creation not their resource. If there was certainty at the outset of passages of scientific activity then there would be no need for science in the first place. The discoveries of science are essentially contestable and frequently contested. To understand the world of science one must recapture the uncertain and provisional 'feel' of discovery and discard the retrospective certainty of the already discovered. But, because of the Experimenter's Regress, uncertainty about the outcome of an experiment goes hand in hand with doubt about whether the experiment has been properly performed. Uncertainty about the outcome is coextensive with uncertainty about whether an experiment is an experiment, or merely a 'preliminary run' or some other kind of errant trial. The same applies to experiments which try to replicate earlier claims. The conclusion is simple: though the replicability of genuine phenomena is coextensive with the very idea of genuine phenomena, knowledge of which phenomena are replicable is coextensive with, not prior to, the discovery of which are real! Neither scientist nor student of scientific knowledge is saved any work by knowing in advance that only genuine phenomena are replicable. This is because the process of scientific knowledge-making is the process of replicability-making. It is only after the discovery has been made, after the process of knowledge-making has been completed, that the replicability of the genuine can be seen. Any set of completed experiments may or may not be replications before the event, just as any statement made outside a philosophical treatise may or may not entail a contradiction. It all depends how things are to be interpreted.

The experimental method does not make science special. The unfolding of scientific certainty is like the unfolding of judgements in every other part of our culture. It is one more part of the unfolding of cultural history and is as deeply enmeshed with every other part as, say, art and literature. Science cannot remove the burden and responsibility of political and moral judgements, for scientific judgement is inextricably mixed up with them. That reasonable persons would agree in advance that science must prefer the replicable to the capricious makes no difference at all in deciding which is which.

Richard L. Gregory

TOUCHING TRUTH

Paradoxically, what we usually *mean* by truth is different from how truth is supposed to be established, or verified. For what 'truth' is generally taken to mean is some kind of correspondence, between the meaning of sentences or perceptions and 'objective' reality. But it is very hard to believe that correspondence between what we appear to know and the reality can be experienced or be in any direct way verified. It might be supposed that God can look down on our perceptions and reality to compare them; but such a comparison to test for truthful correspondence is entirely beyond us. For we cannot step outside our perceptions and conceptions; we can only hope to match reality from within ourselves.

THE PARADOX OF EPISTEMOLOGY

We have confronted the initial epistemological paradox that by 'truth' of perceptions or statements we mean correspondence with reality: but such correspondence cannot be observed or tested directly, or without possibility of error. We cannot reach out to touch reality – so how can we grasp truth?

Or should we abandon this notion of correspondence? The danger here is to fall into solipsism – that nothing, including other observers, exists beyond our own experience. Here we are reminded of a postcard that Bertrand Russell received from Mrs Ladd-Franklin:

Dear Lord Russell,
I am a solipsist. Why are there so few people who think as I do?

The answer seems to be that once we move beyond individual experience to objects or events we live in a mental world of hypotheses. And none of our hypotheses is certain.

It used to be thought that perceptions, by vision and touch and so on, can give direct knowledge of object reality. So that when we see a table as hard and brown we know that it really is hard and brown. But, largely through the physiological study of the senses over the last two hundred years, this has become ever more difficult to defend. For we have every reason to believe that perception depends on fallible neural signals, transmitted down nerves to brain mechanisms which may play up; and on assumptions required for interpreting or 'reading' these signals, which may be inappropriate for interpreting or 'reading' them in terms of 'real' objects. Illusions are attributed to (physiological) signalling errors, and to (cognitive) assumptions which are wrong or inappropriate to the situation. But ultimately we cannot know directly what is illusion, any more than truth – for we cannot step outside perception to compare experience with object reality.

TESTS FOR TRUTH

As we cannot see or touch the object world directly, but it seems that it is only by putting forward hypotheses (which may or may not essentially correspond with whatever reality may be) that we can obtain perceptual and conceptual knowledge, so we must have tests for our hypotheses. These are needed everyday, and they are basic in scientific method. We may emphasize the importance of two kinds of tests.

1. *Testing for Truth by (Failed) Consistency*

Loss of consistency is an important criterion for establishing (though not with certainty) what in perception is illusory. But it is necessary to decide how to resolve the inconsistencies, and this is usually done by ignoring some features of perceptions. Thus, if we see lights clearly hovering outside a window, and we realize they are reflections of lamps and so on optically 'projected' outside the room, then we edit the perception, perhaps calling them 'mere reflections'. They (like all mirror images) are inconsistent with touchable objects. But touch has its own illusions.

We can check for internal consistencies within perceptions. When found, inconsistencies may be written off as minor errors or distortions we can edit out or live with; or as evidence of deep errors, requiring drastic physiological (as by drugs) or psychological (as by analysis) therapy.

We can also check for internal inconsistencies in verbal or written descriptions. Such inconsistencies may be due to logical errors of deduction or to empirical errors of fact. Thus, 'She is a dark-haired blonde' would be a logical inconsistency if 'blonde', by definition, precludes 'dark' hair. No observation could revise such an inconsistency. It cannot be touched by empirical methods. Very different, 'She is a tall blonde' would be an empirical statement whose truth or falsity would be determined (though with possible error) by observation, in more or less standard conditions, and might be deemed false if consistent with observations or reports of her height or colouring. This would be an empirical inconsistency with what is taken to be fact, and so (unlike logical inconsistency) could disappear with a change of evidence. But this kind of inconsistency cannot be observed directly, if indeed, as we believe, perception is never direct knowledge of objects.

Conceptual assumptions change through history, especially of science, and (as argued cogently by Russ Hanson and later by Thomas Kuhn, who labelled them 'paradigm' changes), such changes can be far-reaching and can affect perception.[1] In science such a 'paradigm' change is that from Vitalism to Mechanism in biology; from Special Creation of species to Darwinian Evolution by Natural Selection; from Aristotle's to Galileo's physics, and recently from Newton's to Einstein's concepts of motion, time and force. These are all large dramatic changes of concepts, which largely came about through spotting inconsistencies. Some of these were logical, some empirical.

No doubt there are also many important but small-scale paradigm shifts. They also may produce changes in perception (as perception depends on assumptions) and sometimes changes in how we perceive can affect how or what we think.

2. *Testing for Truth by (Failed) Predictions*

Prediction is a powerful tool for confirming or disconfirming hypotheses. Thus for perception: if what appears to be a wooden table melts or disappears or changes colour when a book is placed on it, the perception is at once in doubt. If it supports the book, and makes the right sort of sound as the book is placed on it, and so on, then the perception (or description) passes these empirical tests of prediction.

Predictions may also be logical, and may test internal consistency of accounts or theories – and possibly also perceptions, for some perceptions, such as the Penrose Impossible Triangle, *appear* inconsistent or paradoxical. For most philosophers successful predictions may confirm hypotheses, though never with certainty for they may fail later, and long runs of successful predictions may occur for 'wrong' reasons. An exception is Sir Karl Popper, who holds that statements or hypotheses may be *disconfirmed* or refuted, but not confirmed by observation or experiment.[2] But is this asymmetry justified? One may, surely, say that it is the *surprise* of a prediction, or observation, which gives it disconfirming – or equally confirming – power. And information is directly related to surprise.[3] Zero surprise gives zero information. Failed predictions may typically be more dramatic than confirmation (which we live by every day to survive), so failed predictions may stand out. But it is hard to argue that surprising successful predictions are not just as important in science. Failed predictions may rule out possibilities, but successes can be direct leads to the next step. Indeed, virtually the whole of applied science depends on *positive* predictions, from theory or experiment, for taking a new practical step and placing reliance on technology. And if one did not accept generalizations as usefully predictive, one must take fright rather than flight in a plane.

To take an example of positive prediction in the history of science: Faraday, in 1831, expected the galvanometer needle to move as he moved the magnet through the coil he had specially wound to try the prediction. It was this *confirmation*, of hunch or theory, which ushered in the whole industry of electric power. To take Popper's favourite example – Edington's measured shifts of the apparent positions of stars near the sun during the total eclipse of 1919 – did these *disconfirm* predictions of Newton's account of gravity and light; or did they, rather, *confirm* Einstein's positive prediction? They are often regarded as confirmation of Einstein's predictions, which in turn revealed inconsistencies, or at least inadequacies, in Newton's account. I at least do not see why Popper takes this as an example of a disconfirming rather than a confirming prediction, or, more generally, why there should be a basic distinction between confirming and disconfirming predictions to test for truth.[4]

'SUBJECTIVE SENSATION' AND 'OBJECTIVE PERCEPTION'

It might be suggested that if we can recognize errors and illusions as departures from truth, we must be able to see and know truth. But one man's illusion, or misconception, can be another's truth. And indeed what we accept as true is clearly affected not only by *what* we know, but also by *whom* we know. Thus, talking to a Cambridge or to an Oxford philosopher are different experiences because they have had different experiences, so for the rest of their lives they select and see facts and concepts differently. And facts may appear very different at different times, as is clear from the history of science.

Among contemporary 'hard' scientists, there is less variety of view than in social science or philosophy, which no doubt is bound up with science's aim for 'objectivity' – though there are fashions for theories, even in the hardest sciences. In biology, through the first half of this century, Vitalism was popular. Now Vitalism is dead. For now we explain the living by the non-living. For example, we draw analogies from man-made machines to life and mind, though the inspiring machines are not claimed to live or feel or think. But this is part of science's long traditional aim to see truth outside mind; though, for most people, most truths that matter are in experience.

Considering 'objective' truth, in statements such as the distance of the sun, or that the Earth moves around the sun each year, suggests that there is an external reality, to which propositions and perceptions more or less *correspond*. But to say that one is in pain, or seeing red, does not so clearly imply that there is anything beyond or in any way corresponding to these experiences. So to *see* that the sun is rising above the horizon at dawn (to take an example from a rather different context from Russ Hanson) though *knowing* it is the Earth beneath us that is moving, is to state a truth against appearance – to appreciate from know-ledge that one is suffering an illusion. It is this that seems imposs-ible for 'subjective' truth, such as experienced pain and red.

This split of illusion – between experienced perception and the truth of the object world appreciated conceptually – is only possible if and when perceptions are not *identical* with the perceived world. So illusions provide a strong case for thinking of perceptions as descriptions or hypotheses of the world. But this holds only for alleged 'objective' conceptual knowledge or perceptal experience. It does not apply to pain, for there is no supposed object 'behind' pain (except for damage to the body, which does not seem to count). And, perhaps more surprising, it does not seem to apply for the experience of red – or indeed to any 'secondary' (as John Locke put it) characteristic.

This seems to be a deep though slippery distinction between Primary and Secondary characteristics. Primary characteristics (such as square and round, hard, and heavy) are susceptible to illusion, as appearance may deviate from conception; but no such separation is possible for Secondary characteristics, whose pres-ence cannot be doubted. But these are limited to individual experi-ence. The impossibility of doubt that one is in pain, or seeing red, is impossible only for the owner. For there are no *shared* sensations – even though sensations may be evidence of shared objects of the 'objective' world.

This may be, paradoxically, because we can (or at least we gener-ally assume that we can) *compare* sensations, though they cannot be *shared*, as objects such as houses or toothbrushes may be shared. But can we compare sensations? It is a truism (but nevertheless true) that your red may be my green – or perhaps some sensation I never have. So how can we claim to be able to compare sensa-tions? A key to this puzzle is how colour-blind people discover that their colour vision is abnormal; for example, that they can confuse what to most people are clearly distinguished, as 'red' or 'green'. John Dalton, in the 1790s, who discovered that his colour vision was abnormal, was a chemist who kept chemicals in glass jars in his laboratory. He found that he confused certain chemicals which his friends could easily identify by their colours. On the other hand he would call grass 'green' and blood 'red' without special problems. The difference was that he recognized grass or blood in other ways and knew that they were called 'green' grass and 'red' blood. So he used these colour names as his friends did, and he seemed to them and to himself as colour-normal – until he came to his chemicals in their glass jars, which he could only distinguish by their colours. For many years colour blindness (or rather red/green anomaly) was called Daltonism. It is remarkable that it was unknown to Classical writers. This same principle is the basis of many tests of colour anomaly, such as the Ishihara colour dots of various brightnesses which reveal numbers according to how they are distinguished by colour. This suggests that, in general, it is the recognition of shared objects (such as grass, blood, etc.) which allows apparent agreement (or disagreement) of sensations. The paradox is that it is the sensations objects give rise to that may allow object-agreement; yet it is object-agreement that allows sensations to be compared.

TOUCHING TRUTH WITH GAMES?

Experiments may be thought of as games played against nature. Often, like games played with people, they are interactive. One can win or lose – except that by 'losing', one may gain information, so in this sense one may almost always win. This is the notion of trial and error; errors can suggest solutions, and so if not too dangerous or costly, errors can be valuable. Thus we may hold that errors can, with intelligence, lead to truth. That is the kind of truth that the experiments and hypotheses of science provide.

The key concept here is interaction. To visualize the importance of interactive experience and experiments, imagine an eye attached to a working brain floating in space without hands or any other senses to allow interactive experiment. What would this passive eye–brain be able to see?

We may imagine that it would see patterns, or light and shade, or movements, but these would be devoid of meaning or significance in terms of objects. So it would, we suppose, suffer supreme agnosia. Could it ever learn, from visual patterns, to see objects? Or does vision require other senses – especially interactive touch? Touch seems necessary to read the Primary physical characteristics of objects from Secondary sensations.

This assumption lies behind the recent emphasis on hands-on experience for introducing phenomena and principles of the world and of science to children and adults in hands-on interactive science centres, such as Frank Oppenheimer's Exploratorium in San Francisco, and our Exploratory in England, in Bristol, as well as other hands-on science centres in America, Canada, India and many other countries. But, if active interaction is so important, can we gain new knowledge from such hands-off experience as television? This is an experimental question. It should be possible to find out, by the methods of experimental psychology, just what people can learn from static or moving pictures and how much is added by interaction through active touch. Physics used to be called, as it still is in Scotland, Experimental Philosophy. What we need is a broad-based experimental investigation of truth. But just as physics cannot say what electrons are made of, and psychologists cannot say what mind is made of – indeed, these may be essentially meaningless questions – so, perhaps, we cannot ask at a deeper level what truth is. For it seems that we can only describe and explain *relations*. The trouble about asking for the 'substance' of matter, or mind, is that we are asking for more than relations, and so for more than we can discover by exploratory behaviour or experiment, or games with or against nature.

The trouble about truth is that the relation or link between perceptions and propositions to 'objective truth' is a bridge with only one visible pier. The other end of the bridge, if there is one, lies in a sea of mystery. This, surely, is something of what Newton meant when he described himself as like a boy playing on the beach, picking up especially beautiful pebbles from an infinity of wonders.

Bruno Latour

CLOTHING THE NAKED TRUTH

> 2.4.8 A sentence does not hold together because
> it is true, but *because it holds together* we say it is
> 'true'. But what does it hold on to? Many things.
> Why? Because it has tied its fate to anything at
> hand that is more solid than itself. As a result no
> one can shake it loose without shaking everything
> else.
>
> Nothing more, you the religious, nothing less,
> you the relativists.

QUAESTIO I : IS SCIENTIFIC TRUTH DISMANTLED BY TAKING REASON AWAY?

SINCE SCIENTIFIC TRUTH is based on a series of rational procedures to sort out legitimate from illegitimate claims, no account of how science proceeds can do away with reason. Depriving oneself of notions like rationality, objectivity, scientific method, rules of logic, is voluntarily to choose dementia since it is abandoning the only touchstone we have left to discriminate dementia from normality.

It is so difficult to do away with these notions that the very people who criticize science in the making, develop social studies of science and claim to be relativists are nevertheless scholars whose works are indistinguishable in practice and in form from those they attack. They constantly imply that rational procedures are necessary to discriminate their truer claims from the wrong-headed ideas of their adversaries. In rationally denying the importance of reason, they vindicate the claims of rationalists.

The links that were forged during the Enlightenment between the scientific research programme, the political emancipation of the people and ethical responsibility are so strong that it is impossible to have one without the two others. Dismantling rationality as the main foundation of science is in effect to advocate reactionary politics and it leads to moral relativism. The Enlightenment comes in one package. To depreciate the importance of reason is to advocate obscurantism.

To do away with rationality is impossible, self-contradictory and dangerous for democracy as well as for the mores.

Sed contra

To this I will answer that there is a confusion being made among rationalists between cause and consequence. A statement is true that *resists* all attempts to bend it or to break it. On this everyone agrees. The disagreement starts when we want to account for the resistance of a statement to dispute and dissent. Depending on their denomination, rationalists claim that the main source of robustness comes from the presence either of consistent logical rules, or of exact representation of an object out there, or of an efficient action. The problem is that, when a study of science in the making is carried out, these three alternative sources of robustness appear along with many others. Moreover the 'coherence' of a logical demonstration, the 'exactness' of a representation, or the 'efficiency' of all action are words used *after* the statement has resisted trials. They are cheers after the victory but do not account for this victory itself. In order for them to be bellowed, hundreds of other allies have to be present at the same time, allies about whom and about which rationalists are strangely silent. The study of all the allies which have to be recruited and mustered for a statement to be held true, that is to resist all attempts at breaking or bending it, is feasible and necessary. Rationalists just confuse cause and consequence, the cheers of the victor with the army that made the victory possible. They confuse what is held together – that is truth – with what is holding the whole lot together.

Exemplum

Louis Pasteur is said to have defeated his opponent Pouchet[1] because he demonstrated rationally and objectively that the spontaneous generation advocated by Pouchet was at best an artifact, at worst a fraud. For the rationalists such a debate is now closed; the winners take all. Not only did Pasteur win, but he also won *because* he was the most rational of the two. There is an asymmetry between Pasteur and Pouchet in their use of reason and their access to truth, an asymmetry which is extended to the way the modern scholar treats the two: Pasteur is studied thoroughly and with respect, Pouchet lightly and with disdain.

For a relativist scholar, reason and truth have to be put aside for a moment, so that a symmetry can be artificially recreated between two equally honest, equally rational, equally hard-working men. Once the scale has been calibrated, the debate is reopened and the allies on both sides of the scale are carefully weighed one after the other. A new asymmetry is going to be visible when the scale tips, but this asymmetry is not to come from the scholars' own handling of the affair, but from the weight of the allies Pasteur brings into the fray.

> Pasteur is a member of the Academy; his opponent is not. He can expound his own point of view at full length in the house journal; his opponent is allowed only an abstract. The Commission set up by the Academy to judge their two claims is made up only of Pasteur's colleagues and admirers; his opponent has no one on the commission sympathetic to his claim. Pasteur invokes God, the support of the Church, Law and Order, on behalf of his demonstration that spontaneous generation cannot occur; his opponent is associated with atheism, darwinism and social revolution. Pasteur traces a complete dichotomy between his religious or political opinions and his science; his opponent, chaffing under the accusation of atheism, mixes moral argument with his experimental set up, etc. . . .

On the two sides of the balance allies are added: the Academy, God, the scientific method, etc. They *all have to be counted* until the scale tips irreversibly. Not only the third one. Not only the first one (see below, *quaestio* 2). Which scholar most resembles the rationalist's portrait of the perfect objective scientist? Is it the one who decides from the beginning that there is a complete asymmetry between the objective Pasteur and the irrationalist Pouchet? Or is it the one who, after calibrating the balance, lets the scale tip under the weight of all the unexpected allies brought into the dispute? The second one of course. But nonetheless it is the first who preaches lessons on scientific method, morality and rationality!

Respondeo

★The only way to study science in the making is to follow how heterogeneous sets of allies are tied together, without ever using words like 'rationality', 'objectivity', 'methodological rules' and such like. All these terms might be useful in a controversy but they do not describe the controversy. They might add some robustness to an emerging network, they do not sum up the strength of this network. To the study of reason we prefer that of network, or, to say it in French, to *raison* we prefer the *réseaux*. We can tell rationalists what Laplace told Napoleon when he asked him what was God's place in his scheme: 'Sire, I do not need this hypothesis.' To confuse rationality with science is like confusing the war cries with the actual moves and know-how of the karateka. To be sure, war cries play some role in intimidating the opponent, but it is not fitting for a scholar to be so easily impressed.

★The accusation of self-contradiction falls by the wayside here too. All scholars, no matter if they believe in rationality or not, do use the same stratagems and get by, mustering as many allies as they can, in order somehow to strengthen their claims and make them more robust so as to withstand trials. Depriving ourselves of rationality is not weakening our own discourse, since we claim, on the contrary, that these allies have *never* been alone on the side of the strong claims. Instead of being self-contradictory as if we were requesting for ourselves a privileged access to truth that we would deny others, we are simply *self-exemplifying*. Our own claims too gain in robustness if we tie their fate to other more solid claims until they withstand trials so well that no one can bend or break them.

★The Enlightenment was conceived two centuries ago as a war machine against religion and the *ancien régime*. Science was supposed to clear up the dark ages of superstition and absolutism, and since ethics was left without a prop, rationality was employed to prop it up. Today, we are entangled in scientifico-political imbroglios that promise total (nuclear) illumination and total darkness at once. The beautiful metaphor of light against night has been so obscured that it is time, after two centuries of loyal service, to give up the 'Enlightenment'. It is *because* we want to disentangle the scientifico-political imbroglios defining our new social links that we should abstain from the notions of 'reason' and 'truth'. Rationalists crown the victors by calling them 'rational' and depreciate the losers by branding them as 'irrational', and such behaviour is taken as the epitome of morality (see below, *quaestio* 3)! On the contrary, using such labels has become unethical since they are what hides from view the hundreds of heterogeneous allies that are contributing to the overall robustness of science and politics.

To do away with rationalism is inevitable, self-exemplifying and necessary in order to understand anew what democracy and ethics are.

QUAESTIO 2: IS RATIONALITY TO BE REPLACED BY SOCIAL
FACTORS?

It is impossible not to use rationality – even though it is far from a good notion (see above, *quaestio* 1) – because of the terrible consequences that its rejection would entail. By jeopardizing the three possible definitions of scientific truth (coherence, adequacy of representation to its object, efficacity) in order to account for the robustness of our sciences, we are left with only one issue: the weak social ties that make up our society will have to bear the weight of all our certitudes. Physics will be explained not by the structure of the world but by the organization of a Science Research Council; astronomy will be accounted for not by the stars and the galaxies, but by the professional interests of Greenwich Observatory; the robustness of genetics will come not from what the chromosomes do, but from the consensus achieved by bourgeois biologists. The rich and robust repertoire of the natural sciences will be explained by the poor and weak repertoire of the social sciences: we will get consensus instead of objectivity; social interests instead of truth; society instead of the world. It is to avoid these dire issues that rationality, as a stop-gap solution, is necessary. Without it, we readily sink.

By doing away with rationality, no reality is left. Everything becomes socially constructed – the Eiffel Tower, quarks, black holes, this table, my mother-in-law, oil reserves. .... The solidity of reality is now replaced by dreams or social ties. It is not only science that is thrown away, it is common sense. Relativism replaces realism. Since everything is socially constructed I could just as well throw myself into the air from the top of the Empire State Building and 'negotiate' with gravity! No, we need to retain some common sense and be able to thump on a table that solidly resists and proves itself not to be a dream or a social construction.

By replacing rationality with mere social factors everything fades away and becomes a plot of devious, interested Machiavellian Princes selling their ideas and grabbing for power. There is no longer any possibility of distinguishing between dream and reality, between archaic and modern thought, between witchcraft and science. Everything is equal. All the cows are equally grey. It is the very principle of all possible discriminations that is taken away when rationality is thrown out.

Sed contra

To this I will answer that there is some misunderstanding on the definition of realism. Reality is what resists (*res* in Latin). Let us call *trial* whatever tests this resistance. The favourite gesture of realists, thumping a table, is a trial of that sort. The table resists their fists. They are right in saying that it is solid and real. Nevertheless, it would be absurd to conclude from this trial by fist that smashing the table with a sledge-hammer will have the same result. Another trial will define another relation and hence another reality. This is what relativists say. They cherish reality as much as anyone else, they simply require us to mention the specific trial that defines a specific resistance and hence a specific reality. 'Realities' is a word defining a plural; it tells of a *relation*, of a front of resistance; it is not something that exists independently among other less real objects, for instance, representations, dreams, imagination.

Now the question is to decide the causes of resistance to a specific trial. Here it is easy to clear up the mistakes made by both realists and social relativists. They both believe that the *list* of causes that explain the resistance can be made *in advance once and for all* and that this list is by and large made of *homogeneous* entities. The first denomination believes that the main sources of resistance come from non-human elements; the second that the main sources come from human or social elements. The first are horrified when human elements invade the list; the second are as horrified when non-human elements get into the dispute. The first one screams: 'This is social relativism!'; the second screams as loudly, 'This is going back to naive empiricism!' However, nothing in the doctrines of realism and relativism makes such a homogeneous list necessary. On the contrary, any trial, including the fist and the sledge-hammer ones, invokes and convokes human *and* non-human allies together. And it is most often because of this mixing up and confusion (see below, *quaestio* 5) that the realists and relativists withstand the pressure, thus defining reality. They are both right – the first in stressing non-human allies, the second human ones – but they both have *too narrow a definition of reality*.

Exemplum

There is nothing to stop us from adding allies, one after another, on the scales on which Pasteur and Pouchet have now become commensurable. In the *exemplum* above (see *quaestio* 1). I purposely limited the two lists to social elements (the Academy, God, publications, gate keepers, buddies). Is it enough to tip the balance? Maybe yes, maybe no, it all depends on the specific controversy. In many other cases calling someone atheist in front of a commission in which he has no friend would have been enough to settle the debate. Here it is not enough because Pouchet is able to use Pasteur's own protocol and to display microbes doing all sorts of tricks; for instance, they reproduce like devils even after he heated the flasks in which Pasteur said that nothing could appear any more because the milieu had been sterilized by heat. Why not add the microbes to the list of allies Pouchet enlists? What stops us? Who said that the Academy commission or God were always enough, and for ever would be, to win over a colleague? If the controversy heats up a bit many other elements have to be brought into the fray. Pasteur has now to bring his own microbes into the dispute to counterbalance his opponent's flasks.

Pouchet's allies	Pasteur's allies	
a lot of them	none	human allies
none	a lot of them	non-human allies

— *dichotomy*

Asymmetric treatment: a dichotomy is made
in the list of allies

Figure 1.

He has to modify his experimental protocol and, for instance,
to increase the heat.

It would be unfair to be realist for Pouchet (he has not got
the microbes in his camp) and relativist for Pasteur (he has got
all his buddies well mobilized on his behalf). It would be as unfair
(*quaestio* 1, *exemplum*) to be relativist for Pouchet (he has a lot
of ideological and social interests to defend) and realist for Pasteur
(of course he won, he was right after all and had the microbes
for him). The only possible fair treatment is to see how each of
them makes the list of human and non-human allies *longer* in order
to resist the settlement of the controversy to their adversary's benefit. There is no reason to impose any compartment or any dichotomy among the types of allies mobilized in the controversy since
the actors make no such compartment and mix them at will. Even
the very distinction between human and non-human elements
slowly fades away to be replaced by a gradient of hybrids arrayed
in tiers.

Respondeo

★It is wrong to believe that we are faced with only two branches
of this terrible alternative: either rationalism or social relativism.

Pouchet's allies	Pasteur's allies	
no supporter	supporters	
accused of atheism	Academy	human
provincial	in Paris	
abstracts only	full articles	
protocols	good protocols	
		No dichotomy
ill equipped	well equipped	
ferments after	no ferments after	
sterilization	more heat	non-human
etc.	etc.	

Symmetric treatment: all the allies are listed, no matter how long and heterogeneous the list

Figure 2.

We do not have to choose between these two equally impoverished versions of reality: the object out there, the social in here. To deny the Scylla of rationalism is not to be thrown on to the Charybdis of sociologism. We do not have to trade black holes for consensus, particle physics for professional interests, or biology for Research Councils' petty politics. Such an alternative would mean that the list of allies one should mobilize to withstand a trial is determined in advance and has to be made either of human or of non-human elements. It would especially mean that we know in advance what society is made of and what nature is made of. It is the refreshing aspect of scientific controversies to play havoc with any definition of both, by unexpectedly tying microbes with gods, heat with Academies, and flasks with commission reports. Rationality is not a solution – not even a stop-gap solution – to untangle these imbroglios brought about by scientists engaged in heated controversies. Far from being what saves us from shipwreck, rationality rocks the boat by forcing us to the most absurd choice – nature *or* society – as if there were a possible *a priori* distinction between the two. Having to choose between realism and social relativism is like having to choose who is the most reactionary and the most despotic between the Shah-in-Shah or

Khomeini – a hard task indeed.

★Who cherishes reality most? Those who try to explain it by depriving the things to be tried out of half of their resources and allies, or those who let the things have on their side as many heterogeneous allies as they see fit? Who offers the fairest and most realistic account of Pasteur's victory and of Pouchet's defeat? Those who make a dichotomy between nature and society – Figure 1 in the *exemplum* above – or those who do not even understand the meaning of such a divide – Figure 2? Are we going to be crucified until the Last Judgement between the Object and the Subject, one being the exclusive property of realist scientists and the other being the exclusive property of social relativists? In this divide and crucifixion, it is reality that suffers most, because the trials of resistance are made up of neither nature nor society. The only people who take reality seriously are those who let the actors plait for themselves weaker and softer ties as in a macramé. Even the decisive realists' acts – thumping a table and pointing their fingers – are studied more precisely by us than by them, because we add to the table the long network that has made the world inscribed on its surface. And if someone claims that it is Newton's law of gravity alone that threw dozens of businessmen from Wall Street skyscrapers on Black Thursday, let him go straight to his retirement home. No! Reality is taken seriously only once the twin brothers of realism and social relativism are put to rest. Fasolt and Faffner are guarding the only treasure worth finding: the world.

★Far from being the only touchstone allowing us to distinguish between truth and falsity, witchcraft and science, pseudo-science and science, myths and reality, rationality is what makes incommensurable all these activities, thus rendering the causes of their distinctions opaque. Rationality is Brennus's word thrown on to the scale; '*vae victis*'; 'you, the losers, you will also be irrational'; 'whoever does not have, even what he has will be taken away from him' (Mark 4:25). The only way to render Pouchet and Pasteur commensurable and then to register why at one point the balance tips on Pasteur's behalf – see below, *quaestio* 3 – is first to do away with rationality, with objectivity, with scientific method or to suppose that the two colleagues are both equally well endowed with them. The only way to detect the practical *asymmetries* among beliefs is to treat them with complete *symmetry*.

The notions of rationality, like that of truth or objectivity, muddle the issues. They add obscurity to obscurity. On the contrary, it is complete relativity that makes all the trials of resistance commensurable.

QUAESTIO 3: IF TRUTH IS DISMANTLED ARE WE LED TO IMMORALITY?

Rationality is indispensable – even though it is fraught with difficulties (*quaestio* 1 and 2) – because it is the only way of maintaining any distinction between might and right. Without it, the powerful are also made right, force and reason are equal, there is no ground left to dissent, no court of appeal to dispute authority and we are led back to obscurantism and despotism.

The adversaries of rationality may be easily defeated. If they were right the winner in scientific disputes would be the one who has the strongest muscles, or the best political connections or the biggest armoured tanks. Since it is almost never the case, this means that there is something else that tips the balance in their favour. It is this 'something else', this unforced consensus, that we call rationality and objectivity. To take this 'something else' away is to abandon any hope of ever understanding why a controversy is settled and consensus eventually achieved.

Rationality is what allows us to distinguish politics or business from science. If we give it away, then there is no reason to resist political influences contaminating the results of the sciences and imposing their definition of what the world should be like. Every objective scientific result will be censored and bent to please elected representatives, businessmen or bureaucrats. It is the end of the only pure and free realm left in the fabric of our societies.

But the worst consequence of irrationalism is that any group endowed with enough resources will be able to impose their truth over everyone else's, and the public, deprived of the notion of reason, will be made defenceless. If Nazis come to power, then 'Jewish science' will be forbidden everywhere, relativism and irrationalism will be defied. If enough people gather together to deny that the Holocaust took place, will that mean that the Holocaust did *not* take place? It is to this horrible conclusion that those who deny rationality are inevitably led. They begin by weakening the objectivity of gravity and black holes, and they end up weakening the objectivity of evil itself. Dismantling scientific truth in any small way leads to immorality in a large way.

Sed contra

To this I will answer that there is a misunderstanding over the notion of force. 'Force' looks very different when it is considered *in opposition* to reason, and when it is seen as what designates the complete *gradient* of resistance where reality is tested (see above, *quaestio* 2). 'Pure force' is an expression that takes meaning only because it is opposed to 'argumentation', 'rationality', 'objectivity', 'rational discussion' and so on. It is devoid of any meaning once this contrast is removed and when a gradient of forces is allowed to settle. When such is the case, arguments also have some force; logical connections are not without strength either; legal barriers exert some pressure as well; taboos seem to have quite a lot of clout also. When the two extremes – pure might and pure right – are forgotten, all the relations of forces may start to unfold. Thus, in order to study the way reality is built through trials of resistance, it is necessary *not to make any* a priori *distinction between might and right*. If such an argument seems too reminiscent of some warlike philosophies of the past, simply substitute the word 'weakness' for the word 'force'. Trials of weaknesses, shows of weakness, that's how reality is shaped. Rationalists seem to ignore that material resistance is better obtained by disseminating the pressures than by concentrating them on one point: if it existed, the rationality they invoke to bear the weight of the whole scientific construction would burst, as Atlas would do had he really to carry the world on his shoulders.

Exemplum

How do we account for Pasteur's victory? Shall we say that he is the one who speaks the loudest? Or that he is the tallest? Or that he has the best showmanship? Or that he is the toughest salesman? Maybe yes, maybe no. As any student of war and politics knows there is no sure recipe for success. The only general rule is that you should have more allies, more resources, that they should be mobilizable, well positioned and have good morale.

Apart from this, victory depends on the specific situation. Pasteur indeed makes *striking* experiments; he uses the energy of the microbes to make them do all sorts of games in front of his audience: at will they infect flasks or respect the pure sterile medium, become visible or invisible, appear or disappear. Is the *force* of his demonstration different *in kind* from the *force* of his argumentation? And are these two different from the forces arrayed by the Academy, or by the invocation of God's name? No. It is their coming together and their being invoked together that eventually tips the balance on Pasteur's behalf, at least for a while. Pouchet gives up, his microbes have deserted him. Is it insane to say that he has been 'forced' to give up? The force of evidence, the force of truth, the force of demonstration are plaited from many different coloured threads. Nothing is made clearer by pretending that a demonstration is not strong *like* an armoured tank is strong – especially not that scientifico-military imbroglio: a tank demonstration.

Respondeo

★If no artificial divide between might and right is made, then the settlement of scientific controversies becomes understandable at last. The source of victory is the same for scientific, moral, philosophical or political controversies – the four being hardly distinguishable. Victory is not to be found in one ally, nor in the sum of allies, but in the $n + 1$ ally that tips the balance of force, *everything else having been made equal by the adversary.* In Pasteur's case it might be the swan-neck flask experiment that eventually breaks the camel's back. In Napoleon's case it might be Grouchy's tardy arrival at Waterloo that eventually turned the tide. In Kennedy's case it might have been 100,000 votes. There are no general causes for these victories. Let us simply weigh the successive resources and ponder the influence of the $n + 1$ ally, instead of messing up the whole account by throwing 'something else' in the balance, that is rationality. Who are more honest, those who say that the $n + 1$ ally is just as necessary as all the others, or those who throw in Brennus's sword and call it 'rationality'? Who is more blatantly trying to impress? Where is the violence? Where is the show of force?

★Fortunately Mrs Thatcher is providing the *in vivo* experiment that shows the absurdity of the belief in the importance of reason. She is really trying to limit the production of science to its bare bones; that is pure rationality. No one had done it before and this is why rationalists had the field to themselves. They claimed that pure, free, objective science was everything, but money and resources were flowing in through the back door. Now, the money is cut. Rationality is left alone to support the scientific enterprise. What will be left? 'Everything' say the mystics of science. 'Nothing' say the sociologists of science like myself. Devious political interests do not bend the straight path of reason. They give science its flesh and its soul. It is not I who mixes up the Empress, God, the Academy, swan-neck flasks and bacteria in order to prove that spontaneous generation does not exist. It is Pasteur himself. It is he who constantly *translates* political interests into microbe cultures and vice versa. Rationalists impute to the analyst's own devious mind what the scientists do. No doubt, this unfair treatment is another proof of their high sense of morality. The pure science untainted by political and industrial interests will be exactly what Mrs Thatcher means it to be: nothing. Is this what rationalists want?

*Since Plato, the touchstone of morality has been the distinction between might and right. Nevertheless, this distinction should be abandoned for morality to be effective again. 'Truth' is what is held together, not what holds together (see above, *quaestio* 1). To confuse the cause with the effect is to overlook the masses of resources that have constantly to be brought in and mobilized in order for an account to resist. To believe that truth can 'defend itself' or 'will eventually triumph' is to deprive it of the only allies that can make one account stronger than the others. If the account 'the Holocaust took place' is in danger of being dismantled, who will defend it best? Those who thump on their table and endlessly repeat that since it has really taken place it cannot be rationally denied by anyone in his right mind? Or those who will look for which resources to bring in, which powers to convoke, maybe which society to rebuild in order for this statement to remain indisputable for a bit longer? There is no way to expect that a terrible statement millions of people would like to dissolve away will require *less* resources and *less* work in order to be maintained in existence, than a small statement about black holes or pions that interests twelve people in the whole world and means nothing to billions of others. Scientists are ready to build a billion pounds' worth of accelerators to answer the latter point and not a penny for the former, which is supposed to glow on its own black light. It is *because* we have studied the resources that are necessary to believe minor points in the natural sciences that we are so concerned by the lack of resources to believe major issues in the historical sciences or in politics. We had to dissolve the distinction between might and right so that the *work* of those who hold on to a belief be made manifest. You cannot have truth on one side and the mixed crowd of allies on another. To believe that you can is to dismantle truth for good. Is this what rationalists really want in the depth of their hearts? Longing for the naked truth is like longing for the purely spiritual: they are both dangerously close to nothingness. I prefer truth warmly clothed, incarnated and strong.

QUAESTIO 4: HAVE THINGS EXISTED BEFORE BEING SOCIALLY CONSTRUCTED?

No matter how subtle they try to be, relativists are unable to escape this absurd consequence of classic idealism: scientific facts did not exist before being 'socially constructed'. How silly! Were there no electrons before Millikan? No microbes before Pasteur? And before Newton's day, was there no gravity acting on stones, planets, apples and stars? Relativists have no way of escaping their rather crude version of the story of the tree falling in the forest unheard by anyone.

Conversely, relativists can be led to accept the existence of everything which has been 'socially *de*constructed'. They will have to say that angels and witches really existed in the middle ages, since people believed in them, that flying saucers are really flying for those who accept them; and that organisms really sprouted spontaneously, at least until Pasteur disproved Pouchet and his fellow travellers.

What is absurd for the *past* existence or inexistence of facts is still more absurd for their *present* existence or inexistence. Relativists are forced to say that gravity exists only 'locally' in the laboratory, as if it were not acting on stones, planets, apples and stars well *outside* the laboratory; and, conversely, they are forced to say that witchcraft also exists 'locally', in the countryside, as if it could be true in one place and false in another!

Witches may depend on the spirit of a period but not gravity. Anyway, what should render relativists eternally silent is the well-known mismatch between what some scientists or artists have done and their time. Many people have been totally unknown in their own country and culture, and only many years later, even after their death, have turned out to be right, respected and credited. So, any attempt to relate the right ideas of scientists with their time and milieu is at best a hopeless task, at worst a cheat.

Sed contra

To this I will answer that there is a slight confusion being made here between *existence* and *essence*, a slight excess in going from one to the other, an excess I wish to avoid. We should be very careful in using verbs in the past tense. Are we allowed to conclude from the fact that something 'existed' between t_1 and t_2 that it has *never* existed? Are we to conclude from the fact that something *has* existed since t_2, that it has *always* existed, even at t_1? The same care needs to be taken as far as space is concerned. From the fact that something exists *only* in between settings s_a and s_b, are we immediately permitted to deduce that it exists *nowhere* else? Conversely, that something exists in between settings s_a and s_b, does this mean that we are allowed to say that it thus exists *everywhere*, even in settings s_c, s_n? The specification of times and settings reveals the temporal and local *existence* of things, that is to say, their *history*. Erasing times and settings defines the *essence* of things, that is their lack of historicity. The transformation of existences into essences, of history into anhistoricity, is made by jumping without warrant *beyond* networks of relations: if angels are deconstructed now, it is taken as a proof that they were always invalid; on the other hand, if electrons are constructed, it is taken as a proof that they were always out there; if witchcraft is still believed in in only a few places, it is immediately taken as a proof that it should really exist nowhere; and if gravity is demonstrated to exist in a few laboratories, it is concluded that it should be everywhere, even where there is no laboratory to show it. In each of the four situations a *supplement* of weakness or of power is added to the networks. I claim that we can live better without this supplement.

Such an excess is not only unjust (see above, *quaestio* 3) and unwarranted, it also has the unhappy effect of distinguishing between the history of things that wax and wane and the anhistoricity of things that know not flux and change. In practice, this means that there can be history only of this sublunar world, our base world of human beliefs and opinions, but that there can be no history of the supralunar world, the world of things that have always and everywhere been patiently awaiting discovery.

Worse, the very distinction between a human society and a non-human nature comes from this transformation of existences into essences: what could have hidden electrons for so long, when they were there all along? What could have made people believe in angels for so long, when really there were never any angels at all? What could make people disbelieve gravity, even when it is demonstrated in laboratories? What could still make people believe in witchcraft in a few faraway places, when it exists nowhere? Answer: society. It is society that is made the source of all the biases and distortions that make people believe in things that do not exist and delay the discovery of those which do exist. Society is in large part the *artificial* solution found to account for all the delays and distortions due to the *artificial* addition of essences to the networks. Take away essences and you will discover this refreshingly new breathing space: a society made only of human and social relations is no longer needed; conversely, things too have their history which is more than occasionally tied to our own.

Exemplum

Let us first treat the Pasteur–Pouchet debate as the rationalists would like us to do. For this we add the adverbs 'never', 'always', 'nowhere', 'everywhere' to the complex networks described in the former *exempla*. Pouchet believed for too long in a spontaneous generation that had never been there. Pasteur, on the other hand, finally discovered, around 1860, the ferments carried by air that had always pestered humanity – corrupting their food and their best-planned experiments everywhere. To account for Fouchet's stubbornness, for Pasteur's discovery and for the belated recognition of micro-organisms, we simply employ the convenient social factors that society generously affords – cultures, traditions, establishment, classes, prejudices – you name them. In a such classic, reasonable, plausible and stale account, one thing is lost: history, and in particular the history of microbes.

Let us now *drain* off this excess of adverbs, so typical of rationalists' accounts, from the Pasteur–Pouchet debate. What is left are temporal and local shifting networks of relations among actors (or 'actants' as they are pedantically known), defined by what they do and what others do to them.

Pouchet accuses Pasteur of destroying the nature of the forces able spontaneously to recreate life because of the heat he employs in sterilizing his culture medium and of the air he excludes. This is a strong objection that Pasteur has to meet head on if he wants to convince his audience. In a famous experiment, he devises a flask with a long swan neck and he leaves the top of the neck open so that air can still get in. In spite of this, liquids which have been sterilized remain clean. However, when he breaks the necks the liquids get dirty after a few hours and, after a few days, they are as full of micro-organisms as Pouchet would have expected. The only modification has been the breaking of the neck. The air, Pasteur concludes, was able to sneak through the neck and reach the liquid, but the slightly heavier micro-organisms got trapped in one of the two curves and could not reach the liquid in which they thrive so well.

Without Pouchet's challenge, Pasteur would not have needed to devise this elegant experiment. Thus Pouchet *constitutes* part of the swan-neck flask, he is tied to it, he is part of it. If Pasteur had not wanted to convince his audience that all contaminations of cultures in the new emerging microbiology were due to external ferments sneaking in because of carelessness, he would not have needed to search for swan necks either. His audience and the new profession are also co-producers of the flasks, they are tied to them, they are part of them. But what about the ferments? In how many other situations during the entire course of history has air been purified that way and, because of the trial imposed by the swan neck, been sorted out into micro-organisms on the one hand and pure air on the other? None. This is what rationalists and social relativists always fail to see. The swan-neck experiment is new for Pouchet, for Pasteur, for the profession of microbiologists, but also *for the microbes*, and, yes, *for the air* as well. You can't imagine ferments independently of the swan-neck flasks, any more than you can imagine Pasteur's career, or Pouchet's

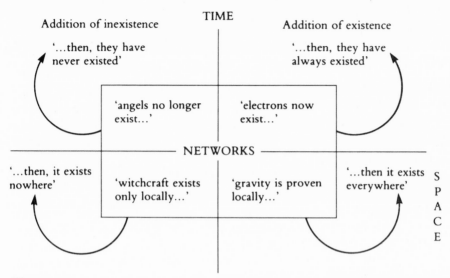

Figure 3.

fate without them, because the shape of all the protagonists –
human and non-human – is being modified by the flasks as much
as the flasks are being modified by all the other actors. This is
why things have a history. This has nothing to do with idealism;
it is not because we impose our human categories to a ferment
out there, it is because the ferment in the swan-neck flask experiment is a *new* ferment, defined in part, like any other actor, by
all the others whose fates are tied to it, including ourselves. The
air itself is not the same air before and after Pasteur, and Pasteur
is not the same after this sorting out of air. Nor is French society.
This is why you should not bungle the analysis of networks by
drowning them with adverbs such as 'never', and 'nowhere',
'always' and 'everywhere'.

Respondeo

★Trees fall in the forest, but those elected to fall in the presence
of men are not exactly the same, since one more element is added
to them – the eye or, more probably, the saw. Newton happens
to gravity, and is an event that modifies it as much as they both
modify England and physics. Is this idealism? How would one
define an electron *before* Millikan? Either you use the definition

that Millikan gave and retrospectively suppose that it was there all along before, even without laboratories, cloud chambers, American physics and Millikan – which is impossible – or you remain silent – which is a much better tack than accusing relativists of absurdity. No one would ask where Caesar was before Rome or where the *Night Watch* was before Rembrandt. Please simply consider that the history of non-human actors is on a par with that of humans. If you find this parity hard to accept remember that it is only your (or Plato's) very urge retrospectively to grant non-humans an empire of essences that creates the very dichotomy between what has and what does not have history.

★Poor Smith, in Orwell's *1984*, was forced to cut and paste the only issue of *The Times* that was used as record of the past. Every new event was rewritten in a way that made it as if it had always existed; and every figure who had been purged away was written off as far back in the past as was necessary. As usual, rationalists admire in science what they hate in politics. If Russian historians claim that there had never been any Trotsky and that he had never been the head of the Red Army, rationalists are incensed by this tinkering with history; but if someone asserts that electrons have always been there even before Millikan tied his fate to theirs, or that spontaneous generation had never been there after all, they swallow those lies hook, line and sinker. In each case, however, it is the very same argument, the same retrospective tampering with historical records, the same denegation of what has and has not been. What happens later in the course of history should never be strong enough to eliminate what has been. You may if you wish act like the pharaohs who erased the names of their predecessors and put their own in their place, but do not accuse *us* of immorality.

★You are allowed to *believe* that gravity exists everywhere outside the laboratories that demonstrate its presence. This is a constitutional right. But suppose you want to *prove* its action here. What will you be forced to do? To build a lab, or to bring instruments *here*. Now, who are the most scientifically sound? Those who say that the conditions of the proof should always be specified, or those who like to believe in things they cannot prove? The local character of an existence cannot be used either by excess or by default, either to expand it everywhere at no cost, or to deny that it exists at all. Gravity and flying saucers circulate in tiny networks that rarely intersect one another. Instead of jumping to unwarranted conclusions about total existence or total inexistence, we prefer to count the nodes of those networks, to see what they tie together and to study how they measure up to one another. Where is the absurdity?

*The idea of a society surrounding works, deeds and facts that would sometimes be in accordance with it and sometimes escape it comes from the same retrospective tinkering with local and temporal networks. Social influence is supposed to be an homogeneous atmosphere that surrounds every deed equally at a given time. It should come as no surprise that lots of events appear to *escape* such an absurd definition of society. But this is no proof that they get free from history. They simply escape the crude definition that some sociologists and historians provide of a *zeitgeist*. If a scientist dies unknown, if his manuscripts are passed along for several generations, if another scientist later on uses them for developing his theories and, by chance, gives credit to the poor fellow who is made the author of a theory he never held, if people launch a subscription for building a statue to the unknown scientist, if texbooks are rewritten to make room for the new old forerunner, I fail to see in what possible way all these events could be out of normal history. When some events are said to escape society and the spirit of a period, first *rework* the definition of that society and that period, and only then reach for your guns to silence relativists.

QUAESTIO 5: CAN WE LIVE WITHOUT A DIVIDE BETWEEN
HUMANS AND NON-HUMANS?

The absurdity of social relativists lies in their denial of the importance of material *constraints*. Not everything is equally possible. Despite the wishes of people or society, *cut-off* points exist at which sheer technical limits render certain avenues possible or impossible, quite independently of our desires. An account of technical and scientific progress that does not pay full justice to these constraints may amuse and sometimes enlighten but, in the end, it is simply wrong. The knowledge of technologists should be added to that of sociologists if we want to get a full picture.

The solution offered by relativists (see above, *quaestio* 2) leads to another extravaganza. They want to treat all actors on a par. In order to avoid the absurd consequences of *social* relativism, they want us to reach a much odder conclusion: people, animal and things are all mixed up in the same huge melting-pot. By erasing all boundaries between human and non-humans, we would be led to claim that scallops think, bicycles argue, microbes fight, computers have volition, trees suffer under the saw, baboons build social theories ... Under the guise of such a naive anthropomorphism is hidden a crude and reactionary form of animism or of futurism. A qualitative distinction between human and non-human is mandatory in order to avoid treating men and women like animals or robots. Relativists want us to weaken the already frail dykes that keep barbarians at bay.

Even if we could accept the moral sequels of mixing up human and non-human, relativists cannot avoid the technical difficulty that only humans talk. Our ability to speak is enough to maintain an absolute gap between us and things. Whenever whales, microbes, stars, scallops or electrons are *said* to speak, it is always through a human intermediary who grants or denies them words. Relativists talk *a lot* about the speech-acts of non-humans – if they were coherent, should that not be enough to silence them?

Sed contra

To this I will answer that, although coherent, I have no reason to remain silent. The very opposition between rationalists and social relativists has already destroyed the absolute divide between human and non-human beyond repair. In order to explain the settling of human controversies, rationalists or technologists must posit an outside non-human essence whose constraints are enough to impose, in the end, a consensus. To this, social relativists answer that the consensus is reached by humans, and only through social means, since there is no outside essence which is constraining enough to silence us. The two positions are both mirror images of each other. The more rationalists insist on the constraints emanating from things, the *easier* it is for social relativists to demonstrate that things are not determinate enough to do that job. The more sociologists insist on the social means to reach consensus,

	Rationalists or technologists	Social relativists
What is asserted in theory	◯ THEY ASSERT THAT there are non-humans out there	THEY ASSERT THAT ONLY HUMANS make a difference ⊗
What is done in practice	⊗ BUT IN PRACTICE THEY SPEAK FOR THEM	BUT IN PRACTICE THEY LET non-humans sneak in ◯
Sum	Non-humans' eminence is both asserted and negated	= Non-humans' eminence is both negated and reasserted

Figure 4.

the *easier* it is for rationalists and technologists to demonstrate that something has been left aside: things and their constraints. The further one side is pushed, the further the other goes (see above, *quaestio* 2). I call this a child's swing. It is fun, but not very suitable for grown-ups.

Steps toward a more intriguing game may be taken if we compare what the twins claim to do with what they do in practice. Rationalists or technologists are quick to mark a cut-off point, after which they invoke the eminent rights of things in themselves; in practice, however, they are still quicker to push things aside while fiercely arguing on their behalf, thus themselves entirely occupying the scene. Conversely, social relativists delight in denying any importance to outside constraints. However, in practice, they demarcate another cut-off point, and then let things sneak in through the back door whenever they wish to settle a dispute *for good*. This is very embarrassing for both schools because if we sum the four quadrants, the two groups end up equal (see Figure 4). They play the *same* game, but in a mirror. One group invokes non-humans while denying them a role; the other invokes humans while denying them a role.

What is wrong in this too predictable game that always ends

up at the same point? The respective *roles* granted to things and to humans. If we modify the attribution of roles the whole game opens up.

Since, in practice, *no one* is able to deny for good the presence of non-humans in achieving consensus (rationalism), *or* to make them play the part of a final arbiter that settles disputes for good (social relativism), why not modify the scenario once and for all? Non-humans are party to all our disputes, but instead of being those closed, frozen and estranged things-in-themselves whose part has been either exaggerated or downplayed, they are actors like all others – open or closed, active or passive, wild or domesticated, far or close, depending on their (and our) negotiating strength. When they enter the scene they are endowed with all the non-human powers that rationalists like them to have, *plus* the warmth and uncertainty that social relativists recognize in humans.

Since, in practice, *no one* is able to make humans play the part of a final arbiter which can settle disputes for good, *or* to deny for good their importance in achieving consensus, why not modify the scenario once and for all? Instead of acting like those social animals whose part has been minimized or exaggerated, humans are *spokespersons* – who talk, represent and interpret non-humans. When they do enter the scene, they are granted all the powers of discussion, speech and negotiation sociologists like them to have, but *in addition* they endorse the fate of all the non-humans for whom rationalists and technologists are so concerned.

Relativists do not enjoy being swung back and forth from 'social factors' to 'technical factors'. They have jumped out of the swing and rewritten the libretto so that they will no longer be faced with these silly twin characters: the social animal on the one hand, the thing on the other.

Respondeo

★The argument about 'constraints' is right only as long as one believes, first, that there could be, on the one hand, someone – or something – free and, on the other, limits imposed on this freedom from the outside, and, second, only if there existed between the two entities a cut-off point at which freedom would give way to necessity. A free, infinitely pliable human being could then be 'limited by' material constraints, or – depending on whether one is a rationalist or a social relativist – an infinitely interpretable thing could be 'limited by' social constraints. However, once you rewrite the scripts and put human and non-human on a par, the whole debate about constraints and cut-off points disappears because there is no longer any place for a free, flexible or infinitely pliable character. We are all for hardness and robustness (see above, *quaestio* 2), but the hard reality does not arise abruptly at some given point. So, instead of identifying cut-off points, let us spread the sources of hardness all along the networks, and instead of constraints let us talk only of *resources*. Gravity is not a 'constraint over' bridge designers' freedom. It is one of their many resources.

★Who mixes up the fate of humans and non-humans? Those hundreds of thousands who bring microbes to bear on our lives, atoms to heat our houses, electrons to carry our voices, fossilized skulls which modify our genealogies, radio-waves which disseminate our President's speeches? Or, we, the dozens of social scientists who try to reconstruct how the former render the boundaries between human and non-human more meaningless every day? Who is building the huge melting-pot where humans, animals, natural things and artifacts exchange properties? We or those we try to follow? Who is extravagant? Those who breed hybrids? Or those who are trying to rework all of social science, so that we might understand how hybrids can so easily be created *in spite* of the 'strict boundary' between human and non-human? What is the more barbarian? To define a politics that considers all spokespersons equally – no matter if they represent a human or non-human constituency – or to cling to version of politics that does not include the politics *of things*?

★It is easy to trace an absolute gap, between humans who speak and non-humans who are mute, only if we do not think about the matter for more than ten seconds. At the eleventh, matter starts to become much less clear. First, lots of humans are talked *about* by others – journalists, politicians, social scientists, to name just a few – but you rarely hear their voices directly. Second, most non-humans are said to communicate, write and answer *directly* in laboratories or through instruments. Microbes, electrons, gravity do the talking and the writing, not Pasteur, Millikan or Newton – indeed this is the very reason why most realists and many rationalists cannot swallow relativists' arguments; they are the ones who most need to blur the absolute distinction between who is speechless and who is not. Third, *who* is speaking when spokespersons speak? The representatives, or their constituency? If they are faithful, they will simply be the mouthpiece of their constituency – as Hobbes would say, they are only the actors of whom the authors are the multitudes. So, it is only when the spokespersons are unfaithful that a distinction may be made between those who are speechless and their representatives. In the absence of a controversy over representation it is impossible to tell apart those who speak directly or those who speak indirectly. But when a controversy flares up, the main argument of the representatives is to say that they 'simply carry out' what the others say, or wish to say . . . See? You cannot silence the spokespersons, either by telling them that they are the only ones who talk or by telling them that they are simply talking in the name of other speechless creatures. Language is a faculty *whose exact distribution is the very outcome* of our fiercest struggles. This is why we cannot grant it all to humans without rendering the politics of things forever obscure.

STORIES ABOUT
REPRESENTATION

Hilary Lawson

INTRODUCTION

REPRESENTATION IS BUILT into the relationship between language and the world and is therefore central to the question of truth. For the realist, language represents the world and if it represents the world correctly a proposition is true. Language literally re-presents the world. But for the non-realist representation cannot mean re-presentation. There is no present to re-present. The possibility is open therefore to explore alternative modes of expression which reinterpret the relationship between language and the world.

Academic papers in factual disciplines tend to have the single rhetorical mode of descriptive assertion. The assumption on the part of the reader is that the paper is conveying the truth, and on the part of the writer that it should give the impression of doing so. The two papers in this section have not completely abandoned this mode of representation but they do suggest alternative approaches.

Steve Woolgar in his paper 'The Ideology of Representation and the Role of the Agent' argues that relativist attacks on the truths of science have not gone far enough. The relativist has not really abandoned truth, instead the truths of science are simply replaced with social truths. Relativism is itself infected with scientism in the sense that it is believed that signs stand for something else, something real that is beyond them, that they can be deemed to represent. The real task is to dismantle the ideology of representation, the assumption that language represents an underlying reality. To abandon the physical reality of science in favour of the social reality of historian or sociologist is to remain firmly embedded in realism. The end of such an ideology is not to be effected by a statement that itself relies on the authority of representation. We are going to need other literary modes, and Woolgar concludes with just such a rhetorical shift.

In the search for a way forward John Forrester proposes psychoanalysis as an alternative model for our understanding of truth. Unlike science, which assumes that the relationship to truth is straightforward, psychoanalysis takes lying seriously. We ask of the scientist not 'Are you telling the truth?' but 'Is that the truth?', as if the scientist were merely a neutral carrier for the proposition. The opposition of truth and lies is a very different opposition from the familiar arguments about truth and falsehood. Forrester argues that an adequate science of lies is necessary if we are to have an understanding of truth.

The search for alternative modes of representation is not an easy one. For althouth truth may be a fiction it is the most powerful fiction we have. The pervasiveness of the assumption of truth is testimony to its power. Even the contemporary wave of dismantling truth is founded on truth. The only weakness in the story of truth is that it reflexively undermines itself. In the ever greater demand to uncover how things really are, we uncover the fictional nature of truth – but in whose name? In the name of truth itself. As we seek reality in the post-modern world, truth has the last laugh.

Steve Woolgar

THE IDEOLOGY OF REPRESENTATION AND THE ROLE OF THE AGENT[1]

OVER THE last twenty years, a large literature has established that science may be understood from what can be broadly termed the 'relativist–constructivist' perspective.[2] There is no point just repeating the standard arguments of this perspective, the idea that science is a social process, that scientific method is not all it was once thought to be, and so on. Let us accept all that. The interesting question is: what comes next? The challenge to objectivism began when sociologists began to take seriously the relativity of scientific truths; sociologists opened the black box of science by insisting that the very content of scientific knowledge was a sociological topic. The sociology of scientific knowledge (with its emphasis on the socially constructed character of the esoteric details of the science itself) supplanted the earlier tradition of the sociology of science (which stressed the institutional arrangements and social relationships between knowledge producers). But what will supplant the sociology of scientific knowledge? This chapter presumes the need for an evaluation of what has been achieved by the relativist perspective on science, as the basis for moving beyond the repeated application of the relativist–constructivist formula.

The 'what comes next?' question is especially interesting given the broader context of challenges to the idea of science as a privileged way of producing knowledge: critiques of science are now to be found in different forms in several disciplines – literary theory, philosophy, history, anthropology and sociology – and in several significant intellectual traditions which cut across these traditionally defined boundaries – deconstruction, the critique of representation, post-structuralism, post-modernism. In this context it is possible to suggest that the radical implications of recent work in the sociology of scientific knowledge are as yet underdeveloped.[3] Despite substantial achievements in the post-Kuhnian epoch, particularly impressive when judged against the legacy of earlier perspectives on science, this vigorous and increasingly influential body of research has yet to realize its full potential. It has failed to push relativism far enough; its proponents are themselves still wedded to an epistemology which supports the notion of truth, albeit one slightly displaced from its familiar venue. Consequently, these proponents of relativism are not dismantling truth *per se*, they are merely in the business of substituting sociological, literary and philosophical truths for the truths of science. Of course, this kind of substitution exercise is healthy enough as a beginning; if nothing else, it still raises the hackles of defenders of the supremacy of science. But it leaves us with the distinct impression that deeper, more fundamental questions remain unanswered.[4]

What accounts for the tangential character of the critique of science, the fact that the kernel of epistemological presumption remains essentially undisturbed, despite all the noise at the periphery? A simple answer is that in at least two senses the relativist critique of science is itself scientific in its own aspirations. First, the disciplinary origins of the social sciences lie in explicit attempts to mimic the aims, methods and achievements of natural science. The scientific pretensions of sociology owe much to the obsession of its founding fathers with the success of nineteenth-century biological sciences. Secondly, and more fundamentally, the disciplines which produce the critique of science share an important epistemological position. Although they might be characterized as distinct from science on disciplinary grounds, they share with science the *ideology of representation*, the set of beliefs and practices stemming from the notion that objects (meanings, motives, things) underly or pre-exist the surface signs (documents, appearances) which give rise to them. A critique of science is empty or, at least, severely restricted, if it fails to address this ideology. The problem for science critics – if one regards it as a 'problem' – is that any attempt to dismantle this ideology, rather than a particular set of truths which happen to emerge from a specific disciplinary application of this ideology, appears tantamount to dismantling one's own discipline.

If the correct (and more challenging) target for deconstruction is the ideology of representation, rather than just 'science' as an organizational phenomenon, we need to remind ourselves that science is no more than an especially visible manifestation of the ideology of representation. Science is, indeed, the tip of the iceberg of the modern obsession with technical rationality and reason; the public face of the ideology of representation. It provides, so to speak, the official party line on an attitude which pervades practices well beyond the confines of professional natural science. Discussions about science may be an obvious place to look for public pronouncements of this ideology, but it is by no means the exclusive locale for its operation. By insisting on a distinction between science (as object) and our own disciplines (as resource), we are in danger of mistaking relativistic critiques of science for an adequate appreciation of the more general problem of representation.

To understand the operation of the ideology of representation we need to appreciate the way it is institutionalized in interpretive practices. In its sociological sense, 'institution' denotes a regularized pattern of activities that are normatively sanctioned. The institution of science thus denotes a regularized pattern of representational practices which are normatively sanctioned in the sense that practitioners (interpreters) routinely display assumptions about the character of representation, and evaluate (both their own and others') attempts at representation by appeal to (often implicit) rules about correct procedure and method. In short, the ideology of representation provides a resource or 'evaluative repertoire'[5] for the evaluation of interpretive practice.[6]

THE ROLE OF THE AGENT

One of the most important aspects of the ideology of representation concerns the role of agency. The key relationship to be negotiated is that between the objects of the world and their representation in terms of signs, records and so on. Agents of representation are those entities (actors, actants) which mediate between the world and its representation. Their role is the relatively passive one of enabling or facilitating representation. However, there is an interesting asymmetry with respect to an agent's relationship to the world and to its representation. Agents are considered passive in the sense that they are not thought capable of affecting the character of the world. According to the ideology, the mediator does not intrude to the extent that s/he is in any way responsible for the character of the de-sign-ated object. However, the agent *is* held responsible for the character of representations. While correct mediation amounts to author-itative speech about the objective world, incorrect mediation can be said to be the source of distorted representations of the (unchanging) world.

The alleged passivity of the agent vis-à-vis the facts of the world is well captured in the idea that facts are neutral, that they are there to be discovered by anybody. A version of this is part of Merton's ethos of universalism in science.[7] But the alleged irrelevance of the agent provides an interesting awkwardness when it comes to acknowledging and rewarding individual scientists for their contributions to science. For these occasions provide a celebration both of the ideology of representation and the part of the (honoured) individual. The dilemma is that the honoured individual is held to be especially capable of obtaining representations of the world, but that such representations do not arise solely in virtue of the individual agent. This accounts for the rather coy, 'lucky bystander' tone of Nobel Prize acceptance speeches: thank you very much, I couldn't have done it without the help of numerous others and (most significantly for purposes) *I just happened to be in the right place at the right time.* The appeal of the ideology of representation is the notion that, given the right circumstances, any other agent could equally have produced the same results, facts, insights and so on. This is the corollary of the view that the same facts were already there, enjoying a timeless pre-existence, merely awaiting the arrival of a transitory agent.

But the scientist is only one kind of agent held responsible for mediating between the world and its representations. The scientific laboratory is populated by a wide variety of inanimate agents: experimental apparatus, oscilloscopes, measuring instruments, chart recorders and other inscription devices. Not all agents of representation share equal responsibility in the business of furnishing representations of the world. Some are reckoned more capable than others, some particularly good at certain kinds of interpretive work, others as having outlived their usefulness and so on. At any time, the culture of the laboratory comprises a highly stratified moral universe of rights and entitlements, obligations and capabilities differentially assigned to the various agents. This moral order can change, for example, with the introduction of a new agent into the community. For example, in a study of solid-state physics investigations into the properties of amorphous metal alloys, it was found that several person-days effort were devoted to assessing the capabilities and performance of a device for measuring changes in electrical resistance during isothermal annealing.[8] These deliberations included negotiations between various agents (the company representatives, the head of the laboratory, putative users of the device) over the capabilities of the device. Even after its eventual purchase, the machine was put through several further tests before being granted the trust necessary for its participation as an adequately socialized member of the community.

The hierarchy of rights and responsibilities is characterized by a particular relationship between human and inanimate agents of representation. Neophyte scientists similarly undergo socialization into the community, imbibing the ethos of representation, but learn to regard inanimate agents as 'machines', that is, as technologies of representation of a different order from them-Selves. While these machines are often credited with the capability of producing direct representations of the world – their rhetorical power is that their representations appear 'automatic', apparently untainted by human intervention – they are presumed to remain under the control of the human agents. Nonetheless, the power of any particular technology of representation can be understood in terms of the amount of work which would be required of an (unaided) human operating in its place.

The capacity (or ability) attributed to various agents and technologies of representation is a reflection of the solidification of past results and knowledge claims. In Knorr-Cetina's terms,[9] the scientific laboratory comprises materializations of earlier scientific decisions and selections. The knowledge products which stabilize and solidify are embodied in technologies which set the scene for the next set of interpretive decisions (representations). This is of significance in three ways. First, established facts become further solidified in the sense that they are no longer just facts by virtue of their utterance; they are embodied in mechanisms which (are said to) enable further work (experiments, inferences, measurement, data collection). Facticity is thus enshrined in terms of instrumental value. Secondly, the rhetorical importance of materialization is that the previous results are turned into a technology which, in the course of further representational practice, can be apprehended as a set of merely passive, neutral instruments. An inscription device[10] with the capability of making an apparently direct connection between, say, the radiation received by a radio telescope and the shape of a pulse on the oscilloscope, in fact encapsulates years of work on the theory of electronics, the wave form of radiation and so on. Thirdly, the instrumentalism and rhetorical neutrality of these technologies conspire to define the next upshot of representational activity. Our apprehension, description and classification of the physical world depends on the technologies which make these activities possible. In other words, the world is constituted in virtue of the technologies of representation available.

It is easy to see that representational practices 'outside' science are similarly informed by the ideology of representation. As writers, practical reasoners, conversationalists and so on, we each subscribe to the view that our writings, reports, practical actions are not merely the whimsical product of individual minds. Despite the possible sources of distortion, bias and so on, we write with the commitment that our signs are – at least potentially – the reflection of real entities in the world, that things other than the signs themselves lie behind and give rise to these mere signs of their existence. The Cartesian dualism of representational ideology thus survives in practices outside 'science' proper. It is sometimes said that 'science' might effect these connections more reliably, in virtue of the prolonged training of its agents. But notwithstanding their relative unreliability, the interpretive practices of everyday life subscribe to the same ideology of representation. This is hardly surprising: science is the institutionalized manifestation of a philosophical tradition which began with the Greeks and which has increased its influence on Western cultures over a period of two hundred years.

Similarly, the role of the agent and other technologies of representation is central to interpretive practices as institutionalized in areas 'outside' science. We assign differential rights and responsibilities to different kinds of agents of representation: tape recorders can be regarded as more faithful than mere recollection, but only if correctly operated by a (trained) knowledgeable user. There are of course differences between science and non-science. The extent and variety of inscription devices available to the social scientist and literary critic hardly compare with those used by science. Particle accelerators on the one hand; pens, typewriters and word processors on the other. But despite the difference in scale, the notion of agent and his/her relationship to the technologies of representation remains central. The main difference is one of resources, not of ideology.

ONTOLOGICAL GERRYMANDERING

Now we are clearer about the importance of the ideology of representation and the concept of the role of agency in interpretation, we are in a better position to assess the status and achievements of critiques of science. The relationship between science and those non-sciences which purport to provide a critical edge upon science is obviously crucial. It is fairly clear that the success (or, at least, the plausibility) of critiques of science is that they suppose (and present) themselves as something separate from the science which is being deconstructed. This is especially important, given the main conclusion of the sociology of scientific knowledge that there is no essential difference between science and non-science. The critic of science is the mediator between the objects of his or her study (science, scientists' behaviour, etc.) and the signs (texts) which represent those objects, just as the scientist (observer) is the mediator between objects and their representation. More practically, this means that the course of deconstruction entails various implicit claims at differentiation between deconstructer and deconstructed. In short, the former presents the argument as if she or he was immune from the strictures applied to the target of the argument. This involves the establishment and manipulation, in the course of the argument, of boundaries between those assumptions and arguments susceptible to deconstruction and those which are not.

This is done implicitly and with some subtlety; the relativist argument highlights the susceptibility of those claims and assumptions to relativism, while simultaneously backgrounding the fact that the very assumptions of relativism are equally susceptible to the same treatment.

The process of establishing and manipulating a boundary between arguments which are and are not susceptible to relativism is called 'ontological gerrymandering'.[11] Again, the role of the agent is crucial. The susceptibility of claims to relativism is enhanced by spotlighting the role of the agent, and emphasizing the possibility of arbitrariness, or distortion, or motivated, actively constructed representations. The critical gaze focuses on agencies such as the police, the courts in the case of the sociology of deviance; on the news services in media studies; and on the scientist in the sociology of science. Meanwhile, in all these studies, the role of the agent which makes *these* representations (about the police, etc.) is hidden, subdued and silent.

The ideology of representation has been roundly criticized in general terms by a number of influential scholars: in philosophy of science,[12] in anthropology[13] and in social studies of science.[14] It is important to note, however, that most of these criticisms have deployed a form of ontological gerrymandering: their authors have produced texts which develop and elaborate arguments for the deficiency and/or historicity of conventions of representation; but the texts themselves tend to trade upon the same conventions or, at least, they fail to address the extent to which this might be true and whether or not it is consequential. Within the sociology of scientific knowledge tradition, a number of authors have produced admirably detailed, fine-grained analyses of representational practices in the natural sciences.[15] But, once again, the focus is predominantly on the representational practice of *others* (in this case, of the scientists). The analyses remain unreflexive, unconcerned with the way in which representation is used to produce stories about representation. Another way of making the point is to observe that despite a substantial move to replace the passive conception of agency by a more active conception of the scientist (police, news media, anthropologist), the 'author of criticism' remains a passive agent, depicted as disengaged and apparently aloof from the practice of criticism itself.

We can now see that . . .

Just a minute . . .
Go away . . .
But you surely need to point out . . .

Not yet. Go away . . . Where was I? Ah, yes . . . We can now
see that although science is a highly institutionalized form of representation, representational practices beyond professional 'science' are also subject to an ideology of representation which
sustains a Cartesian dualism between objects and their representation. Critics of science, especially those who espouse an avow-
edly 'relativist' line, have by and large failed to try to step outside
this ideology of representation in their own research and argument. They have had to continue to engage in ontological gerrymandering in virtue of their inattention to the way their own
practices are subject to the ideology of representation. The failure
to move on corresponds to their operation within, and hence their
reproduction of, an established moral order of agency and technology. It follows that the more radical challenge to the concept
of science must take issue with conventional ideas about the relative
capacities of different agencies of representation and interrogate
some of our deeper preconceptions about the adequacy of those
technologies by virtue of which the world is made available to
us.

The ideology of representation is institutionalized in the sense
that representational practices are normatively sanctioned. Of
course, much is already known about instances of fraud and deception in science. These undoubtedly constitute a violation of expectations about correct scientific behaviour. They do not, however,
constitute a violation of the ideology *per se*. Fraud in science
amounts to the distortion of findings and results, but it does not
challenge the very distinction between results and the objects from
which they purport to derive. For example, the 'bogus' claim
to have discovered N rays, while subsequently said to have been
the upshot of improper behaviour, nonetheless trades upon the
concept of separation between phenomenon and their ostensive
signs. It is thus useful to distinguish between methodological deviation and ideological deviation. While critics of science have been
very good at pointing out the former, little has been done on
the latter.

Garfinkel's prescription for revealing the fundamental structure
of practical actions was to take ordinary, everyday scenes and

see what had to be done to cause trouble.[16] His notion is that these 'breaching experiments' expose the character of what was taken for granted. The degree of consternation caused by the breach is a reflection of the strength of adherence to the norms being violated. What then would constitute a breach of the ideology of representation? Clearly, we require some mechanism which suspends or makes problematic the distinction between object and its representation and, in particular, disrupts our assumptions about, or our inattention to, the role of the agent. This could be done, for example, by disrupting the supposed neutrality and authority of the agent, perhaps in making this very argument! For example, the hidden hand of the author (observer) – the agent for presenting this argument – could be revealed just at the point when readers least expect it.

Is this where I come in?

If you must.

I don't much like your tone. I thought we had agreed that my entrance was to be the major highlight of the whole argument, that the appearance of a different *voice would be the best way of making the point.*

Which point?

That it is not possible effectively to demonstrate the importance of the role of the agent of representation using the standard univocal textual form.

Yes, I agreed it would be better to try to *demonstrate* the point rather than just to keep stating it. And we did agree that some sort of dramatic, unexpected interruption by a second voice would convey a sense of how much the conventional form of text assumes a straighforward relationship between author and text. This is entirely in line with what has been called the search for 'new literary forms'.[17]

But it's clear that for most of this essay you resisted the appearance of a second voice just so you could produce a straight *text, presumably under the illusion that it carried some kind of conviction ...*

No ...

... You only allowed me into the text right at the end, when you started to run out of ideas ...

But ...

... I am beginning to wonder if the only reason for my appearance is so that we can quarrel about whether or not I should be present!

No, no! That's not it! Let me be absolutely clear: you are not here just as some kind of heckler. The point is not that readers should now consider some alternative to the argument developed earlier in the chapter. Instead, your inclusion is meant to exemplify all that was said about the need to become aware of our dependence upon conventional textual forms.

So what exactly is my function as a second voice supposed to be?

Well, put it this way, your appearance is intended to remind the reader that conventional textual forms depend on a conception of the author as a passive, neutral agent of representation. That if we are going to take deconstruction seriously, we also have to consider what it takes to disrupt our own efforts at producing representations.

But we were getting on fine until you started this dialogue business. (Or should I say you were getting on fine . . .)

Yes, although that's exactly the point. By 'getting on fine', I think you mean that the argument was starting to become per-suasive. I'm flattered, of course. But the point is that in order to achieve this effect, I (or maybe we) had to pretend I was a neutral agent in order to unmask the pretence to neutrality, to engage in ontological gerrymandering so as to articulate the tactic of onto-logical gerrymandering, to accede to the ideology of representation in order to expose the ideology of representation and so on.

But has my appearance added anything to the argument?

Yes, very much so. Although not in the usual sense of 'adding something'. It is precisely the usual linear form of argument, sus-taining the author's silence about his own role as agent, which we are trying to disrupt.

You think this is a disruption?

Isn't it? One of the points of a breach, as I understand it, is to surprise the reader, to get him or her to recognize features of the taken-for-granted world (in this case features of the role of agents of representation) which had hitherto been seen but unnoticed. The element of surprise is important, so I was rather disappointed when you gave the game away with your premature entry a few pages back.

But the point of a breach is that the reader can't tell whether or not one is occurring. So on that score we have clearly succeeded.

Maybe.

So let's see if I've got this right. I appear as a way of interrogating the concept of self in representation?

Exactly.

But what does it mean to 'interrogate'.

A pessimistic view about representation is that, since representation is all-pervasive, it is clearly not possible to try and evade it, so all attempts to 'step outside' representation are doomed. But this response only follows if we think of explorations of new literary forms as an attempt to escape representation; as a way of side-stepping the ever threatening methodological horrors[18] and thereby more reliably grounding representational practice. The idea of interrogating self is that without wishing to try and escape representation, it is none the less worthwhile to pursue the possibility of developing alternative forms of literary expression which might modify existing conventions. The notion of interrogation is meant to contrast with the aims of either *explaining* representation (as in those attempts to analyse scientific discourse which unreflexively redeploy the central axiom of representation for their own ends) or trying to *escape* it (which, we have already said, is impossible in the sense that all interpretive activities involve representation).

And I suppose attempts to interrogate self are all part of the more general (and highly fashionable) interest in 'de-centring'.

Quite. Not that I would want to make too much of this, but you could construe the interrogation of self in representation as just the latest step in a long historical progression: self was radically displaced by the Copernican revolution, and took refuge in science; then self was displaced from science by the relativist sociology of scientific knowledge, and took refuge in the Author, the unreflexive social scientist. With the exploration of new literary forms, the spotlight is turned on Author in an effort to chase out self again.

Hmmm. I see why you don't want to make too much of that! And you have to admit that (y)our use of dialogic form hardly meets the rather grand objective you spelled out earlier: to 'interrogate some of our deeper preconceptions about the adequacy of those technologies by virtue of which the world is made available to us'.

No, of course not! This is just an initial attempt to broach issues in the ideology of representation, a first tentative effort to open questions which go beyond the usual style of relativist analysis. And I (we) should stress that dialogue is only one possible kind of exploration of literary forms.[19] I certainly wouldn't want to suggest that this effort provides some sort of 'solution' to the 'problem' of representation. Indeed, it would be quite misleading to try to seek a 'solution'.

And you feel this sort of exercise carries conviction?

Well in terms of 'convincing' or 'persuading' people, I'm not so sure. After all, the one thing we can say with any confidence about conviction is that it requires unreflexive operations within the ideology of representation. I think perhaps we should avoid taking conviction or persuasion as our objective.

What's the problem? I know one of the editors said he really liked the idea.

Yes, but the other editor didn't! And those two different reactions underscore the difficulty. Even in a volume devoted to assessing the fate of science at the hands of post-modernism, we meet quite contrary editorial reactions to the attempt to break with conventional forms of representation. More generally, it seems that those interested in the pursuit of alternatives to current conventional forms of representation will quickly recognize what's going on in this kind of dialogue; but for those to whom this seems strange, no amount of arguing the case is going to convince them otherwise.

Right, I know the reaction: 'trivial'.

'Frivolous'.

'Playful'.

'Fancy stuff'.

'Doesn't tell us anything'.

'Smart–arse'.

Er, do you think it's a good idea to mention these reactions in front of our readers?

Definitely not! Although, of course, they may have already reacted in these ways. The point is that these reactions testify to the entrenchment of ideas about what counts as serious textual form. In the standard view, a condition for seriousness seems to be the suppression of any demonstrative attention to the role of the agent.

But what if you want to be serious in demonstrating the hidden role of the agent?

Well that, of course, is what we're trying to do. We have to develop a form of non–serious seriousness.

Okay, I like that. But what are the ground-rules for this kind of exercise? I can imagine critics complaining that anything seems good enough, that there don't seem to be any criteria of adequacy. What exactly counts as a 'good' exploration of 'new literary forms'?

Well, you won't be surprised to learn that the issue of adequacy is still highly controversial. For example, in the particular case of the so-called 'two voices' device, a number of authors have sought to use it[20] and others have contested its value.[21] The interesting problem is precisely to renegotiate what adequacy might mean in a situation where conventional forms of written expression are being challenged. For example, Pinch and Pinch deploy dialogic form to argue *against* the use of the 'two voices' device.[22] The very striking effect of their experiment is the way in which it celebrates the form of text it seeks to criticize; the success of the argument against using two voices actually depends on the use of two voices. So you should not jump to the conclusion that the enterprise is not serious, simply because participants are unable to come up with a clear-cut definition of adequacy.

Hmmm . . . So ideas like adequacy, conviction and persuasion are all in the melting-pot. We have to resist deploying these notions in their conventional sense, because they too buy into the ideology of representation.

Yes.

And I suppose that also applies to the idea of a conclusion?

Quite.

John Forrester

LYING ON THE COUCH

> So what is truth?... truths are illusions one has
> forgotten are such, metaphors which have become
> habitual and lost their sensory force, coins which
> have been effaced and which from then on are
> taken to be, not pieces of money, but metal....
> To be sure, man forgets that things are like this
> for him; so he lies unconsciously in the required
> manner and in accordance with age-old custom –
> and, precisely because of this unconsciousness and
> this forgetting, he arrives at a feeling of truth.
> (Nietzsche)[1]

IT HAS BECOME a simple truism to say that the sciences, or more
particularly those philosophers concerned with the sciences, have
developed a privileged claim on the truth. The truth of science
goes without saying. Other truths – moral, religious, aesthetic,
personal – require special pleading, even a special epistemology.
Truth thus now has an intimate relation with *knowing* things.

However, it has also become commonplace to consider the business of 'knowing things' and of truth as primarily a consequence
of the properties of propositions, couched in language. The propositional focus is by no means new, although it became, as a
result of the 'linguistic turn' of twentieth-century philosophy, a
peculiarly comfortable one. Historically, the discourse of truth
has been so saturated with the twin model of conformity with
the real ('conformity with the facts, with the real'), and conformity

with what exists in the mind ('having the intention to tell the truth, not to deceive'), that the turn towards the proposition, as the site in which the real and the mental meet, has not entailed a revolution. Dismantling truth, then, may well entail a closer look at this propositional model of truth – the model that, for epistemological conservatives and radicals alike, has always followed Hobbes in saying: 'For *True* and *False* are attributes of Speech, not of Things. And where Speech is not, there is neither *Truth* nor *Falshood*. *Errour* there may be, as when we expect that which shall not be; or suspect what has not been: but in neither case can a man be charged with Untruth.'[2]

I

> The former are convinced that among the false
> books flooding the world they can track down the
> few that bear a truth perhaps extrahuman or extra-
> terrestrial. The latter believe that only
> counterfeiting, mystification, intentional
> falsehood can represent absolute value in a book,
> a truth not contaminated by the dominant pseudo
> truths. (Italo Calvino)[3]

Something peculiar did happen in the course of the recent history of the propositional notion of truth. Having established that truth can only be predicated of propositions, it somehow became accepted that the most important function of propositions was to have truth predicated of them. And then a further step was taken: propositions *necessarily* possess a truth value or function. The truth of a proposition became something like a necessary property, inherent in the proposition, rather than an accidental feature of it. Or to put it more plainly: the very *notion* of a well-formed proposition became inseparable from the question: is it true or false? In short, the narrowing-down process started by claiming: 'Only propositions have truth value', and then continued, by claiming: 'What makes a proposition important is the precise truth value we can assign to it'. To utter a proposition automatically now came to entail that one had made a truth claim that could be examined according to canons of proof.

This elementary mistake has certainly led to the excessive con-

cern of philosophers with evaluating the truth claims of propositions. However, it could be claimed that scientists have ignored
it, even when the stylistic canons of their profession have made
them paragons of epistemological virtue for many philosophers.
Scientists, it should not be forgotten, conform to a pattern of
discourse, or a pattern of rhetoric, that is more concretely agonistic
than this model has allowed for: most scientists are more like
commandos in the field, or lawyers in a court, than they are like
generals at GHQ, or judges on the appeal bench. It could be conceded to the 'propositions possess truth functions' lobby that all
statements in scientific publications are drafted with an eye to
possible contestation as to their truth. However, not only do most
of these statements never have to face such a challenge, they are
specifically drafted so as to resist any simple confrontation of their
content with whatever other features of the world (usually other
propositions) are taken to constitute a test of their truth value.[4]
Given this, one might think that, even within science, the search
after unambiguous means of ascertaining the truth value of propositions is not only a blind alley, but also a red herring. What use
can they possibly be?

It is possible that the importance attached to truth does not
come from its recent sequestration by the self-appointed spokespersons of the scientific community. Before the hegemony of science, the concept of truth gained much of its purchase through
the conviction that the fate of a man's soul may hang on his adherence to the truth. The importance we in the West attach to truth-
telling may well owe much to the 'accidental' importance that
the public profession of faith and martyrdom took on in the
expanding evangelical origins of the Christian West. Certainly
Augustine's famous preoccupation with lying is in part an attempt
to guarantee that one's capacity to witness to the truth of Christ
is not impaired by any social mores that sanction secret allegiances.
The attention to the state of the individual soul required by Christianity required an extremely vigilant attitude towards lying.

Augustine conceived of lying as consisting in a doubling up:
saying one thing in speech and another in one's heart. This doubling
conception indicates its affinities with – not to mention its origins
in – Platonic philosophy, in which the entire dialectic of truth
is founded on the doubling, the splitting of appearance and reality.
The dialectic must stop somewhere, and its end is always on the

'other side', the side of reality, rather than appearances. Hence the idea of truth residing 'behind' appearances.

The truth that lies behind – this is common both to Platonic conceptions of truth and to the Augustinian conception of lies: the truth the liar conceals is to be found in his heart. When truth becomes hidden behind appearances, the world takes on a depth, becomes a series of layers. Yet the possibility of depth may well be primarily given in the experience of deception – the experience of being deceived by the world, or by others, or that of *deceiving* others. The dimension of duplicity, of doubleness, is common then to both Platonic conceptions of the epistemology of truth and to moral discussions about the sinfulness of lying. Indeed, it may well be lying that gives one the possibility of conceiving of an 'appearance' in the first place. And this division of appearance from reality is an effect of the exercise of the will – perhaps the exemplar of this exercise. As Jankélévitch puts it:

> In any case, if sin, far from being error, is something one commits on purpose, the lie becomes the sin *par excellence*, not necessarily the most serious, but the most characteristic, the quintessence of sin. Because one never lies without willing it. Hence the gravity of the first lie of an infant. The day of this first lie is a truly solemn day where we discover in the innocent the disturbing depth of '*conscience*'.[5]

Nor perhaps is it an accident that Augustine's preoccupation with lying was paralleled by his introduction into philosophy of the problem of the existence of 'other minds' – the original question he posed arose from a consideration of the Last Supper, when Jesus, without naming names, says that one of those around the table will betray him. The problem of other minds arises as the disciples look from one to another, searching out the signs of a betrayal yet to come . . .[6]

In this way, the very act of enquiry into the world, the very act of understanding, is seen to involve a duplicity that is akin to that of lying. Again, Jankélévitch: 'the power to deceive is given at the heart of the power to make oneself understood, not as a secondary effect of it, but as its ransom – the other side of the alternative'.[7] A similar conclusion, via a different line of thought, is reached by Nietzsche:

> Insofar as it is a means for the preservation of the individual,

the intellect develops its principal forces through dissimulation; the latter is in effect the means through which weaker, less robust individuals survive, given that they are unable to conduct a struggle for existence with horns or the sharp jaw of the beast of prey. In man, this art of dissimulation attains its peak: illusion, flattery, lies and deceit, whispers, posturing, borrowed . . . are in man so much the rule and the law that there is almost nothing more unimaginable than the arrival of an honest and pure instinct for truth amongst men.[8]

The depth of consciousness, the dissimulation proper to the life of human intelligence, on occasion the capacity to lie itself have been equated with the capacity to imagine (to imagine things other), to *negate*, and thereby to create fiction, even hypothesis – and thence to science. Popper argues that:

the moment when language became human was very closely related to the moment when a man invented a story, a myth in order to excuse a mistake he had made. . . . I suggest that the evolution of specifically human language, with its characteristic means of expressing negation – of saying that something signalled is not true – stems very largely from the discovery of systematic means to *negate* false report. . . . Indeed it [lying] has made the human language what it is. . . .[9]

In this way, what is an attempt to erect a morality and a theology may verge over into a phenomenology, and a naturalistic one at that (as in Popper and Nietzsche), which describes, as it were from the inside, the development of the capacity to lie, and renders it the mainspring of human creativity, as well as sin. This other side of truth may seem a far cry from the assigning of truth functions to formal propositions. But I have made what may seem like a detour in order to remind us of the difference between traditional discourses on truth and what has now become the traditional discourse on scientific truth. Scientific truth does not pay attention to the dilemma or experience of the individual subject, in which deception bulks large. If it does so, it is only in the form of questions such as: what constitutes grounds for justifiable belief? *Having reasons* is the normal way of setting boundaries around this question. In science, theories, hypotheses and models are taken to exist in their own right, independent of the subjects who might hold them. Or rather, and this is where the force of the system we call science is said to arise, they are taken to exist solely in relation to what we may call, for simplicity's sake, the indivisible, homogeneous, self-identical subject of science – the subject who is always interchangeable with someone else. The truth of scientific discourse is evoked when one wants to disclaim the possibility that the 'subjectivity' of the scientific subject is at issue.

On the other hand, in non-scientific discourse, in the Western tradition, usually that of ethical and moral discourse, truth is evoked precisely in order to put the subject on the line. 'Are *you* telling the truth?' – a strange question for the scientist to hear, although he or she knows what it means, and reacts in the knee-jerk way that we all do. The scientist wishes to convert this question into another: 'Is *that* the truth?'

Of course, this practice runs against the entire metaphysics of Western science. Not only does the Platonic conception of truth, as being conformity with an ideal world of pure forms, hang heavy, but the heritage of the Protestant world of truth being a unique relation to God and his Creation has left indelible marks. The Cartesian grounding, while not being explicitly Protestant, bears the mark of the Reformation: the brave, defiant 'I', despairing of the medieval world of the authority of the Church and Book, yet refusing to join the vociferous sceptics who sweep away any certainty that derived from any other source but faith, finds its certainty in the private, but indubitable, world of reason. At the same time, the metaphysics of modern physical science brings Nature as a witness to court – and not only the court of the Lord Chancellor Francis Bacon, or the *noblesse de robe* whose scepticism Descartes, also a lawyer, was combating. In the court of natural philosophy, Nature is presumed never to perjure herself – Nature does not deceive.

This refrain is a familiar one to historians of science. Descartes secured the certain foundations of modern science by invoking a God who, in his very nature, could not deceive him, Descartes – even though Descartes, being human, may, probably will, lie to God. Descartes thus founds science by placing this crucial constraint upon the nature of God; Einstein founds his science by placing an analogous constraint upon God: 'Subtle is the Lord, but malicious he is not.' For Descartes – though this is less true for modern scientists – the major threat to knowledge comes from the possibility of *being deceived*: the sceptics had emphasized the impossibility of man attaining truth, in large part because of the inadequacy of his sensory and intellectual equipment. It was not so much a matter of someone, Descartes' malicious demon, deceiving man, but of being perpetually under threat of being deceived, despite one's own efforts to make the best of one's equipment. The non-deceiving God allows at least one or two certainties to be laid down across the swamp of potential self-deception.

The urgency of finding some grounds for certainty clearly did not, in the sixteenth and seventeenth centuries, stem from the need to find a proto-ideology for a science that did not as yet exist, but rather from the requirements of religion and morals. These discourses about truth may not have originally been primarily concerned with knowledge so much as with ethical questions. Yet as old as the debates about scepticism are the tirades launched against lying, the practice that undermines the possibility of truth from within. An examination of these tirades will help us to see more clearly the issues underlying the discourses on truth, whether they are 'epistemological' or 'ethical'.

2

It seems to me that the possibility exists for fiction
to function in truth, for a fictional discourse to
induce effects of truth, and for bringing it about
that a true discourse engenders or 'manufactures'
something that does not as yet exist, that is,
'fictions' it. (Michel Foucault)[10]

Extremism of conclusion, extremism of argument have been the characteristics of philosophical views of lying.[11] Augustine regarded lying as a mortal sin, since the doubleness of deceitful speech – having one thing in one's heart, saying another – subverted the God-given purpose of speech: to tell the truth.[12] This Augustinian concentration on the intention to deceive held sway, through Aquinas' reiteration and reformulation, pretty well until the seventeenth century. However, it is worth considering the context of Augustine's hard line. His major discussions of lying occur in his *De mendacio* of 395 and his *Contra mendacium* of 420. The first enunciated the doctrine of the intention to deceive; but the second text, when replaced in its context, is far more revealing of the issues at stake in lying.

The occasion for the writing of this tract was the emergence of the Priscillianist heresy, which included the doctrine that lying is sometimes justified, especially in order to conceal religious doctrines from strangers. Augustine was quick to point out that a consequence of this doctrine would be that one would not be able to tell who was a Priscillianist and who wasn't. Indeed, certain zealous Catholics pretended to be Priscillianists in order to discover who the Priscillianists were, including one, Consentius, who asked Augustine to comment on this means of detecting them, this 'pious fraud'. The Priscillianists argued that speaking the truth in one's heart was sufficient – there was no necessity for speaking it out loud. As so often, Augustine's arguments centre upon the egotistical task of saving one's own soul; the Priscillianist doctrines are mistakes, not lies. Hence: 'For, what they say when they are lying is one thing; what they say when they are mistaken is another. When they teach their heresy, they say those things about which they are mistaken. . . .'[13] In consequence, if one believes their professed dogmas one dies (i.e. goes to Hell); whereas if one believes them to be Catholics when in fact they are not, one does not put one's own soul at risk. Following their doctrine on lying will ensure that true Catholicism is no longer visible. But if Catholics profess *their* dogmas in order to catch them, those who hear may end in death. That is, once one admits a lie, for whatever purpose, the outcome becomes *uncertain* – when you reveal yourselves to them, they will not know what to believe, since they know that you are a liar.

Augustine's attack on this doctrine indicates how truth for him was conceived of as identical with the eternal nature of God, indeed that God and truth were the same thing. The notion that truth supplies a fundamental reference point of stability, taking over this function in philosophical discourse from the function that God has in theological discourse, is a crucial theme in the historical dialectic of lying and truth. The other great hard-liner in the history of lying, Immanuel Kant, indicates this well.

The core of Kant's doctrine was that: no lies are admissible, since in lying one denies one's own humanity, that is, one denies one's right to one's own truthfulness (and not a right to the truth). Every lie 'vitiates the source of law itself'[14] – it harms mankind generally.

The background to this position is to be found in Grotius' reformulation of doctrines of truthfulness in terms of natural law: it is only wrong to lie to those who have a right to the truth. Implicit here is the beginnings of the idea of society as a contract between certain equal parties. Those who have contracted in do have rights and duties; those who haven't don't. To lie to those who do not belong to the society is not a transgression of the social contract. What the contract thus amounts to, and what a society now amounts to, is a convention, a *rule* (rather than a natural law) of truthfulness, whose only guarantee is the social itself. As even Kant put it in combatting this notion: 'truthfulness is a duty which must be regarded as the ground of all duties based on contract, and the laws of these duties would be rendered uncertain and useless if even the least exception to them were admitted. Society now takes up the place of God as a guarantor of truth. And, as we shall see, the Priscillianist heresy can emerge in a new and different form.

The critique of the absolutist position on lying focuses first on the givens of human life, in particular those of humans in society, rather than on the morality of truthfulness. Alexandre Koyré spelled out the underlying structure of this critique, in a paper called '*Réflexions sur le mensonge*', published in 1943, and bearing, one surmises, directly upon the state of truth to be found in Vichy France.

Koyré's analysis starts with the anthropological claim: 'It is certain that man is defined by speech, that the latter brings with it the possibility of lying and that – pace Porphyry – the lie, much more than the laugh, is what is unique to man.'[15] Lying is the favoured weapon of the oppressed – to fool the oppressor is to humiliate him. Koyré articulates his account of when lying becomes acceptable around the relation of the subject and the other, of 'us' and 'them'. Societies that tolerate lying are those in which conflict and heterogeneity are paramount; persecution from 'outside' is necessary for the lie to become a fundamental part of the order of society. In particular, it presupposes contact between hostile elements of different societies – a mythical agonistically social state of nature, prior to the constitution of 'true' society. In order to cohere, this ideal society requires a firm base, which we might as well call the truth. But, in the face of a hostile world, the lie will have to become the principle of the existence of the society. As a consequence, the society will, in the limiting case, now disappear either *in fact* (how could we know this?) or in the eyes of the others. The society disappears into the night of the secret. 'Hence, a total inversion has taken place: the lie, become the group secret, will be the condition of its existence, its habitual mode of being, fundamental and primary.'[16] The perfect Priscillianist society has now come into existence. To quote Koyré again:

> as a consequence, the supreme duty of a member of this secret grouping, the act in which he expresses his attachment and his faithfulness to the group, the act by which he affirms and confirms his adhesion to the group, consists, paradoxically, in his dissimulation of this fact. To dissimulate what is and in order to be able to do so, simulate what isn't: such is the mode of existence that, necessarily, all secret societies impose upon their members.[17]

Once constituted, a social grouping will, given a hostile environment, necessarily constitute itself anew not as a secret society, but as something more profound – what Koyré calls 'une société à secret', a society *of* the secret, a society whose existence is now predicated upon the secret. And complete loss of foundations seems to follow from here: does it exist, how could one possibly detect its existence, from what standpoint could one judge of the existence of both an inside and an outside to such a society?

Koyré indicates how such a society will bring into existence an entirely new topography of the relations of the lie and the truth. No member of such a society will believe what the leader says, knowing that public pronouncements are for the benefit of the others. But, equally, it is possible for the leader to make use of this rhetorical move to employ the double lie: saying the truth because he knows it will not be believed by the 'others', and only in a manner of speaking by 'us' – *Mein Kampf* is the classic example. It may well be such a society that makes it quite proper for a high official jestingly to ask, 'What is truth?', knowing no reply is possible except martyrdom.

What is clear is that the absolute refusal of lying, following Kant and Augustine, and the canny defence of lying espoused by Nietzsche, Oscar Wilde and others, all depend upon the black opposition that is painted between the two. Even the subtleties of Wilde, no matter how true they might be, are quite clearly mounted so as to *epater la vérité*. Yet what would it be like to countenance, in an equable manner, rather than donning the cloak of the *enfant terrible*, the symmetry of truth and lies? Could such a methodological principle, derived from the working practices of anthropologists, imported into the history and philosophy of science by Bloor and others, be countenanced, let alone found effective?

The whole issue may seem irrelevant to the cynics. Lying is as old as speech, they would say, just as adultery is as old as marriage. How can one expect to draw a watertight distinction between the two, let alone get everyone to agree to it, when, as soon as your back is turned, like the bourgeoisie, the vow will be broken? Indeed, one will expect far more lying than adultery, since, following Augustine's argument, just being unfaithful in *thought*, never mind words, constitutes a lie. And we know how cheap words are.

So: 'everyone lies'. But is this necessary, or is it just a weakness which moral reform could hope to rectify? In his paper entitled 'Everyone Has to Lie', Harvey Sacks wonders whether this statement, and others like it that crop up in everyday conversation, is true or false.[18] Specifically, he proposes that finding 'cases' for which the statement does not apply is not an appropriate way of evaluating the truth or falsity of such conversational statements. He thus shifts the question from 'Is this true or false!' to 'Under what conditions is the question "is this true or false?" a legitimate, or even comprehensible, one?'[19] Sacks notes, as Austin had done before him, that a more fundamental criterion, and one that has to be settled before truth–falsity is raised, let alone decided, is whether a statement is serious or a joke. We can, and should, multiply these criteria: we have to decide whether the person who makes the statement is acting or not (is it a joke to ask if it is *true* that Macbeth has no children,[20] whether he is being childish or not and so forth?)[21] Sacks' solution is as subversive as Derrida's. He proposes that the criterion for deciding whether 'true/false' is a suitable criterion is the 'sequential relevance': if a certain speech–act is often followed by a true/false assignation (e.g. a complaint or excuse is followed by 'That's true'), then one has a criterion of relevance of the true/false criterion. Since 'Everyone has to lie' is often itself a complaint or an excuse, one sees that the true/false criterion is a response to a complaint or an excuse.

This criterion may seem overly legalistic in its nature: after all, law courts are supposedly the institution in society that, in the last resort, in the last instance, decide upon the validity of complaints or excuses. Sacks' criterion would make the legal model of truth the *only* standard of truth. While it is important to be reminded that any society has a range of regimes of truth, ones that are almost certain to be mutually inconsistent, this does not address the question we are obliged to confront: the specific nature of the regime of truth in science, and its relation to the moral discourse on truth and lies.

There is another discourse that has a kinship to the ethnomethodological approach, and also recognizes the cynic's response. And it sets up the conditions for a scientific study of lies through a set of rules for the conduct of its discourse that speak to all the questions we have raised concerning the morality, epistemology and everyday practice of lying.

3

> Publication of this article does not imply
> Department of Defense endorsement of factual
> accuracy or opinion. (Article on 'Lie Detection',
> *International Encyclopaedia of Psychiatry, Psychology,
> Psychoanalysis and Neurology.*)[22]

To put this direction of argument at its most forceful, I want to argue that psychoanalysis is the science of lying in two different senses. First, it is the *only* science that does not find the prospect that the 'object' of its enquiry may intentionally deceive the scientific investigator subversive of its pretensions to truth. Secondly, the verbal material upon which it *concentrates* its attention (although of course everything the subject says has *some* significance) is very much akin to methodical deviations from the truth: fantasies and dream-texts.

The first attitude, the aplomb with which the analyst greets lies, might be thought to be an extension, albeit an exceedingly rare one, in both natural and social scientific discourses, of its 'realism', or perhaps cynicism; it is founded on the expectation that the subject will, inevitably, being human, lie. The truth-saying properties of language, which are often taken to be both the *a priori* condition of possibility of language, and the *telos*, the final

end and justification of language, are bracketed off, as being idealizations – important, primal idealizations, of much the same sort
as are our idealizations of our parents, who, we imagine, gave
us this fickle and all-powerful tool. Whereas the techniques of
social psychology are continually tempted into deceiving the subjects in order to render them unconscious of the true nature of
the observer's interest, the boot is on the other foot in psychoanalysis: it is the 'objective observer', the analyst, who will be the
butt of any deception that is to be practised. Whereas the social
psychologist hopes to *forestall* the possibility of the subjects of
the experiment deceiving the experimenter, either by insisting that
the experimental subjects be completely naive and *innocent* of the
experimenter's goals, or by placing them in a situation in which
they have, according to the experimenter, minimal *motive* for such
deception, the psychoanalyst places them in a situation in which
they have minimal incentives *either* for telling the truth *or* for telling
lies. Which way they go is entirely up to them. The analyst is
professionally disinterested in the difference between truth and
lies.

What is more, the place of reality in psychoanalysis is highly
idiosyncratic. The extent to which psychoanalysis takes no account
of reality has recently become something of a scandal.[23] However,
this particular practice, rather than being the quirk of a complacent
bourgeois profession turning a blind eye to social reality, or of
a family-centred idealism, bracing itself against the long waves
of history, is embedded in the basic rules for the practice of psychoanalysis. The fundamental rule of analysis states: 'Say whatever
comes into your head, no matter how nonsensical, insulting,
objectionable or irrelevant.' This rule thus implicitly excludes all
normal criteria by which one judges whether a statement or utterance is pertinent, a faithful representation of reality, goal-directed
– *whatever* the goal might be – or 'serious'. Implicitly, the fundamental rule excludes the criteria by which one decides 'the truth'.
As Lacan puts it: 'In analysis one lets go of all the moorings
of the speaking relationship, one eschews courtesy, respect, and
dutifulness towards the other. . . . All our attempts and instructions
have as their aim, at the moment when we free the subject's discourse, to deprive him of every possible genuine function of
speech. . . .'[24]

Although patients are asked to obey this rule – that is, they are asked to give up all the criteria by which speech is made sensible, is made to conform to the real, is made so as to entertain the other, and so forth – no patient ever succeeds in so doing. Individual patients are always sliding back into rhetorical modes they have been asked, and have agreed, to forgo: they attempt to persuade the analyst they are right, they attempt to seduce the analyst into believing in at least *something* (whether it is the cruelty of the Thatcher government or the blissfulness of their childhood years), they try to coerce the analyst into distinguishing fiction from reality, jokes from the serious, dreams from nightmares. But the implicit requirement of the fundamental rule, and the attitude that the analyst in consequence adopts towards what the patient says, is that all these rhetorical ploys or varieties of speech-act be separated off from the other discourse the patient also engages in, the discourse that is in basic conformity with the fundamental rule. In other words, when the patient complains about the analyst's incompetence, he recognizes the speech-act as a complaint, when the patient declares his admiration for the analyst's technique or taste in husbands, she hears it as a compliment, yet the analytic technique is always to *separate off* this aspect, this illocutionary force, of the utterance, so as to analyse it. Thus, for instance, Freud spells out that when a patient expresses doubt about the content of a dream – 'I'm not sure who the person was, it might have been the *au pair*' – the doubt is taken to be as much a part of the dream-content as the *au pair*.[25] The radicality of this interpretative stance of the analyst is most clearly seen in his attitude towards negation – the integrity of which, after all, is the cornerstone of logical analyses of the truth or falsity of propositions: '"You ask who this person in the dream can be. It's *not* my mother." We emend this to: "So it *is* his mother." In our interpretation, we take the liberty of disregarding the negation and of picking out the subject-matter alone of the association [*den reinen Inhalt des Einfalls*].'[26]

Similarly, for the affects, which include spite and self-righteousness, as well as anger, fear, love and hate: 'the release of affect and the ideational content do not constitute the indissoluble organic unity as which we are in the habit of treating them, but that these two separate entities may be merely *soldered* together and can thus be detached from each other by analysis'.[27] Hence, the lack of interest the analyst displays in the question of whether

something 'really happened' is entirely a consequence of the interpretative technique of putting to one side certain rhetorical
markers, bearers of illocutionary force, in utterances, whether they
be claims as to honesty, urgency, importance, reality – or truth.
It is not so much that the analyst is *only* interested in fantasy,
and *disregards* reality; rather, he is interested in *both* fantasy and
reality, and *disregards* the distinction between the two. As Freud
put it, in the letter marking this epistemological turning point:
'... there are no indications of reality in the unconscious, so that
it was impossible to distinguish between truth and fiction invested
with affect'.[28] 'Impossible to distinguish between truth and fiction'
... It is on the recognition of this 'fact' about human beings that
psychoanalysis is built. What distinguishes Freud's project, then,
is to recognize this 'fact' *and* not to throw up his hands in despair
(as he seemed tempted – but not that tempted – to do). Freud
was obliged to discard the idea that there is any criterion by which
one can distinguish what a person says as being truth or fiction,
as long as one concerns oneself solely with their utterances.
Instead, however, of seeking the truth criterion *outside* their utterances, he discarded the *necessity* for finding a criterion of truth.
What matters is the fact that they *said* it, not whether it is true
or not.

It is not as if this issue of fiction and reality was something
new that Freud stumbled on, though I hope I have made it clear
how novel was his decision to bypass the issue. Hysteria presented
nineteenth-century doctors with the possibility of a 'disease' with
variable, unpredictable symptoms – a disease in which the body
deceived the doctor, led him on a wild goose chase. In addition,
and often in consequence of this anti-scientific possibility, it
seemed probable that it wasn't the body that was lying, but rather
the mind of the patient – it was probable that the patient was a
'hysterical malingerer'. Rather than believe that nature could lie,
could deliberately deceive and mislead, by presenting false clues,
clues that changed as soon as they were found, doctors attributed
the cause of this protean entity to the patient's will. Hysteria highlights the frustration of a doctor who says he deals only in bodies
and observation, the look, when confronted with a patient whose
variable symptoms may only denote a movement of deception.
The hysteric highlights the doctor's impotence in the face of a
patient who will not name his pain in the correct way. The medical

response was twofold: first, an attempt to find a sure physiological index for when the patient is lying. The first lie-detectors grew out of this preoccupation with the truth of the patient's pain, by reaffirming the veridicality of the body's clues: the polygraph, the skin-galvanic response. On the other hand, the doctor began to play the same game as his patient: began to deceive his patient through the art of hypnosis. Hypnosis had this double edge: it was intended as a sure physiological means of duplicating and reproducing hysterical symptoms, thus bringing them under the sway of a physiological model in which nature cannot lie. On the other hand, it was intended as a means for securing total dominion over the patient's mind, through control of the body, and the suggesting away of the pains and symptoms. Now, instead of the patient deceiving the doctor, it was the doctor who assessed his priviledged relation to the truth by deceiving the patient.

Freud originally conceived of his relations with the hypnotized patient as dependent for their efficacy on the freedom of choice with which they both entered into the 'compact', as he called it.[29] It was this awareness of the freedom of choice underpinning the cure – and the implicit enlightenment baggage of justice and equality that came with the freedom – that made it doubly ignominious for Freud to be forced, as he inevitably was, into the hearty reassurances and trivial deceptions which any slight setback in the process required of him. 'The physician must constantly be on the look-out for a new starting point for his suggestion, a new proof of his power, a new change in his hypnotizing procedure. For him too, who has, perhaps, internal doubts about success, this presents a great and in the end exhausting strain.'[30] Indeed, Freud occasionally hinted that hypnotism could never be entirely satisfactory, precisely because the authority of the physician was fraudulent, and the entire success of the operation rested on deception:

Whereas no patient ventures to be impatient if he has still not been cured after the twentieth electrical session or an equal number of bottles of mineral water, with hypnotic treatment both physician and patient grow tired far sooner, as a result of the contrast between the deliberately rosy colouring of the suggestions and the cheerless truth. Here too, intelligent patients can make it easier for the physician as soon as they have understood that in making suggestions he is, as it were, playing a part and that the more energetically he disputes their ailment the more advantage is to be expected for them.[31]

So, even when relying on suggestive (rather than rememorative) hypnotism in his practice, Freud's attitude was double: weary distrust of the deception it necessitated, a deception that both doctor and patient freely colluded in; and, in addition, belief that the playing of the parts assigned to them, so long as they were recognized as parts and not subject to the exacting and fatiguing standards of truth, could bring success.

This dialectic of lying, deception and truth, played out between doctor and patient in a malign form in hysterical malingering, in a more benign form within hypnotism, posited a truth of the disease as its alpha and omega. But within the very practice of hypnotism lay the recognition that fiction can cure as well as truth. And Freud was then led by his quest for the causal memory or mental event into the world of dreams, where he discovered, not that dreams were the opposite of reality, as had been conventionally supposed from Descartes on, but that dreams transcended the distinction between reality and non-reality. He thus discarded the distinction between truth and fiction, and created a new reality, which he called psychic reality, whose very principle of operation is fictionalizing (whether it be of reality or of anything else).

Psychoanalysts do not talk about lying, however. They talk instead of fantasy – and this indicates just how indifferent they are to the dimension of truth (and of lies). The consequence of the fundamental rule is that *all* modalities of discourse – whether it be the scientific regime of truth, the legal regime of truth, the dramatic regime in which disbelief is suspended so as to arrive at some 'other' mode of truth – all these are grist to the mill of analysis.[32]

A useful way of understanding the consequences of this is to start by noting that a discourse is as much defined and constituted as it is limited by the rules which permit the resolution of disagreements. These means often include some irrevocable (*sic*) call on the real, the court of final appeal. In law, this appeal is to the legal system itself (and not the 'facts' of the case); in science, the appeal is to nature, or the object, but in reality to a natural object that has become so precisely defined and instrumentalized by the procedures involved in its agonistic interrogation that it answers in *place* of the real, which always recedes before the onward march of instrumentation, symbolization and accepted procedure. As Latour and Lacan agree, the real is the impossible, 'reality as the Latin word *res* indicates, is what *resists*'.[33]

Psychoanalysis, however, is *founded on* the exclusion of this call on the real. Psychoanalysis, like all sciences, overcomes resistances: in physics, what resists soon becomes an 'effect', soon is symbolized, for preference in mathematical symbols and instrumental procedures – it becomes a symbolized reality, which no longer offers resistance to the scientist. In psychoanalysis, the resistance, namely 'whatever interrupts the work of analysis',[34] soon becomes sought out so as to furnish the brute reality of the work of analyst and patient; yet it is precisely what is to be eliminated, so that something new can emerge.

So the emphasis on resistance in psychoanalysis is not new or novel; it simply makes explicit a 'realist' move in much scientific practice. What is *psychoanalytically* 'real', what is unique to the reality constructed by psychoanalysis, is the transference. Now, everyone knows that this is a construct, an artifice, of the psychoanalytic situation. To verify the transference by, say, the patient asking a parent if he *really* behaved like that towards his father when he was three years old, is to undo the very conditions that gave rise to the phenomenon in the first place – namely, the thirst or demand for knowledge, for love, for the past, embodied in the very idea of addressing oneself to a psychoanalyst, rather than to one's parent, in the first place.

Hence any call on the real in analysis is immediately seen only as a call. It is not a matter of outrage that psychoanalysis deals only in fantasy and not with 'the real world'; it is like asking to see what the stars look like when you shine the sun on them, and then protesting that they are a product of night-time dreams, since one cannot see them in the full light of day. The apocalypse of the meeting with the real that an empiricist philosophy of science relies upon is only encountered by the psychoanalytic patient in a meeting with the real of the analyst – who, by definition, is not real in that sense for the purposes of the encounter. The call on him or her to be real is rather like asking a jealous lover who has, like Proust's Marcel, constructed a world of knowledge by spying, by inferring, by investigating, to test that knowledge by confronting himself with the real of his loved one – an encounter that can never resolve the question jealous knowledge is address-ing.[35]

We might have deduced all this simply from the fact of the psychoanalytic situation being immersed in speech, in words – and nothing else. Traditionally, human deception stems from two sources: the senses and from language. Nature is invoked by scientists as the arbiter of decisions as to the truth – on the assumption that nature does not lie, that God does not trick the scientist, that, in sum, God is *unconscious* of anything other than himself. Otherwise he would respond in some way to what is happening in his other (the universe). If God cannot lie, then the duplicity of the world has to receive other explanations. Obviously one of these is the invocation of the Devil: it is the Devil, the demon of the *Meditations*, who tricks, the devil who can lead man astray.

The other path is to isolate what it is about human beings that make them liable to be tricked, to be deceived. The traditional themes appear here: first, the untrustworthiness of the senses, through which we are led into the dialectic of rationalism and empiricism, with all its attendant contradictions. The second theme, however, introduces the idea that it is human *nature*, the inheritance from the natural, that makes human beings liable to be tricked: in particular, the function of speech. If all truth stems from propositions, then all lies also stem from these: from the fact that a proposition can not only be false, but can also be intended to mislead. One misleads the other on the assumption that he or she believes in the truth-telling functions of propositions. If God is exempt from the suspicion of being a liar, it must be man who introduces lies into the world, man who impersonates the Devil, who takes on the godlike function of leading away from the truth (since it as godlike to lead away as it is to lead towards, as godlike to se-duce as it is to e-ducate). Indeed the semantic aura of seduction is exactly opposed to the rigours of truth: leading away, away from truth, into ignorance.

Curiously enough, this helps us to understand Lacan's bizarre interest in the question 'Why don't the planets speak?'[36] He concluded that we have silenced them, in order to turn them into something that does not deceive us, that does not lie. *We* have silenced them, as Lacan says, attributing this definitive move to Newton. So the attack on animism, and on anthropomorphism, which is often so closely identified, for the reason we are now

exploring, with animism, is an attempt to deprive nature of intentionality – specifically of the intention to deceive. We do not care
if nature intends to wear down newly raised mountain ranges,
in order to keep the geological system a steady-state one – this
can easily be translated into feedback mechanisms and the like,
which we do not take seriously as truly intentional agents. What
really disturbs us is if nature intends to do something in order
to deceive *us*, intended to produce the appearance of age-long
erosion in the South Weald specifically so as to deceive Charles
Darwin about the age of the world;[37] one might argue that the
voluntaristic God of the seventeenth and eighteenth centuries, who
could be invoked as placing fish fossils in the Alps so as to make
the earth *look* as if it had been completely covered by water, this
God, who can create the world as a stage for man, a metaphor
in which the 'stage' brings with it its ancient connotations of make-
believe, this voluntaristic God could easily turn into a deceiving
God – as he did for Philip Henry Gosse, the author of *Omphalos*.
If an intention to deceive *us* (which I would prefer to write as
an intention-to-deceive-us) were a viable hypothesis, we would
be irretrievably implicated in the observed system, not only in
that our presence *changed* that system (the weak form, the Heisen-
berg form) but because the system changed *because* of us. Our
uncertainty would not be a reflection of the indeterminacy of the
system, but a consequence of the system recognizing our existence,
and accommodating it. Nature would be deceiving rather than
indeterminate. A nature who is as active as the scientist, producing
as many lies in his (nature's) works as she (the scientist) produces
truths in her propositions, is not to be countenanced. If it were,
it would amount to letting God play dice with the world, letting
the planets speak, letting God be a deceiver, while still remaining
God. One might say that the freedom of the universe depends
upon this relaxation of the restrictions imposed upon science.

Let us return to the analysis of propositions, to follow out the
psychoanalytic logic most forcefully. Confronted by the world,
propositions have to conform to the real in order to be true. Turning inwards, propositions have to conform to what is in the heart
not to be lies. The simplest way of stating the Freudian doctrinal
starting point is: the evidence is not immediately available to make
a firm claim as to what the heart says – its reasons may not quite
surpasseth understanding, but they may well be unconscious. It

is this infinite regress opened up by asking propositions to 'correspond' to something else, something 'within', that persuaded Sartre
that the concept of the unconscious gained us nothing in the way
of understanding, and lost us much in the way of clarity. Yet
all the moralists agree that, on anything worth posing the question
about, a declaration as to true intentions is not likely to be very
truthworthy. As Adam Smith put it:

> There are two different occasions upon which we examine our
> own conduct, and endeavour to view it in the light in which
> the impartial spectator would view it: first, when we are about
> to act; and secondly, after we have acted. Our views are apt
> to be very partial in both cases; but they are apt to be most
> partial when it is of most importance that they should be
> otherwise.[38]

We all know this. We all know that we do not know what prompts
us to act, what meaning our act has for us, precisely when it
is most important that we do know this. Perhaps we are lying
to ourselves. . . . Perhaps we are not. It is this constitutive doubt
that the practice of psychoanalysis eliminates, so as to restore the
possibility of *someone* (maybe ourselves, maybe not) finding out
these reasons of the heart.

If the science of lies, in following its neutral methodology,
in which it is not so much a question of symmetry between two
knowledge claims as studied indifference to any *particular* knowledge claim (i.e. withholding, for as long as is useful, the decision
as to what is real and what is imaginary), if this science is also
committed to the recognition of individual truths, but has no
secure, objective means for elaborating a generality upon them,
then surely this is what we are to expect from any theory that
takes lying seriously. Surely, in order to defuse the potentially
destructive effect of lying, we will always have methodically to
ignore the knowledge-claim to truth, while recognizing that any
enquiry will inevitably establish its own truth, in the same way
as the patient establishes his or her truth. To talk about the truth
of my life, even about my destiny, does make sense, even if it
is not the sense of objective true-for-all truth, even if it is always
subject to the discovery that I have been lying (to myself, to
others) – and that I have been lied to. Why would we expect
anything more from the truth-claims of human beings en masse?

Notes and References

Stories about Stories: Hilary Lawson

1. K. Mannheim, *Ideology and Utopia* (London, Routledge & Kegan Paul, 1936); J. Fraser, *The Golden Bough, a study in magic and religion* (London, Macmillan, 1922); B. Malinowski, *Crime and Custom in Savage Society* (London, 1926).
2. P. Winch, *The Idea of a Social Science and its Relation to Philosophy* (London, Routledge & Kegan Paul, 1958); T. Kuhn, *The Structure of Scientific Revolutions* (Chicago, Univ. of Chicago Press, 1964); P. Feyerabend, *Against Method* (London, Verso, 1978).
3. A. Bloom, *The Closing of the American Mind* (New York, Simon & Schuster, 1987).
4. H. Putnam, *Reason, Truth and History* (Cambridge, Cambridge Univ. Press, 1981), ch. 1.
5. H. Lawson, *Reflexivity: The Post-Modern Predicament* (London, Hutchinson, 1985).
6. J. Habermas, *Der Philosophische Diskurs der Moderne*, (Frankfurt, Suhrkamp, 1986).

Richard Rorty: Science as Solidarity

1. T. S. Kuhn, *The Structure of Scientific Revolutions*, 2nd edn (Chicago, Univ. of Chicago Press, 1970), p. 206.
2. Ibid., p. 171.
3. T. S. Kuhn, 'Rationality and Theory Choice', *Journal of Philosophy*, LXXX (1983), p. 570.
4. Ibid., pp. 569–70.

W. H. Newton–Smith: Rationality, Truth and the New Fuzzies

Notes and References

1. T. S. Kuhn, *The Structure of Scientific Revolutions* (Chicago, Univ. of Chicago Press, 1982).
2. Nicholas S. Jardine, *The Fortunes of Inquiry* (Oxford, Clarendon Press, 1986).
3. Richard Rorty, *Consequences of Pragmatism* (Brighton, Harvester, 1982), p. xliii.
4. Ibid., p. xix.
5. W. H. Newton–Smith, *The Rationality of Science* (London, Routledge & Kegan Paul, 1981).
6. Rorty, *Consequences of Pragmatism*, p. 193.
7. Ibid., p. 165.
8. P. Feyerabend, *Against Method* (London, New Left Books, 1975).

Hugh Tomlinson: After Truth: Post-modernism and the Rhetoric of Science

1. P. Feyerabend, *Against Method* (London, New Left Books, 1975), p. 171.
2. See Hilary Putnam, *Reason, Truth and History* (Cambridge, Cambridge Univ. Press, 1981), pp. 50ff.
3. Ibid. p. 49.
4. See W. H. Newton–Smith, *The Rationality of Science* (London, Routledge & Kegan Paul, 1981), pp. 24ff.
5. See Putnam, *Reason, Truth and History*, pp. 64 and 73.
6. Ibid., p. 74.
7. See, for example, Karl Popper, *Conjectures and Refutations* (London, Routledge & Kegan Paul, 1963), ch. 10; and Newton–Smith, *Rationality of Science*, ch. 2.
8. P. Feyerabend, *Science in a Free Society* (London, Verso, 1978), p. 99; see generally, Feyerabend, *Against Method*, ch. 15.
9. Cf. Feyerabend, *Against Method*, pp. 269ff. and 284.
10. Ibid., p. 155.
11. Hilary Putnam, *Meaning and the Moral Sciences* (London, Routledge & Kegan Paul, 1978), p. 126.
12. See, for example, Newton–Smith, *Rationality of Science*.
13. T. S. Kuhn, *The Structure of Scientific Revolutions*, 2nd edn (Chicago, Univ. of Chicago Press, 1970), p. 206.
14. Feyerabend, *Science in a Free Society*, p. 70.
15. For a discussion of this argument see Putnam, *Reason, Truth and History*, pp. 119ff.
16. Friedrich Neitzsche, *Will to Power*, translated by Kaufmann and Hollingdale (New York, Random House, 1968), para. 540.
17. Putnam, *Reason, Truth and History*, p. 74.
18. Richard Rorty, *Consequences of Pragmatism* (Brighton, Harvester Press, 1982), p. xiii.
19. Richard Rorty, 'Habermas and Lyotard on Post-Modernity', in Richard J. Bernstein (ed.), *Habermas and Modernity* (Cambridge, Polity Press, 1985), p. 161.
20. See Rorty's article in this volume, above, p. 6.
21. Richard Rorty, *Philosophy and the Mirror of Nature* (Oxford, Basil Blackwell, 1980).
22. Rorty, *Consequences of Pragmatism*, Introduction.
23. 'Solidarity or Objectivity', in John Rajchman and Cornel West (eds), *Post-Analytic Philosophy* (New York, Columbia Univ. Press, 1985).
24. See Rorty, *Consequences of Pragmatism*, Introduction, pp. xiv–xv.
25. 'The Contingency of Community', *London Review of Books*, 24 July 1986, p. 10.

26. See generally Richard Rorty, 'Le Cosmopolitisme sans emancipation', *Critique*, 456 (Mai, 1985), pp. 573–6.
27. 'Habermas and Lyotard on Post-Modernity', p. 166.
28. 'Le Cosmopolitisme sans emancipation', p. 577.
29. Ludwig Wittgenstein, *On Certainty*, translated by Anscombe and von Wright (Oxford, Basil Blackwell, 1969), para. 110.
30. Rorty, *Philosophy and the Mirror of Nature*, p. 176.
31. Gilles Deleuze, Vincennes Seminar, 7 March 1978.

David Ruben: Realism in the Social Sciences

1. David Ruben, *Marxism and Materialism*, 2nd edn (Brighton, Harvester Press, 1979), p. 19 and passim.
2. For this distinction, see for example David Ruben, *The Metaphysics of the Social World* (London, Routledge & Kegan Paul, 1985), pp. 32–5.
3. Ernest Gellner, 'Cause and Meaning in the Social Sciences', reprinted in *The Concept of Kinship and Other Essays* (Oxford, Basil Blackwell, 1987); and Peter Winch, *The Idea of a Social Science* (London, Routledge & Kegan Paul, 1958).
4. Colin McGinn, 'Philosophical Materialism', *Synthese*, 44 (1980), pp. 173–206.
5. See David Ruben, *Marxism and Materialism*, pp. 127–39.
6. I discuss the distinction between the social and the non-social generally, and offer a criterion for the former, in David Ruben, *The Metaphysics of the Social World*, ch. 3.
7. A. MacIntyre, 'The Idea of a Social Science', in B. R. Wilson (ed.), *Rationality* (Oxford, Basil Blackwell, 1970); also A. MacIntyre, 'Is a Science of Comparative Politics Possible?', in P. Laslett *et al* (eds), *Philosophy, Politics, and Society*, Fourth Series (Oxford, Basil Blackwell, 1972).
8. See for example Russell Keat and John Urry, *Social Theory as Science* (London, Routledge & Kegan Paul, 1975); and Ted Benton, *Philosophical Foundations of the Three Sociologies* (London, Routledge & Kegan Paul, 1977).
9. See David Ruben, *The Metaphysics of the Social World*, pp. 167–72.

H. M. Collins: The Meaning of Experiment: Replication and Reasonableness

1. For a fascinating glimpse of an imaginary world in which constancy is not preferred see the story of 'Tlon' in Borges' *Labyrinths* (New York, New Directions, 1964).

    Actually, the relationship between magic, science and constancy is not so straightforward. The standard account of the Azande poison oracle seems to suggest that Zande magic rests on a 'physical contradiction'. The Azande test for the presence of witchcraft by poisoning a chicken – if it dies, witchcraft is suggested. To test this they poison a second chicken. The hypothesis is *confirmed* if the second chicken *lives*. One might think of this as a paradigm of magical practice, or one might argue that the Zande are testing for the constant qualities of witchcraft by revealing its ability regularly to confound the natural world.
2. Karl Popper, *The Logic of Scientific Discovery* (London, Hutchinson, 1968), p. 45.
3. Ibid., p. 99.
4. For the consistency of the worlds of schizophrenics see the works of R. D. Laing.
5. For the origin of this argument see R. Brown, *Social Psychology* (New York, Free Press, 1965). For a use of this idea which criticizes the Festinger case study *When Prophecy Fails* see H. M. Collins and G. Cox, 'Recovering Relativity: Did Prophecy Fail?', *Social Studies of Science*, 7 (1976), pp. 327–80.
6. Examples and illustrations in the rest of this paper, unless otherwise referenced,

are new or taken from H. M. Collins, *Changing Order: Replication and Induction in Scientific Practice* (London, Sage, 1985). In particular, full accounts of the building of the 'TEA-laser' and the non-detection of gravitational radiation will be found therein. There is also extended discussion of the nature of experimental replication and the Experimenters' Regress. A guide to the existing literature on case studies of scientific disputes will also be found in *Changing Order*, as well as references to useful review articles.

In this paper I have tried to draw out the particular consequences of these ideas for the notion of reasonable agreement about scientific method as discussed by W. H. Newton–Smith in this volume.

7. P. Atkinson and S. Delamont, 'Mock-ups and Cock-ups: The Stage-Management of Guided Discovery Instruction', in P. Woods and M. Hammersley (eds), *School Experience: Explorations in the Sociology of Education* (London, Croom-Helm, 1977) provide a fascinating case study of experiment in the classroom. S. Shapin and S. Schaffer, *Leviathan and the Air Pump: Hobbes, Boyle, and the Experimental Life* (Princeton, Princeton Univ. Press, 1985), show us how the same confidence trick was first invented and worked in grown-up 'natural philosophy' by Robert Boyle.

8. The distinction between ordinary and contentious science referred to here is close to T. S. Kuhn's division between normal and revolutionary science. Contentious or 'extraordinary' science, however, need not be so 'grand' as revolutionary sciences.

9. Many lay-persons' impressions of experiment are formed by seeing 'demonstrations'. Demonstrations are quite different – they have been rehearsed many times, and deal with well-established phenomena, not new and contentious phenomena.

10. Michael Polanyi, *Personal Knowledge* (London, Routledge & Kegan Paul, 1958), first set out the idea of tacit knowledge. Polanyi reads more into the idea than I would wish.

11. For example, see M. Hesse, *The Structure of Scientific Inference* (London, Macmillan, 1974).

12. See H. M. Collins, *Changing Order*, esp. ch. 2.

13. Ibid., p. 88.

14. For selectivity of results in Robert Millikan's famous 'oil-drop experiment', see G. Holton, *The Scientific Imagination* (Cambridge, Cambridge Univ. Press, 1978). For a fascinating account of Eddington's famous 1919 eclipse experiment which 'verified' general relativity, see J. Earman and C. Glymour, 'Relativity and Eclipse: The British Eclipse Expeditions of 1919 and Their Predecessors', *Historical Studies in the Physical Sciences*, 11 (1980), pp. 49–85.

Richard L. Gregory: Touching Truth

1. Russell Norwood Hanson, *Patterns of Discovery* (Cambridge, Cambridge Univ. Press, 1958); Russell Norwood Hanson, *Observation and Explanation* (London, Allen & Unwin 1972); T. S. Kuhn, *The Structure of Scientific Revolutions* (Chicago, Univ. of Chicago Press, 1962).

2. Karl Popper, *Objective Knowledge* (Oxford, Clarendon Press 1972).

3. Claude E. Shannon and Warren Weaver, *The Mathematical Theory of Communication* (Urbana, Univ. of Illinois Press, 1949).

4. Richard L. Gregory, *Mind in Science* (London, Weidenfeld & Nicolson, 1981), pp. 249–62.

Bruno Latour: Clothing the Naked Truth

1. The debate between Pasteur and Pouchet about the possibility of spontaneous generation took place in the 1860s. Pasteur was against its possibility and Pouchet for it. It is not a very important event in the history of science but it has become a convenient *topos* for historians and sociologists since a famous article by J. Farley and G. Geison 'Science, Politics and Spontaneous Generation in 19th-Century France: the Pasteur–Pouchet Debate', *Bulletin of the History of Medicine*, 20 (2), (1974), pp. 257–70. The debate over spontaneous generation has now become a debate over the possibility of a non-rationalist explanation of science; see N. Roll-Hansen 'Experimental Method and Spontaneous Generation: The Controversy between Pasteur and Pouchet, 1859–1864', *Journal of the History of Medicine*, 34, (1979), pp. 273–92. For the history of Pasteur see Bruno Latour, *Pasteurization of France* (Cambridge, Harvard Univ. Press).

Steve Woolgar: The Ideology of Representation and the Role of the Agent

1. A more elaborated version of this argument appears in S. Woolgar, *Science: The Very Idea* (London, Tavistock/Horwood, (1988), esp. ch. 7), albeit with an entirely different ending. My thanks to Lisa Appignanesi and Hilary Lawson for their interesting comments on an earlier draft.
2. D. Bloor, *Knowledge and Social Imagery* (London, Routledge & Kegan Paul, 1976); H. M. Collins, *Changing Order: Replication and Induction in Scientific Practice* (London, Sage, 1985); B. Latour and S. Woolgar, *Laboratory Life: The Construction of Scientific Facts*, 2nd edn (Princeton, Princeton Univ. Press, 1986); K. D. Knorr-Cetina and M. J. Mulkay (eds), *Science Observed: Perspectives on the Social Study of Science* (London, Sage, 1983).
3. 'Radical' here denotes an epistemological rather than a political radicalism. Much of the Marxist literature on science is disappointing in that its concentration on the distribution and resources of science appears to accept the fundamental auspices of science: the ideology of representation. See Latour and Woolgar, *Laboratory Life*, p. 277.
4. This way of posing the question unproblematically adopts the rhetoric of progress. It is unclear to what extent practitioners in the sociology of scientific knowledge are willing to apply a constructivist view of progress to their own field of research. For an attempt to interrogate the notion of progress in this context, see S. Woolgar and M. Ashmore, 'The Next Step: An Introduction to the Reflexive Project', in S. Woolgar (ed.), *Knowledge and Reflexivity: New Frontiers in the Sociology of Knowledge* (London, Sage, 1988) pp. 1–13.
5. M. Mulkay, 'Interpretation and the Use of Rules: The Case of the Norms of Science', in T. Gieryn (ed.), *Science and Social Structure: A Festschrift for Robert Merton, Transactions of the New York Academy of Science, Series 2* (1980), pp. 111–25.
6. It is important to note, however, that neither rules nor ideology *determine* interpretive activity.
7. Robert Merton, *The Sociology of Science* (Chicago, University of Chicago Press, 1973), chs 12 and 13.
8. S. Woolgar, *Science as Practical Reasoning: The Artful Management of Epistemological Horror* (forthcoming).
9. K. D. Knorr-Cetina, *The Manufacture of Knowledge* (Oxford, Pergamon, 1981).
10. Latour and Woolgar, *Laboratory Life*, ch. 2; Bachelard, *Le Matérialisme Rationnel* (Paris, P.U.F., 1953).

11. S. Woolgar and D. Pawluch, 'Ontological Gerrymandering: The Anatomy of Social Problems Explanations', *Social Problems*, 32 (1985), 214–27.
12. R. Rorty, *Philosophy and the Mirror of Nature* (Oxford, Basil Blackwell, 1980); I. Hacking, *Representing and Intervening* (Cambridge, Cambridge Univ. Press, 1983).
13. C. Geertz, *The Interpretation of Cultures* (New York, Basic Books, 1973); P. Rabinow, *Reflections in Morocco* (Berkeley, Univ. of California Press, 1977).
14. See note 2.
15. G. N. Gilbert and M. Mulkay, *Opening Pandora's Box: A Sociological Analysis of Scientists' Discourse* (Cambridge, Cambridge Univ. Press, 1984); B. Latour and J. de Noblet (eds), *Les 'Vues' de l'Esprit*, special issue of *Culture Technique*, 14 (1985); M. Lynch and S. Woolgar (eds), *Representation in Scientific Practice*, special issue of *Human Studies*, 11, nos 2–3.
16. H. Garfinkel, *Studies in Ethnomethodology* (Englewood Cliffs, New Jersey, Prentice Hall, 1967).
17. M. Ashmore, 'A Question of Reflexivity: Wrighting the Sociology of Scientific Knowledge', DPhil. thesis, University of York (1985); M. Mulkay, *The Word and the World: Explorations in the Form of Sociological Analysis* (London, George Allen & Unwin, 1985); Woolgar (ed.), *Knowledge and Reflexivity*.
18. Woolgar, *Science as Practical Reasoning*, ch. 2.
19. For other kinds of exploration of literary forms, see note 17.
20. See note 17 and Woolgar and Ashmore, 'The Next Step'.
21. Woolgar and Ashmore, 'The Next Step'; A. Wynne, 'Accounting for Accounts of Multiple Sclerosis', in Woolgar, *Knowledge and Reflexivity*.
22. T. Pinch and T. Pinch, 'Reservations about Reflexivity or Why Should the Devil Have All the Best Tunes?', in Woolgar (ed.), *Knowledge and Reflexivity*.

John Forrester: Lying on the Couch

1. Friedrich Nietzsche, *Das Philosophenbuch*, 1873, Part III: 'Knowledge Theoretical Introduction on Truth and Lies in an Extra-Moral Sense' (Paris, Aubier Flammarion Bilingue, 1969), p. 182.
2. Thomas Hobbes, *Leviathan*, 1651, ed. with an introduction by C. B. Macpherson (Harmondsworth, Penguin, 1951), p. 105.
3. Italo Calvino, *If on a Winter's Night a Traveller*, trans. William Weaver (London, Picador, 1982), p. 104.
4. Bruno Latour, *Science in Action* (Milton Keynes, Open Univ. Press, 1987).
5. Vladimir Jankélévitch, *Du Mensonge*, 2nd edn (Lyon, Saint-Amand-Montrand, 1945), p. 14.
6. Maxime Chastaing, 'Connaissez-vous les uns les autres', in *Psychologie comparative et art: hommage à I. Meyerson* (Paris, PUF, 1972), pp. 255–64.
7. Jankélévitch, *Du Mensonge*, p. 21.
8. Nietzsche, *Das Philosophenbuch*, p. 172.
9. Karl Popper, 'Replies to My Critics', in Paul Arthur Schilpp (ed.), *The Philosophy of Karl Popper* (La Salle, Illinois, Open Court, 1974), pp. 1112–13.
10. Michel Foucault, 'Interview, "The History of Sexuality"', in Colin Gordon (ed.), *Power/Knowledge: Selected Interviews and Other Writings, 1972–1977* (New York, Pantheon, 1982), p. 193.
11. Sissela Bok, *Lying: Moral Choice in Public and Private Life* (Hassock, Sussex, Harvester Press, 1978).
12. Saint Augustine, *De mendacio* (Lying), 395, in *Treatise on Various Subjects*, ed. R. J. Defarrari, Fathers of the Church, vol. XVI (New York, Fathers of the

Church, 1952), pp. 51–110; Saint Augustine, *Contra mendacium* (Against lying), 420, in ibid., pp. 121–79.

13. Saint Augustine, *Contra mendacium*, p. 130.

14. Bok, *Lying*, p. 38; Dominique Colas, 'Mensonge pédagogique et sexualité infantile chez Kant', *Ornicar?* 2 (1975), pp. 73–5; Immanuel Kant, 'Réflexions sur l'education', 1776–87, trans. with an introduction by A. Philonenko (Paris, Vrin, 1966), p. 147.

15. Alexandre Koyré, 'Réflexions sur le mensonge', in *Renaissance* (New York, Ecole libre des hautes études, 1943), vol. I, p. 95.

16. Ibid., p. 102.

17. Ibid., p. 104.

18. Harvey Sacks, 'Everyone Has to Lie', in B. B. Blount and Mary Sanches (eds), *Sociocultural Dimensions of Language Use* (New York, Academic Press, 1975), pp. 57–79.

19. See J. L. Austin, 'Performative Utterances', 1956, in *Philosophical Papers*, ed. J. O. Urmson and G. J. Warnock, 2nd edn (London, Oxford Univ. Press, 1970), p. 249.

20. See L. C. Knights, 'How Many Children Had Lady Macbeth? An Essay in the Theory and Practice of Shakespeare Criticism, 1933', in *Explorations*, 1946 (Harmondsworth, Penguin, 1964).

21. See Jacques Derrida, 'Signature Event Context', *Glyph 1*, 1977, pp. 172–97; and 'Limited Inc a b c . . .', *Glyph 2*, 1978, pp. 162–254.

22. *International Encyclopaedia of Psychiatry, Psychology, Psychoanalysis and Neurology*, edited by Benjamin B. Wolman (New York, Van Nostrand Reinhold, Aesculapuis, 1977), 12 vols.

23. Jeffrey M. Masson, *The Assault on Truth: Freud's Suppression of the Seduction Theory* (London, Faber & Faber, 1984).

24. Jacques Lacan, *The Seminar. Book 1: Freud's Papers on Technique, 1953–1954*, ed. Jacques-Alain Miller, trans. with notes by John Forrester (Cambridge, Cambridge Univ. Press, 1988), pp. 174–5.

25. Sigmund Freud, *The Interpretation of Dreams*, in *The Standard Edition of the Complete Psychological Works of Sigmund Freud*, trans. under the general editorship of James Strachey in collaboration with Anna Freud, assisted by Alix Strachey and Alan Tyson, 24 vols (London, Hogarth Press, 1953–74) (henceforth 'SE'), vol. V, pp. 515–16.

26. Sigmund Freud, 'Negation', in *SE*, vol. XIX, p. 235.

27. Freud, *The Interpretation of Dreams*, *SE*, vol. V, pp. 461–2.

28. Sigmund Freud, *The Complete Letters of Sigmund Freud to Wilhelm Fliess, 1887–1904*, trans. and ed. Jeffrey Moussaieff Masson (Cambridge, Mass./London, Harvard Univ. Press, 1985), p. 264.

29. Sigmund Freud, 'Hypnotism', in *SE*, vol. I, p. 110; see also *SE*, vol. XXIII, p. 239.

30. Freud, 'Hypnotism', p. 113.

31. Ibid.

32. John Forrester, 'Freud, Dora and the Untold Pleasures of Psychoanalysis', in Lisa Appignanesi (ed.), *Desire* (London, ICA Publications, 1984), pp. 3–8; and 'Contracting the Disease of Love: Authority and Freedom in the Origins of Psychoanalysis', in W. F. Bynum, Roy Porter and Michael Shepherd (eds), *The Anatomy of Madness: Essays in the History of Psychiatry*, vol. I: *People and Ideas* (London, Tavistock, 1985), pp. 255–70. Both papers are to appear in John Forrester, *The Seductions of Psychoanalysis: Freud, Lacan, Derrida* (Cambridge, Cambridge Univ. Press, 1989).

33. Latour, *Science in Action*, p. 93.
34. Freud, *The Interpretation of Dreams*, SE, vol. v, p. 517; see also Lacan, *The Seminar. Book I*, pp. 33ff.
35. Malcolm Bowie, *Freud, Proust and Lacan: Theory as Fiction* (Cambridge, Cambridge Univ. Press, 1987), p. 55.
36. Jacques Lacan, *The Seminar. Book II. The Ego in Freud's Theory and in the Technique of Psychoanalysis, 1954–1955*, ed. Jacques-Alain Miller, trans. Sylvana Tomaselli, with notes by John Forrester (Cambridge, Cambridge Univ. Press/New York, Norton's, 1988), pp. 234–42.
37. Joe D. Burchfield, *Lord Kelvin and the Age of the Earth* (London, Macmillan, 1975).
38. Adam Smith, *The Theory of Moral Sentiments*, ed. D. D. Raphael and A. L. Macfie (Oxford, Oxford Univ. Press, 1979), p. 157.

Index

Index

Index